To my dismay, as I left my charge's room, my candle flame was quenched at once by a strong draught.

The door to the cupola, I thought in strange panic, must have opened again. "Be sensible, Harriet," I told myself in my Aunt Alice's voice, "it is only darkness after all, and the breeze you feel on the back of your neck is a perfectly natural occurrence! Simply feel your way along the wall and find your door!"

So I felt my way along the wall, but in my panic and disorientation, I did not find my door. Instead, shaking with cold and fright, I found myself outside the open door to the cupola itself, where I stood transfixed as a light, thin at first, swelled to a sudden blaze as it descended the winding stairs.

"Exploring, Miss Newcombe?" a cool voice greeted me.

Above me loomed the master of Ravensfall, a cold smile on his saturnine face.

A Memorable Collection of Regency Romances

BY ANTHEA MALCOLM AND VALERIE KING

THE COUNTERFEIT HEART   (3425, $3.95/$4.95)
by Anthea Malcolm

Nicola Crawford was hardly surprised when her cousin's betrothed disappeared on some mysterious quest. Anyone engaged to such an unromantic, but handsome man was bound to run off sooner or later. Nicola could never entrust her heart to such a conventional, but so deucedly handsome man. . . .

THE COURTING OF PHILIPPA   (2714, $3.95/$4.95)
by Anthea Malcolm

Miss Philippa was a very successful author of romantic novels. Thus she was chagrined to be snubbed by the handsome writer Henry Ashton whose own books she admired. And when she learned he considered love stories completely beneath his notice, she vowed to teach him a thing or two about the subject of love. . . .

THE WIDOW'S GAMBIT   (2357, $3.50/$4.50)
by Anthea Malcolm

The eldest of the orphaned Neville sisters needed a chaperone for a London season. So the ever-resourceful Livia added several years to her age, invented a deceased husband, and became the respectable Widow Royce. She was certain she'd never regret abandoning her girlhood until she met dashing Nicholas Warwick. . . .

A DARING WAGER   (2558, $3.95/$4.95)
by Valerie King

Ellie Dearborne's penchant for gaming had finally led her to ruin. It seemed like such a lark, wagering her devious cousin George that she would obtain the snuffboxes of three of society's most dashing peers in one month's time. She could easily succeed, too, were it not for that exasperating Lord Ravenworth. . . .

THE WILLFUL WIDOW   (3323, $3.95/$4.95)
by Valerie King

The lovely young widow, Mrs. Henrietta Harte, was not all inclined to pursue the sort of romantic folly the persistent King Brandish had in mind. She had to concentrate on marrying off her penniless sisters and managing her spendthrift mama. Surely Mr. Brandish could fit in with her plans somehow . . .

Available wherever paperbacks are sold, or order direct from the Publisher. Send cover price plus 50¢ per copy for mailing and handling to Zebra Books, Dept. 3945, 475 Park Avenue South, New York, N.Y. 10016. Residents of New York and Tennessee must include sales tax. DO NOT SEND CASH. For a free Zebra/ Pinnacle catalog please write to the above address.

MISTS OF RAVENSFALL

VIVIEN FISKE WAKE

ZEBRA BOOKS
KENSINGTON PUBLISHING CORP.

ZEBRA BOOKS

are published by

Kensington Publishing Corp.
475 Park Avenue South
New York, NY 10016

Second printing: October, 1992

Printed in the United States of America

DEDICATION

To Doctor John Schwartz's Thursday Night Group (which usually meets somewhat erratically on Sundays) and especially to Patricia Wallace-Estrada.

SPECIAL THANKS TO:

The staff of the Alexander Public Library, Wanganui, New Zealand. The Staff of the Davis Wanganui City Library, Wanganui, New Zealand. The staff of the Wanganui Regional Museum, Wanganui, New Zealand. Johanna Wren: friend, helpful critic and typist, Fullerton, California.

Prologue

Ravensfall
September, 1892

There are still some who call me murderess. Perhaps they are right; there is guilt yet within my soul, else why should I avoid the river walk at night, why tremble at a certain tone of voice or trill of laughter.

Yes, there is guilt. In my nightmares, I feel those hands again slipping from mine, and see that grey, distorted face that even below the churning waters still holds its haunting, demoniacal smile.

I wake, shuddering, and in the candle's flickering flame (for always now, I have candles burning throughout the night) I gaze about my bedchamber seeking comfort from red plush hangings, from the darkly polished mahogany tallboy and massive wardrobe.

In the fireplace, dying embers glitter still within the grate, while above the enshrouded mantle, the Queen and her Albert stare sternly into space. A very British scene—cozy, tranquil—but the heavy curtains swell in a sudden draught and the candlelight flutters, sending huge spider shadows flickering about the walls. Outside, I hear a morepork's plaintive cry and the illusion is shattered, for I know that out there beyond this British house in its very British garden lies the strangeness of an ever-encroaching, tangled forest—bush, they call it, in this outlandish place—and a dark dangerous river, swathed in mist.

The morepork cries again and I remember old Moana muttering angrily to Malvina. "Not morepork, not owl—he is *ruru*." She had sucked at her gums a moment, her rheumy old eyes glistening with malice. "You want to change everything, but one day, one day . . ."

"That's enough!" Placing an arm about Malvina's trembling shoulders, I stood my ground.

She cackled. "Who you think you are, hey?" Smiling at me slyly, she pointed a gnarled forefinger toward the house at a certain window glinting in the sun.

It was my turn to tremble for I knew that she had guessed my secret.

I am trembling now, but it is not of Moana that I am afraid, though she still lurks here after all the rest have fled. No, I am not afraid of old Moana, though she watches me continually as I go about my lonely rounds, laughing at me soundlessly from odd corners. Like a Greek chorus, she notes my actions and awaits my doom—for she knows, as I know, that somewhere out there in the darkness of the bush, lurks my fate.

The curtain sways again. The moon will have risen by now, shining down on the encroaching trees and turning the river mist to silver. If I go to the window

8

now, will I see a pale face gazing up at me? Will I see *his* face? Will he be waiting for me as he threatened?

Dear God, what shall I do?

Here I am in my bedchamber at Ravensfall, isolated in a foreign land: Harriet Newcombe, twenty-three years old, alone, terrified. How did I come to such a pass?

One

"Miss Newcombe? I'm Callum Douglas, manager to Mr. Raven." He had smiled down at me, his face under the brim of his slouch hat lean, suntanned; his eyes with their long, dark lashes, a curious shade of light blue-green. "But you're such a little thing," he added, amused.

I drew myself up. "I believe I am sufficiently tall, sir!"

He laughed; then added, his words lilting a little with a soft Scottish burr, "Indeed, yes. Sufficiently so, ma'am. But I forget myself!" Raising his hat to reveal dark red hair, he sketched an exaggerated bow. "Welcome to New Zealand, Miss Newcombe. Welcome to Wanganui!"

Wanganui. I whispered the soft syllables slowly to myself—Wang-a-nu-ee. I was here at last—at the end of the earth, as my Aunt Alice had warned me. Behind me the train puffed steam out over a wide river estuary lined with shipping, and I thought fleetingly of my three-month voyage to this strange land and the dark, dismal rectory I had left behind me in Manchester.

"Your portmanteau, Miss Newcombe . . . please allow me . . ."

Startled, I looked up. From under the slouch hat, the blue-green eyes looked quizzically down at me. "Your portmanteau, Miss Newcombe. Allow me to take it. You have, of course, other luggage?"

"My steamer trunk is to be shipped up from Wellington on the *Stormbird* next week, but I do have a box in the guard's van—a few books and things . . ."

"A few books and things. Naturally, Miss Newcombe . . ."

Why, beneath that mocking gaze, did I feel the necessity to defend myself? "I am a school teacher, sir. Books are the tools of my trade."

"Of course, Miss Newcombe. Just so." Tossing a coin to a lounging youth, he gave instructions to fetch my box and, giving me his arm, led me past the goods shed to a gig waiting on the unpaved street by the station. "So you are our latest governess," he said pleasantly, taking up the reins.

I dragged my eyes away from the wooden one-and two-story buildings lining the street, with glimpses of the river in between. "School teacher, sir," I asserted firmly.

"School teacher? I had thought that school teacher and governess were . . ."

"Quite different."

He raised his eyebrows and looked down at me, amused.

"Under the terms of my agreement with Mr. Raven's solicitors," I continued, tilting my chin, "I shall tutor his children from eight until four o'clock each day—my evenings will be my own!"

He laughed; a broad Scots laugh that frightened the horses of a passing dray. "And what will you do with these evenings of yours, far from civilization, in the middle of the bush?"

"Bush, Mr. Douglas?"

"The colonial word for the native forest."

"Oh, I see. Well, sir, I assure you I shall have plenty to do—I shall certainly not be at a loss for occupation!"

"I wonder, Miss Newcombe, what your occupation will be?"

I thought of my box with its precious, secret contents and smiled a little; then glanced over the crowded masts across the river to its further bank. "So Wanganui has spread from its little mudhole?" I asked, pointing to the tiny dwellings dotted here and there on the low, green hills opposite.

"You have been here before, Miss Newcombe?"

The query was abrupt and the strong, brown fingers tightened about the reins. Surprised, I glanced up. "Why no, Mr. Douglas," I explained, "but my father was here over twenty years ago. He was a missionary and he told me all about his experiences before . . . before . . . he died . . ."

"Your father is deceased. I'm sorry, Miss Newcombe."

I thought about my poor father a moment, and of Aunt Alice in whose charge he had left me—and of her husband, the Reverend Mr. Pugh, and the rectory in Manchester, and I shuddered.

"Miss Newcombe, you have gone quite pale!" For

an instant, the strong, brown fingers covered mine.

"It is nothing, sir. Merely fatigue—the journey from Wellington was interesting but long." I cast about for a change of subject. "Is Ravensfall far from here?"

Another bellow of a laugh. "You could say so! Tonight, you will spend at Mr. Raven's town house in Wanganui. Tomorrow, you will travel by river steamer . . ."

"Oh, no! Not another boat!"

"Not just a boat, an elegant lady of a vessel—newly acquired by Hatrick and Sons and fixed up with all sorts of falderals just to please the fair sex on their excursions up-river. Look Miss Newcombe," he added, pointing with his whip beyond a bridge spanning the river now shining in the sunset. "There she comes, the *Wairere!*"

Callum Douglas was right. Toward us surged a gallant little vessel; as we watched it paused beside the quai to disgorge a scattering of passengers.

"Tomorrow morning at seven. Will you be ready, Miss Newcombe, to sail into the unknown, to tackle gorgons, ogres, unimaginable giants?"

"Gorgons, sir? Giants? I hardly imagine that Mr. Raven or any of his family . . ."

In the gathering dusk, the face under the slouched hat was lost in shadow. "Perhaps, not gorgons nor giants, Miss Newcombe—this is New Zealand, after all—but, perhaps . . . other . . . beings . . . ?"

The Scottish burr had lost its laughter and I shivered in a sudden chill breeze. I gave myself a shake. "I suppose, sir," I answered matter-of-factly, "that you are referring to Maori mythology. I must admit that I know little about it; but I shall be most interested to learn."

There was a short silence.

Callum Douglas laughed brusquely. "How serious you are, Miss Newcombe! Interested to learn, indeed—we shall have to see what we can do! But here we are at Victoria Avenue, the main street of our metropolis . . ." With a deft flick of the reins, he guided the chestnut drawing our gig round a corner onto a broad gaslit thoroughfare.

I looked about with interest. Though here and there were imposing edifices of stone, the unpaved street was sheltered by the usual wide verandahs arching from simple, wooden buildings.

"Not exactly Manchester, Miss Newcombe, though we do well enough, I suppose . . . apart from these wretched dirt streets!" Expertly, my companion steered the chestnut around two potholes and a deep rut in the road. "You are fortunate," he continued, "that April, so far, has been dry; for Victoria Avenue can be a mudhole indeed!"

I held onto the side of the swaying gig. "Now, let me see—April—spring in England . . . so . . ."

"Autumn, here; and going into winter . . ."

"Ah . . . 'Season of mists and mellow fruitfulness' . . . Is autumn here, the same as in England?"

"Not as harsh, not nearly as harsh—at least, here in the North Island . . . but . . ." His voice softened suddenly, his words almost lost in the passing traffic. "But up-river, Miss Newcombe, you will find mists aplenty."

I glanced up at him, puzzled, but his profile—outlined against the gaslight's soft glow—was unreadable.

Another expert flick of reins and, making a right turn, we left the gaslight behind as we clattered up a short hill into a darkness relieved only by an occasional lamplit window.

"We are almost there, Miss Newcombe." The words were soothing, as if my unease was sensed. "Mr. Raven *maintains* his *establishment* in Wicksteed Street . . ."

Was it my over-heightened sensibilities or in the high-flown words did I detect a note of irony? Before I could make up my mind, the gig swung left and after a short while we stopped before a bay window glowing beyond a sloping lawn swathed in darkness.

"Miss Newcombe . . ." The words seemed strangely hesitant for such an assured man, the tone oddly diffident. "Miss Newcombe, If . . . if Ravensfall is not . . . er . . . quite what you had expected . . ."

The words faded into the silence and I looked puzzled into the darkness where his face should be. "I am hardly *expecting* anything, Mr. Douglas! This is a new land after all and I know little about it . . . what can I expect but the unexpected?"

A soft laugh. "There now! There's a logical mind for you! What, no woman's intuition?"

I resisted an impulse to slap his face.

"What I meant," he continued, "was that Ravensfall is an isolated spot and a young woman such as yourself—and such an *intelligent* young woman—might prefer not to bury herself in the wilds. Wanganui might . . . offer you more congenial employment?"

I sat aghast at his impertinence but before I could reply with a well-deserved setdown, he swung down from the gig, remarking that he would rouse Mrs. Hargreaves, Mr. Raven's housekeeper. She and her husband, he told me, would look after me well enough and Hargreaves would see me onto the *Wairere* the following morning.

I found my voice at last. "Then, I shall not be seeing you again?"

Perhaps he detected my lack of disappointment for his words, though respectful enough, seemed to float on an undercurrent of laughter. "Alas, no—at least, not tomorrow." A short pause as he reached the door and raised his hand to knock. "I have some business of Mr. Raven's to conclude . . ."

The door swung open and he stood a moment, a long, lean silhouette against the glowing light. "But we shall meet soon enough at Ravensfall . . ."

Two

Mrs. Hargreaves, behind a somewhat sour-faced and prim exterior, proved unexpectedly communicative. She and Hargreaves, she explained, setting before me a dish of scrambled eggs and excellent country ham, had not themselves been in Wanganui long. Mr. Raven, she explained with a sniff, had hired them on one of his visits to Wellington.

"Mr. Raven travels frequently?"

Another sniff and a twitch of her apron. "On business, Miss, or so they say . . ."

What business, I wondered, but, of course, could not ask. "And Mr. Raven's children?" I continued, "Do they come to Wanganui often?"

The hint of a smile. "Once a month, Miss, of a weekend, to take Holy Communion at Christchurch . . ."

A pause.

"You'll like the children, Miss . . ."

Was it my imagination, or was there the slightest emphasis on the word *children?*

"Miss Malvina and Master Reginald, such quiet, little things—just like little mice, as I tell Hargreaves—and that Miss Ishbel with her pretty ways . . ."

"Miss Ishbel?"

"Miss Isobel, as I should say; but she goes by her highland name, her having been born in the Scottish Hebrides . . ."

"In the Hebrides? I had thought that Mr. Raven was an English gentleman. Does he not own an estate in Yorkshire?"

"Lord love you, yes, Miss. English, yes; a proper landed gentleman, as they say . . ."

Another sniff and a wry twist of the mouth.

"But Miss Ishbel is Mr. Raven's stepdaughter, her mother, who passed away, poor lady, was a widow when she met Mr. Raven. She was married first to a Scottish gentleman, Miss Ishbel's father . . ."

A pause, as my empty plate was whisked away.

"Miss . . . er . . . Ishbel is seventeen, as I collect?"

"Yes, Miss, and as pretty a thing as you ever did see. It's a crying shame . . ."

A thump, as a rice pudding was deposited before me.

"A crying shame that the poor, young lady should be kept so close."

In answer to my questioning look, "Away up-river, Miss, buried alive in the bush. She should be here in town, gadding about with other young people . . ."

"But I thought you said . . ."

"That they come to Wanganui? Yes, Miss, so they do, but Miss Ishbel never mixes freely . . . there's always that Mrs. Mannering—Mr. Raven's cousin,

19

you know—or Mr. Raven himself, keeping an eye on her. Of course, they do say that she's a great heiress. Perhaps, they're afraid of fortune hunters . . ."

A knock at the door. Enter Hargreaves—who, as silent as his wife was garrulous, put a damper on the conversation.

Later, however, at the door to my bedchamber, Mrs. Hargreaves, her sour face glistening yellow in the candle light, paused for a last word. "I do hope, Miss, as you'll be happy here . . ."

The implication being clearly that I should not.

"Hargreaves and I find it a mite quiet even in this so-called town; but you, Miss, away up-river, with nothing but the bush . . . like being in the middle of nowhere . . . at the end of the earth, as you might say . . ."

Thanking her, I took my candlestick and closed the door firmly.

At the end of the earth, I thought as I glanced about the room, that was what Aunt Alice had declared when she had learned of my decision to go to New Zealand.

"Of course, Harriet, you realize that you will be far away from family and friends . . . entirely by yourself, child, at the end of the earth. And this Mr. Raven— he is a widower, you say?"

"He is a gentleman, Aunt, and entirely respectable. An elderly cousin supervises his household."

Behind her pince-nez, my aunt's grey eyes had regarded me coolly. "I must say, child, that I cannot understand why Mr. Raven's solicitors would be willing to employ a young woman as inexperienced as yourself—and as a *teacher*, only, with your evenings free of other duties! This is most unusual, Harriet, and I must admit I cannot like it!"

"As I am now two and twenty, I believe I am old enough to make my own decisions!"

The narrow face had flushed. "Harriet, you forget yourself. I await an apology!"

Biting my lip, I brought myself to apologize, "I am sorry if I have offended you; I am well aware of all you have done for me . . ."

"We took you in, Harriet, when you were ten years old . . ."

Sighing mentally, I had tried to ignore the usual diatribe, but despite my best efforts, the well-known phrases had penetrated my consciousness . . .

"Took you in . . . when my poor brother . . . such a harum-scarum as you were . . . no wonder, considering . . . and even now, after all my training, after all the admonitions of Mr. Pugh . . . you still . . . of course, considering your background . . . why look at you, even now, a veritable hoyden! I declare your hair is again escaping from its pins and the top button of your gown is half-undone! Really, child, you look just like your . . . your . . ."

Folding her hands, she had turned away.

Just like my mother, she had been going to say, but of course, did not; as my mother's name and all reference to her, were forbidden in that dreary place.

"Come, Harriet," I said to myself firmly, setting my candle on a walnut dresser, "you have left Aunt Alice and the Reverend Mr. Pugh far behind!" I smiled a little at the thought that if I were at one end of the earth, then my aunt and her wretched husband, were, most certainly, safely at the other.

Putting up my hands to unpin my unruly hair, I found that several locks were already drifting down, having become undone when I had earlier removed my hat. I wondered, laughing a little, what Aunt Alice would say, if she could see me — "A true lady is never obtrusive, Harriet, and always tidy. You must draw your hair straight back and restrain it in a bun! My dear, surely you do not wish to look like . . . like . . . like your . . . really, child, after all my training and after all the kind admonitions of Mr. Pugh . . ."

Mr. Pugh, I thought now with a shudder; Aunt Alice's husband.

I remembered my last interview with him, in his study, after I had received notice of my employment from Mr. Raven's solicitors.

"My dear Harriet," he had rumbled, his face brick-red between its grey Dundreary whiskers, "to be so far away from us . . . to be quite without our supervision . . . is this wise? Considering your . . . er . . . background, my dear, I fear you lack the strength of will to refrain from . . . er . . . temptation."

A heavy arm was placed about my shoulders. "You know, my dear child, you frequently lack decorum . . ." His clasp tightened and I could feel the heat from his arm through the thin bombasine of my gown.

"Have you informed Mr. Raven's solicitors of your . . . um . . . *background*, my dear? I fear that you must do so!"

A stern finger was wagged before my face.

"My dear Harriet, you are not a proper model for young children, and I fear, I very much fear that . . . not to put too fine a point on it, my dear, there is bad blood in you . . . and that without a restraining influence, it will out . . . it will out . . ."

His arm slipped about my waist, but twisting free, I had run off down the stairs.

I had not, of course, informed Mr. Raven's solicitors, but taking my steamer ticket when it had arrived, I had gathered up my few possessions and had left the rectory as quickly as possible.

Now, in my bedchamber at the other end of the earth, I stared at myself in the glass above the dresser. My untidy hair drifted about a face flushed by Mrs. Hargreaves' strong hot tea. Definitely indecorous, I thought, trying to smile, but somehow managing only a little sob. "Bad blood," Mr. Pugh had said; and of course, he was right . . . I must be very careful, I told myself, to make sure that it would not "out." Grabbing my hair, I combed it back and plaited it for the night.

What did life hold in store for me, I wondered. Then, turning toward the bed, I noticed my precious box that Hargreaves had deposited on the floor near the window. Of course, I thought, therein lay the way to my ultimate independence, indeed, to my salvation.

Three

Hatrick's wharf at six-thirty—a dismal dawn of spitting rain and low, heavy clouds. In the dim light, the river stretched endlessly into stormy darkness.

The taciturn Hargreaves, depositing me on the quay, shouldered my box and trudged off to the loading zone.

"Miss Newcombe?"

A lilting Scottish burr, the doffing of a hat.

"Mr. Douglas? I had thought you were about Mr. Raven's business . . ."

In the breaking dawn, the shadowy features twisted into a sardonic smile. "Why, so I am, Miss Newcombe, so I am—and *Mr. Raven's business* takes precedence over all, does it not?"

Hardly knowing what to say, I bit my lip.

"As I find myself here, on *Mr. Raven's business,* I had thought to bid you *Bon Voyage* . . ."

"Indeed? Thank you . . ."

Another figure loomed in the half-darkness.

"Mr. Douglas, I believe? You travel on the *Waiwere,* this morning?"

Did I imagine it, or did Callum Douglas give a slight start? In any event, his voice, when he replied, was cool.

"No," a sideways glance at me, "I shall travel to Ravensfall later in the day."

"Ah," the voice, a bass, rich with a colonial twang, continued, "then perhaps you can tell me if Mr. Raven is at home . . . but excuse me, I do not wish to intrude on your conversation . . ."

"No conversation; Miss Newcombe and I were merely exchanging . . . pleasantries. But I forget myself! Miss Newcombe, allow me to introduce the Reverend Mr. Takarangi. Mr. Takarangi, this is Miss Newcombe, the newest addition to our household — and fresh from England."

Takarangi, I thought in some bewilderment; that was a native name. Sure enough, the face revealed beneath the raised hat proved to be that of a Maori.

"Miss Newcombe," the bass rumbled, "How do you do?"

"How do you do, sir?" I responded automatically. I searched about for something to say. "Will there be many traveling up-river?"

"A great many, I expect." Beneath the solemn rejoinder was a slight quiver of restrained laughter.

"If you'll excuse me, Miss Newcombe, I must attend to Mr. Raven's business. But . . ." On a sarcastic note. "I leave you in excellent hands!" Flashing a mocking smile, Callum Douglas turned toward the loading zone.

There was an awkward pause.

"The *Waiwere* will not be ready to leave for another half hour." Mr. Takarangi informed me, at last. "Perhaps you would like to take a short stroll . . . the Courthouse is nearby and Moutoa Gardens has a statue that might interest you . . . allow me to escort you." There was no mistaking now, the laughter trembling behind the words. "Of course, my dear young lady, fresh from England as you are, perhaps you are a trifle perturbed at being left alone with me?"

"Oh, please, sir . . ."

"I assure you, that some of us are quite civilized . . . I, myself, for instance, have not eaten anyone within these past three months!"

The rumbling laugh was so infectious, I found myself joining in.

"There now, that's better!" A kindly hand took my elbow and directed me across the road behind the wharf.

As I looked up at my new companion, the breaking light revealed a wide-featured, open face with a deep olive complexion. From under a bowler hat, the hair, though thick and dark, appeared somewhat grizzled at the temples—a man of about forty-five, he seemed to be.

I blushed, as I found myself studied in return.

"You are taking Miss Inglewood's place at Ravensfall, Miss Newcombe?"

"Yes, I believe so, though my duties will not be quite the same . . . that is, sir, if you are referring to the former governess of Mr. Raven's children?"

"I am." A sad shake of the head. "Poor, young lady . . . however, here we are—Moutoa Gardens."

26

In front of us, stretched a lawn dotted here and there with shrubs. In the background, at the top of a gentle slope, was an imposing wooden building, which Mr. Takarangi assured me was the Courthouse. "And here," he continued, pausing before a statue, "is the Moutoa Monument . . ."

In the gloom, the statue appeared to be that of a weeping woman clasping a funeral urn.

"Most interesting," I murmured politely, my mind elsewhere. Miss Inglewood, I thought; why, *poor* Miss Inglewood?

" . . . Commemorates the Battle of Moutoa in 1866," Mr. Takarangi continued, "an island, up-river . . ."

"Ah, yes, of course!" With difficulty, I pulled my thoughts together. "During the . . . er . . . Maori Wars, I suppose. My father told me about them, but I must confess, I don't quite understand what they were about . . ."

A short pause.

"Land, Miss Newcombe. Land. But you are just arrived . . . I shall be glad to explain another time."

I leaned forward the better to read the names on the statue's plinth. "But there are Maori names here . . ."

"Indeed, yes. The settlers were helped by the lower river tribes who objected to the Hauhaus breaking the mana of the river."

"How-hows?"

A rumbling laugh. "Hauhau; yes. A religion that sprang up during the Wars and so-named from the battle cry of its devotees."

I shivered a little, thinking of the early settlers in

27

their little clearings in the bush, listening to the wailing cries. As if to complement my thought, from the wharf the *Waiwere* hooted its signal for departure.

"And . . . *mana?*"

Another pause; this time, longer.

"Oh, as for that, Miss Newcombe . . . perhaps, when you have been here a little longer . . . but, come, the *Waiwere* is about to leave . . ."

The steamer hooted again as we made our way back to the wharf. Quite a crowd had gathered and as we came near, an elderly, blanket-wrapped Maori woman approached Mr. Takarangi. Taking her hand, he bent down and to my astonishment, lightly pressed noses with her.

Another rumbling laugh at the sight of my face. "The *hongi,* Miss Newcombe—the greeting between old friends of my race. What letters you will have to write home, what letters! But, excuse me! May I present a member of my flock, Mrs. Potaka?"

"Er . . . How do you do?"

I was rewarded with a toothless smile, above a tattooed chin.

"A member of your flock, Mr. Takarangi?"

"Yes, I minister to an Anglican mission up-river. Mrs. Potaka is visiting her niece."

Behind Mrs. Potaka, a handsome young woman smiled at me shyly. From the folds of the blanket, tucked behind her shoulders, a plump, bright-eyed baby regarded me curiously.

"My wife, Mere, teaches at the mission school," Mr. Takarangi continued, as we withdrew. "In fact, it is partly on her account that I am here, obtaining some supplies."

As he spoke, a ray of sunshine sifting through the

heavy clouds reflected on the metallic waters of the river. The immediate shore was crowded with carved Maori canoes and as I watched, several of these slender vessels — each piled high with supplies and powered by three to five men — were launched out onto the river.

"Don't be fooled by the sunlight," Mr. Takarangi smiled down at me. Raising his head, he sniffed at the air. "It's bound to rain again and heavily — especially up-river, and . . ." Again, the laughter, "they say, we Maoris always know! But, come, I must see you on board."

He took my arm, but as we make our way toward the gangway, he paused a moment, his broad open brow furrowed a little in thought. "Miss Newcombe," he continued, at last, "forgive me, but you seem a young lady of great good sense — for a *pakeha,* that is!" The hint of a roguish smile, but the brown eyes remained serious. " 'Pah-kay-hah' is what we Maoris call you Europeans. However . . ." Another pause, but this time with no hint of laughter. "However, Ravensfall . . . you'll be surrounded by the bush, you know; nothing for miles on end, but trees and shrub and fern and yet more fern . . ."

"But . . . surely . . . Ravensfall . . ."

"Ah, yes. Ravensfall. A little world in itself — and very *civilized* of course — Miss Inglewood, your predecessor, you know, spoke always of the musical soirées, the social niceties, the . . . er . . . civilities of Mr. Raven —"

A raised eyebrow, a half-smile.

"You mean, sir . . . ?"

"I mean nothing, Miss Newcombe. How could I? I

have not yet been to Ravensfall myself, though Mr. Raven, through his manager, Mr. Douglas, has asked me to call—he has, it seems, an interest in our mission, which lies not too far from Ravensfall . . ."

Callum Douglas, I thought—and remembered his cool reception of Mr. Takarangi. There was something, here, I thought. But what?

"As I was saying, Miss Newcombe," the rumbling voice recalled me to my senses. "Ravensfall is isolated—or so Miss Inglewood found it, poor soul. She was wont to visit my wife, you know—as indeed, *you* must do, for Mere likes nothing better than meeting strangers from afar."

We found ourselves at the foot of the gangway.

"So, Miss Inglewood did not . . . er . . . like Ravensfall, Mr. Takarangi?"

"Oh, not to say 'like'—or 'dislike' for that matter; but she had strange fantasies. Strange fantasies, it seems to me, brought upon her by the separation from her kind . . ."

The broad brow was turned away from me; the intent brown eyes gazed toward the river.

The clouds drew in again and there was a sudden splatter of rain.

An urchin grin. "As you see, Miss Newcombe; we Maoris are always right—at least, about the weather!"

I summoned all my courage. I raised my chin. "Mr. Takarangi, will you please tell me what this is all about! Where is Miss Inglewood? What happened to her?"

Down in the estuary the gulls shrieked, and all about us was a hustle and bustle as my fellow passengers swarmed aboard; yet Mr. Takarangi and I stood in a small well of silence, as if in the eye of a cyclone.

The brown eyes, suddenly opaque again, gazed down at me. "She died, Miss Newcombe, she died . . ."

Four

A melancholy whistle and the *Waiwere* drew into the lee of a big bend in the river.

"There you go, Miss. Watch your step!"

The mate—a huge, kindly man—helped me down the gangplank. "Sorry about the engine trouble," he continued. "We should have been here hours ago!"

I found myself on a wooden landing at the base of a steep hill covered with a wild, dark green tangle of ferns, bushes, and twisted trees.

The mate smiled down at my puzzled face. "The house is on the other side of the bend, Miss, on a bluff overlooking the river. You can't see it from here because of the ridge and the trees in between."

I gazed at the inpenetrable bush. "Er . . . How does one get there?"

"There's a path—they call it the River Walk— leading from the landing up round the edge of the cliff."

I looked where he pointed and, sure enough, in the dim light I could make out a faint track lined with huge, feathery ferns mounting steeply from the landing and winding upwards between the bush and the edge of the cliff.

"You just stay put," he continued, "until they send someone down to meet you. We'll blow the whistle again as we go past the bluff, so they'll know you've arrived."

"Perhaps," I suggested, "I should start walking . . ."

"Bless you, no!" he exclaimed. "You just stay put as I said." He scratched his fair head, tipping his peaked cap forward, and gazed down at me worriedly. "They may come this way, see," he continued, gesturing toward the path, "but with all this rain, it could be dangerous, and especially after what . . ." He stopped and scratched his head again. "They may come by the bush path, instead," he explained, pointing to the trees in front of us. "So you just stop where you are."

He turned, putting one foot on the gangway, then hesitated, looking back at me. "You're a little bit of a thing to be burying yourself out here in this wilderness. The Girls' College in Wanganui, now, they need an English mistress; seems to me, you'd just fit the bill. If things aren't . . . to your liking out here at Ravensfall . . ." he paused a moment, fumbling again at his cap, "the river steamer sails by here three times a week."

"Thank you, Mr. Phelps," I answered, somewhat stiffly, "I appreciate your concern but I'm sure I shall be more than satisfied with my position at Ravensfall."

He looked down at me then, quietly, biting his lip as if he would say more; but at that moment, the whistle sounded urgently again and he leaped over the side, drawing the gangway up after him. "Remember," he called again, "the steamer sails three times weekly."

Left alone in the silence and the gathering darkness, I gazed disheartened at the rain-drenched bush-enshrouded hills. 'The other side of nowhere.' My aunt was right, I thought, shivering.

At that moment, there was a flurry in some giant ferns up on the hillside to my right. Two birds squawking angrily rose in an agitated spiral. A small animal, I thought, must have disturbed them; but out of the corner of my eye, it seemed to me that the bushes fluttered again. The birds concealed once more in some nearby tree continued to punctuate the silence with nervous chirps of alarm. I was telling myself that it was merely my overwrought nerves that made me imagaine that I was being observed, and that the shadowy form I thought I had seen among the ferns was only a trick of light, when a long wailing cry suddenly sounded throughout the bush.

So startled was I, that I stepped backward, nearly falling into the swiftly flowing river. It was completely unlike any human cry I had ever heard and seemed to come from the direction of the path through the bush that the mate had pointed out to me. The cry sounded again, and as I watched, horrified, the bush directly in front of me suddenly parted to reveal a small pale face.

Before my startled gaze, a slight white-haired figure stepped forward through the gloom.

"Mademoiselle Newcombe, I presume?" questioned this apparition politely.

I dropped a small curtsy. "The same," I replied, endeavoring to restrain relieved hysterical laughter. On closer inspection, I observed that the white hair

34

was actually a makeshift wig made out of cotton and tied back with a black ribbon in the style of a century ago. The face below it belonged to a boy of about ten.

"Allow me to introduce myself," he begged in a strong French accent. "I am the Comte de Puissey Choiseul de Rambouillet."

He executed a deep and graceful bow. He was wearing jacket, shirt, and breeches of a former age, but the effect was spoiled by his bare shins and feet.

"Indeed?" I replied, somewhat faintly. Then recollecting myself, I hastened to curtsy again, adding "Enchantée, Monsieur! I am honored by your welcome and would appreciate your escort to Ravensfall."

He frowned solemnly up at me. Then, as I watched in fascination, he fixed a blade of grass between his thumbs and, lowering his head, blew the same blood-curdling shriek I had heard before, "Oh, hurry up, Hemi, do!" he shrilled up the path behind him.

Through the trees glimmered the light of an approaching lantern. As it drew closer, I saw that it was held by a stout elderly Maori who, though barefooted, was dressed respectably enough in shirt and trousers.

"Good evening," I greeted him.

However, apart from grinning at me cheerfully, he said nothing; but, giving the lantern to the comte, he shouldered my box and, taking my portmanteau in one hand, started back through the trees.

The comte politely offered me his arm, then raising the lantern, showed me the path we were to follow. It was then, in the lantern's glow, that I saw his face clearly for the first time; it was small and delicately shaped, but it was the eyes that attracted immediate attention. Set under dark, well-defined brows, they

35

were of such a light brown as to be almost yellow. Topaz-colored, I thought, following him up through the trees.

So intrigued had I become with my new companions, that it was not until much later that I was to remember my silent observer among the trees.

Five

The path through the bush was steep and uneven. Huge trees crowded in from all sides, rising from a tangled undergrowth like a chaotic but silent army. The lantern cast little light and, hampered by my long skirts, I was forced to stumble along, slipping and sliding in the mud and disentangling myself from the encroaching fronds of low-lying thorny bushes.

At the top of the hill, I was relieved to find myself at the edge of what, in the lantern's dim glow, appeared to be a sloping lawn.

"The house, Mademoiselle," my young companion announced politely, pointing to a huge, sprawling shape opposite, about fifty yards away. With a courtly bow, he handed me the lantern and disappeared back into the bush.

Somewhat at a loss, I followed Hemi, who plodding along at a continued steady pace, led me over the lawn. On closer acquaintance, the house, as with most I'd seen since arriving here, proved to be made of wood. As far as I could see in the darkness, it was built in the colonial style. It was at least three stories high and had two galleries, one bordering the ground floor and another at first-floor level, which ran its entire width. The windows were dark, but from behind the shutters of one a faint light glowed.

Mounting wide stone steps, I waited while Hemi knocked at an imposing front door. After my long trek through the bush, I had expected a more primitive setting. Now, wet, weary and cold, I wondered with some trepidation what awaited me inside.

As if in answer to my thoughts, the door suddenly swung open to reveal a hall so grand, that for a moment I remained speechless. Beyond me, its broad shallow steps glinting in mellow lamplight, curved a graceful wooden staircase. The banisters, flute-shaped and elegant, led up to a landing lost in shadows. However, it was the newel post at the foot of the stairs that really caught my eye. Intricately carved, it supported a large wooden bird, whose wings were upraised in flight.

Beyond the stairs green baize-covered doors led into the back regions, and inset in the polished wooden panelling on either side of the hall were ornately carved double doors. Through the doors on the left floated a murmur of voices, a soft tinkle of glasses.

"Please to come in, Miss!"

I came out of my daze to find a plump, rosy-faced maid servant—immaculately clad in dark dress with white apron and lacy cap—gazing at me reproachfully.

"I'm Jenny, Miss," she informed me in—to my delighted surprise—a soft Lancashire accent. She bobbed a curtsy. "Please to follow me, Miss. Mrs.

Douglas says as how you'd want to visit your room first and freshen up. I'll bring you your supper on a tray and afterwards, if you feel up to it, perhaps you'd like to visit the family in the drawing room?"

Smiling at me shyly, she took up a lamp from a small rosewood table at the foot of the stairs and, with Hemi clumping along behind, led me to a chamber on the second floor. We paused a moment before entering, Jenny shining her lamp down the dark passage.

"There's Miss Malvina's room," she said, pointing to a door on the right. "Then the governess' room—your room, now," she added, nodding her head at the dark brown door in front of us. "Then the schoolroom with Master Reginald's room on t'other side. Down at the end of the passage are Mrs. Douglas' rooms—a bed-chamber and a sitting room. Mrs. Douglas used to be a nurse to Miss Malvina and Master Reginald—and to Miss Ishbel, also. She's housekeeper now, though . . . she said to send you her compliments, Miss. She would have welcomed you, but she has a chill and is confined to bed."

Jenny paused a moment, looking at the door to my chamber. In the passage it was icy cold and damp; a breeze from some hidden source drifted past us, ruffling the lace of her cap. Hemi shuffled beside us, uneasily shifting my box, which all this time had rested on his broad shoulder. His plump brown face had a greyish tinge and he gazed at my door, a wary look in his deep brown eyes.

Taking a deep breath, Jenny pushed open the door, entering before me to light the way.

"This is the governess' room," she said, chattering

nervously. She set the lamp on a low table and bent to stoke up the small fire that smouldered in the grate. "Mrs. Douglas said as how a fire would warm the place up," she explained. Taking a taper she set it in the fire, then straightening up, she lit the candles in their brass sconces over mantel and dresser. "There now," she exclaimed, "the place looks right cozy!"

There was a thump behind me. Hemi had set down his burden at last. Bobbing his head at me, without further ado he headed out the door.

"Well, now," Jenny said, shaking her head in disgust. "Don't take no notice of that Hemi. Bats in the belfry, he has! I hope as how you'll be comfortable, here, Miss Newcombe."

I glanced about the small room, taking in the dark mahogany, the red plush hangings. "I'm sure I shall," I agreed warmly, when I noticed two small bowls of violets: one on the low table where Jenny had set her lamp and another on the escritoire by the window. "Oh, how pretty," I exclaimed, touching one delicate purple blossom.

Jenny looked pleased. "Those are Miss Ishbel's," she explained. "Very particular, she was, that you should have them. 'You must make Miss Newcombe welcome,' she says to me. 'After all, you both come from Lancashire' . . . and she put those into my hands. She raises them in the conservatory — though it's so mild here, she could probably grow them outside. In New Zealand we have flowers all year round. You may think *this* cold, Miss, but it ain't as cold as England!"

"Then you like it here, Jenny?" I asked, needing reassurance.

"I miss my mam and my dad, and everyone.

Sometimes, it's right lonely here in the middle of the bush . . ." She paused a moment, her blue eyes direct, very honest. "But folk are friendly here, friendlier than they are at home — perhaps because there are fewer of them!" She giggled and thrust out her left hand. For the first time, I noticed the simple ring with its blue stone on her third finger. "And anyways, Miss, I'm bespoke!" She smiled again and blushed.

"I'm happy for you, Jenny," I was replying, when a sudden draught billowed out the red plush curtains behind me.

To my surprise, Jenny turned quite pale.

"There must be a wind rising," I said soothingly. Looking at her, I was puzzled; I could not understand her distress.

"Very likely, Miss," she agreed crisply. Seeming to pull herself together, she crossed the room and pulled aside the curtains.

The sash window was, of course, closed; but the strong draught was seeping through between the edge of window and sill.

"There, you see," I pointed out to her. "It's only a draught."

I joined her at the window and we stood together, looking out on blackness.

"What's out there, Jenny?" I asked. Since coming up the stairs, I had become quite disoriented.

She hesitated a moment, her hand tightening on the curtain. "Bush, Miss, and the river. Always the river . . ."

She turned to me, her blue eyes full of concern and I believe then that she would have spoken, if there had not been a knock at the door. "That will be Ngaire," she said, "with the hot water." I wondered later if I had imagined the relief I thought I saw in her eyes.

The door opened to admit a tall young Maori girl, dressed like Jenny in a dark dress with cap and apron. She was carrying a copper can of steaming hot water which she took over to the washstand for me and began to pour into the basin.

To my disappointment, Jenny and Ngaire left the room together. Though my aunt had dinned it into me that one should never gossip with servants, I already felt that Jenny with her friendly smile was something more and that she was on the verge of telling me something important. I looked forward to seeing her again, but it was Ngaire who brought up the lamb and peas that was my supper and who later came to take me down to the drawing room.

By that time, I had washed and changed my mud-bespattered skirt for another; but there was little I could do about my hair. Frizzied as usual by the damp, it hung about my face in a heavy, tangled mass. If only it were a definite color, I thought in disgust, but it was neither brown, blond, nor auburn, but some muddy color in between. To towel it dry, as I well knew, would only make the tangle more riotous than ever. Instead I dampened my brush and dragged my wild locks back as tightly as possible, plaiting them into a braid which I pinned into a knot on the back of my head.

What would the Raven family think of me, I wondered? They would see me, I decided, a triangular-shaped face with slanting eyes that, like my hair, were of a indeterminate color, being neither brown, nor blue; a nose of no particular distinction, with a scattering of freckles across the bridge; and a mouth too full and red. "My dear Harriet," my aunt had exclaimed, her monotone rising in intensity, "try to subdue your lips, my dear, try to subdue your lips . . . it's almost as if you painted. Bite them inwards, my dear, bite them inwards. You don't want people to think that . . . that . . . well, that you are . . . um, *immodest*, like . . . like . . ."

Would the Raven family consider me immodest, I wondered now. Would they guess at my 'tainted blood'? Perhaps, I thought to myself, in this new friendly country that Jenny had described, it would not matter. I smiled at myself cynically. Not matter! It was obvious from the evidence of wealth I had seen around me, that these were people of consequence and to such people, blood lines always mattered; as in the past I had learned to my cost. For the first time since I had begun my journey, I wondered if Mr. Pugh had been right: if, indeed, I should have written to Mr. Raven about my background.

Six

There was a knock on the door. Ngaire, the Maori maid, bobbed a curtsy and led me down the two flights of stairs to the front hall. As we descended, soft notes from a pianoforte floated up to us, the melody faint, nostalgic.

The family always gathered in the drawing room after dinner, Ngaire informed me in her soft voice, and tonight, Miss Malvina and even Master Reginald had been allowed to come down to welcome me. In the hall, she paused a moment before the great double door opposite the ones through which I had heard the tinkle of glasses. I could hear the music more clearly now, and recognized the gentle, floating strains of Beethoven's "Moonlight Sonata."

"That will be Mrs. DuPrès," Ngaire murmured. "She's a friend of the family," she added, grinning a moment as if at a secret joke.

Looking up at her velvety, deep brown eyes, I experienced a sudden start of recognition. "Of course," I exclaimed. "You must be Hemi's daughter!"

As if by magic, the smile vanished. She looked down at me silently, almost — to my surprise — scornfully.

"I'm Hemi's granddaughter," she announced. "*Rangi* was my father!" She looked as if she would say more, then shrugging her broad shoulders, she threw open the double doors.

Beyond was a large handsome room shining with light. Two gleaming chandeliers hung from an ornate high ceiling and candles in gilt sconces further lit up the dark panelling. Over a rich pink and mauve Aubusson carpet, plum-colored chairs and sofas in the style of Louis Quinze held sway. Another world, I could not help thinking to myself, another age. It was as if, like Prince Florimund of ancient legend, I had struggled through a nightmare forest to come at last upon an enchanted castle.

The music rose in a passionate crescendo and Ngaire's announcement of my name was not at first heard. Thus it was that the occupants of the room, unaware of my presence, remained still for a timeless moment, ranged before me as if in a *tableau vivant*. And on looking back, it seems to me that in that tableau were hints of all the troubles yet to come — if only, then, I had had the prescience to see.

Dominating the scene in front of a huge stone fireplace, complete with roaring inferno, stood a tall, dark-haired man. He was looking quizzically at a large sketchbook that he held up to the light. Beside him, her gleaming auburn head bent close to his, one delicate, long-fingered hand placed carelessly on the sleeve of his elegant evening jacket, stood a tall slender girl. Hunched on low stools, at some distance

45

to the right, were two young children; a girl pale and fair-haired, was playing cat's cradle with a dark-haired boy, whose back was turned to me. To the left of the fireplace, a lady of uncertain years sat tatting, while conversing from time to time with a broad-shouldered gentleman who was peering into a glass-fronted cabinet. It was as if, I thought with some amusement, they had arranged themselves for a family portrait.

After her announcement of my name, Ngaire had withdrawn, and I stood for an uncertain moment in the doorway, wondering whether to announce my presence with a delicate cough. At that moment, however, with a flutter of notes, the sonata drew to a close, and in the midst of the ensuing soft applause, the young lady by the fireplace looked around and saw me.

She moved gracefully toward me, her lavender and white striped skirts seeming almost to float over the pink and mauve carpet.

"Why," she exclaimed, smiling pleasantly while clasping my hands, "you must be Miss Newcombe. I am Isobel McCleod—but you must call me Ishbel: everyone does, for I was born in the Highlands, you know! But what a dainty, little thing you are: I declare, beside you, I feel like a lamp post!"

Slipping an arm protectively through mine, she drew me forward to meet the company.

"Papa, Cousin Lydia!" she exclaimed in her musical, bell-like tones. "Here is Miss Newcombe come to us!" She turned to me smiling again, the light gleaming on her smooth, auburn curls. "Allow me to introduce my stepfather, Miss Newcombe—Mr. Marcus Raven—and the lady, brave enough to look after us all, our cousin, Mrs. Mannering."

Mrs. Mannering, a plump lady in widow's weeds, paused from her tatting to bestow on me a benevolent smile; while Marcus Raven, Master of Ravensfall, bowed slightly, his handsome dark-featured face without expression. Slowly he placed the sketchbook he had been holding on a low table.

"Welcome to Ravensfall, Miss Newcombe." His voice, a low baritone, was distant.

There was something familiar about his face, which at first I could not place. Then, with a little start of surprise, I recognized what it was: his eyes of course, of so light a brown as to be almost the topaz eyes of my young companion of the early evening.

"I have a smudge on my nose, Miss Newcombe?" The low baritone was pleased to be amused.

I was annoyed to find myself blushing furiously; then, refusing to be put further out of countenance, I raised my head and answered stiffly, "Pray forgive me, sir, you remind me of . . . of an acquaintance of mine, and I was startled by the resemblance."

"Indeed?" There was a look in the pale eyes I could not fathom, and the thin lips twitched suddenly.

"My dear," Mrs. Mannering said suddenly to Ishbel. "You are keeping Miss Newcombe standing, and after such a journey she must be tired. Pray be seated, Miss Newcombe, and allow Ishbel to introduce the others of our company."

"Why, of course, Miss Newcombe. Do take this chair near the fire — it is quite the most comfortable — and allow me to introduce our guest, Mr. Gideon Tavish of Edinburgh. Mr. Tavish is writing a book about New Zealand birds."

47

Mr. Tavish, a stern-faced bearded gentleman of middle height, turned from the glass-fronted cabinet and bowed politely.

"How do you do?" His voice, deep and full, possessed a slight Scottish accent that was pleasing to the ear. "I trust you are recovered from the rigours of your journey, Miss Newcombe?"

"Thank you, sir."

There was a sudden rustle of skirts from the other end of the room.

Turning, I saw a curtained alcove, which rising two steps above the level of the drawing room acted as a little stage. Through the draperies, I saw the outline of the pianoforte, a long, low music stool set before it. From the stool, with a froufrou of her elegant puce and gold skirts, was rising quite the most handsome woman I had ever seen. Advancing to the steps, she paused a moment, looking down at us — an actress, ready to receive acclaim.

Though scarcely taller than myself, she had a presence which drew immediate attention. Not precisely beautiful, she nonetheless possessed an elegant hourglass figure, and her gleaming chestnut hair — piled high in a fashionable pompadour — and flashing green eyes gave the appearance of great vitality.

"Mrs. Joseph DuPrès," Ishbel introduced quietly. Her manner, vivacious until that moment, was suddenly subdued. I sensed a certain wariness about her.

Mrs. DuPrès nodded her head slightly. "Good evening, Miss Newcombe, I trust that you will find life here to your liking." Her green eyes surveyed me curiously, then evidently deciding that I was of no importance, she looked past me toward Mr. Raven.

"Marcus," she demanded, a slight French accent underlying her voice, "When you travel next to Wanganui, I should like above all things to accompany you. I understand that Collingwood's has a new shipment of music and both Ishbel" this with a brilliant smile at Ishbel, "and I need to add to our repertoire."

"Of course, Hélène, if you wish," Mr. Raven replied. Then, his pale gaze encountering mine, he added coldly, "You will, of course, accompany us, Miss Newcombe. Mrs. Mannering, the children and myself—when I am at Ravensfall—visit our townhouse in Wanganui one weekend each month to partake of Holy Communion at Christ Church. You are, of course, Church of England?" he asked repressively, raising a haughty dark eyebrow.

I agreed that I was. How, I wondered to myself, could I dare be otherwise!

Mr. Raven turned toward his children, still hunched upon their stools.

"Malvina, Reginald," he commanded suddenly, "come and greet Miss Newcombe."

The boy turned toward me and for the first time I saw his face. Though the cotton wig no longer adorned his dark hair and he was now respectably dressed in sailor suit, black stockings and boots, I recognized the comte—my young companion of the early evening.

I was about to greet him with a smile and a joke, when I realized that the child was looking toward me with no hint of recognition.

"Good evening, Miss Newcombe," he said woodenly. Gone was the French accent, and the animation of

49

the early evening was now completely lacking. He stood still, gazing before him expressionlessly.

"Your bow, Reginald, your bow!" his father reproved impatiently.

The boy bowed awkwardly, the grace and verve of the former occasion a mere memory hovering in the air between us.

"Good," said Mr. Raven surprisingly. "Very good, Reginald. You have improved!"

I looked at him, amazed.

Reginald, stepping backwards, managed to trip over his own feet, causing him to sit abruptly on the floor. With an exasperated sigh, his father turned aside to speak with Mrs. DuPrès, who with Mr. Tavish was tactfully studying a display of eighteenth-century snuff boxes in the cabinet.

Mrs. Mannering smiled conspiratorially at me and whispered "Poor Reggie, he is not . . . that is, he is a little . . . I'm afraid, Miss Newcombe, that you will find our poor Reggie is . . . rather . . . er . . . *slow* . . ." she sighed and tapped the side of her head significantly. "But his mother, you know, poor woman—he was just old enough, you know, when—and I dare say," she finished brilliantly, "that, that must have . . . *affected* him, don't you know!'

I looked at her, dazed.

"Affected him?" demanded Mr. Raven suddenly. "What do you mean, Cousin Lydia? *What* has affected Reginald?"

Unbeknown to us, Mr. Raven had parted company with the snuff boxes and now hovered eaglelike about Mrs. Mannering's chair.

Mrs. Mannering, her large watery blue eyes,

50

moonlike behind her spectacles, gazed at me appealingly.

"My arrival has made Reginald nervous, Mr. Raven," I explained.

There was a short silence as my employer gazed down at me expressionlessly. "I think," he suggested coolly at last to Mrs. Mannering, "now that Miss Newcombe has been introduced, that we should ring for coffee."

"Of course, dear Marcus," Mrs. Mannering agreed, with a grateful glance at me, "and perhaps Jenny can now take the children up to bed."

"Jenny?" asked Mr. Raven, one dark eyebrow raised.

"Why, yes, Marcus; Mrs. Douglas, as you know is confined with a chill to bed."

"Ah, yes," a sidelong glance at me, "poor woman, I had quite forgot." He gazed down at me, his dark brows glowering. "Mrs. Douglas on occasion still acts as nurse to my children, Miss Newcombe," he explained. "And to Ishbel also, sometimes. Indeed . . ." Here he paused as if he would say more, but thought better of it. "But, no matter, Miss Newcombe. Perhaps, you will see me in my study tomorrow."

'Study,' I thought, and my tired mind conjured up a picture of a red-lipped Mr. Pugh. Perhaps this was reflected in my face, for an anxious Mr. Raven leaned over me. "Whatever is the matter, Miss Newcombe?" he asked with cool concern. "I meant only that you must wish to discuss with me my children's education!"

"Indeed, yes, Mr. Raven," I remembered, stammering. "Hours of study must be arranged and texts, also—perhaps, when I have seen the schoolroom and what it contains . . ."

"Precisely, Miss Newcombe. Perhaps, then, we can agree upon tomorrow morning?"

"Of course, Mr. Raven," I answered with relief. "I'm sure I shall be able to present you with plans regarding Miss Malvina and Master Reginald, but as for Miss Ishbel—"

"Ishbel, Miss Newcombe? What of her? What has poor Ishbel done?" Though the tone was jocular, the light brown eyes were guarded.

"Why, nothing, Mr. Raven. But it seems to me, that she is a young lady and in little need of further formal teaching." I stared up at him questioningly.

He looked down at me, his eyes smoky amber in disapproval. "Ishbel is only seventeen years old—though she may, indeed, seem old for her years. I assure you, Miss Newcombe, that she is greatly in need of mature female companionship."

"But, a young lady, Mr. Raven, out here in the middle of nowhere? Surely, you could at least have her board at . . . at . . . the Wanganui Girls' College?" At last, I remembered the mate and his kindly words. "She could at least associate with young ladies of her own age. She could go on outings. She could, perhaps, appropriately chaperoned, of course, even meet with members of the opposite . . ."

My voice trailed away under the icy glare of my employer.

"Why, Miss Newcombe," his frigid baritone suggested, "I do believe you have been gossiping."

To my mortification, I felt my face flush. "Mr. Raven, I am not in the habit of gossiping." I began hotly, when the door opened and Jenny came in to lead away the children. In the ensuing 'good nights' and the arrival of Ngaire with the coffee, it was Ishbel's turn to play. She had chosen some Chopin Études, and I know I should have been pleased, but to my exhausted ear, surprisingly, they seemed mechanical, entirely lacking in emotion.

"My Ishbel plays well, does she not?" inquired a husky voice by my side.

Looking up, I found Mrs. DuPrès gazing down at me, an enigmatic light in her green eyes.

"She does indeed," I agreed, insincerely.

"Miss Inglewood, I'm afraid, did not challenge her sufficiently."

"Miss Inglewood?" I asked. "Ah, yes, Ishbel's former governess, I understand. I believe, that she is . . . deceased?"

For a moment, Mrs. DuPrès looked out of countenance. She paused a moment, biting her lip. At last, in her deep voice, she said, "Yes, poor woman, she had an unfortunate accident. While the river was in flood last year, she fell in and . . . drowned."

In between études, Ishbel had stopped playing for a moment. Except for a clink of coffee cups and the crackling of the fire, there was complete silence. Mrs. DuPrès and I stared at each other, her green eyes cold and measuring.

Softly, Ishbel started to play again.

"As I said," Mrs. DuPrès continued with a little shrug, as if she had spoken of nothing untoward, "I have had the guidance of Ishbel's music, and I think, in the circumstances, that she has turned out very well . . ."

"You are to be congratulated, Mrs. DuPrès," I answered vaguely, my mind still on Miss Inglewood. All of a sudden, the events of the day seemed overwhelming. I wondered when I could possibly excuse myself to go to my room.

"You will, of course, be teaching only the two younger children," Mrs. DuPrès continued. "Ishbel is seventeen and needs only —"

"Companionship," interrupted a deep, gruff voice.

I looked up to find Mr. Tavish looming up over me. "Miss McCleod is delicate," he assured me through his beard. "You must be an elder sister to her . . ."

I was about to ask him why, if Ishbel was too old for formal teaching, she was kept in such an isolated spot, when Mr. Raven joined the group.

"You are tired, Miss Newcombe," he remarked coldly. "I think we must bid you good night. Ishbel, I know, will be glad to escort you to your chamber."

Ishbel, having finished her playing, came out of the alcove and added her entreaties.

"Oh, do allow me to take you to your room, dear Miss Newcombe. I haven't spoken with someone directly from 'home' in such an age. Perhaps we could gossip a little before you go to bed?"

And I, thinking of the billowing curtain, of Jenny's and Hemi's uneasiness, of Miss Inglewood's unfortunate demise, decided that I should be glad of her company.

Seven

Out in the hall, Ishbel took up a lamp from the rosewood table. Raising it high, she paused a moment on the stairs, looking back over one shoulder, preparing to light my way.

Sometimes now, in my desolation, I think of Ishbel as she was then, poised for a moment on the rich Persian carpeting of the stairs: slender and tall in her lavender and white striped gown, her auburn hair glowing dully in the mellow light, her pale, patrician features thrown half into shadow against the dark wall panelling. *If only I had known,* I think now; if only I had known then of her secret fears, of the dangers besetting her, perhaps I *might* have saved her.

But I did not know. And so concerned was I with my own consequence, that I did not realize fully the horror of it until it was too late.

I looked up at her, wreathed as she was in an aura of youth and beauty, and thought with some humor how much she was the complete antithesis of my short dowdy self. What ironic fate, I wondered, had brought it about that I, a simple missionary's daughter of dubious background, should have the guidance of a young lady of such wealth and breeding.

"Pray follow me, Miss Newcombe," Ishbel said, gathering up her skirts as she mounted the stairs. "I declare, in our enormous house, you must feel quite lost! But don't worry, you will soon have the way of it!"

As she spoke, the lamp's glow alighted on the carved wooden bird, where it hovered in perpetual flight atop the newal post.

"A raven, of course," explained Ishbel in response to my questioning look. With a tinkling laugh, she added, "The badge of my stepfather's family. They are descended from the Vikings, you know, and used to rampage into battle with their raven banners flying! Black ravens on a red ground . . ."

"Then the name does refer to the bird?"

"Indeed, yes!

I paused a moment, looking down at feathers so intricately carved, they seemed almost to quiver. With a sudden shock, I suddenly realized that the wings were raised, not in flight as I had supposed, but rather in the act of landing. Under one carved claw, a small mouse struggled in its death throes, while the bird's cruel, sharp beak thrust down toward it.

With a little shudder, I followed Ishbel up to the first floor landing. In the well of the landing, unnoticed by me on my earlier trip with Jenny, hung a small portrait of an elderly man.

"Josiah Raven," Ishbel enlightened me. "Steppapa's uncle. Very wicked, or so they say . . ."

"Ishbel!" I exclaimed, thinking it my duty to reprove

her.

She smiled at me, unabashed. "Oh, come, Miss Newcombe, even Steppapa tells stories about him sometimes! He met him, you know, when he visited New Zealand as a young man." Then, seeing my puzzled look, she added apologetically, "But how I do run on! I ought to explain that Josiah Raven, though born in England — indeed as a young man, he lived at our Ravensfall in Yorkshire — became the captain of a whaler and ended his days in New Zealand. It was he who built this house, and named it Ravensfall."

She raised the lamp to help me see the portrait better, saying as she did so, "Apart from the painting of poor dear Mama in the dining room, we have no other family portraits here. Steppapa shipped out all kinds of furnishings from our estate in England, but the portraits, he felt, should remain at home against our return."

Despite Ishbel's remarks, the face that peered at us from the portrait seemed ordinary enough: frowning black brows that recalled those of Mr. Raven, narrow brown eyes, a craggy nose, and a full spade beard that almost disguised the faint line of a straight-lipped mouth.

"Mr. Raven actually met him?" I asked.

"Yes, when he traveled to New Zealand several years ago. They suited each other, it seems. When Great-uncle Josiah passed on, he left him this house and land."

Turning away from the portrait, Ishbel continued up the stairs.

On the second floor she paused a moment, explaining that the stairs to the servants' quarters on the third floor were down the hall to the left, behind a green baize door. The servants' stairs led right down to the kitchen, she was explaining, when the chill draught I had noticed earlier in the evening drifted by, softly patting our faces like the soft touch of unseen fingers.

"Bother," exclaimed Ishbel, "someone has left a window open in the cupola and has not closed the door." Her voice, usually so soft and musical, was sharp suddenly.

"Cupola?" I asked, puzzled.

"Indeed, yes. It is quite a landmark hereabouts; Josiah's Turret, it's called . . . or Josiah's Folly! You would not have seen it when you first arrived, for it was too dark."

So saying, she raised the lamp and there, on the landing at the head of the stairs, was a partly open door through which an icy current emanated, lifting the tendrils at the nape of my neck. I shivered.

Ishbel pushed open the door, revealing the first few steps of a spiral staircase twisting up into yawning blackness. "The stairs twist right up to the roof through the third floor. The dome can be seen for miles around," she explained. "They say that Great-uncle Josiah used to spend hours at a time up there with his telescope, watching the river . . ."

"Watching the river?"

"Yes, there's a lot of traffic, you know—mainly Maori canoes—traveling up and down between Wanganui and the centre of the island. And from up there," Ishbel continued, nodding her head toward the stairs, "one can see right down to the coast. Miss Inglewood, our former governess, used to climb up there a lot; she felt hemmed in, she always said, and needed to see above the trees . . ."

Ishbel paused a moment, biting her lip and casting me a questioning glance.

"I know about Miss Inglewood," I said gently. "Mrs. DuPrès told me."

"Ah." Ishbel expelled her breath slowly, in seeming relief, but her expression, I noted, altered subtly at my mention of Mrs. DuPrès. A relationship, I thought, to be explored later.

"She was a pretty thing, Miss Inglewood," Ishbel murmured in a muffled voice, "not unlike our dear Mama, actually; small and fair-haired, blue-eyed . . ."

"You must miss her," I said softly.

"Miss her?" Ishbel stared down at me, her face pale, wraithlike in the dim light. "Oh, yes indeed. She looked after us all like — like *mother*. Though," she added, smiling, "at times, she had the oddest fancies! I think sometimes, that she must have listened to the servants too much. They're very superstitious, you know."

In response to my puzzled gaze, she gave her tinkling laugh. "They say, you know, that old Josiah 'walks' among us still." She raised the lamp again to shine it up the winding stairs, glancing back as she did so at me. In the heightened glow, her eyes, a clear light aquamarine, shone with a brilliance that was almost magnetic.

I glanced up the stairs twisting their way to dark infinity and against my will saw in my mind's eye the bearded face of the old whaling captain in the portrait on the landing. Nonsense, I thought to myself

59

abruptly; Ishbel was right, superstitious nonsense! I folded my arms to prevent my shivering.

Ishbel was all apology. "My dear Miss Newcombe, pray forgive me, keeping you here in the cold! Let me take you to your chamber; we must not have you catching an inflammation of the lungs!" Closing the door firmly, she led me along the passage.

Inside my room, she rested the lamp on the mahogany tallboy and busied herself lighting the candles above the washstand.

I looked about the cosy room, still shivering despite myself.

The governess' room, Jenny had called it, and had paused nervously before the door; and Hemi, once inside, had put down my box and fled. The governess' room, I thought to myself—Miss Inglewood's room and now mine.

"My dear Miss Newcombe, I do believe you have taken a chill!"

I came to my senses to find Ishbel regarding me, her fair brows bent in a concerned frown. "Do come to the fire and warm yourself. I have got up quite a blaze!"

Indeed she had. After lighting the candles, she had busied herself at the small fireplace, stirring the still glowing embers in the grate. Having set a new log on top, she was now sitting back on her heels, her skirts billowing about her. "Come," she pleaded with a smile, patting the red cushioned seat of a low armchair drawn up before the hearth.

Sinking with a grateful sigh into the chair, I thanked her for her kindness.

"Oh, it's a mere nothing, I assure you, Miss Newcombe. I do so want you to be comfortable." Smilingly, Ishbel eased herself up onto a low footstool and we sat for a moment, gazing companionably into the fire together.

"I must remember, also, to thank you for your violets," I added, catching sight again of the delicate flowers in their porcelain bowl. "They are among my favorite flowers."

"Oh, really?" asked Ishbel, pleased. "Miss Inglewood loved them, too. I used to bring her the first of the season and she would wear them as a nosegay. In fact, now, when I smell them — they have a very delicate scent, you know — I almost imagine her still with us. But, poor Miss Inglewood, she is gone, isn't she, quite gone . . ."

With a sigh, Ishbel turned her head away. In the grate, the flames dimmed as with a crackle the log sank into the embers. The room, at first so cosy, now was lost in shadows.

"They never found her, you know," Ishbel continued, her head turned from me, "for she was swept away in the flood." Then, giving herself a shake, she added, "But what dismal talk is this; and on your first night with us! Pray forgive me. I think, perhaps, I had better retire and leave you in peace!"

She rose gracefully and moved toward the door, where she paused a moment, glancing back with a kind smile. "Good night, Miss Newcombe, I hope you will be happy with us. Sleep well!" And she was gone.

I sat for a few moments gazing into the embers. Had Miss Inglewood sat here once, as I did now, nervous and uncertain in her new position? Had she asked herself questions about the people in this huge, dark house? Impatient with myself, I rose and, briskly unbuttoning my blouse, approached the washstand in the corner near the window. The curtain swayed in the draught and it seemed to me that the breeze conveyed a delicate fragrance from the violets on the nearby escritoire.

Had Miss Inglewood washed from this bowl, I wondered, as I did now, admiring the pink cabbage roses reflected under the cool water? Had she gazed into this selfsame glass?

With a little shiver, I finished undressing and brushed out my hair. It had dried and, in a fit of rebellion, I brushed it into a cloud, letting it drift loose about my face and down my back.

Someone, I saw with pleasure, had unpacked my portmanteau for me and had placed my nightgown over the turned down sheets of the high mahogany bed. Looking in the huge wardrobe, I discovered my spare blouse, cloak, and traveling suit neatly cleaned and pressed, hanging from the rail. "Jenny", I thought and resolved to thank her warmly in the morning. At least, I had made a friend, I thought.

With a lighter heart, I slipped into my nightgown and even smiled as I picked up my wrapper. "Such colors, Harriet!" my aunt had exclaimed, at the sight of my one extravagance. "Such colors! A true lady, my dear, should never be obtrusive; and you of all people, should not draw attention to yourself!"

It was true, I thought, smiling happily, the colors were anything but restrained. I gazed down with pleasure at the bright peacock blue and gold patterned silk.

"I'm so tired of dark clothes, Aunt," I had said, "and

anyway, no one will see me!"

"I should hope *not*, Harriet!"

Still smiling, I blew out all the candles save one on the mantelpiece. I should stay by the fire a few minutes, I decided, for I needed time to collect myself. So much had happened to me in such a short space of time, and my mind whirled with thoughts and impressions. I stoked up the embers and with a sigh sank again into the armchair.

It was then I heard a scream.

Thin and wailing, it sounded faintly through the wall behind my bed. For a moment, I started in superstitious horror, then, pulling myself together, I rose and firmly grasped the candle. Malvina, I remembered, was in the room next to mine. The poor child was probably suffering from a nightmare.

Malvina's door opened easily. All was darkness, but the flame from my candle hollowed out a cave of light, dazzling the immediate prospect and reflecting on the brass knobs of a bedstead half-hidden in one shadowy corner.

"Malvina?" I queried softly.

The child was sitting bolt upright, her large, blue eyes staring straight ahead.

"Malvina?" I asked again, and drew closer. It was not until I had shone the candle directly in her face that I realized that the poor child was still fast asleep and in the midst of some dreadful nightmare.

Before I could put out a hand to wake her, she muttered swift and low, so that I could hardly hear her, "I did not! Truly, I did not! Oh, *poor* Miss Inglewood! Oh, Papa, you must not! No, Papa, no . . ."

Gently, I eased her back into her pillows, murmuring soothingly as I did so. Slowly, she closed her eyes and, mumbling once again, "Oh, *poor* Miss Inglewood!" she turned on her side and with a sigh, drifted off to sleep.

I stood gazing down at her in her small, narrow bed; her fair hair spread across the pillow, her pale face flushed in sleep.

Some childish misdemeanor, I reasoned, worried her still, poor little mite. Something she had done and her Papa had found her out. But *poor* Miss Inglewood? Why *poor* Miss Inglewood? Of course, I thought, my mind clearing, she would think Miss Inglewood blamed for *her* mistake.

That was it, I declared to myself with firm satisfaction. Shining my light once more, I satisfied myself that she was indeed in a peaceful sleep.

Poor child, I thought, what had she done to suffer such a nightmare? Was Mr. Raven truly such a stern father?

She and Reginald, though thin and pale, were certainly well groomed and well dressed, and my candlelight as I shifted it about the room shone on furnishings both suitable and elegant. Materially, I decided, with a doubtful shake of my head, she was well provided for; but if Mr. Raven was a truly caring father, why was she so frightened of him? Shaking my head, I made my way carefully out of the room.

To my dismay, once out into the corridor, my candle flame, though carefully guarded by my hand, was quenched at once by a strong draught.

The door to the cupola, I thought in strange panic, must have opened again. Or perhaps Ravensfall, such

64

a rambling, enormous place, was *full* of draughts. "Be sensible, Harriet," I told myself in my Aunt Alice's voice, "it is only darkness after all, and the breeze you feel on the back of your neck is a perfectly natural occurrence! Simply feel your way along the wall and find your door!"

So I felt my way along the wall, but in my panic and disorientation, I did not find my door.

Instead, shaking with cold and fright, I found myself outside the open door to the cupola itself, where I stood transfixed as a light, thin at first, swelled to a sudden blaze as it descended the winding stairs.

"Exploring, Miss Newcombe?" a cool voice greeted me.

Above me loomed the master of Ravensfall, a cold smile on his saturnine face.

Eight

"Exploring, Miss Newcombe?" the disdainful voice asked again. Raising his lamp higher, the better to observe me in my embarrassment, Marcus Raven bent his sardonic gaze on me.

I stood before him, miserably conscious that my too-bright wrapper had slipped from my shoulders, exposing my defenseless self clad only in a thin, white nightgown. I was horribly aware of his cool eyes raking me from indecorous top to ill-clad toe.

"An emergency, Miss Newcombe?" The light eyes played about my fall of hair, now drifting across my face, and the thin lips quirked in a crooked smile as I hurriedly dragged my wrapper back into place, pulling it tightly about my trembling shoulders.

He loomed enormous in the doorway to the cupola, the light from his lamp outlining his broad shoulders and narrow waist. His black bow-tie had, I noticed, become undone and his white stiff-collared evening shirt gaped open about his brown, muscular throat. He swayed a little, and the lamplight surged a moment about my feet.

"Don't run, Miss Newcombe," pleaded my employer in amused contempt, as I began to back away. "I am not under the influence of spiritous liquor!" He shifted the lamp slightly and I noticed a graze on the side of his head.

"You are hurt, sir," I exclaimed in concern.

"Nothing to signify, I . . . slipped on the stairs and . . . bumped my head."

"I should be glad to offer you some assistance . . . perhaps, a damp cloth . . . ?"

"Ah, I shelter a Nightingale under my roof! Although," his cool gaze flicked over me again, "perhaps, your present attire would indicate a bird of more . . . exotic . . . plumage?"

I retreated, blushing.

"Come, Miss Newcombe; you are no coward, surely?" he chided me in tones of gentle raillery. "In fact, I know you are not!" Then, as I looked at him in great surprise, he added, his voice sharpening. "But I believe, I asked you if there were an emergency, or do you," he asked with deadly politeness, "make it a practice to roam about a gentleman's halls in such . . . charming . . . déshabille?"

"No, sir, I do not!" I flared, unable to help myself, as the tensions of the day and the humiliations of the evening conspired to make me reach my breaking point. "I left my room, sir, in answer to a scream — a *scream*, sir! — from your daughter, Malvina, who was suffering from a nightmare, of which, sir, *you* seemed to be the main participant!"

"I, Miss Newcombe?" The dark brows rose in delicate surprise.

"*You*, Mr. Raven! Your daughter is frightened of you. Did you know? Or, instead of getting to know your daughter, do you spend your time *roaming about your halls* at dead of night?"

"Oh, bravo, Miss Newcombe! Touché!"

"And when I left your daughter's room," I continued, trying to keep my voice from trembling, "my candle blew out and I lost my way. If you will kindly shine your lamp down the hall, Mr. Raven, I shall no doubt be able to find my way back to my chamber."

Turning from him abruptly, I surreptitiously hitched at my errant wrap slipping again from my shoulders and stalked stiff-legged down the corridor.

"Good night, Miss Newcombe!" An amused baritone followed me down the hall as I returned to my room.

I turned to see him, tall and alert, one hand on the door to the cupola, the other holding the lamp. In the dim light, I could no longer discern his expression. I felt, rather than saw, his contemptuous smile. With burning cheeks, I opened my door. "Good night, Mr. Raven," I managed at last, with as much dignity as I could find, and slipped thankfully into the anonymous gloom of my chamber.

Once inside, I paused, my back to the door, tears of humiliation stinging my eyelids. What had he thought, I asked myself, to see his children's governess disporting herself about his halls in such wanton disarray?

Resolutely, I crossed to the fireplace, and with a

taper lit from the last glowing embers, I lighted again the candles above the washstand. Slowly, I moved to the glass and forced myself to look into it.

It was as I thought; worse, even. Unruly hair, I saw, tangled by the breeze, flushed high cheekbones and eyes sparkling with angry tears; and above all, the wrapper, the shameful gaudy wrapper, slipping even now from my thinly clad shoulders.

"A lady, Harriet," I could hear my Aunt Alice saying, "in no matter what circumstances, should always be well covered!" She had sniffed and then handed me her 'going away' present, a heavy, woolen dressing gown in a glorious shade of muted, dark brown. "I have done my best, Harriet, to bring you up a lady. As I am sure, your poor father—in his right senses—would have wished . . . but your mother, child," her glance had fallen away, embarrassed, to the despised wrapper flaunting itself amidst my more humble attire waiting to be packed away. "You are very like her, you know, not only in . . ." she looked toward the wrapper again and shuddered, "your choice of dress, but also in your refusal to adapt yourself to woman's lowly position. Your tongue, dear, is much too sharp. I fear, Harriet, that one day your impertinent remarks will lead you astray."

My impertinent remarks, I thought now, gazing into the glass. How could I have addressed Mr. Raven in such a way; accusing him of neglecting his own daughter! What must he have thought?

I shuddered, studying my colorful and scantily clad appearance, remembering too late all my aunt's advice about remaining in the background.

"You must learn, Harriet, not to attract attention

to yourself; for I fear you are very like your mother . . ."

Like my mother, I thought in despair, looking at my flushed cheeks and sparkling eyes. I had tried so hard to follow Aunt Alice's admonitions, but as Mr. Pugh would have said, my "tainted blood would out."

"I fear, Harriet," he would rumble, patting my shrinking shoulder, "that your mother was wanton — for she was a slut, you know; an Irish servant girl, without proper home or family. She wandered into your father's mission in Manchester one day, and he — poor, misguided fool — was caught in her snare and married her out of pity. I warned him, of course, warned him that it would not do, that she would bring nothing but trouble, would in fact drag his good name in the mire. And, of course, I was right, for she ran off, shortly after you were born . . ."

Here, Mr. Pugh would pause, one plump forefinger pointing toward heaven. "And when you were ten years old, Harriet, God in his infinite wisdom took your father, and so you were left to us . . . a Christian obligation . . . but in this life, we all have our cross to bear. You have been a great trial to us, Harriet, a great trial, for you are like her, you know, very like . . . but we shall see to that, shan't we! Oh . . . hmm . . . yes, we shall see to that . . ." His damp hand would press me to my knees to, as he put it, seek out my salvation in prayer. I shuddered and dismissed that and subsequent memories from my mind.

A new life, I thought bitterly, as I reached up to snuff the candles, that is what I had sought in New Zealand; a new life in a romantic land, far from all who knew about my shameful background — that had

70

been my plan and I had ruined it. What was the use, I asked myself in despair, of leaving Manchester behind, if myself, my true self—that wicked, untameable self—was still with me?

Slowly, I made my way over to my bed. After such an incident, I asked myself, would I be allowed to keep my present situation? I doubted it. Mr. Raven, by his earlier cool reception, had already made clear his doubts concerning me, and I had seen by his air of haughty surprise, that my ill-considered remarks concerning Ishbel's education had also met with his disapproval. If, I thought then, he had seen fit to find fault with my earlier conduct, what must he have thought of my later disheveled appearance outside the cupola? What, too, of my outrageous remarks concerning his treatment of his daughter, Malvina?

I thought again of his ironic gaze and shuddered. A "bird of exotic plumage" he had called me. I wondered, then, if he had had any inkling as to how close he had come to the truth. Choking back a sob, I climbed up into the bed. I would pack again in the morning, I told myself, and be ready to leave with as much dignity as possible.

As I sank down into the deep feather mattress, however, I remembered the kindly words of the mate of the *Waiwere* as he had helped me onto the Ravenshall landing . . . that the Girls' College in Wanganui needed an English mistress and that he was sure that I just 'fit the bill.' All was not yet lost then, I told myself. I would leave Ravensfall the day after tomorrow and seek both board and employment in Wanganui and then . . . reaching out to snuff my candle, my eyes alighted on my box. In all the tension of my

71

arrival, I had given it scarcely a thought; but now, as I looked at it, the familiar excitement surged through my veins. I thought of the books and the precious papers inside; those papers that I had managed to hide from my Aunt when she had instituted a regular search of my belongings, after she had discovered me — at the age of sixteen — reading *The Mill On The Floss*.

"My dear Harriet, what are you about, to be reading such rubbish! So this is why you have such unfeminine ideas about female education! This author, you know, is quite notorious! Not only are her writings quite unfeminine, but . . ." Blushing painfully, my aunt lowered her voice. "but, I understand that she lives with a man who is not her husband and not only that, but . . . I hear she *smokes!*"

Shortly after this, my aunt found my copy of *East Lynne* concealed under my neglected pile of mending.

Confined to my room for a week on bread and water, I spent the time scribbling my own stories, the papers of which I hid among the pages of my copy of Fox's *Book Of Martyrs*.

Feeling somewhat more confident, I snuffed out my candle and snuggled down under the quilt. Not only would I find a position as a teacher, I assured myself, but released at last from the need for secrecy, I would be able to spend as much of my spare time as I wanted at my writing. Perhaps I would become an author myself! Tentatively, I stretched out, my feet seeking the flannel-wrapped, stone hot-water bottle that Jenny or Ngaire had so kindly placed in my bed. This was a new land, I told myself; a land of opportunities and I *would* make a new life for myself — I *would;*

but on the verge of sleep at last, Mr. Pugh's face—huge, monstrous—floated to the edge of consciousness. "We shall see to that, Harriet," it mouthed in frightful silence, "we shall see to that!"

Nine

After such a day, it was not surprising that I slept fitfully, my rest disturbed by uncertain dreams verging on the edge of nightmare. It was with some relief that I finally awoke fully to find a dim white light filtering in through the red curtains.

Struggling out of bed, I groped for Aunt Alice's brown wool dressing gown and, making my way to the window, threw back the curtains. Moisture had condensed on the glass, and the air I breathed was damp and chill. Throwing open the window, I leaned out into a cool damp world. The rain had stopped. In its place a fine white mist rose like steam from the unseen river in its chasm far below, dispersing itself in wraithlike wisps amongst the dark green shrubbery of the surrounding bush.

Immediately below my window was a balcony forming the roof of the first-floor verandah. Beyond the narrow balustrade, I could see the tops of giant feathery ferns with parts of a gravelled walk interspersed in between; then on the other side of the walk a narrow strip of bluff bordering the long drop to the river. On my left, far away to the southwest, was a glimpse of the sea, and on my right many miles to the northeast, a lonely snow-enshrouded mountain top rose delicately above the enveloping mists.

New Zealand, I thought. I was truly here at last. All at once, my doubts of the preceding night fell away. A new country, I thought again, a new life. All would come right, I told myself—poor fool that I was—for I felt it in my bones. It was at that moment that I heard the gravel crunch on the walk below my window, far to my right.

On looking down, I spied Hemi walking below with a male companion—a European, as far as I could tell. As I peered out, he lifted his head suddenly and I found myself looking down into the lean, pale face of Callum Douglas. Before I could withdraw, he raised his fingers in an ironic half-salute. How, I wondered, had he reached Ravensfall so soon? He had not, I knew, been on the *Waiwere*.

Lowering my window in some embarrassment, I hastened to answer a subdued knock on my door. In the hallway was Malvina, already clad in a ruffled white pinafore over a brown merino dress, her fair hair confined by a brown velvet Alice band. Smiling at me shyly, she wished me a good morning and announced that breakfast would be served in the schoolroom when I was ready.

She was turning to leave, when I said casually, "I hope you had better dreams after your nightmare last night, Malvina."

To my surprise, she looked at me in fright. "I had a nightmare last night, Miss Newcombe?"

"Oh dear," I replied, concerned, "perhaps I should not have reminded you of it—but I wondered if you often suffered from them?"

"Wh—what did I say, Miss Newcombe?" The tip of her tongue flickered around her lips and her blue eyes widened in apparent fright.

"Oh, nothing much. I can scarce recall," I lied. "Nothing to worry about, at all events." I crossed over to her quickly and, laying my hands on her thin shoulders, I smiled down into her upturned face.

To my surprise, I saw tears sparkling in her eyes. "You won't t—tell, Miss Newcombe, will you? You won't tell that I had nightmares again, that I talked in my sleep?"

"Won't tell whom, child?"

"Why . . . any . . . anyone. I don't want *anyone* to know!"

"Not even Mrs. Douglas?" I asked gently. "Surely, my dear, if you are subject to nightmares, Mrs. Douglas—or even your Papa—should be informed—and a doctor summoned."

"Oh no, Miss Newcombe! Pray do not tell my Papa! He must not know . . . he must never know . . ." She broke off, biting her lip, her blue eyes, though tearful, wise beyond her years.

"Must not know *what*, Malvina?" I asked in consternation.

"Oh, nothing, Miss Newcombe. Nothing at all. I am twelve, you know, and of an age, as Mrs. Douglas says, for girls to have strange fancies . . . but you will not tell Papa, will you? Promise me, you will not."

As she spoke, a knock sounded again at my door. Malvina's face, if possible, turned even whiter than before. "Promise me, Miss Newcombe," she begged. "Please don't tell . . . oh, promise me!"

What could I do? Though unbeknown to the poor child, I had already discussed her nightmare with her father, I could not in the urgency of the situation do anything other than nod my head and smile. "I promise," I assured her, crossing my fingers behind my back at the same time and feeling like a traitor. "But of what are you afraid, Malvina?"

She opened her mouth as if to speak, but a knock sounded again at the door and as I went to open it, Malvina, a white, terrified look at me, slipped past me into the corridor. "You promised!" she hissed at me, as she fled.

It was only Jenny carrying a copper can of hot water. She bobbed a curtsy in the doorway, a cheerful smile on her pleasant plump face. "I hope as how you've slept well, Miss?" she beamed, her familiar Lancashire accent comforting to my ear. "Mr. Raven presents his compliments, and asks that you wait on him as soon as you've had breakfast." Still smiling, she carried the can over to the washstand and splashed some hot water in the basin for me.

So, I thought, watching her grimly, I was to be dismissed: for what other reason could he possibly wish to see me so early in the day, before I had had time to find out my students' capabilities? My face must have reflected my thoughts, for Jenny said, "Why, Miss, whatever is the matter?"

I forced myself to smile. "Forgive me," I apologized, "my mind was on something else! While I remember," I continued, "I should like to thank you for being so kind as to press my clothes. I declare, my traveling suit looks hardly the worse for wear!"

Crossing to the wardrobe, I threw open the door to

display my serviceable herringbone tweed hanging neatly from the rail, my spare shirtwaist neatly pressed beside it. Jenny's face cleared, as if by magic. "Oh, it were nothing, Miss, I'm sure. I was glad to do it for you—you coming from Lancashire, an' all!"

With a shy smile, she put down the hot-water can and joined me at the wardrobe, putting out a hand to finger the tweed. "Besides," she added, "I love working with good stuff. I double as lady's maid to Mrs. Mannering, you know, and to Miss Ishbel too, betimes, when she's off to some social evening . . ."

"Social evening?" I interrupted in surprise. "Out here in the bush?"

"Oh, lor', yes, Miss. There's always summat going on. Though we're cut off by miles of bush, there's other houses scattered here and there. We get about by pack horses mostly, or by canoe up the river. We usually stay overnight and come back next day. It's lots of fun, Miss. Folk get sick of their own company, don't they?"

She stopped a moment and smiled at me again. "You'll be going too, Miss, for you'll have to chaperone Miss Ishbel."

I sighed and looked away. I was going to miss Jenny, I thought.

"Miss?"

"What is it, Jenny?"

A silence, while she twisted her hands and looked toward the floor.

"Oh, nothing, Miss . . . it's just that . . . oh, Miss, why do you wear your lovely hair the way you do?"

"*Lovely* hair?" I asked with a sarcastic laugh.

"Oh, yes, Miss. Now come here, do!"

I found myself guided toward the glass and seated in a chair.

"Look, Miss . . ."

I watched, fascinated, as my hairpins were removed, and my hair, a heavy curtain, fell about my shoulders. A brush whisked about my locks, reducing them to some kind of order.

"Oh, look, Miss, all those highlights — copper, gold, amber — I'll bet this has never been cut!"

"Well . . . no!"

A pair of scissors was flashed out of an apron pocket. "Now, Miss, don't take on . . . All you need is a snip here, a snip there; you need some hair about your face, see. All soft and pretty, like; never scrape it back — makes you look like a scalped chicken!

She dragged my hair back to demonstrate and we both giggled.

"Oh, come on, Miss; let me cut it . . . *do!*"

A fit of madness seized me; I found myself nodding my head.

Snip, snip, snip. I was mesmerized as I watched the flashing scissors.

"There, Miss, see how it curls about your face? Now, all we have to do is pile it high in a chignon — give you a bit of height, like — there, we are. Oh, I know some as would give their right arm for this; so thick and with a natural curl — never the tongs for you, Miss! Now, then. What do you think?"

Flushed and breathless, Jenny smiled at me in the mirror.

"Oh, Jenny . . . I . . . I hardly recognize myself!"

"But, do you like it, Miss?"

"Yes. Oh, *yes*. But, don't you think . . . that it is

. . . Well, doesn't it make me look . . . a little . . . er . . . frivolous?"

"Frivolous! What, you, Miss?"

"Now, Jenny, don't laugh at me. But, I am supposed to be a teacher, you know!"

"So, who said teachers shouldn't be pretty?"

"Now, Jenny . . . !

"And, while we're on the subject—oh, Miss, I do hope as you won't be offended—but with that pale skin, you didn't ought to wear black nor dead white, neither . . ."

She stepped back and looked at me consideringly. "What I'd like to see you in is rose pink or maybe a light glowing blue . . . if you get yourself some dress lengths, Miss, I'd be glad to help you make them up. Mrs. Mannering says I've quite a knack with my needle . . ." Then pulling herself together with an obvious effort, she added with an apologetic smile, "Here I am, keeping you from your breakfast. My mam always said I talk too much and she was right!" Then, as I continued to gaze at myself in the glass, she added diffidently, twisting her hands a little in her apron, "I hope as how I haven't offended you, Miss— me and my big mouth!"

There was real anxiety in her tone and I turned to her quickly. "Of course not, Jenny. You've just make me look at myself in a different way, that's all! Like all of us Lancashire women, you're plain spoken—and I thank you for it!"

"Bless you, Miss. Thank you!" she exclaimed. Then dimpling at me as she went out the door, she added, "Be careful when you dress, Miss. I don't want that chignon to come tumbling down!" With a cheerful laugh, she closed the door, leaving me still gazing at my embellished appearance in the glass.

With an effort, I pulled my eyes away and, slipping off my dressing gown, prepared to wash. I should have to take the chignon down, of course. The curls were bad enough, I told myself as I splashed some more hot water into the basin. I couldn't possibly go downstairs with my hair dressed in such a frivolous manner, I found myself informing the pink, cabbage roses gleaming translucent through the soapy water. *Whatever* would Aunt Alice say! I sneaked another glance at myself in the glass: yes, I should have to take my hair down again, I decided. However, instead of jerking off my nightgown as usual, I found myself pulling it off gently, careful not to disturb a hair on my head.

Thoughtfully, I looked into the wardrobe. All of a sudden, my spare skirt looked impossibly dowdy to me, its black bombasine folds dull and lusterless. As I was going to leave so soon, I decided, I might as well wear my traveling suit, and while I was about it, I told myself, instead of the black blouse Aunt Alice had made me to wear with it, I would don my spare white shirtwaist, which happened to have a froth of lace at the neck. If, I decided, jutting out my chin, I was going to be dismissed, then I might as well be dismissed in style.

One of the buttons of my jacket had become loose and as I delved into my sewing bag to find a needle and thread, my eye encountered something bright. It was a little ornament made out of gaily colored gauzy ribbons that an elderly lady on the ship had given to me in return for a favor. Though I thanked her at the time, I had put it away, never thinking of wearing it. Looking at it now, its brightness seemed a symbol of all my hopes. After fixing the button and slipping on my jacket, I pinned the ornament to the lapel and then stood back to look at myself in the glass. I was right, I decided; with its silver-edged blue and rose ribbons interspersed with tiny, silver beads, the ornament was just the thing to brighten my dull herringbone tweed.

Perhaps it was the ornament, perhaps it was my softly piled chignon; but it seemed to me that my whole face was livelier. There was even a flush in my normally pale cheeks. As I put up my hands to take down my hair, I thought over again what Jenny had said about my appearance. Pretty, she had said I was! I laughed to myself as I reluctantly removed the first hairpin. Pretty, indeed! I half-removed another hairpin and then hesitated. What would Aunt Alice say about all this, I wondered suddenly. My fingers paused a moment, the hairpin quivering between them. But Aunt Alice was not here to see, I thought. Slowly, I replaced the hairpin. As for Mr. Raven, why should I care what he thought about my appearance, if in any case he was about to dismiss me?

I stared at myself in some astonishment as I realized that, for the first time in my life, I was free to please myself, make my own decisions. My hair would stay as it was, I told myself firmly. Tucking a fresh pocket handkerchief into my breast pocket, I swept out of the room, my head held high.

Ten

Would I have left my room so confidently, I wonder now, if I had known the consequences of that decision made in a moment of vanity? Yet, how could I have known? How could I have guessed that a change in appearance of a mere teacher would lead to a chain of events so terrible that even now I shudder as I write?

Such awareness was denied to me as, on that cold, foggy morning only a few short months since, I stepped into the hall. Indeed, so convinced was I that I was about to be dismissed, that I had already determined that Ravensfall was not going to be a part of my future.

The hall, though dim in the early morning light, was lit from each end by large windows which were themselves decorated with a diamond motif of red and yellow glass. As I stood admiring them for a moment, I heard the sound of a door opening far to my right. A man emerged into the hall. Though I did not see his face, for he had turned immediately and disappeared through another door at the end of the passage, the set of his broad shoulders helped me to recognize the Scottish visitor, Mr. Tavish. In some surprise, for I had not realized that there were also some guest rooms on 'the children's floor,' I turned to my right and entered the schoolroom.

The room, large and airy, was furnished comfortably with overflowing walnut bookcases, a large table covered by a blue and white chequered cloth and several chairs of various shapes and sizes. A small fire flickered in the grate and, as in my room, the two large windows were hung with red plush curtains.

The children were kneeling on a red cushioned window seat, gazing out into the mist. As I closed the door, Malvina jumped up to greet me, her blue eyes widening slightly at, as I supposed, my changed hairstyle. Reginald turned more slowly, his face, I was sorry to see, as blank of expression as it had been in the drawing room the night before. I should certainly have to mention his strange behavior to his father before I left, I thought; and I realized with a stab of guilt, I should also have to explain to Mr. Raven the situation with Malvina.

Smiling at me shyly, Malvina rang for breakfast and, as we seated ourselves at the table, I pondered again the strangeness of the children I had been hired to teach: Malvina with her fear that expressed itself in nightmares and Reginald with his odd behavior. Ishbel, I considered, though evidently delicate and high-spirited, was by far the lest troubled of the three. What a pity, I thought again, that she was stranded here in the middle of the bush. Perhaps, I decided, I could put in another plea for her to her father before I left.

Breakfast was delivered by a young maid I had not seen before. Though the meal was good and wholesome, consisting of porridge and soft-boiled eggs, neither child—despite my gentle urging—would eat much. Neither did they respond when I attempted to converse with them, though Malvina occasionally sent me one of her shy smiles.

If only, I found myself thinking wistfully, I had more time to spend with them. With the untimely death of their mother, hinted at by Mrs. Mannering the night before, and the shocking circumstances of Miss Inglewood's sad demise; they were probably overwhelmed by tragedy. They were, I thought, close to the age I had been when Mr. Pugh had taken me from my father's house. I had a longing to put an arm about their shoulders, to soothe away their fears with a loving hand. But it was not to be, I reminded myself with regret, for had not Mr. Raven summoned me to his sanctum with the intention of dismissing me?

Mr. Raven, I thought with a sudden pang. Rising to my feet, I dabbed hastily at my lips with my table napkin. Condemning myself for my nervous anxiety, I hurried to the door and there paused a moment looking back at the children. They gazed solemnly back at me, Malvina with her arm about Reginald's thin shoulders and in that moment, I thought I saw at last, a gleam of understanding in Reginald's eyes.

On an impulse, I asked, "Perhaps you could lead me down to your father's study?"

I looked at them both, but it was Malvina who joined me at the door. Reginald, his face blank again, sat still, gazing silently at his plate.

85

"Your brother?" I began tentatively, once we were out in the hall, but Malvina, with a veiled look at me from under her long fair lashes, walked quickly ahead, saying, "Oh, pay no attention to Reggie, Miss Newcombe; once he gets to know you, he will soon be himself, I dare say."

There was a frigidity about her tone that did not invite further questions. Resigned, I followed her to the stairhead. I noticed that she kept to the opposite side of the passage as we passed the cupola.

As we descended, Malvina chattered brightly, as if to make up for her reticence over Reginald. The guest rooms, she explained, were all on the second floor, while the morning room, Mr. Raven's, and Mrs. Mannering's suites of rooms occupied the first floor. Ishbel, since she had reached the age of seventeen, had been promoted to a bedroom and sitting room on the first floor. The ground floor, she explained, held the library, drawing and dining rooms, as well as Mr. Raven's study and, in the back of the house, the kitchen quarters.

"The guest rooms are all situated on the second floor?" I asked, puzzled.

"Indeed, yes, Miss Newcombe."

"But surely I saw Mr. Tavish just now coming out of a room along the passage from the cupola?"

Malvina looked at me in surprise; then, her face clearing, she suggested innocently, "Perhaps, Mr. Tavish was visiting Mrs. Douglas, Miss Newcombe. She is our housekeeper, you know, and looks after all our problems."

Indeed? I thought, with a raised eyebrow—alone with a gentleman in her room, at seven o'clock in the

86

morning? Still, I reminded myself hastily, it was none of my affair. I was, after all, about to be dismissed!

Like the others, the first floor, I soon discovered, was lighted from each end by large windows studded with diamond panes of red and yellow glass. In this diffused light, old Josiah's portrait on the first-floor landing assumed an almost saintly aura.

"Our Great-uncle Josiah," Malvina was explaining, when I turned my head and caught my breath in surprise.

Below us the entrance hall on the ground floor was flooded with light from two large stained-glass windows set on either side of the front door. On the left, in a blaze of reds, golds, blues, and greens, St. George was depicted slaying a fire-breathing dragon, while on the right the hapless maiden — her golden locks floating about her delicate face — writhed against the bonds that tied her to a tree.

When the sun was shining, I thought, how glorious would be the light in the hall. Even now, in the dim vague whiteness of a foggy morning, the pictures stood out in startling relief, dispensing a glow both delicate and subtle.

Below us, to the left, a door closed and muffled footsteps sounded on the rich Persian carpet. Looking down, I saw the top of a familiar, slouched hat.

"Callum Douglas," Malvina whispered, drawing back a little. "Mrs. Douglas's son, you know, and my father's manager."

The footsteps paused and the lean face looked up.

"Who's there?" The Scottish burr was abrupt. The pointed-down shotgun he was carrying quivered a little.

"M-Miss . . . N-Newcombe, this is M-Mr. Douglas."

The hat was doffed and in the varied light from the windows, the dark red hair glowed with a fire that was touched with gold.

"Miss Newcombe and I have already met. Good morning, I hope you have quite recov—" His words faded into silence as he gazed up at me, his eyes widening. "Well, Miss Newcombe! I was about to say that I hoped you had recovered from your journey, but I see you have! You have indeed!" His tone was jocular, but his face remained serious and as I watched, a shadow—almost of sadness—passed over his features; but so quickly, that afterwards I wondered if I had imagined it.

"Good fortune, Miss Newcombe!" All of a sudden, he was his old self again. After a mocking half-salute, he passed in front of the stairs and padded off down a passage that led behind the dining room to the right.

"Cousin Callum is Mrs. Douglas's son," Malvina repeated, as we descended the stairs. "He is a sort of cousin of ours, for his father was related to Mama's first husband."

"Indeed," I asked, surprised. "Then, you all came out to New Zealand together?"

We had reached the bottom of the stairs, before Malvina finally replied. "Yes. That is, Papa thought it best that we should all stay together . . . after . . . after . . ."

After what, I wondered, but seeing her distress, I did not force her to go on.

We turned into the passage entered by Callum Douglas and Malvina stopped before a polished oak door. "Papa's study," she announced. She looked at me hesitantly for a moment, as if she would have said more, then turning from me suddenly, ran off into the shadows.

I looked at the door shut uncompromisingly against me. What was on the other side, I wondered. Rejection? Humiliation? My confidence, so hardly won by the change Jenny had wrought in my appearance, began to ebb away. I had to tell myself to lift my head, to throw back my shoulders.

"Courage, Harriet," I whispered to myself aloud, and standing still for a moment, I forced myself to remember Mr. Raven's looks of cool contempt, his disparaging remarks. This time, come what may, I decided, I would not be patronised, I would not be humiliated. Furthermore, I told myself firmly, rapping sharply on the door, there were a number of things I felt obliged to tell Mr. Raven about his children before I left.

So it was, head raised for battle, eyes sparkling, and cheeks flushed, I entered the study in response to the summons.

Eleven

The door opened into a small but pleasant booklined room furnished with several leather upholstered chairs and an enormous teak desk. To one side was a large rough stone fireplace, surmounted by a small oil of a clipper in full sail, while opposite the door were blue curtained French windows letting out onto the ground-floor verandah. I could see a patch of damp green lawn under the spreading branches of an ancient tree of a type I had not before seen.

Mr. Raven was not alone. With Callum Douglas, he was standing at his desk looking down at an open ledger.

"Ah, there you are, Miss Newcombe," he announced, glancing reprovingly at a small ormulu clock ticking on the mantelpiece.

I was about to make my excuses, when I remembered just in time my vow not to be on the defensive. After all, I thought to myself angrily, I had received Mr. Raven's summons scarcely an hour before—did he expect me to dress and have breakfast in five minutes flat?

I stood on my dignity, giving him a cool look.

Unfortunately, this seemed lost on Mr. Raven, who barely glancing in my direction, instructed me to be seated. I should have preferred to stand, but could not do so without seeming churlish. As if sensing my mood, Callum Douglas grinned at me. "We shan't be long, Miss Newcombe. Mr. Raven is just giving me his last instructions before he leaves." He turned back to the ledgers, saying as he did so, that he and I had met in the hall.

Paying no attention, Mr. Raven studied the ledgers for another minute or two, before remarking, "That's all, then, Callum. Unless you have any questions?"

Shaking his head, Callum Douglas picked up his hat and gun from a nearby chair and bade a pleasant journey to his employer. Then, seeing my eyes on the gun, he explained, "Opossums, Miss Newcombe. The countryside abounds in them; they destroy our fruit, you know, and have to be exterminated . . ."

He paused a moment, then observing my obvious incomprehension, explained, "A small animal, Miss Newcombe, something like a cat that carries its young in a pouch, and lives in trees . . ."

"A native of Australia," Mr. Raven interrupted with some asperity. "God knows," he added, "what our early settlers were thinking of to introduce it to this innocent land . . ."

Grinning at me, Callum raised a humorous hand in farewell and left.

Mr Raven continued for a moment to consider the ledger, then frowning a little, he turned at last to me.

"Miss Newcombe," he began, then stopped, his dark

91

brows quirking upwards questioningly.

I found myself blushing under his raking gaze. It was the chignon, I told myself, that had attracted his attention — that, or the frivolous ornament pinned on my lapel. In any event, I thought miserably, I was about to be dismissed.

Mr. Raven continued to study my appearance for a moment, a look on his face I was unable to decipher. A pulse throbbed in his temple, and I noticed a faint bruise from his fall the night before. Remembering the circumstances, my face grew hot again. Most certainly, I was about to be dismissed. Raising my chin, I waited for the blow to fall.

After another long look, the import of which I could not understand, he spoke at last, in a voice stiff with disapproval. "You wished to discuss texts and hours with me, Miss Newcombe?" he asked to my amazement.

"Texts?" My voice quivered uncertainly. "Hours?"

Mr. Raven glowered down at me. "Precisely," he agreed impatiently. "Texts and hours," he continued, slowly and distinctly, as if speaking to a young child. "I do believe, Miss Newcombe, that you expressed such a desire to me last night in the drawing room?"

So I was not to be dismissed, I thought.

Some of my astonishment must have shown on my face, for with a sigh, Mr. Raven closed his ledger and, coming from behind his desk, crossed the room to tower over me; a grim, broad-shouldered figure in a rough tweed jacket, brown corded breeches, and polished riding boots. "I do hope, Miss Newcombe," he gritted between clenched teeth, "that you are not proving to be feather-brained!"

"Feather-brained, sir?" Despite all my good intentions, I found my temper flaring. Rising proudly to my feet, I caught a heel in my long skirts and pitched forward straight into his arms.

"Good God, Miss Newcombe, what are you about?" Enveloped as I was in a masculine odor of tweed and tobacco, I found it impossible to reply, the more especially as my head appeared to be riveted to Mr. Raven's chest.

"I should be obliged, sir," I managed at last, "if you would unhand me."

"Nothing would give me greater pleasure,"Mr. Raven's baritone voice assured me, "if only your damned — pray excuse me, Miss Newcombe — if only your hair were not entangled with my waistcoat buttons!"

It was at that moment that the study door opened.

"Marcus?" a quavering voice questioned. "As you did not answer when I knocked, I thought perhaps that you had not . . . Oh! . . . Pray, excuse me . . . I see you are engaged."

"I am not," Mr. Raven remarked with admirable restraint, "engaged, Cousin Lydia. It is merely that, that . . ."

"That Miss Newcombe's hair has become entangled with your waistcoat buttons? I see . . . Allow me to help!"

Between the ministrations of Mrs. Mannering and Mr. Raven, I was at last set free.

"As I was rising from this chair," I explained, blushing to Mrs. Mannering, "I . . . caught my heel and . . . fell . . ."

"Of course, dear child." Above her shining pebble

spectacles, her shortsighted blue eyes smiled at me blandly. To my surprise, she patted me on the hand, then turning to Mr. Raven, she murmured rapidly, "You did ask me, Marcus, that if . . . if . . . a . . . *Certain Matter* . . . should arise, I should see you immediately."

"Ah. Just so, Cousin Lydia; you did quite right!"

A long look passed between them, then turning to me, Mr. Raven continued, "I'm afraid you must excuse me, Miss Newcombe. Mrs. Mannering needs to consult with me privately. And afterward, of course, I shall have to leave immediately. I have been called away unexpectedly to one of my properties near Upokongaro, which is why I asked you to present yourself at such an early hour. We shall discuss my children's education when I return on Thursday. Perhaps by then," he added in sarcastic tones, "you will be able to give me *some* inkling of your plans?"

Blushing with mortification, I turned to leave the room, but not before I heard Mrs. Mannering murmur in her bleating way, "I fear, Marcus, that she *suspects*, for when I took up her drops this morning, she would *not* . . ."

At a warning sound from Mr. Raven, she broke off and I—obliged to close the door—heard no more.

If only, I think now, I could have heard what Mrs. Mannering had to say; what danger might have been avoided! But that is hindsight, I suppose. As it was, I stood there in the dark passage, so overcome by humiliation that I did not pay attention to what I had heard. It was only later in the midst of all that was to follow that I was to give the words their true significance—and then, of course, it was too late.

On my right, as I came out of Mr. Raven's study, I noticed a side door leading onto the verandah. Perhaps, I thought, a little fresh air would help me gather myself together before I was forced to face the schoolroom again.

Outside, the air was cool and damp. To my right, a pathway led to the bluff overhanging the river, while before me, a large well-kept lawn swept away to the left. Around its edges, encroaching bush loomed through the still hanging mist. It was then, as I stood inexpertly tidying my hair, that I became slowly aware that I was not alone.

It was the same feeling I had experienced on the river bank the night before; the feeling that someone hidden nearby was observing my every movement. With a shiver, I looked toward the mist-enshrouded bush, but as I turned my head, I could see no one. I was about to give up and seek refuge inside, when the ancient tree outside Mr. Raven's study caught my attention. Was it my imagination, I asked myself, or had the tree trunk changed shape? Surely there was a thickness that had not been there before? Strangely nervous, I peered through the mist, a chill running along my spine as I gradually made out a small human figure, standing so still it seemed almost a part of the trunk. From the short stature, I thought it might be a woman, but the face was lost in shadows.

"Aha, Miss Newcombe," a hearty Scottish voice suddenly boomed into my ear. "You are observing our pohutukawa, I see!"

Turning with a gasp of fright, I bumped into a tweed-clad Mr. Tavish.

"Oh, my dear Miss Newcombe! How thoughtless of

me — I see I have startled you!" He put out a steady-ing arm.

"Think nothing of it, Mr. Tavish," I assured him in some confusion. Was there to be no end to my faux pas, that day, I wondered ruefully. "My mind was elsewhere," I admitted. I turned to look back at the tree, and noticed at once that the figure was no longer there.

"Why, what is it, Miss Newcombe? You have turned quite pale!"

I laughed nervously. "You will think me a complete ninny, Mr. Tavish, but a moment ago, I could have sworn that I saw a woman under that tree."

"Old Moana, I expect," Mr. Tavish remarked care-lessly. "Hemi's mother, you know." He smiled at me through his dark beard. "No wonder you were star-tled, she has a way of turning up unexpectedly. Don't let her bother you. She keeps an eye on all of us pakeha!"

"*Pakeha?*" I asked. I remembered that Mr. Takarangi had used the same word.

"Pa-kay-ha," Mr. Tavish repeated slowly for my benefit. "What the Maori call us Europeans." He smiled at me again, his brown eyes moist and warm. I remembered uncomfortably that I had seen him leav-ing Mrs. McKnight's room and removed myself hur-riedly from the sheltering comfort of his arm.

"But, as I said," Mr. Tavish continued, "pay no attention to her. She's quite harmless, you know — or she would be, if she didn't fill the children's ears with nonsense . . ."

"What sort of nonsense?" I asked with interest.

"Oh, tales of monsters and faeries. The Maoris

have all kinds of folk tales, you know."

He paused and looked at me a moment, a broad-shouldered, comfortable-looking man in his mid-forties. "But come, Miss Newcombe, I see you have recovered from your fright. In fact, if I may say so," he added, his eyes straying to my hair, "you are looking particularly fine today!"

Unused to the attentions of gentlemen, I lowered my eyes hastily and hurriedly changing the subject, asked, "That tree, outside Mr. Raven's study. What did you say it was called, Mr. Tavish?"

"Pohutukawa."

"Po-hoo-too . . . ?"

He chuckled softly at my attempts at pronunciation. "I doubt you will be able just to twist your tongue about such a word, Miss Newcombe. In fact, we *pakeha* call it the New Zealand Christmas Tree because on that day—in the middle of summer, you understand!—it flowers all over with bright red blossoms."

Smiling at me still, he delved into his waistcoat pocket and hauled out his watch. Flicking open the lid, he remarked with obvious reluctance, "I'm afraid you must excuse me, Miss Newcombe, but I must see Mr. Raven before he leaves—he has been called away, you know, on urgent business."

Not waiting for a response, he gallantly offered me his arm. "Perhaps, I may escort you along the verandah to the front door? That way," he remarked with a twinkle, "you will have time to see the front gardens and Mrs. Mannering—whom I observed just now entering Mr. Raven's study—will have had time to state her case!"

We followed the verandah around the side of the house to the front door, Mr. Tavish talking the while about his experiences in New Zealand.

"So good of Mr. Raven to invite me here, so good. We met in Wellington, you know, when I first arrived. When Mr. Raven heard of my project through a mutual friend, he suggested—nay, insisted—that I should come to Ravensfall. The bush, he said, is teeming with native birds!"

"Ah, yes," I agreed politely. "You are writing a book about New Zealand birds, I recollect? And does New Zealand have a great many rare birds then, Mr. Tavish?"

"Indeed, yes! Perhaps, to make up for its lack of native animals!"

He smiled at my look of surprise. "That is correct, Miss Newcombe. New Zealand has no native animals—apart from a small dog, now extinct. But then," he wagged a playful finger at me, "unlike Australia, New Zealand has no snakes, either!" He paused a moment, then added more somberly, "Unless of the human kind!"

We had reached the front of the house by then and, having taken me out onto the front lawn—the better, he said, to observe the noble facade of the house—he looked up at the first floor. But to which of the windows he directed his eyes, I could not determine.

Silently, he ushered me up the stone steps to the front door. "Well, here we are, Miss Newcombe!" Rather brusquely, I thought, he began to open the door. Had he regretted his revealing comment, I wondered? As if to underscore my sudden anxiety, he turned toward me, his soft warm eyes concerned; but what he was about to say died trembling on his lips, for through the half-open door a musical voice pealed out a greeting.

"Good morning, Mr. Tavish! And —why, Miss Newcombe, I do declare! So early abroad. You are to be commended after such a journey yesterday!"

There in the hall stood Ishbel, clad in a simple blue morning dress, her auburn curls shining in the varied light from the stained glass windows. Over one slender arm, she carried a flat straw basket laden with violets, and as Mr. Tavish—after another warm look at me—made his excuses, Ishbel nodded her head toward the dining room door.

"My daily pilgrimage to my mother," she said, quite without conceit. "Perhaps, if you would like to come with me, Miss Newcombe?"

At my nod, we turned toward the dining room, but she paused a moment, looking back at me, a puzzled look on her delicate features. "Oh, I see what it is," she exclaimed at last. "It is your hair! Oh, pray forgive me, dear, Miss Newcombe—but . . . but . . . the difference is quite startling! Last night, you know, you were like nothing so much as a little bird blown out its nest by a storm, but now . . ."

"Oh, Ishbel!" I objected, blushing hotly.

"But now," she continued, ignoring my interruption, "there is something . . . something about you that I cannot explain. Something, something, almost invincible . . ."

She stared at me a moment, her beautiful, aquamarine eyes calm, considering. Then, raising one delicate dark brow, she shrugged her shoulders and turned toward the dining room. "In any event," she smiled back at me in a parting shot, "you have captured Mr. Tavish, for I see that he is quite enamoured of you!"

"Ishbel!" I exclaimed, quite shocked.

But, with a trill of laughter, she disappeared into the dining room.

It would never do, I told myself sternly, to have such an informal relationship between mistress and pupil. Thoughtfully, I followed her through the doorway.

The dining room, long and narrow with dark panelled walls, was furnished almost entirely in gleaming mahogany. There was a somber air about the room that the muted gold of the heavy curtains and the dark reds and purples of the Turkey carpet did little to dispel.

Perhaps because of this, the large oil painting that faced the door was even more striking. It was of a dainty fair-haired young woman who looked out on the world with timid dreaming eyes.

"My mother," said Ishbel simply, advancing to place her offerings in small vases at the portrait's foot.

There was something familiar about the picture, which I recognized at once. "Malvina," I exclaimed, "how like her she is!"

A shadow passed over Ishbel's fragile countenance. "Yes, she is," she agreed. Then, as if to explain her discomfiture, she added, "My mother was consumptive, you know, and I fear that Malvina . . ."

"Oh, no!" I comforted briskly. "Malvina, though highly strung and delicate, is healthy enough, I'm sure. You need have no fears for her."

"I had no fears for my mother, Miss Newcombe,

but she died!"

"Of consumption?"

"No, Miss Newcombe . . . of laudanum poisoning."

The room was still suddenly.

"Of laudanum poisoning?" I asked at last.

Ishbel busied herself with her violets. "Yes, Miss Newcombe," she replied at last, her voice muffled. "My mother had been taking the drops, you know, to help her sleep at nights. And then, one morning, I went to her room early, before her maid had called her, and found her lying there."

"Oh, Ishbel!"

"It was almost two years ago, you know, while we were still in Scotland."

"Scotland?"

"Yes, Miss Newcombe. My mother had an estate up there in the Hebrides, you know. We went up there at least once a year, and it was there that she . . . died."

Two years ago, I thought. Ishbel, poor child, could have been no more than fifteen — and as for Malvina and Reginald, ten-and eight-years old, poor lambs.

"And so your mother in her extremity, poor soul . . ."

There was a short silence, then Ishbel turned toward me again, her eyes hidden by her long dark lashes. "My mother did not take her own life, Miss Newcombe." Carefully, she gathered up the old violets now discarded from their vases, placing them, it seemed to me, with reverence into her straw basket. Slowly, she walked toward the door.

I looked at her, stunned. "An accident, then," I suggested at last. "Your poor mama, or perhaps her nurse, was mistaken in the dose one night . . ."

101

Ishbel paused a moment before leaving the dining room. "Oh no, Miss Newcombe, it was no accident. My mother was murdered."

In the muted light, her beautiful green-blue eyes shone large, haunted. At the sight of my frozen countenance, she nodded as if in satisfaction, then vanished abruptly into the hall.

Twelve

Murdered, I questioned in consternation! Surely I could not have heard right. Questions hovering on my lips, I rushed swiftly into the hall. There was no sign of Ishbel, but from the drawing room opposite I heard the first faint strains of a Strauss waltz. Could she be practicing, I wondered astounded, and after such a statement!

In the drawing room, rose velvet portières had been drawn back to reveal large French windows ranging along two sides of the room. As in Mr. Raven's study, they looked out onto the ground floor verandah, beyond which loomed the inevitable bush. In between, however, stretched an expanse of lush, green lawn edged with rhododendron and hydrangea bushes. Here and there were beds of early spring flowers. Daffodils, I noticed with pleasure, starry narcissus and clumps of cream and purple polyanthus. I was surprised at such a riot of color in the middle of what I had taken to be midwinter.

"You are looking for someone, Miss Newcombe?"

The music had stopped and turning I saw Mrs. DuPrès poised beside the piano in the raised alcove. As I watched, she carefully lowered the piano lid and, stepping from the dais, crossed the room to talk with me.

"I was looking for Ishbel," I admitted. "I was talking to her just now in the dining room—and now she's nowhere in sight!"

"Oh, Ishbel!" Mrs. DuPrès exclaimed with an indulgent laugh, "that young lady seems to appear and disappear at will!"

I was tempted to tell her of Ishbel's astonishing remark and to ask her the truth of it, but I refrained, telling myself that after all I was not aware of Mrs. DuPrès' actual position in the household. Also, although her manner, compared with her demeanor of the night before, seemed friendlier, there was still a watchfulness about her which I found disconcerting.

She studied me in silence a moment, a totally elegant woman. Even in the cold morning light, her creamy complexion was flawless, while her elaborate russet and leaf-brown velvet morning dress accentuated the shining coils of her chestnut hair.

At last, lifting a delicately arched brow, she remarked in her husky French-accented tones, "I hope you rested well, Miss Newcombe? Your appearance has certainly changed from last night—and for the better, I think!"

I stared at her, taken back at her patronizing tone.

As if she sensed my thoughts, she smiled in a superior fashion before changing the subject. Glancing out the window, she remarked, "You are surprised, I dare say, to see so many spring flowers. But we are very sheltered here in the valley and, in any event, New Zealand—being more temperate than England—has flowers all year round."

"How delightful," I murmured, in an attempt to be

polite — Mrs. DuPrès was, after all, a guest of my employer. "I must admit," I added, "that I am glad to be away from English winters."

A delicate shudder, Yes, indeed." A smile, faintly amused, "Who could even think of vineyards in those circumstances."

"Vineyards?"

"Yes, indeed, my husband and brother-in-law work a vineyard next to Ravensfall."

She smiled slightly at my surprise, then continued, "They are up north at the moment, considering the acquisition of another property. I always stay here at Ravensfall when they are gone . . ."

Pausing a moment, she added pointedly, "But I must not keep you from your duties, Miss New-combe."

Turning away, she drifted slowly toward the door, her head tilted as if she were listening.

Flushing with annoyance at her implied order, I deliberately walked slowly about the room, stopping every now and then to examine a picture and the sketchbook that Mr. Raven had been examining when I had first seen him on my introduction the night before. As I picked it up to glance curiously through its pages, I heard voices out in the hall. Mr. Raven, it seemed, had emerged from his study at last, and if I recognized the rumbling tones of the other voice aright, he was accompanied by Mr. Tavish.

With a soft exclamation, Mrs. DuPrès slipped out of the room. Mr. Raven, I thought with a wry smile, was indeed a popular man that morning.

Having no wish to meet with him again before he left on his travels, I stayed in the drawing room a moment, glancing idly through the pictures in the sketchbook. One or two of them had been washed over with watercolor, and it was at those I looked first. They were mainly outside scenes of places presumably about the estate, and though they seemed ordinary enough at first glance—and of no particular distinction—I soon realized with a shock that there was a strangeness about them that warranted closer attention.

One picture, for instance, of a corner of the garden, depicted a scene of seeming innocence until one noticed that from out the bush that formed the background peered a small, brown face, the features of which were twisted into a mask of indescribable malignancy. In the next picture—a study of a particularly wan Malvina drooping on the lawn—the same face peered again, its expression, if anything, more evil than before.

It was the third picture, however, that really made me shudder. In it I recognized the broad sweep of the river near the spot where I had waited the evening before. Because it was also evening in the picture, the shadows were long and it was not immediately apparent that oozing out of the water was a loathsome beast, half snake, half dragon, with an air about it as evil as the small face in the pictures going before. From under the waters behind the beast, another face gazed up; this, a human one, pale, twisted, its eyes staring, its mouth shrieking in silent agony.

Though I was vaguely aware that someone had entered the drawing room, I continued to stare at the picture in revulsion. What kind of mind, I wondered, could have conjured up such a scene?

"Good morning, Miss Newcombe," a pleasant lilting voice greeted me, "welcome to Ravensfall. I am Mrs. Douglas. I'm sorry I could not greet you last night."

Standing before me, dressed in a housekeeper's correct black bombasine, was a large handsome woman in her later forties. Under her starched, white cap, her brown hair, though streaked with grey, was abundant and glossy, and her broad, high-cheekboned face and light blue eyes reflected a pleasant expression.

"How do you do, Mrs. Douglas?" I greeted her politely. "I hope you are feeling better. I understand you have been suffering from a chill?"

"I'm much better, thank you, Miss Newcombe. Mr. Tavish was kind enough to give me a nostrum that cured him quickly when he suffered recently from a similar complaint."

"Mr. Tavish?" I asked, remembering his stocky figure emerging from Mrs. Douglas' room that morning. Surely, I thought now, looking at those candid blue eyes, there must be some innocent explanation.

"Yes," Mrs. Douglas continued, "our visitor from Edinburgh, you know. Apparently he travels with all kinds of medications. He has been so very kind. He even came to my sitting room last night and again this morning to show Jenny exactly how to mix the ingredients."

"How kind, indeed," I murmured, blushing at my former unkind thought. Thank God, I thought, Mrs. Douglas, with her open honest looks, seemed just the sort of person I could talk to about the children — and, after all, as I reminded myself, she still acted sometimes as their nurse.

I gestured toward the sketchbook. "Am I right in

thinking this is Ishbel's?" I asked diffidently.

The book was still open at the picture with the beast. Mrs. Douglas looked at it, her lips pursing in distaste. "Yes," she admitted, "I'm afraid it is Ishbel's. Poor child! I hardly know what to say, Miss Newcombe, but Ishbel—all the children, in fact—are still suffering from Miss Inglewood's sad demise, which in their minds has been made even worse by old Moana's stories."

"Old Moana?" I asked. "Oh, yes, I remember now. Mr. Tavish warned me that she filled the children's heads with nonsense."

Mrs. Douglas shook her head unhappily. "I asked Mr. Raven to speak with her and so he did, but . . ." Her voice faded unhappily, then she added, "It's strange, though, that Ishbel should be so influenced. Though Moana speaks more than I would like with Malvina and Reginald, Ishbel she usually avoids."

I looked again at the picture. "Is this some dreadful creature of myth and legend, then?"

"Yes. A *taniwha*, I believe it's called."

"Tan-ee—?"

Mrs. Douglas smiled faintly. "Tan-ee-faa, Miss Newcombe—the letters 'wh' are pronounced like an 'f' in Maori. Yes, the taniwha are said to be savage monsters who prey upon humankind. According to the Maoris, the Wanganui River has several. They live mainly in rivers, I understand; though, I believe there are supposed to be some that fly . . ."

She rubbed a hand across her forehead and laughed a little—a despairing sound. "I'm afraid, Miss Newcombe, that in the great flood last year, when Miss Inglewood . . . poor Miss Inglewood . . . was swept away, that Moana said . . ."

She paused a moment, looking distressed, and I, glancing again with a barely repressed shiver at the face mouthing its terror under the water, took pity and finished her sentence for her.

"Moana said the taniwha had taken her?" I questioned.

"I'm afraid so, Miss Newcombe. And although Ishbel is too old to believe such things . . ." She stopped, looking at the picture.

"She had to get it out of her mind, perhaps?" I suggested.

Mrs. Douglas looked at me, respect dawning in her light blue eyes. "Yes, Miss Newcombe, I believe you're right. Poor bairn, she's had so much tragedy to cope with lately. But no doubt Mr. Raven's solicitors told you all about that?"

Now at last was my opportunity. "No, Mrs. Douglas, they did not. I knew the children's mother had passed away, of course, but until half an hour ago, I did not know how."

Mrs. Douglas turned toward me, disconcerted.

Flushing with embarrassment, but determined to go on, I continued. "Ishbel said—forgive me if I disturb you, but if I am to help the children, then I must know the truth—Ishbel said that their mother was *murdered*."

Though I had spoken in low tones, the word seemed to rebound about the room.

Mrs. Douglas bit her lip. "I'm sorry, Miss Newcombe, that you had to find out in such a way—what Mr. Raven's solicitors were thinking of, I don't know—the truth is, the late Mrs. Raven *was* murdered."

We looked at each other in silence, that foul word hanging between us, a dark menace. Then Mrs. Douglas continued, reciting as if from a legal paper. "Mrs. Raven was given an overdose of laudanum by the hand of a person or persons unknown . . ."

"Then no one was arrested?" I asked in disbelief.

"I did not say that, Miss Newcombe."

Mrs. Douglas turned away, then, as if forcing herself to go on, she braced her shoulders and faced me again.

"You may as well hear it all, Miss Newcombe, and it would be better coming from me. Mr. Raven was arrested for the death of his wife."

"How dreadful," I exclaimed incredulously, "I can hardly believe such a thing! How those poor children must have suffered. And Mr. Raven, too," I added as an afterthought. "Still, that is all behind him now, isn't it . . . ?"

I stopped at the stricken look on Mrs. Douglas' face. "Oh, come, Mrs. Douglas. Obviously, Mr. Raven was found to be innocent."

"No, Miss Newcombe, he was not."

We stared at each other a long moment; myself stunned, she white, a kind of desperation about her face.

At last, she went on. "The family was on Mrs. Raven's estate in the Hebrides at the time, so . . . so . . . Mr. Raven was tried by a Scottish court. Mr. Raven was found to be neither 'innocent' nor 'guilty,' Miss Newcombe. The jury brought in a verdict of 'unproven.'"

. . . *The candle flame dips and outside, the morepork—* *ruru-cries again and I think about Maona. Perhaps, if I* *had listened to her, paid heed . . .*

And yet, how was I to know that this little old woman *with her walnut face and gnarled hands, would be the key to* *all of this?*

Thirteen

A fluttering of wings and a small brown bird darted past my head, its long tail feathers gently brushing my cheek.

Malvina giggled: a rare sound. "Just a fantail, Miss Newcombe." She reached up as the bird hovered delicately.

"My goodness, are they tame? Do they come to one's hand?"

"Oh, no! They're after the insects in the air, you know, that we stir up as we move about. Look there's another one!"

"And another!" Laughing, I held up my hands, but the small creatures continued to flutter tantalizingly just out of reach. "But I dare say, they could be tamed?" I looked thoughtfully at the open front door behind us. "Do they ever come inside?"

"No!"

The word, harshly sibilant, emanated from the shadows at the back of the hall behind the stairs.

My eyes adjusted to the light at last; the darkness

shifted and old Moana shuffled forward. I had often been aware of her in my week at Ravensfall, but this was the first time she had approached me. My nose crinkled as she came closer; in one hand, she clutched a small clay pipe and the tattered shawl draped about her shrunken shoulders stank strongly of tobacco.

"Good morning, Moana!" Keeping my voice pleasant and low, I resisted a temptation to stand back.

A glare was my reply. The rheumy brown eyes turned malevolently on Malvina. "Never inside! Never!" The words uttered in a voice harsh and cracked, shattered the peaceful silence of the hall.

"Why ever not?" I asked, as Malvina shrank against me.

Another glare and a silence, the curved blue lines of the tattoo about her mouth writhing as her wrinkled lips worked together.

In contrast with her previous harshness, her words, when they came, were soft almost gentle. "You pakeha, you know nothing . . . that bird, he come inside . . . he bring death . . ."

"What utter nonsense . . ."

My exclamation faded into silence as Maona glanced past me, her hooded eyes dimming suddenly to narrow slits.

Turning, I saw a cream and gold-clad Ishbel crossing the lawn, an empty basket on her arm. When I looked back, Moana was slipping away across the hall.

"Good morning, Miss Newcombe!" Ishbel's voice, musical as always, penetrated my thoughts. "Is something wrong?"

"No . . . that is . . . Tell me, is Moana always so strange?"

A trilling laugh. "Oh, pay no attention to Moana. She's full of odd superstitions!"

Such as the taniwha, I thought, that Ishbel herself seemed so obsessed with. I remembered her sketch-book with a shudder.

I forced a smile. "Where have you been so bright and early?"

"Up on the bluff. We have a memorial up there to Miss Inglewood and I like to go there on Sundays to leave some of my violets."

Why was it, I wondered irritatedly, that conversations with Ishbel tended usually to be morbid?

As if guessing my thought, she smiled suddenly and in her cream and gold dress with the winter rays of the early morning sun gilding her auburn curls, she glowed all pink and white and gold like a Renaissance angel. "Forgive me, Miss Newcombe, I do tend to run on so . . ."

A pause as pearly teeth bit at a blushing underlip. "I'm sorry, Miss Newcombe . . . It's just . . . Well, Miss Inglewood is dead, I realize that — but, Miss Newcombe, it — it happened so short a time ago, just a few months in fact, before you come to us."

Another pause as the clear aqua eyes sparkled with unshed tears. "And as I told you, her body was never found. It's almost, you know, as if she went away for just a little while and may come back at any moment."

A cold hand slipped into mine. "Miss Newcombe, it's almost time for Sunday Prayers." Malvina's timid tone were scarcely above a whisper and her little face was pale and strained. No wonder the child was so nervous, I thought, in such an atmosphere.

I glanced at the grandfather clock by the dining

114

room door. "Goodness me, a quarter to nine already! Where has the morning gone?"

As if on cue, the clock chimed the three-quarter hour and the dining room swung open to reveal a slightly breathless Hélène DuPrès. Behind her, holding open the door, stood Marcus Raven. So he had returned from his excursion, I thought. This was the first time I had seen him since Mrs. Douglas' revelation and I looked at him now, dark clad and sombre, and shivered a little as I wondered yet again if he could possibly have perpetrated such a despicable crime.

"You have caught a chill, Miss Newcombe?" The baritone penetrated my thoughts and the cool eyes bearing down on me were pleased to be faintly amused.

I found myself blushing as I wondered if he had guessed at the cause of my shiver, but before I could reply, he had turned to Ishbel and Malvina.

"Good morning Ishbel, Malvina; but where is my son? Where is Reginald?" He looked inquiringly at me.

Out the corner of my eye, I observed Hélène DuPrès pressing fluttering fingers to her brow. Was it my imagination, or was her color a little high?

"Reginald, sir, has had a minor upset and is confined to bed."

"Poor Reggie!" This from Ishbel, as she set down her basket on the rosewood table before disappearing into the drawing room. "I expect he ate something disagreeable."

Mr. Raven frowned down at me. "Reginald is not to be pampered, Miss Newcombe."

115

Bother the man, why did he seek always to put me in the wrong? I felt my face flush, but before I could speak out, Hélène DuPrès—surprisingly—came to my rescue.

"Oh, come now. Marcus. You know very well that Reggie is delicate and needs to be cosseted from time to time." She had recovered her color and her breath and now spoke in a light amused, somewhat patronising tone that I liked even less than Mr. Raven's disapproval.

As if guessing at my discomfiture, she gave me a condescending smile and taking Mr. Raven's arm, drew him across the hall into the drawing room.

Left alone with Malvina, I looked through the dining room door. Though the mahogany sideboard was laiden with chafing dishes of deviled kidneys, scrambled eggs and—so my nose informed me—fried lamb chops, there were only two used place settings—set close together—at one end of the long dining room.

They had sat tête-à-tête then. Discussing what? I remembered the flushed cheeks of Hélène DuPrès, her heightened breathing. Above the dining table the portrait of the late Mrs. Raven gazed down with Malvina's wistful smile. Who had killed her, I wondered? Why? Surely, Mr. Raven could not have done so . . . and yet?

"There you are, dear!" Mrs. Mannering beamed down at me from the stairs, her pebble glasses glinting in the sun now pouring in through the stained glass of the hall windows. "What a glorious morning. Such a change from all that fog! I was wondering, my dear, if you would care to take luncheon with us?"

A pause as the last few steps were negotiated. She stood, panting a little, one plump hand resting on the carved raven of the newel post. "I really feel quite remiss . . ." absentmindedly, her hand slipped to the carved wooden mouse writhing in its death throes. "Really, quite remiss . . . Oh, Malvina to be sure! There you are, child!"

Beside me, Malvina stiffened.

"You are a treasure, child. An absolute treasure! So well-behaved, so obedient, so caring for your little brother. Now run along child, do, or you will be late for Sunday Prayers, and you do not wish to offend your dear papa."

An agonized look at me; then a flurry of lace-edged petticoats as Malvina scurried into the drawing room. I turned to follow.

"A moment, Miss Newcombe!"

The pebble grasses were turned full force on me; an ingratiating smile lit up the plump face. "As I said, I feel quite remiss . . . but time passes so quickly, does it not? It seems only yesterday that you arrived . . . and yet almost a week has passed by already . . . I really should have inquired if you are quite happy here."

"Quite happy, thank you!" I stemmed the babbling brook at last.

"But so much alone, as you are! After England life must seem so dull. A young woman such as yourself, shut away in your room . . . I thought, perhaps, that in the evenings, you . . ."

I rushed in to avert the invitation I sensed was coming. "Please, Mrs. Mannering, there is no need for concern. I have much to occupy my time . . . my

117

lessons to prepare, letters to write . . . um . . ." I paused, desperately searching for excuses. (My writing, I thought, but of course did not wish to say so!) Luckily, just then, at the back of the hall, the green baize door opened and through it filed the servants on their way to Sunday Prayers in the drawing room. They were led by Mrs. Douglas, who bestowed a smile on me and a pleasant 'Good morning' as she passed by. In her wake, Jenny and Ngaire smiled at me also while Hemi ignored me altogether.

In the train, I observed other faces that I was half familiar with from my past few days of roving about the house and grounds: Martha, the whey-faced maid who had served me my first breakfast, Cook (a Mrs. Murchison, a scrawny woman introduced to me by Malvina) with Murchison, her husband—a sort of butler—and two or three others, followed by a freckle-faced boy with a thatch of bright blond hair, about Reginald's age. This last, unlike the others, was not carrying a prayer book.

Immediately, I saw my means of escape from Mrs. Manning. "Oh, my goodness, my prayer book—I had quite forgot—I shall fetch it at once!"

"No need to worry, my dear! We always keep one or two on hand, in case of visitors. You will find one by the drawing room door—and a hymn book also! But, come, we must go in. Dear Marcus does not like to be kept waiting!"

In the drawing room, the chairs had been arranged in two rows supplemented with two hard benches behind and a lectern in front.

Ishbel was playing softly on the piano, while the servants seated themselves on the benches and Mrs.

118

Douglas, Malvina, and Hélène DuPrès settled themselves in the front row of chairs. Behind the lectern stood Marcus Raven, riffling through the pages of his prayer book. He looked up as we took our places in the second row of chairs and frowned significantly at the clock on the marble mantelpiece. As it still wanted three minutes to the hour, I stared back at him, unabashed.

As I did so, masculine voices rumbled from the hall and in hurried Gideon Tavish and Callum Douglas. Both men were attired in tweeds and brought in with them a brisk aroma of the outside air.

"Pray excuse us, my dear Raven—completely my fault, I'm afraid! Mr. Douglas was kind enough to show me the nesting place of some bellbirds and I became so involved with my sketches that . . ."

"Think nothing of it, my dear fellow! In any event, it still lacks two minutes to the hour." Marcus Raven smiled—an expression which brought about a remarkably salutary effect to his usually sombre features.

However, I could not help a sarcastic glance toward the clock. It was one thing for Harriet Newcombe to be late, I thought in irritation and quite another apparently for Gideon Tavish!

"And what has brought such hectic color to those fair cheeks?"

Beneath the whispered words was a note of merriment. Callum Douglas had slipped into the chair next to mine and now was looking down at me, a devilish gleam in his blue-green eyes.

"Your question, sir, is impertinent!" I hissed, as we rose for the first hymn. Unfortunately, in my agitation, my hymn book slipped from my hands and fell

119

upon Malvina as she was about to rise from the chair in front of me. Poor child, she could hardly help but give a muffled shriek and then a string of whispered apologies that gradually faded into embarrassed quiet.

"Perhaps, Malvina, you could return Miss Newcombe's hymn book." Mr. Raven's tone was frigid, his expression glacial. "We shall begin with singing hymn number five hundred and forty. Ishbel. . ."

Resounding chords sounded which seemed familiar but which—in the turmoil of the moment—I could not place. From beside me, a smothered laugh immediately disguised as a cough.

I had to restrain a laugh myself as my nervous fingers finally found the right page. "Fight the good fight with all thy might," was the first line of the hymn and—I had to agree with the smothered mirth beside me—singularly appropriate in the circumstances!

No wonder the opening chords seemed so familiar, I thought with a strangled giggle. I remembered endless hours teaching Sunday School under the aegis of Mr. Pugh. "Fight the Good Fight" had been one of his favorites. I remembered his visitations to my class and his booming voice dominating the quavering treble of my pupils.

Unfortunately, I also remembered overhearing some of my urchins secretly singing their version of the fine old words:

"Fight the good fight with all thy might,
Sit on a barrel of dynamite.
Strike a match and thou shallt be
Blown into Eternity!"

At the time, it was Mr. Pugh I had imagined sitting on the barrel, but now I pictured Marcus Raven.

Somehow, I regained my calm. Sunday Prayers turned out to be a brief and reverent condensation of the service for Morning Prayer as outlined in the Book of Common Prayer, interspersed with various hymns that, as Malvina had told me earlier, were chosen by each member of the family in turn. With wry humor, I wondered who had chosen "Fight the Good Fight." And why? Perhaps, it had been Marcus Raven himself, I thought, as I watched him reading the Collect for the Day. After all, according to Mrs. Douglas, he had certainly had to fight. Though with such a tarnished victory!

A brief pause after the closing words of the Collect. I looked up and found the light eyes fixed on me, the expression in them for once not arrogant but solitary, vulnerable. A moment later he announced the next hymn with his usual aplomb and I wondered if I had imagined the whole thing.

What must it be like, I wondered, to live under such a cloud? I understood now, of course, the propitious terms of my employment: the generous salary, the limited hours — the willingness of Mr. Raven's solicitors to accept a female as young and inexperienced as myself. They had been hoping, I told myself, for someone who had heard nothing of the trial and who after having heard would, because of the great distances involved, be obliged to stay — perhaps, considering the salary, even willing!

Beside me, Mrs. Mannering, the black ribbons of her widow's cap fluttering as she bent over her hymn book, quavered in a shrill soprano that the "Rock of ages" was indeed "cleft for her." In front of me, Malvina sang earnestly, one thin finger carefully following the words, and I thought of her brother upstairs in bed. It was not the salary that kept me there, I thought, but my poor little charges captive in a house of gloom.

Though I had been at Ravensfall so short a time, I had developed a fondness for the children; for Malvina and her shy winning ways and even for Reginald with his blank stare and the ingenious mind that I was sure lurked behind. What a mystery the child was! I wondered yet again how I might win his trust.

"A penny for those thoughts!"

It was Gideon Tavish who spoke, his deep voice with its hint of a Scottish burr almost a growl.

I came to myself with a start. Prayers had ended and the small congregation was leaving accompanied by Ishbel's loud though expressionless rendition of "Praise my Soul, the King of Heaven." Behind us, Hemi and another manservant were taking away the wooden benches and Callum Douglas had left my side to talk to Mr. Raven at the lectern.

Warm, brown eyes smiled down at me; an avuncular arm was presented. "Perhaps you would care to take a turn about the garden, Miss Newcombe? Unless, of course, your duties take you elsewhere?"

"Thank you, my time is my own today and a walk in the garden is just what I need. With all that fog, I was beginning to feel quite a prisoner!"

"Then, my dear young lady, allow me to be your liberator!"

Unfortunately, just then, Ishbel stopped playing

and the words, "Allow me to be your liberator," swept into the silence. Out the corner of my eye, I noticed Mr. Raven's eyebrows rise as he glanced first to Gideon Tavish and then to my hand resting on his arm. Callum Douglas, a puckish quirk about his long thin lips, looked in amusement from one to the other of us.

Another warm look from Mr. Tavish as he patted my hand, pressing it down into the rough tweed of his jacket sleeve. " 'Come into the garden, Maude,' " he quoted with a jocular smile. "Do you read Tennyson, Miss Newcombe?"

"Y . . . yes. I . . . I quite enjoy him—the *Idylls* in particular."

A flutter of papers and a click as Ishbel bestowed her hymn book inside the music stool. Like Callum Douglas and Mr. Raven, she also looked toward us, her brows knit thoughtfully. I could almost feel the eyes of all three of them burn into my back as we left.

"Something worries you, Miss Newcombe." It was not a question, but a statement, the deep voice soothing, mesmeric, lulling me to gentle dreams.

I dragged my eyes away from the giant tree fern before me, its spacious, green leaves tinged on the underside with streaks of white. "Something worrying me?" I hesitated, wondering if I should go on. Mr. Tavish was, after all, not a member of the family and Marcus Raven might prefer that I keep my impressions of his children to myself. "Not to say worrying, sir . . . exactly."

"Come, come, my dear young lady. I am the

discreetest of fellows, I do assure you!" The warm brown eyes gazing down at me were, like the voice, mesmeric and I was lost.

"It's Reginald," I admitted frankly, "He—"

"Reginald?" The surprise in the brown eyes was quickly disguised and the words that followed, it seemed to me, were uttered almost in a tone of relief. "Reginald. Yes, of course. You are worried, naturally, about his slowness of mind and wondering how best you may bring him along."

"But Reginald has no slowness of mind, he—"

"How kind you are! My dear Miss Harriet—If so I may call you? If you are not offended by the informality?" The pat on my hand was fatherly, the expression in the eyes was not.

Mesmerized, I shook my head.

"My dear Miss Harriet, this is your first teaching position?"

"I have taught Sunday School . . ."

"Ah, yes! But not the same. Not nearly the same!" Another kindly pat and through the beard, a smile. "As I said, you are so very kind and inclined, in your inexperience, to over-rate the abilities of your pupils. You would like to think that Reginald is of . . . sufficient . . . er . . . strength of mind? And when he does not perform, you blame yourself."

"But—"

"Put your qualms to rest, my dear! You are not to blame. And apart from his natural inability, Reginald—and Malvina and Ishbel, too, of course—has been afflicted by all the tragedy in his young life." A pause, a sideways glance at me. "You know of course about Mr. Raven's . . . ordeal?"

124

I nodded.

A sigh. A fingering of the beard. "A tragedy, a great tragedy. But of course, on the part of Mr. Raven, totally undeserved." Another sideways glance, the brown eyes bright, glistening almost.

"Of course, sir, I understand. However, Reginald . . ."

"Poor child, to have lost first his dear mother to whom he was devoted and then Miss Inglewood who was like another mother to him. She was very like the late Mrs. Raven, you know: the same fairness, the same slight build . . . the same delicacy of temperament."

I looked at him in surprise. "You knew them, sir? I had thought that you had met Mr. Raven for the first time after you had arrived in Wellington."

A look of surprised respect—but at the back of the eyes, a certain wariness. "How quick you are, Miss Harriet! I see that Reginald and Malvina must look to their laurels!"

"Oh, pray excuse me, I did not wish—"

A rumbling laugh, the eyes still wary. "Come, come, my dear, I was merely congratulating you! For you are right, of course! I did indeed meet Mr. Raven for the first time in Wellington. However, I was briefly acquainted many years ago with Mrs. Raven when her first husband, James McLeod, was yet alive."

"Indeed, what a coincidence!"

Did he detect an element of doubt in my voice? "Not a coincidence at all, my dear young lady. Merely a mutual acquaintance, who hearing of my project, gave me a letter of introduction to Mr. Raven."

Why, I wondered, did he feel the need to explain

the circumstances in such detail?

He paused a moment, fingering his beard, his eyes watchful. "Of course, I was not acquainted with Miss Inglewood. However, Mrs. Douglas, who knew her well, has a likeness of her in her sitting room. You must ask to see it and compare it with Mrs. Raven's portrait in the dining room . . . you will then understand, I think, why the children were so fond of her and how this additional tragedy has doubly affected poor Reginald!"

"But, Reginald," I began again in irritation, only to be again interrupted.

"Excuse me, sir, Miss Newcombe!" Behind us, her footsteps muffled by the lush green grass, Jenny was approaching.

"Excuse me, Mr. Tavish, sir, but Mr. Raven sends his compliments and asks if you will please wait on him in his study. He said to tell you he has found a book of particular interest. And you, Miss, Mrs. Douglas hopes you'll join the family for luncheon at one o'clock."

"Oh, yes, thank you! Mrs. Mannering already asked me."

A humorous look. "So she said, Miss." A smothered giggle. "But she doesn't remember your reply."

"I'll take my leave, then, Miss Harriet, if you will excuse me. Unless you would like me to escort you back to the house?" Gideon Tavish smiled warmly down at me. "How glad I am that you are to join us at luncheon!"

"Thank you, sir. I believe I shall stay here a while in the fresh air."

He nodded and Jenny and I watched his broad

back as he crossed the lawn, turning once more before, with a friendly wave and bow, he disappeared into the house.

"Well, Miss, you've made a right conquest there, and that's a fact!"

"Jenny!"

"But he's too old for you Miss. Why he must be at least five and forty! Of course, they do say that older gentlemen well set up in the world . . ."

"Jenny, for shame! I assure you I have no feelings of . . . of . . . *that* nature for Mr. Tavish, nor he for me. He is merely friendly, that is all!"

An unrepentant grin. "Yes, Miss! Oh, while I remember, Mrs. Douglas asks if you would like to take afternoon tea with her in her sitting room at three-thirty?"

"Of course, I'd be delighted!" Surely, the one person in the house, I thought, I could talk to about Reginald.

"I should explain, Miss, that luncheon on Sundays is really dinner — the evening meal being of cold meats only, to give Cook a rest."

"I see." I bit my lip worriedly. "Is the meal formal?"

"No, Miss." A critical look at me. "Your suit will do well enough for today. When your trunk arrives, we'll have to see what we can do about your dresses."

"Now, Jenny —"

"Oh, I almost forgot, Miss. The family meets in the drawing room at twelve-thirty to take a glass of sherry. That's informal, too! Mr. Raven serves the sherry himself. He says he likes to make our work on Sundays as light as possible. But, I've got to go, now, if you'll excuse me. Sunday mornings are always

127

hectic, what with the formal prayers and all . . ."

Grinning cheerfully, she trotted back across the lawn and into the house.

Through the open door of the hall, I could hear the faint chimes of the grandfather clock striking the quarter hour. It must be a quarter after ten, I thought. Another two hours, at least, before I had to report to the drawing room. I thought of my box upstairs in my room. Now would be a good time, I told myself sternly, to settle down and write, not having had much opportunity to do so within the past few days. Yes, I really ought to go up to my room, but Gideon Tavish's face rose before me in my mind and I saw again the wariness in his brown eyes. There was something about him that . . . but what? I shook my head. No, I would not go to my room, I decided, I knew I should not be able to settle to my writing. Besides, I really ought to check on Reginald.

Fourteen

Reginald's room was situated down the hall from the school room. To my disappointment, as I raised my hand to knock voices sounded on the other side of the door. He was not alone, as I had hoped.

Suddenly, as I waited, wondering what to do, a series of thumps sounded, followed by an ear-splitting scream.

"Help! Help! Murder! Have mercy — oh, please!"

I flung open the door.

By the bed, kneeling on the floor, his hands in an attitude of prayer, was the freckled-face boy I had seen with the servants at Morning Prayer. Above him, on the bed, reared a nightshirt-clad Reginald, his eyes glaring and his face twisted with a diabolical grin. Both boys were wearing tricorne hats constructed out of newspaper and Reginald, with deadly accuracy, was pointing a newspaper-made sword straight at the throat of his opponent.

"*Canaille!*" shrieked Reginald in fury. "Filthy dog of a filthy peasant! You think you will take me — ME — to the guillotine!"

"Monsieur," replied Freckle-face, his colonial twang

making the French title almost unrecognizable, "I ain't a filthy peasant, I'm the Duc de Berry in disguise!"

"Cur," snarled Reginald. "I don't believe you. If you are the Duc de Berry, why did you cross swords with me?"

"Because you ain't the Comte de . . . de . . . de Thingamejig, that's why. Now put up your sword, there's a good fellow!"

"I," said Reginald with a vicious thrust of his sword, "am the Comte de Puissey Choiseul de Rambouillet! And don't you forget it!"

"You ain't a count. You're a bloody Pom!" shrieked Freckle-face.

In the midst of their drama, neither boy had noticed me and considering the language now being used, I decided it best to step in. Composing my features with an effort into an expression of great solemnity, I sank into a full curtsy. "Monsieur le Comte, s'il vous plaît!"

A dead silence. A blush from Freckle-face; an enigmatic stare from Reginald.

I plunged straight into speech. "Oh, Monsieur le Comte, spare him, spare the Duc de Berry!" My hands fluttered across my eyelids. "He saved my sister from the guillotine!" (Bravely, I restrained my sobs.)

A ghost of a smile from Reginald, then a grave bow, managed as best he could from the feather mattress billowing about him.

"Mam'zelle, it will be as you wish." He removed his sword. "Monsieur, please rise. This beauteous demoiselle has convinced me of your innocence!"

Unfortunately, the effect of his words was lessened

as he lost his balance and fell face downwards into the blankets.

"Stupid pommy!" immediately yelled Freckle-face.

"Pig Islander!" rejoined Reginald, but without rancour. He struggled to rise, but again fell over.

Both boys dissolved into helpless giggles.

"Pig Islander?" I asked, bewildered. "Pommy?"

Another blush from Freckle-face spreading over his features to his mop of bright blond hair. "Sorry, Miss! It's a word we use for you new chums."

His accent, close to Cockney, but not quite, was hard for me to follow. "New chums?"

The blush—if possible—deepened, but then was followed by an urchin grin. "Yes," (more like 'yis' to my unatuned ear) " 'new chums,' people who've just got here, like you! Sorry, Miss, didn't mean to offend!"

"No offense! Now, let me see, you, I take it—" (I could hardly keep the laugh out of my voice—the small, pointed face was so earnest) "have been here a long time?"

He drew himself up. "I was born here, Miss. Me and my dad, we're *real* New Zealanders!"

A pillow hurtled through the air, catching my new acquaintance neatly on the side of his head. "Pig Islander!" screamed Reginald.

"Come, now, boys!" I moved quickly between them. "You'll break something! Perhaps, later, when Reginald is well again, you can both have a pillow fight outside?"

"You mean it, Miss? Really?" The blue eyes shone and the freckled cheeks relaxed in a sunny smile.

"Of course I do! I'm sure that Mrs. Douglas will

131

have some old pillows somewhere—I shall have to ask her. But I don't know your name?"

"Jim, Miss. My dad's Greg Parker. He gardens here and does odd jobs. He lives in the old *whare* beside the stables."

He grinned at my puzzled expression and gave me a patronizing, kindly look. "That's a Maori word for cottage."

"I don't believe I saw your father at Prayers, today?"

A veiled look. "Well, no, Miss. You wouldn't, would you?"

On the mantel, the clock chimed the three-quarter hour.

"Oh, cripes—begging your pardon, Miss—almost eleven o'clock! My dad'll have my hide. Got to go, Reg—sorry!" He rushed out of the room.

"What a lively young man, Reginald. I'm so pleased you have another boy to play with; and so near your own age. How old is he?"

A silence. Reginald had fallen back against his pillows, the bedclothes pulled up to his chin, his eyes shut.

I picked up the fallen pillow from the floor and wondered what to do. I gritted my teeth. Really, the child was as obstinate as his father! I determined that no matter what, I would make him talk to me!

"Monsieur le Comte, s'il vous plaît! I know that you have enemies, that the *canaille* would drag you to the guillotine . . ."

The long, dark lashes fluttered and the delicate lids flew open.

I clasped one pale hand in mine. "Oh, monsieur, the guillotine! How many lives has this dreadful

132

monster taken? And *you*, the great Comte de Puissey Choiseul de Rambouillet to be in its awful shadow!"

The eyes watching me became less guarded. "Oh, Monsieur, I am, as you know, a poor exile from the land of my birth—and I am in danger! Mon Dieu, what danger am I in! Oh, monsieur, may I speak to you?"

A lively intelligence lit up the little face. "You may speak, mademoiselle!"

"Oh, monsieur, perhaps we could join forces—but always, of course in secret! When we are in the presence of others, we shall pretend to know nothing of their plots!"

"Mam'zelle!" The cool, little voice was firm. "You are right—this *is secret* business. But how do I know that you are not a spy sent by my enemies?"

"Monsieur, how could you think such a thing of me? How could you think me a creature of such dishonor?"

(I smote my brow.)

"Very well, Mam'zelle, calm yourself! But we must have a pact!"

I remembered my little urchins in Manchester. "And a password, monsieur!"

A gleeful look, then a return to aristocratic dignity. "Bien sûr, Mam'zelle! Of course! But what shall the password be?"

"But, you must choose, monsieur. You are monsieur le comte!!"

"Indeed, Mam'zelle. Then, let it be—" A pause and his eyes sparkled, I could have sworn, with tears. "Then, let it be *Rogue*." He turned his head away, his flushed cheek pressing into the pillow.

I laid a gentle hand on his shoulder and kept my voice low. "And this Rogue, monsieur, who is he?"

Another pause. "He . . . he was my dog, mam'zelle . . . when I was young."

The small form curled tightly into the bedclothes while I looked down, shattered. There were questions I must ask, I thought, but this was not the time.

Jim Parker had left the door partially open and footsteps in the corridor provided me with a heaven-sent distraction.

My voice was urgent. "Monsieur le Comte! One approaches! What shall we do?"

The quilt quivered as Reginald grew more tightly into a ball.

"Oh, please, monsieur! I beg of you!"

A sudden throwing aside of bedclothes and Monsieur le Comte was back again, leaning against his disordered pillows. "Mam'zelle, we must conduct ourselves as we agreed! Calm yourself!"

The door opened slowly and there was Jenny, holding a tray bearing a pitcher, a glass, and a covered platter.

"Time for your luncheon, Master Reggie! It's a bit early, but Mrs. Douglas thought as how you'd be hungry after so little breakfast. Oh, Miss, I didn't see you sitting there!"

She placed the tray on a small table. "Why, Master Reginald, what a fix you've got yourself in. All these clothes and pillows in such a tangle. My word, you must have been in a fight!"

As I rose to help Jenny straighten the bed, I smiled secretly at Reginald, only to be rewarded with a wooden stare. I should have been expecting it, I suppose, but the effect was devastating. In fact, so wooden was his gaze, so completely lacking in animation, I found myself wondering if indeed my preceding interview with him had been nothing but a figment of my imagination.

"Now, there you are, all comfortable again. And see what I've brought you!" Jenny placed the tray across Reginald's knees and whisked the cover from the platter. "A real treat, Master Reginald—and just because you're poorly. A regular spoiled lad, you are!"

Nestled in a small dish was a gleaming, golden brown pie.

"There now, what did I tell you! A chicken pie, just as cook likes to bake—and just for you, you naughty boy!"

I had breakfasted light and early and my nose crinkled longingly as wisps of steam unfurled into the cool bedroom air. Reginald, however, looked down with no apparent interest. I could have killed him.

"Well . . ." Jenny shot a helpless glance at me. "I have to be going."

To my surprise, at the door she paused again and, as in the garden, looked me over critically. "Yes," she said as to herself, "that suit will do . . . but that hair, well . . ." she looked at me impishly, "it needs tidying. I'll be with you in your room, Miss, in a quarter of an hour from now."

"Jenny, what . . .?"

"Oh, it's nothing, Miss!" A warning glance at Reginald, who apparently paying no attention, was doubtfully examining his pie.

"All I'll say now, Miss, is that I'll see you in your room in a quarter of an hour from now!" Another laugh and a whisk of her skirts and she was out the door.

I looked after her in wonderment, coming to my senses only when Reginald sneezed suddenly.

"Monsieur, you have a chill?"

"Non, Mademoiselle."

It seemed to me that the light eyes looked at me warily again.

I hesitated a moment. "Jenny is our friend, surely, Monsieur?"

"Perhaps."

The tone was doubtful and the small face stony. What, I wondered had caused such distrust, such distress of heart?

"Oh, Monsieur, Jenny is a *good* person. She would harm neither of us!"

"Perhaps not, but . . . she talks . . ."

"I . . . I see. Then, Monsieur, if you do not wish it, I shall not speak to her—or to anyone—about the danger surrounding us." I thought again of my Manchester urchins. "You have my word! You talked about a pact, Monsieur?"

I imagined some childish demand, a paper perhaps written in milk and then dried to invisibility before the fire in his bedroom grate in which we would agree to support the other to the death.

Reginald still had the power to surprise me. From under his pillow he fished out a small knife. "We must share blood, Mademoiselle!"

Fifteen

At twelve o'clock, after Jenny's mysterious ministrations—she still would not tell me what all the fuss was about—and having nothing better to do, I decided to visit the library opposite Mr. Raven's study.

It turned out to be a long narrow room running parallel with the dining room—indeed, fortunately for me as it turned out later—there was a connecting door, but so cunningly concealed in the dark panelling to be not at once apparent. At one end, French windows—as was the case in Mr. Raven's study— looked out onto the south lawn and the huge tree under which I had first spied Moana. Around the walls were six-foot bookshelves burdened with a variety of leather-bound tomes, and above the bookshelves were oil paintings of sailing ships interspersed with a landscape or two.

So, Josiah Raven had been a "reading man," I thought, and looked with awe on the volumes before me. I thought again of the portrait at the head of the stairs, of the thin line of mouth through the spade beard, and the shrewd brown eyes above. "Josiah's Folly" Ishbel had told me the cupola was called. No Folly, I thought now, looking at all the books and thinking again of the portrait; there had been a reason for that cupola—and, I thought, thinking of the dishevelled Mr. Raven I had met on my first night at Ravensfall, there still was!

Across the passage, masculine voices sounded. I recognized the deep tones of Gideon Tavish as he began to open Mr. Raven's study door.

"There's nothing for it, my dear fellow, we shall just have to disguise the drops as best we may—at night, now, it should be easy enough—in hot milk, perhaps. However, in the mornings . . ."

His words faded as his voice softened and he again closed the door.

I stood, riveted, remembering suddenly the words of Mrs. Mannering that I had overheard on my first morning at Ravensfall—"I fear, Marcus, that she suspects." About whom were they talking, I wondered? Why should drops have to be disguised? I remembered Mr. Tavish's wary look in the garden when I questioned him about his first meeting with Mr. Raven. There was something going on, something clandestine and—I was sure of it—sinister.

The study door started to open again. "In Wanganui, then." It was the end of a statement, as if a decision had been made. "Of course, there may be other ways. I shall check in the library."

Hardly thinking what I was doing, I rushed to the library door leading into the dining room and scurried through.

The sideboard had been cleared of the breakfast dishes; Ngaire and Martha, the whey-faced maid, under the enigmatic smile of the late Mrs. Raven, were busily setting up the long table for luncheon.

At my sudden entry, Martha gave a little shriek and Ngaire dropped a knife.

"Lord, Miss, you startled us!" Ngaire looked at me curiously. "Why . . . you're panting! Is something wrong?"

What could I say, that her employer and his guest of honor were apparently engaged in subterfuge of a dubious kind? Embarrassed, I cast about for something harmless to say. "Something wrong? No, of course not . . . it's just that . . . that . . ." Inspiration came to me at last, "I believe I saw—"

Martha's whey-face, if possible, paled even further and Ngaire, her brown eyes suddenly still, gave me an intent look. "Saw what, Miss?"

"Oh, nothing, really. Perhaps it was a mouse . . ." I paused, hating to lie and feeling somewhat ridiculous. Martha gave a sigh (could it have been of relief?) and began again to set the table but Ngaire continued to look at me closely.

I plunged on. "Of course, I didn't actually *see* it. It was just out the corner of my eye. I have an aversion for the creatures, you know and . . . and . . . I expect the whole thing was my imagination."

Feeling a complete fool, I retreated through the dining room door into the hall, aware that both girls had again paused from their task and were gazing at me, their eyes wide. So overcome with embarrassment, was I—and with the nervous confusion I had been thrown into by Gideon Tavish's remarks—that it

139

was not until much later that I wondered at the girls' apparent fright.

To my relief, there was no one in the drawing room; I needed time to be alone to sort out my thoughts.

A log fire sparkled now against the chill and this, with the sun's pale rays sifting through the heavy portières, sent out a golden welcome. The chairs had been rearranged about the fireside and on a side table sat a silver tray bearing crystal glasses and decanters.

Standing in front of the fireplaces, I gratefully held out my hands to the flames. The aromatic scent from the burning logs combined with the sharp fragrance from vases of white and gold freesias placed here and there about the room, had a headiness that, acting upon my nervous condition, almost made my senses reel.

"A glass of sherry, Miss Newcombe?"

The familiar lilting Scottish burr brought me to myself with a start. Callum Douglas had crossed the soft carpet and stood by the decanters.

"Thank you. Not quite yet, I think."

The thin lips pursed primly. "Not quite yet, I think."

To my annoyance, the imitation was almost perfect.

"Come now, let's not stand on ceremony!" A glint in the blue-green eyes. "I assure you, you will not be dismissed if you indulge in a glass of wine before the entrance of the Master of Ravensfall."

The tone was sarcastic but a smile all at once softened the sharp features. "Pay no attention to me.

140

Mr. Raven and I do not always rub well together, that is all and just now . . ." He bit his lip and grinned at me ruefully. "Forgive me, I did not intend to embroil you in our goings-on. Come now, a glass of sherry!"

Without the sarcasm, the eyes shone with a gentler more kindly light. I wondered briefly why he and Mr. Raven did not get on.

"Perhaps . . . a small glass."

A clink as glasses and decanters were maneuvered. Of course, I thought, Callum, though Mr. Raven's manager, was also a "poor relation." Perhaps he was taken advantage of? At least, I smiled to myself, I was not alone in my dislike of Mr. Raven's manner.

A glass was handed to me. "Your health! But I see you are smiling. Would you care to share the joke?"

The sherry was warming and smooth and helped to stifle the hunger pangs that had bothered me since I had sniffed the aroma of Reginald's chicken pie. "No joke. It's just that . . ." I took another sip; the sherry really was good! "Forgive me, I do not wish to be indiscreet . . ."

"No, of course not!" One eyebrow arched in mock disapproval. The eyes glinted wickedly.

I took another sip to fortify myself. I felt pleasantly warm, relaxed — the heat from the fire, as I supposed. I remembered my former nervousness with a little shudder and wondered if I could possibly confide in Callum Douglas. Why, I asked myself, had I felt such an antipathy toward him. Surely, he was at Ravensfall on much the same footing as myself . . . and surely, if one considered his circumstances . . .

I looked up into the blue-green eyes; there were smokey brown circles about the pupils, I noticed.

141

"So you won't tell me why you were smiling?" The tone was gently mocking. "Perhaps you don't have to; perhaps I can guess. We Scots are said to have 'second sight,' you know!"

Another puckish grin with — I could not help it! — an answering smile from me.

"I can hardly believe, Cal — Mr. Douglas, that you are serious!" To my embarrassment, I felt myself blushing at my near use of his Christian name.

A light laugh. "Perfectly serious, *Miss Newcombe!*"

I blushed again at his mock formality and hardly knew where to look.

A pause, as he grinned down at me, his left eyebrow raised devilishly. "Let me prove my clairvoyance!" He looked abstractedly into the far distance, the fingertips of his right hand pressed with mock drama against his temple. "You were thinking . . . you were thinking . . . ah, I've got it! You were smiling of course, at your discovery!"

"Discovery?"

"Indeed, yes; your discovery that you and I have something in common. That Mr. Raven . . . finds fault . . . with both of us."

I attempted a light laugh and with deliberate casualness sipped slowly at my sherry. "How can you say such a thing? I'm sure that Mr. Raven and I—"

"Oh, come now, no prim protestations! You are no actress . . . Harriet . . ." A pause, as he registered the shock in my face. "Your features reveal your every thought."

He smiled and gently touched my cheek with the tip of one lean brown finger. "You will let me call you Harriet, will you not?"

The room really was rather warm, I thought, so much so, that I felt a little dizzy; I had the insanest urge to cling to the waistcoat in front of me and rest my head against the strong chest beneath. I pulled myself together with difficulty. "I hardly th . . . think, that . . . that Mr. Raven would approve of such informality!"

"Tut, tut! Indeed, not! And, of course, you must have Mr. Raven's approval!" The tone was teasing again, but the eyes were serious. "Very well, Harriet; then let us keep our informality a secret for now." An expression flitted across his face that held a sadness I could not understand. "You need an ally and it is just as well that Marcus Raven does not know who that ally is!"

"I don't understand!"

"Do you not? Hasn't that sharp mind of yours discovered a certain — atmosphere — here, at Ravensfall?"

Despite the draw of the blue-green eyes, I resolved to be discreet. What, if after all, Gideon Tavish's remarks about the drops turned out to be perfectly innocent, how foolish I should look!

I sipped the last of the wine. "I know of course about Mr. Raven's . . . difficulty . . . and naturally the loss of the late Mrs. Raven, and in such circumstances, has greatly affected those she loved. But that is now in the past and I hope that I . . ."

Over the lean features flickered another expression I could not fathom. Was it grief, bitterness — or even, fear? "Oh, aye, poor Minna, poor rich Minna." A pause and a considering look. "In the past, you say? My poor girl, don't you realize . . . but, no, I see you

143

do not!"

"Whatever are you talking about?"

Another considering look, this time the eyes shadowed. When he spoke again, his words echoed the advice given me by the mate of the *Waiwere*. "This is a lonely place, Harriet, and there are things going on here that are not of your concern. If you must stay in New Zealand, then settle in Wanganui. I understand they need an English mistress at the Girls' College . . ."

"But . . ."

His eyes swept over me and a slight smile relieved his urgency as he noted Jenny's latest efforts with my hair. "I doubt you'll stay there long before you're snatched up by some young fellow."

The dizziness I had experienced earlier returned— really the room was *very* warm! "That . . . that is . . . (a slight hiccup) . . . impertinent!" I drew myself up as tall as I could—about as high as his middle waistcoat button. 'I do not intend to leave Ravensfall," I managed at last, my voice shaking. "I have Malvina to consider and Reginald, also. I . . . I have developed a . . . a fondness for them, and perhaps, if only just a little, I believe they have for me."

A sigh. "Yes, of course . . . the children. That was just what Miss Inglewood said, poor soul, before she . . . and that is why you need an ally—someone to whom you may turn when you are in doubt, when you feel you are . . . in danger. Because like Miss Inglewood you are stubborn. No matter what the warning, you are determined to stay, are you not!"

The face above me was a blur, I felt distinctly faint. "Miss Inglewood? What has she to do with this?" I tottered forward.

"Harriet, you are indisposed! Here, let me take your glass and help you to a chair. There now, are you quite comfortable?" A strong hand arranged a cushion behind my head.

"Yes, thank you. How foolish of me . . . but the . . . warmth of the room . . ."

"*Not* the warmth of the room," the voice was harsh. "My words, my mention of Miss Inglewood in such a context."

"You mean that Miss Inglewood was in some kind of danger?"

An exasperated sigh. "Harriet, that is what I have been trying to tell you! Mary—Miss Inglewood—asked too many questions, she probed too much and so . . ."

"Mary," I thought. So Callum Douglas had been on first name terms with Miss Inglewood. In the gradually clearing haze, I gathered my wits together. "I had thought that . . . Miss Inglewood . . . was accidentally drowned when the river flooded?"

"So she was. The question is—how did the 'accident' come about?"

I looked at him puzzled but before I could demand an explanation, voices sounded from the hall. Callum, a finger to his lips, moved away toward the fireplace and stood looking down into the flames.

Mrs. Mannering and Hélène DuPrès entered, closely followed by Marcus Raven, a smiling Ishbel clinging to his arm—smiling, but not for long. As I watched, Mr. Raven disengaged himself from his stepdaughter—rather abruptly, I thought—and turned toward the decanters. Ishbel's face at once lost its glow; she drifted away toward a window seat and kneeling, shoulders drooping, gazed at some finches twittering in a shrub outside. After a few moments, Callum, an expression almost of tenderness on his face, moved over to the window to engage her in quiet conversation.

How alike they were, I thought. From a distance, the differences in their features were not so noticeable; the similarity of shape of head and, of course, their intense coloring being more remarkable.

At least poor Ishbel had one friend! I watched Marcus Raven serving sherry to Mrs. Mannering and Hélène DuPrès, who after greeting me had seated themselves near by, their heads close together in earnest conversation. What was the matter with the man, that he could show his stepdaughter no affection when she so obviously needed it? I looked again at the arrogant profile, the hawk nose, and decided that perhaps he had no affection to give. I thought about his late wife. Minna, Callum had called her, "poor, rich Minna." Had Mr. Raven any affection for her or had he married her for her money . . . and then . . . oh, surely not! And Mary Inglewood? What had Callum said—that she "probed too much!" My thoughts in a whirl, I could not believe what I was thinking!

"A glass of sherry, Miss Newcombe?"

I looked up startled, to find the object of my horror standing before me, a smile, for once, lighting up his saturine face.

He noted the shudder I tried to restrain. "Or, perhaps you are teetotal. How very admirable!" His eyes strayed toward the occasional table beside me and observed my empty glass. His lips twitched. "Ah, I see you are not! Perhaps another glass?"

In my overly sensitive state (doubtless brought about by my shattered nerves) his tone — though perfectly polite — seemed to imply that this would be at least my third glass of the morning!

I was about, with dignity, to decline, when Ngaire came to the door to usher in a pleasant-faced young man I had never seen before.

"Oh, there you are, dear Jonathan! I am so pleased that you could come!" Mrs. Mannering broke off her conversation with Hélène DuPrès to welcome her guest.

"The pleasure is mine, ma'am!" The voice, a pleasing tenor, was from its accent a colonial one. A real New Zealander, then, as Jim Parker of the freckled face, would say, I thought with some amusement.

I looked at him with interest. Of medium height and build, he had a rugged "open-air" quality about him that was enhanced by glossy, light brown hair, deep blue eyes, and a robust complexion.

"I believe you know everyone, here?" Marcus Raven asked handing him a glass of sherry. "Except, of course, Miss Newcombe, our latest arrival — she is here to teach my children. Miss Newcombe allow me to introduce Mr. Jonathan Turner, my solicitor's son and junior partner."

"Very junior partner, I'm afraid." Smiling, the young man shook hands with me, then turned to Mr. Raven. "I've brought the deeds to your new property, sir, and the other papers you wanted."

"Ah. Yes . . . just so! We'll talk about them after luncheon." Mr. Raven spoke rapidly and low — an

147

unusual style with him — as if he did not want his words to be overheard. In his more usual tones, he added, "Good of you to come all the way from Wanganui!"

A pleasant smile. "I seize every excuse to come up-river. And my father doesn't mind — he likes to have first-hand news of his grandchildren!"

"And how are they all?"

"Very well . . . though the youngest has just had an attack of croup." He turned to me. "My brother farms across the river from Ravensfall, Miss Newcombe."

I looked at his spotless attire, the neat dark suit, and high-collared shirt with a correct dark tie. "Then how . . ."

A mellow laugh. "Hemi came for me from Ravensfall in his canoe — though I could have come in our old dinghy, if it were not being repaired!" He laughed again at my surprise. "We're not as isolated as you might suppose. Especially of course with the *Waiwere*. What a blessing that boat is," he turned back to Mr. Raven, "and so comfortable! I came up in her on Friday and was able to work on briefs all the way. And I suppose I'll do the same when I return tomorrow."

The door opened and Jenny appeared to announce luncheon. She saw me with Jonathan Turner and her face broke into a beaming smile. So that was it, I thought with inner amusement. She had known of the guest for luncheon and had done her best to make me look as fine as possible!

Unfortunately for Jenny, Ishbel came forward at that moment from the window seat where all this time she had been talking with Callum.

"And what do you think of New Zealand, Miss

Newcombe?"

"Most interesting," I was beginning when I realized that he was paying no attention to my reply. The intense blue eyes were fixed on Ishbel as she advanced across the room, one hand on Callum's arm and her delicate face upturned to his. She laughed at that moment, a musical laugh; a carillon of tiny bells.

"Excuse me, I don't believe I have met . . ."

"My stepdaughter, Ishbel McLeod." Marcus Raven interrupted smoothly. "I had quite forgot, Jonathan, that Ishbel was not . . . er . . . present, when last you came."

The topaz eyes were guarded and I did not believe the words. Marcus Raven, I was quite sure, never forgot anything.

"Come, Jonathan, I shall introduce you and then we must all go into luncheon."

And after luncheon, I thought, he would take Mr. Turner off to his study and remain closeted there until we were all safely about our various tasks. I remembered my night in Wanganui and the sour-faced Mrs. Hargreaves dumping my rice pudding before me, while exclaiming that it was a "crying shame" that Ishbel was kept so close. What else had she said? It was important, I knew. I racked my brains . . .

"My dear Miss Harriet, allow me to take you into luncheon!"

An arm was offered to me and I looked up into the warm brown eyes of Gideon Tavish.

He had changed out of his tweeds and was now attired in a suit of charcoal-grey superfine with an amethyst pin clipped to his mauve and silver-striped tie and a single pink carnation peeping nattily from one lapel.

"Ah, I see you observe my buttonhole!" He bent forward, his voice soft and his eyes dancing. "Now, I wonder if you can guess who gave it to me?"

Dazed, I shook my head.

"Why, my delicious young ladyfriend, of course! Come now, Miss Harriet, can't you guess who she might be?"

"I'm afraid I . . ."

A booming laugh; all heads turned our way. "Well, here she is!"

Malvina peeked shyly around the door. Her face brightened when she saw me and then to my surprise relaxed into a happy smile when she recognized Gideon Tavish.

"And now, I have two beautiful young ladies to escort! Come, my dears!"

As Jenny had said, luncheon was really dinner and turned out to be pleasantly informal. Mr. Raven carved the meat himself and the servants withdrew immediately after bringing each course to table.

"I am not at all sure that I approve of our informality, Miss Newcombe. But these colonials, you know . . . of course Jenny is from Lancashire and properly trained . . . but the others . . . Do you know," Mrs. Mannering lowered her voice in horror, "that in some households, the servants do not even wear uniforms, and they speak to their employers in the most informal terms!"

I tried to look suitably shocked. Gideon Tavish who was seated opposite gave me the ghost of a wink. I glanced hurriedly away.

We were seated at the foot of the table, one of us on either side of Mrs. Mannering, who acted as hostess. At the head of the table sat Mr. Raven, with Mr. Jonathan Turner on his right and Hélène DuPrès on his left. Mrs. Douglas, who had joined us on our way into luncheon, and Malvina were seated on my side of the table, while opposite between Mrs. DuPrès and Mr. Tavish, were Callum and Ishbel.

Mrs. Mannering sighed. "Of course, one is fortunate to have servants at all! Mrs. Watt—an acquaintance of mine in Wanganui—was complaining that it is hard to hire anyone at all. The young people here are so independent . . ."

She paused long enough to nibble a piece of roast potato.

"Ah, the pioneering spirit!" Gideon Tavish plunged in, while he had an opportunity to speak. "The young men set out to clear the land and take the young women with them!"

I half listened with one ear as Mrs. Mannering began another of her interminable monologues, bravely interrupted now and again by Gideon Tavish.

Beneath the portrait of the late Mrs. Raven, her bereaved husband made pleasant conversation with Jonathan Turner and Hélène DuPrès. Mr. Turner participated politely but his eyes strayed repeatedly across to Ishbel. Evidently not averse to his advances, Ishbel responded with little smiles and swift glances from beneath her long fluttering lashes. Poor girl, I thought, that was of course what she needed most; a lighthearted social life and the attentions of good-looking young men! I resolved there and then to

151

tackle Mr. Raven on the matter.

I was not the only one to notice the flirtation — if so strong a word was indeed suitable! Beside Ishbel, Callum, a small frown wrinkling his brows, kept an intent watch on the proceedings.

I remembered his tender look toward Ishbel when Mr. Raven had deserted her in the drawing room and his long conversation with her at the window seat. Was there something there, other than mere cousinly affection? And yet his attentions to myself had been so very particular. I remembered, could still feel, the soft touch of his finger on my cheek. You are getting above yourself, Harriet, I told myself sternly. Whatever Jenny has done to your hair; beside Ishbel, you are still small and insignificant! Callum was merely concerned about me, as a friend would be.

"Miss Newcombe?" I looked round to find myself being addressed by Mrs. Douglas.

"I'm sorry, Mrs. Douglas, I'm afraid I was daydreaming!"

She smiled at me from the other side of Malvina, who as usual was picking at her food.

"I only asked if you have felt homesick, yet?"

I thought of the rectory in Manchester and shuddered. "Indeed, no. There have been too many things to interest me! And as a matter of fact . . ." I looked around at the panelled walls and at the main course that we were now completing, of roast beef and potatoes in a rich brown gravy accompanied by peas, roast carrots, pumpkin, and Yorkshire pudding. "If it were not for the tree ferns outside the windows, I could almost swear that I had not left England!"

There was a slight lull in the conversation and Mr.

Raven overhearing my last few words, leaned forward, directing his remarks to me down the table. "A common enough feeling, Miss Newcombe." He smiled slightly. "Most people here think of New Zealand as being a 'young' country — and so it is in *pakeha* terms — but away from the houses we build and the roads we establish, there are still the old gods in the dark forests, the ancient myths and legends. There was, you know, another people here before us . . ."

A slightly embarrassed laugh from Jonathan Turner. "Come now, sir! The Maoris let us into the country quite willingly — the Treaty of Waitangi, you know — and they've benefited from it. Most of them, you must admit, are quite civilized now. Even here, upriver . . ."

Rescue for Mr. Raven came — as might be expected — from Hélène DuPrès.

"Civilized, you say! Have you met Moana, Mr. Turner?"

A boyish grin. "I have indeed. Your point is well taken!"

They both laughed.

Marcus Raven looked down the table at me, his eyes rueful. He opened his mouth as if he wished to say something but just then Ngaire entered to take away our plates and he shrugged his shoulders and turned away, his words unspoken.

Sixteen

A timid knock. Three o'clock on a winter's afternoon, the shadows already drawing in. I was writing my novel at last.

"Miss Newcombe?"

Malvina's voice. Regretfully, I left Sir Percival and his tiff with the Lady Ariadne.

"Malvina?"

At the door in the half-light, her little face stood out pale, strained.

A deep breath. "Miss Newcombe, I know you are taking tea with Mrs. Douglas at half past three."

"Oh, so I am—I had quite forgot!" I looked with regret at my manuscript scattered about the small table I had asked to be supplied to my room. I smiled. "Thank you for reminding me!"

A timid smile in response, but a smile none the less—and then a blush. "Oh! Well, that is . . ."

I came to the rescue. "That is not what you have come about," I suggested gently.

"N—no, that is . . ."

"Come in, Malvina, do! And sit down."

She sank down on the cushioned stool by my fireside chair, her Sunday lace-edged pinafore and blue merino skirts billowing about her.

I left my papers and sat on the chair beside her. I wanted to take her in my arms but could not. There was something about the set of those thin shoulders that did not invite familiarity. Daringly, I reached out and touched her lightly on her hair, on the slim curve of her shoulder—the bones were delicate, brittle, and there was a tremulousness that vibrated throughout, reminding me of a lost sparrow I had caught once inside the church in Manchester and had held for a moment in my hands before releasing it to the outside air.

"There is something troubling you?"

The wide blue eyes looked up at me and I was reminded again of her likeness to her mother. There was a difference however; a resolution about the mouth that was completely lacking in the delicate features of the portrait of the late Mrs. Raven. Malvina, it seemed, had inherited something from her father.

"It's n . . . nothing, really. It's just that I was talking to Reggie and he told me . . ."

"That I know his secret?"

An anxious glance through the long, dark lashes. "Well, yes."

"And you are worried that I will tell your papa?"

A look of sheer terror. "Oh, please, Miss Newcombe, you must not!"

"Why not, child? Why are you so afraid of your papa?"

155

A veiled glance through the lashes and an evasive answer. "You promised, Miss Newcombe!"

"So I did! And of course, I shall keep my promise."

A sigh of unutterable relief. "So you won't tell Papa? You won't tell anyone?"

"What is it, Malvina? Please tell me!"

A doubtful look, but the little mouth remained firm. "You won't tell *anyone*, Miss Newcombe?"

"Of course not. Not if I have given my promise!"

"Not even Mrs. Douglas?"

So that was it! I took a deep breath and burned all my boats. "Not even Mrs. Douglas."

I was rewarded with a tremulous smile.

Mrs. Douglas, I thought in despair. The one person I could talk things over with—but a promise was a promise!

"But, surely Mrs. Douglas knows about Reggie? She was your nurse after all."

"We had another nurse when we were young; but when Mama . . . left us . . . she decided she could not stay."

Poor little things, I thought, to be left so much alone. I gave her a quick hug and a cheerful smile. "Well, you have me now, my dear. I shall certainly not desert you!"

An answering smile but the blue eyes were doubtful. And who could blame her, I thought, after such a life!

My little clock chimed the quarter hour.

I sighed. "I suppose I must go. Malvina, don't you feel you could tell me why you and Reginald are so frightened?"

Her eyes widened and I thought for a moment that

I had at last caught her off guard.

I was doomed to disappointment. The long dark lashes swept down and the little mouth pursed itself in a thin line.

"Now, Malvina, don't be difficult! You have nightmares, Reggie hides himself in a dream world — there is something that is troubling you both, something awful. What is it? Why won't you tell me?"

The eyes were naked again suddenly, naked and afraid. "Miss Inglewood asked us that — and she is dead."

A scurry of petticoats. Malvina rose from her stool and fled.

Sugar, Miss Newcombe?"

"No, thank you."

I accepted my cup and saucer (fine Doulton china) and a finger sandwich (boiled egg and watercress).

The correct housekeeper's cap nodded inquiringly and the blue eyes smiled. "Your room is comfortable; you have everything you need?"

"Oh, yes. Thank you, Mrs. Douglas!"

I looked about me. The tall windows with the red plush curtains half-drawn against the lengthening shadows, looked out over the front lawn and the thick ever-encroaching bush. In contrast, a bright fire flickered within a well-blackened grate and a lamp cast a rosy glow over a Wedgwood teapot, buttered scones, finger sandwiches, and a Dundee cake.

"Your sitting room is very cosy, Mrs. Douglas."

A small laugh. "Yes, indeed. Mr. Raven has been so kind . . . He insists always that I have all the

157

comforts of 'home.' "

"You miss Scotland?"

"Indeed, I do! Though, I must admit that parts of New Zealand are very like it — especially down in the South Island."

"I expect the children miss it, too — Scotland?"

"Scotland and England; Mr. Raven's estate lies in Yorkshire, as you know. However, twice a year, Mrs. Raven would visit her Scottish estate in the Highlands and take the children with her."

I swallowed the last of my finger sandwich. "And Mr. Raven, he went with them?"

"When he could, poor gentleman. Do try these date scones, Miss Newcombe. Cook made them specially. But as I was saying, Mr. Raven traveled to Scotland when he could — but his Yorkshire estate . . ." A shake of the head and a sip of tea. "His Yorkshire estate was all but bankrupt."

"Bankrupt!"

"Aye, bankrupt. Mr. Raven, you see, inherited his estate from his older brother."

"His older brother?"

"Mr. Peregrine Raven. A spendthrift and a wastrel as ever there was — *and* a gambler!"

"Indeed!"

"Indeed, yes! Poor Mr. Marcus — to inherit so much . . . and so little. Another date scone?"

"Thank you. They're very good. Better even than Mrs. Porter's, my aunt's cook. But you were saying?"

"So much and so little. You see, the estate was large but encumbered. It took some time, I assure you, for Mr. Raven to bring things about. And then, of course after the late Mrs. Raven's — demise — he decided to

158

bring his family here, away from all the notoriety . . ."

I rushed in to soothe. "Of course, I understand. However," I dabbed at my lips with my napkin. "Don't you think that, now *that* is all in the past, the children, and of course, Ishbel, should mingle more in society?" I laid down my napkin. "It can do them no good, you know, to be so isolated here . . ."

The blue eyes met mine, with as I thought at the time, a look of respect. "You are of course, quite right, Miss Newcombe. Just as I said to Mr. Raven, this very afternoon. But you must try a piece of Dundee cake—or Mrs. Murchison will be very disappointed."

"Thank you." I accepted a piece of the light fruit cake and nibbled at the split almonds and chopped glacé cherries scattered about the top. "You were saying, Mrs. Douglas . . . ?"

A humorous look. "You are a determined young woman, Miss Newcombe!"

"Please excuse me . . ."

A faint smile. "I meant only that you really care about your charges."

"Of course."

"Well, as I was saying, I was talking to Mr. Raven only a short while ago. Apparently, Mr. Raven, Ishbel, and of course, Mrs. Mannering, have been invited to a ball in Wanganui when next the family is in town. Mr. Turner brought the invitation with him this afternoon."

"Oh, that's wonderful. That is just the thing for Ishbel—" I stopped at the look on Mrs. Douglas' face. "Oh, don't tell me that she is not to be allowed to go!"

A slight hesitation. "Ishbel is so highly strung, you

159

see . . . however, Mr. Raven did say he would think it over." A sigh. "Well, we shall just have to see."

We shall indeed, I thought grimly; but managed to restrain my unruly tongue from saying so. "Does the whole household go to Wanganui?" I asked instead.

"Yes; including most of the indoor servants — Mrs. Hargreaves needs the help, you see." A sudden smile — perhaps relief at the change of subject? "You will enjoy being back in a town again!"

"Yes . . . yes, I suppose I shall." To my surprise, I realized that even after so short an acquaintance the thought of leaving Ravensfall so soon quite bothered me.

Mrs. Douglas laughed at my apparent lack of enthusiasm. "Yes, the place does grow on one, despite the isolation and . . . and . . ." Biting her lip, as if she had said too much, she busied herself, pouring out another cup of tea.

I wanted to question her but of course could not. Instead, glancing about the room, I spied a silver-framed photograph on a side table. It was of a serious-faced woman of about thirty or so — and there was indeed a likeness to the late Mrs. Raven. "Miss Inglewood!" I exclaimed, before I could help myself.

"So it is. But how did you know?" The tone, I thought, was wary.

"Mr. Tavish told me that you had a likeness of her."

A sigh almost of relief. "Yes, poor woman. She was an orphan, you know, and had no other family and after . . . after it happened, there was no one to whom we could send back her personal effects.

"The children seemed to have been very fond of her."

"Poor little souls. For all she was here such a short time, they took a great fancy to her."

"She did not come to New Zealand with the family?"

"No, she came out independently. But another piece of Dundee cake, Miss Newcombe?"

"Perhaps, just a small piece—it really is delicious!" We munched companionably.

A reminiscent smile from Mrs. Douglas. "In fact, it was over a piece of Dundee cake, that I first met Miss Inglewood!"

She enjoyed my surprise. "In the tearooms on Victoria Avenue! It was crowded, you see, and so I did not object to sharing my table with a strange young woman—especially when I recognized from her accent that she had just come from 'home,' we're always agog, as you will find out, to hear the latest news. She ordered Dundee cake with her tea and when they said they had none left, I offered her a piece of mine. And so we got to talking and when I found out that she was in search of a post, I mentioned the fact to Mr. Raven, as he was becoming concerned about the children's education. It's not so easy to find a young woman willing to isolate herself in the bush."

"She was happy, here?"

"She seemed to be; although, she was always so quiet, slipping about the house like a little mouse. One was never sure where she would appear next! However, she certainly was good with Reggie and Malvina; though she did have some rather odd ideas about their education. Some more tea?"

I handed her my cup and saucer. "Odd ideas, Mrs.

Douglas? In what way?"

A thoughtful pause as she poured out my tea and gave me back my cup and saucer. "Well, for one thing she would read to the children by the hour out of books which to me seemed too advanced — Dickens' *A Tale of Two Cities*, for instance! She had the oddest notion that poor dear Reggie was brighter than he seemed."

I bit my tongue.

"Poor soul. She meant well, I suppose — but this is a very dreary conversation and I have been doing all the talking! I'm sure that by now, you must have questions about the children that I may be able to help you with — about their little foibles and so forth. Please ask whatever you wish and I shall see what I can do!"

I drank the last of my tea and set my cup aside. "Not really, at least, not at the moment; although, as time goes on, I'm sure there will be things I shall need to ask you about." I handed her my cup, saucer, and plate to be placed on the tea tray. "There's just one question at the moment. Apparently, Reginald had a little dog once that he seems to be still upset about. I wondered what had happened to it?"

A silence and then a deep sigh. "That was Rogue, a little Airedale. It was most unfortunate and I hardly like to tell you, but for Reggie's sake I suppose I must." Another pause as she placed her own tea things on the tray. "The truth is that one day after Mrs. Raven . . . died . . . Reggie's dog was found. . ."

"Found . . . dead?"

"I'm afraid so. And also from laudanum poisoning."

A long silence.

We both jumped at a knock on the door and remained staring at each other as Martha entered to remove the tea tray.

Seventeen

Needless to say, after such a day I could not concentrate on my writing. In fact, it was enough for me to endure the rest of the evening without suffering a nervous fit.

And yet, I wondered as I readied myself for the night, what had I learned? My mind was a mishmash of vague information: remarks half-overheard, veiled threats, and accounts of mysterious — even brutal — happenings in the past.

What did it all mean?

As I buttoned Aunt Alice's ugly brown woolen dressing gown over my flannel nightdress, I could hear her voice in my mind, mouthing her favorite speech to me, "Get yourself in hand, Harriet! Really, so headstrong and impulsive as you are! And such a flibbertigibbet — I declare that over-active mind of yours will cause you trouble yet!"

I took the pins out of my hair and dragged my brush through the usual tangles. Was I being too imaginative, now, I asked my reflection in the glass above the washstand. Was I misinterpreting remarks half-heard. And what about that most improper encounter with Callum Douglas in the drawing room before lunch? Had the effects of that glass of sherry on my empty stomach caused me to exaggerate his warning. And why on earth should anyone want to harm *me?*

What was there of *any* substance, I wondered, as I braided back my hair? Mrs. Raven had been murdered, that was true, and a poor little dog killed. But both events had happened in the past and in another country . . . and in any case, what had one to do with the other? Mr. Raven may or may not have committed the murder, that was true. But what had that to do with the present situation? And as for Miss Inglewood, whose tenuous presence seemed still to "slip" as Mrs. Douglas had said, "like a little mouse from room to room." How could she, a complete stranger, have been a threat to anyone?

In the glass, the room behind me glowed in the light from the lamp I had brought in from the school room. Miss Inglewood's room, I thought . . . always, Miss Inglewood. What had been her hopes and fears, I wondered? The draft from under the door stirred the frill round the legs of the fireside chair and the valance about the bed. Despite the small fire in my grate, the air was chill. I buttoned the dressing gown up to my throat and turned in irritation from the glass. Bother Miss Inglewood, I thought, and told myself that I had to rid her image from my mind.

What was there of any substance, I asked myself again? What about the drops? After all, I had heard the actual words. And not, I thought, blushing at the memory, when I was under the influence of sherry! "I fear that she suspects," I had overheard Mrs. Mannering say, and later Gideon Tavish had suggested that the drops be placed at night in milk . . . and what else had he said? That they could "perhaps, find other ways"? Other ways of disposing of the drops, I wondered, or other ways of . . . ?

"Stop it, Harriet!" I whispered to myself out loud. Much as I hated to admit it, Aunt Alice had been right. I did let my imagination run away with me! Mr. Raven could possibly be a murderer, but it was hardly likely that an elderly widow and a respectable author of books about birds would be in league with him!

There had to be a perfectly harmless and logical explanation, I assured myself: which I should find out about in due course — and then I should have a good laugh!

The same was true about the children's state of mind, I told myself sternly. Surely considering the tragic circumstances and the situation in which they presently found themselves, this was only to be expected? I straightened my papers on my writing table and glanced about the room. Despite the chill, how bright and cosy everything was! All that was needed was a padded roll of cloth along the bottom of the door to keep out the draft. I should begin making one tomorrow, I decided. I looked toward the fireside chair — how inviting it was, with its matching cushioned stool. I thought of Malvina sitting there that very afternoon, her skirts billowing about her, her eyes wide with fear. "We told Miss Inglewood," she had responded to my question, "and she is dead."

I shivered. Miss Inglewood again! Was there no escape from her presence? As Ishbel had intimated, it was almost as if she were alive and about to appear at any moment. I gave myself a little shake. Really, I was becoming as bad as the children! I wondered what it was that Malvina had told Miss Inglewood. Something, no doubt, that her childish mind had conjured up as serious and when Miss Inglewood had drowned, doubtless, Malvina had somehow connected the two and now felt forever guilty.

The whole situation was ridiculous and there had to be a practical solution! The root of the whole problem, I decided angrily, lay with Marcus Raven; it was he of whom his children were so afraid and it was he who kept his children in such gloomy isolation. If Mr. Raven was afraid to mingle with society because of his tortured past, that was one thing; but keeping his children in a paroxysm of fear was quite another. And, I decided, I should certainly tell him so! I looked at the clock—it lacked five minutes to eleven. Unless he had retired, he would probably be with the family in the drawing room. Very well, I would leave a note in his study, asking for an interview tomorrow morning.

Before I could lose my courage and change my mind, I hastily scribbled a note, draped my black crocheted shawl over my shoulders and took up the lamp.

I was glad of the shawl. The chill was back in full force and with it a dampness that penetrated the bones. I guessed that the fog would be back again in the morning. I was glad, too, of the lamp. After my encounter with Mr. Raven on my first night, I had determined not to be caught again in the draughty halls with only a candle.

The wide passage stretched out in front of me, the darkness almost tangible, my lamp casting about me only a faint glow of light. For once, the cupola door was shut, but (laughing at my silliness!) I had to force myself to walk by it, rather then move to the wall opposite, as Malvina always did.

The stairs and landings on the way down were just as dark and remained so until a thin haze of light greeted me as I descended the stairs leading to the first floor. There to my surprise, on a little table by Josiah Raven's portrait on the first-floor landing, stood a small lamp. I was puzzled. Downstairs, in the well of the hall, all was darkness — so the family had retired for the night; perhaps, I thought, someone intended to go downstairs again. As I stood on the last stairs, half-hidden by the wall, I heard a door open down the corridor to the right.

Peering round the wall, (if it were Marcus Raven, I had no desire to meet him, attired as I was!) I saw Hélène DuPrès. She was leaving the room nearest the landing. I watched as she made her way to another room further down the hall, the light from the candle she was carrying, highlighting her chestnut hair cascading down the back of what appeared to be a diaphanous rose and silver wrap. Where was she going, I wondered, so scantily clad? To visit Ishbel or Mrs. Mannering? Surely not, at that time of night — and dressed in such a manner!

Hélène DuPrès so occupied my mind, that I

reached the ground floor almost without realizing it. Down in the front hall, the lamp beside old Josiah's portrait became merely the faintest of glows and the passage leading from the other side of the stairs to Mr. Raven's study, a tunnel of darkness. I held the lamp up high, trying to penetrate the shadows. The library door was partly open I noticed and opposite, the study door was shut, but at the end of the passage, I could hardly make out the shape of the outside door. I stood for a moment, remembering suddenly the reaction of Ngaire and Martha to my sudden entrance into the dining room that morning. They had been frightened, I realized now. Frightened of what, I was beginning to ask myself, when Ishbel's words on my first night at Ravensfall came unbidden into my mind. "They say," she had said outside the cupola, "that Josiah Raven still walks."

Somewhere a board creaked and my hand holding the lamp shook, the light dipping and wavering among the shifting shadows.

"You are a coward, Harriet Newcombe," I informed myself aloud. "Josiah Raven is probably in Hell, where doubtless he belongs — and you must accomplish what you have set out to do!"

Somewhere in the darkness, I could have sworn I heard the whisper of a laugh; but clutching my shawl with one hand and the lamp with the other, I marched as quickly as I could down the hall, my face resolutely turned from the open library door.

I had thought to push my note under the study door. Unfortunately, the paper had slipped well down into my dressing gown's capacious pocket and somehow had become entangled with my handkerchief and my laundry list that I had absentmindedly tucked into the pocket that morning. I realized that I should have to put the lamp down; but I was worried that I might spill the kerosene if I bent with it all the way to the floor and besides I now saw that the door seemed particularly flush with the thick carpet. I decided to go in and rest the lamp on Mr. Raven's desk while I searched for the note in my pocket; the whole thing would take only a moment or two.

Taking a deep breath, I opened the door. To my surprise, the study was not entirely dark. Embers still flickered in the grate and a lamp on the desk — though turned down very low — gave out a muted light. Had Mr. Raven then been the one to leave the lamp beside Josiah's portrait, in readiness to come back downstairs again? Perhaps, I did not have much time?

I hurried across the room, set down the lamp and began to search in my pocket. It was then that a fleeting odour caught my nostrils, I looked about. Sure enough, at one end of the desk was an earthen crock (somewhat soil-stained) and an almost empty glass. My nose crinkled as I recognized the smell — I had sniffed it often enough when with Aunt Alice I had visited the derelicts at my father's former mission in Manchester ("My dear Harriet, one must always do one's duty, no matter how unpleasant!"). Was my employer a tippler then, as well as a possible murderer? I remembered my meeting with him at the cupola on my first night at Ravensfall. "I am not under the influence of spiritous liquor," he had said — *as he had swayed on the stairs.*

I stared angrily at the glass, telling myself that I had been an idiot. What kind of a man was this, I wondered, to be in charge of a delicate girl and two young children?

"A tot of whisky, Miss Newcombe?"

Marcus Raven leaned against the door jamb, his hands tucked negligently into the pockets of a capacious topcoat. He smiled politely but his eyes remained watchful, cold.

I looked at him, speechless.

A long silence.

I found my voice at last. "I assure you, Mr. Raven, that *I*," the slightest emphasis on the pronoun, "do not indulge myself with whisky."

An approving nod. "Nicely done—and true to form!"

A brief grin at my puzzled face. "Attack is the better form of defense . . . especially if one is in the wrong."

My cheeks burned. *"I,"* again a slight emphasis on the pronoun, "have done nothing wrong!"

A cocked eyebrow. "Then what are you doing— uninvited—in a gentleman's private study in the middle of the night and dressed only in your . . . night attire?" A doubtful look at my black crocheted shawl and Aunt Alice's dressing gown. "I take it, Miss Newcombe, that *is* your night attire? Not that I wish to be rude, but your ensemble when last I met you on your nighttime wanderings, was rather . . . more . . ."

"Mr. Raven, I came to your study to bring you *this*." I held out the note in a trembling hand.

"Ah. A letter! But I forget myself—I must not keep you standing. Please sit down . . . that chair by the fire . . ."

I looked longingly at the door but Marcus Raven

continued to stand in the way.

He smiled pleasantly. "Tell me, Miss Newcombe, do you consider that I murdered my late wife?"

"Excuse me?"

"Your ears did not deceive you. Do you think that I murdered my late wife?"

"Well . . . I . . . I . . ."

"You have not as yet made up that decisive mind? You have not cast me yet in the role of villain? You surprise me. Not wishing to rob you of the pleasure of shocked discovery, I am not at the moment going to admit to either yea or nay. I shall say only, that at times, my mood is distinctly murderous—and this is one of them. Sit down, Miss Newcombe!"

I sat down.

He quickly closed the door and took the chair opposite mine, completely cutting off my route of escape. Leaning forward, he took the note from my hand.

"It is only a request, Mr. Raven. I was going to slip it under your door, but I had difficulties with my lamp and . . ."

He opened the note and bent his head to read.

There was a short silence, followed by a cough. When he looked up at last, his face was expressionless.

"A request, you say, Miss Newcombe?"

"Yes, I thought it would be better if . . ."

He smiled politely. 'If you are short of funds, Miss Newcombe, I should of course be glad to advance your first quarter's salary."

"Oh, no, it's not that. I just thought . . ."

One eyebrow was raised. "You would like me to

attend to this personally?"

"I don't understand. Of course, I should like . . ."

A shake of the head. "In that case, I shall certainly do my best. Now, let me see . . . four pairs of stockings (black wool), three pairs of cambrick drawers, three chemises . . ."

"Mr. Raven, please, that's my—"

"My dear Miss Newcombe, what is this? Two pairs of *stays?* Have you not heard Mrs. Amelia Bloomer's opinions about such torturous underwear and its pernicious effects upon the female anatomy. I should have thought that *you* would be in the forefront of the reformers!"

"Please, Mr. Raven . . ." Desperately, I held out my original request for an interview.

"What's this, another request?"

To my utter humiliation, I felt tears spring to my eyes. Desperately, I looked away and blinked.

"Come now . . . I fear I have gone too far!" Quickly, he rose and standing momentarily beside me, briefly rested a hand on my shoulder. "I am sorry, please forgive me. I fear that today has been . . . and this evening . . . in other words, I forgot myself and when I saw your laundry list and you sitting there so very prim . . ."

"My Laundry list? You knew . . ."

"That it was your laundry list? Of course, and I'm afraid I let my sense of humor run away with me."

"How could you, sir! How could any gentleman . . ."

"Come now, I have been a husband after all! I assure you that I am well acquainted with the more intimate articles of feminine attire."

He paused a moment and an expression — was it of pain? — passed so quickly over his face, I wondered afterward, if I had indeed observed it.

"Come!" A hand clasped firmly above my elbow. "What you need — what we both need — is a hot cup of tea!"

"Cup of tea?"

He gave a short laugh. "Miss Newcombe, you are not a cuckoo clock. There is no need to repeat every word I say."

I found myself at the door. "But where are we going?"

Silence as the door was opened and Mr. Raven peered down the passage — almost, as I thought later, as if he were expecting someone. "Going?" he remarked at last. "Where to, but to the kitchens. But first, I believe we shall need a lamp." He quickly crossed the room and took up my lamp from his desk.

"But the servants will have gone to bed."

An amused glance. "I should certainly hope so. I have no wish to compromise your reputation!"

He returned to the door and then peered again up and down the hall. "Brrr, how cold it is. How sensible of you to wear your shawl."

An extra strong draught blew up the passage. With a muffled exclamation, Mr. Raven shone the lamp to the right. The outside door was swinging gently in the soft breeze.

"How remiss of me, I must have neglected to latch the door when I came in!"

In answer to my questioning look. "After my walk."

That explained the topcoat, I thought, my mind regaining at last some of its former astuteness, but on looking down at the well-polished shoes, I could discern no dust or clinging grass — and surely, after a walk over the lawn on a damp night . . ."

"Come along, Miss Newcombe!"

Marcus Raven closed the study door but interestingly did not go down the passage to close the outside door. Instead he led me past the dark library to the stairs and the green baize door beyond.

Eighteen

The big kitchen range had, of course, been banked down for the night, but to my surprise, Marcus Raven seemed to know how to get it going again and soon had a tea kettle singing cheerily into the shadowy reaches of the stone-flagged kitchen.

An amused glance at my raised brows. "I assure you, I am not completely helpless, Miss Newcombe."

"So I see, sir!"

I watched, fascinated, as the Master of Ravensfall moved about the kitchen of his residence, producing in quick succession, teapot, cups, and saucers, sugar and milk and some shortbread in a tartan-decorated tin.

Another amused glance. "There is really no reason why a gentleman should not know how to brew a pot of tea!" Deftly, he warmed the teapot with hot water from the kettle and measured three spoons of tea from the caddy on the plush-covered mantelpiece. "Especially when the gentleman has had to fend for himself at sea . . ."

"You were in the navy, Mr. Raven?"

"Not the navy, precisely." Expertly, boiling water was poured into the teapot. "I sailed with my late uncle—Josiah Raven—the former owner of this house. There now, we'll just wait for that to brew." After stoking up the fire again, he slipped off his overcoat and hung it on a nearby hook.

He leaned a moment against the mantel, tall and elegant in his perfectly cut dinner suit and gave a short laugh at the surprise which was no doubt reflected in my face. "Really, Miss Newcombe, do you always judge by appearances?"

"It's just . . . that . . ."

An ironic lift of an eyebrow. "You can not imagine me out of my present element? What a matter-of-fact young woman, you are! I assure you that despite my apparently civilised veneer, a pirate lurks beneath!" The light eyes narrowed, the voice softened suddenly.

I attempted a light laugh. "Really, Mr. Raven . . . is this a warning? Are you trying to tell me that you emulate those remote Viking ancestors of yours that Ishbel told me about?"

A wolfish grin. "Suffice it to say, that I have roamed, if not the high seas, then at least a fair stretch of the South Pacific."

"Your uncle was a whaler, I understand."

"In his younger days, yes." A pause as he poured the tea, adding milk in response to my nod. "However, by the time I came to live with him, he had been settled for some time in Wanganui—though he still liked to sail about the coastal waters and sometimes further afield. I traveled to Tasmania with him two or three times and to Fiji also."

177

"You had intended to settle in New Zealand, then?"

A wry smile. "Indeed, yes. As a younger son, I had my own way to make in the world and my uncle offered to make me his heir." He seated himself on a kitchen chair opposite mine and stretched out his long legs to the now glowing stove. "Mind you, I liked New Zealand from the beginning, I would have been quite content to stay here . . . however, I was obliged to return to Yorkshire when my elder brother died . . ."

Peregrine, I thought; and remembered Mrs. Douglas telling me of Peregrine's debts — and how Marcus Raven had paid them off. Was that why he had married Minna McCleod, I wondered. Had he used her fortune to pay off his debts? Peregrine, the gambler, I thought, Josiah . . . the . . . what — reprobate? And now, Marcus — the murderer?

I looked at my employer, the tips of his well-shod feet stretched out to the glowing grate, his long-fingered, elegant hands cradling, of all things, a thick crockery cup and saucer of hot steaming tea. Perhaps it was the informality of the situation, but his facial expression, the way in which he held himself, seemed gentler somehow, more relaxed — as if beneath the harsh outer crust lurked a persona at once friendlier and more humane.

"Some shortbread, Miss Newcombe?"

I came out of my reverie to find the tartan-decorated tin wafted beneath my nose.

"Thank you, yes; perhaps a small piece."

The shortbread, rich and crumbly, prevented speech for a while.

"You were glad to return to Yorkshire?" I asked at last, dusting some crumbs from my skirt.

"Yes . . ." A surprised look. "No . . . no. That is, at first . . ."

"I'm sorry, that was unthinking of me—your brother . . ."

"Please don't apologize. Peregrine—I liked him well enough when he was not in his cups—but he was my half-brother, you know, and much my senior. Though he was kind enough to me, in his way, motherless waif that I was."

I looked at the lean figure before me and suddenly visualized a small, tousle-headed boy, searching, always searching for affection.

A light laugh. "Miss Newcombe, I am not a cast-off spaniel! There is no need to watch me with those great eyes of yours! My mother—I swear it—died at my birth and I never missed her!"

"Sir, I . . ."

"But in answer to your question. Yes, I was glad to return to Yorkshire at first, the dales, the moors—the ancient stones of Ravensfall, the first Ravensfall—but after a while . . ." A pause, as he sipped thoughtfully at his tea. "It's almost as if once visited, this country sends out a call and one sees again the dark forests, the Pacific waters breaking over lonely shores." A crooked grin. "Or perhaps, what called me back was the thought of my carefree life with my Uncle Josiah!"

I sipped at my tea. "From what I have heard, your uncle must have been somewhat unconventional."

An amused gleam. "You could say so—in his younger days, especially. I'm afraid he did not always sail on the right side of the law. Have you heard of Bully Hayes, Miss Newcombe?"

"I don't believe . . ."

"A pirate, well known here in the South Seas—my uncle was perhaps too well acquainted with him—but I'm afraid I offend your sensibilities?"

"Not at all." I looked about me at the spacious kitchen and thought of the well-stocked library. "I'm sure that Mr. Josiah Raven must have had his good points."

"Doubtless; but not many, I fear." A wicked glance at me. "At the moment, I expect he is *where he belongs*, receiving his just deserts!"

I bit at my lip, embarrassed. I remembered the half-whispered laugh in the darkened hall after my remarks concerning Josiah Raven's probable present location. The thought that I may have been overheard was unbearable!

A short laugh. "However, enough of my uncle! Tell me—now that you are more relaxed—why did you want to see me so urgently? It must be something very important to necessitate a night time delivery!"

More relaxed! I gritted my teeth. "Not really urgent, but certainly important. I understand you have received an invitation for Ishbel to attend a ball in Wanganui?"

All of a sudden, the eyes watching me were no longer friendly. Marcus Raven slowly sipped his tea, his face, above the rim of his upturned teacup, completely lacking in expression.

I gazed back, determined not to be intimidated.

The cup was lowered into the saucer. An amused stare. "Indeed, yes. As your . . . er . . . source has probably informed you, the invitation was delivered to me this afternoon by Mr. Jonathan Turner."

I gave him a steely look and replied with calm

dignity. "My *source*, sir, was Mrs. Douglas. She happened to mention the invitation when we were taking tea together, this afternoon."

"Naturally! And to what conclusions did you and that esteemed lady come to regarding Ishbel?"

I drew myself up, ready to face the fray. "We believe that Ishbel should be allowed to go!" I waited for the explosion.

A puzzled stare. "Naturally, Miss Newcombe. I agree wholeheartedly. In fact, I sent my acceptance for Ishbel via Mr. Turner, just this afternoon."

"Oh!"

"I am glad that I have made a decision that has won your approval, Miss Newcombe!" The tone was light but one eyebrow quirked ironically.

"Yes. That is . . . thank you . . . I don't quite know what to say . . ."

"You will, of course, as Ishbel's companion, accompany her to the ball. I have already written a note to that effect."

"But . . . but . . ."

A repressive stare. "You have some objection, Miss Newcombe?"

"No, no . . . of course, not! It's just that—"

"Mrs. Mannering will also be there; and, of course, myself. However, you being closer in age . . ." Another pause, this time longer. "You are aware, of course, that Ishbel is . . . delicate . . . and somewhat . . . highly strung?"

"I am aware that Ishbel is a young girl in need of companions of her own age."

A wry smile. "And you think me an ogre to keep her from her natural milieu?"

I looked him straight in the eye. "Yes, sir!"

A short laugh. "Bravo, Miss Newcombe—for bearding the dragon in his den! However, the fact remains that Ishbel needs careful supervision."

"Really? I have not noticed anything untoward in Ishbel's behavior. She is a little withdrawn perhaps, inclined to be morbid. But nothing that could not be remedied by a more active social life in an atmosphere less . . . less . . ."

"Gloomy? Repressed?"

"Well . . . yes!"

Silence. The face before me was expressionless. I wondered if I had gone too far, but squared my shoulders prepared to see it out. The words, when they came, were a total surprise.

"You are, of course, quite right. And that is why I have decided to let Ishbel go to the ball. However, I should like you to keep watch over her. As I said, you are of an age, you may mingle where Mrs. Mannering and I may not."

"Surely Ishbel does not need to be so closely supervised!"

A raised brow. "That is hardly for you to question, Miss Newcombe. But since you do, I should like to remind you that Ishbel, besides being young and inexperienced in the ways of the world, is also a considerable heiress."

I wanted to speak out, but under the haughty gaze, I decided that silence was the better part of valor. The informal, even affable, Marcus Raven of just a few minutes before seemed completely to have vanished.

"But I see by your expression," the baritone broke into my thoughts, "that you still are somewhat hesitant. Don't you *want* to go to the ball? I thought that all young women liked to dance!"

"It's not that." I bit my lip in embarrassment. "It's just that my trunk has not yet arrived and I fear that even when it does, that . . . that . . . I shall have nothing suitable to wear."

To my surprise, he threw back his head and laughed a loud full laugh. "I might have known," he managed at last. "My dear Miss Newcombe, you are full of surprises! Here I was imagining from your disapproving gaze that . . . that . . . well, never mind!"

"I am glad you find me amusing, sir!"

With an apparent effort, he was serious again. "Forgive me, I do not mean to mock. You must not, of course, worry your head about such a matter. We shall be leaving for Wanganui a week before the ball and I believe that will give both you and Ishbel time to prepare yourselves more than adequately. I shall, of course, advance your first quarter's salary! But, you must be tired. Let me escort you to the stairs."

I found myself led firmly back through the hall to the foot of the stairs.

"Marcus? Is that you, at last?"

Hélène DuPrès peered down from the first-floor landing. In the glow from the lamp, her silken wrapper appeared more diaphanous than ever, the rounded curves of her figure clearly visible beneath.

"Good evening, Hélène!" Marcus Raven's voice was expressionless. "It is indeed, I — and Miss Newcombe, also." He handed me the lamp and stood back to let me up the stairs.

A muffled gasp from the stairhead as Hélène DuPrès in a flurry of floating draperies promptly disappeared.

"I must bid you good night, Miss Newcombe. I have some business I must attend to."

"Do you not need a lamp?" I tried to keep my voice level, disguising the shock I had felt at the sight of Hélène DuPrès.

"No, thank you. I shall find my way easily enough." He stood for a further moment, looking down at me, his dark brows coming together in thought. Then, as if coming to a decision, he raised his head and turned to go. "I believe that we shall leave for Wanganui on Wednesday. Pray see to it that Malvina and Reginald have their school books with them. We should be away for at least two weeks. Good night, Miss Newcombe!"

I watched as he disappeared into the darkness, then, my mind seething with questions, I made my way up the stairs.

Hélène DuPrès, I thought. Had Marcus Raven's apparently sudden decision anything to do with her unexpected—and somewhat startling—appearance at the head of the stairs? And what was she doing there anyway, clad so immodestly? "Is that you, *at last?*" she had asked. She had been expecting Mr. Raven, then. I paused on the first-floor landing and glanced down the corridor, remembering my earlier glimpse of Mrs. DuPrès as she had made her way from one room to another. I could scarcely bring myself to believe it, but had my employer made an assignation to meet with a married woman in the middle of the night? Surely not! Suddenly, I remembered Hélène DuPrès and Marcus Raven only that morning as they had left the dining room; her face had been flushed and her breathing heightened. Could it be, I wondered, that

Mr. Raven had made Hélène DuPrès his paramour?

It was only when I reached my chamber and noted the time on my little clock—half-past one—that another somewhat unpleasant thought occurred to me. If I had wondered at Hélène DuPrès and her appearance in the middle of the night; what must she now be thinking of me?

In my agitation, my hand shook as I placed the lamp beside my bed. Though the fire in my grate was completely out and the air in my room sharp with a damp chill, I felt the need for a breath of fresh air. Parting the heavy curtains, I raised the window sash and leaned out, taking deep breaths to calm myself down.

As I had thought, mist was again wreathing about the river far below, but the pathway they called the River Walk was still clear. As I watched, the moon dipped behind a cloud and then reappeared, shining down with sudden bright intensity on a dark figure slipping in and out of the tree ferns lining the path just below my window. I made some small movement in surprise, sending a loose wooden chip from the windowsill skittering down onto the roof of the second floor verandah. The figure stopped and a pale face looked up. It was Marcus Raven.

I place a fresh candle in the candlestick and think of Marcus Raven's face gazing up at me from the River Walk that night. What would have happened, I wonder, if I had gone with my tangle of suspicions to someone in authority? Would a life have been saved?

The shadows seethe and tumble as the candle flame wafts in the draught and I wish I had the courage to fetch the schoolroom lamp — but I am loath to step into the black darkness of the hallway, a darkness that may not be empty. I gaze into the shadows and think again of my former charges, Malvina and Reginald (bless his little heart!) and Ishbel — I blame myself most for her. If only I had known, surely the signs were there and myself to blame for not having understood.

Nineteen

A breezy sparkling afternoon. Clouds above and clouds reflected in the river beneath. Were we floating on air or water?

"Miss Newcombe!" A familiar deep voice.

"Mr. Takarangi. How nice to see you again!" I struggled up from my reclining position against the bow of the tethered canoe.

"And my young friends, I see!"

"You have met Malvina and Reginald?"

"Indeed, yes. They came with Miss Inglewood once or twice when she was visiting my wife at the Mission school." He and the children exchanged easy smiles. I could see at once that they liked him. "But what brings you here?"

"Ishbel has been invited to a ball and Mr. Raven decided that we should all come to Wanganui for a holiday—although Malvina and Reginald must continue with their lessons, of course." I put on a suitably solemn look and both children burst into giggles.

A deep chuckle. "I can see that you all take learning

very seriously! That, no doubt, is why you are in that canoe. I expect you are studying tides and their influence on marine life?"

"Yes, indeed! I always think that *doing* is so much more entertaining—and memorable—than reading *about* things in some stuffy book. Oh, you are joking! I'm sorry!"

"No need for an apology! I was joking to begin with but not now, for your philosophy agrees with my own." A slight smile. "How your face lights up when you are filled with enthusiasm! You must be a splendid teacher!"

I felt myself blushing. "Oh, no! Not at all! Very inexperienced, I fear! However, it's probably about time we were going back. I promised Mrs. Hargreaves faithfully that we should be home in time for tea!"

"Here, let me help you!" Mr. Takarangi bent down to help me up the short wooden ladder of the landing stage to which the canoe was tethered.

Ruefully, I looked down at my long skirts. "What a bother skirts are—how I wish . . . oh, please excuse me!"

"Excuse you for what? For the inpropriety of wishing for a more practical garment?"

We both laughed. What a sensible man he was!

He helped Malvina up the ladder next. Reginald, of course, scrambled up by himself.

We stood for a moment, looking at the river with its busy traffic skimming up and down. Overhead, the gulls screamed and I remembered the first time we had met. "Mr. Takarangi, you talked about the *mana* of the river. What did you mean?"

A long pause. *"Mana.* How can I describe it? Honor, integrity, perhaps . . . sanctity. Miss New-combe, *mana* cannot be explained, especially to a pakeha." A kindly smile. "Forgive me, I mean no discouragement. One day, I am sure that *you* will understand and without having to have it explained . ." Of a sudden, the words faded and the hand guiding my elbow tightened perceptibly. "But here is Callum Douglas. Is he perhaps looking for you?"

"I shouldn't think so."

We watched as the long-legged figure approached along the river bank and then paused by the storage shed at the head of the landing.

The raising of hats and, on the part of Callum Douglas, an exaggerated bow toward myself.

"So you have discovered the Ravensfall canoe — *Miss Newcombe?*" The tone was deeply respectful but there was the hint of a laugh at the back of the blue-green eyes. Beside me, Mr. Takarangi stiffened. Why, I wondered, looking from one to the other, were they so antagonistic?

"Yes," I answered, "Mrs. Hargreaves told us where it could be found and we made it the object of today's walk."

" 'Object of today's walk'? How very serious you sound! But then learning is a serious business, is it not!" The mocking blue-green stare turned its full force on the children. "What a great deal you must be learning from Miss Newcombe — such a serious person as she is!"

An uncertain smile from Malvina. A blank stare from Reginald.

189

Mr. Takarangi raised his hat. "If you will excuse me, Miss Newcombe, I believe I must take my leave!" The deep voice was friendly but the brown eyes lacked their earlier camaraderie.

An enigmatic stare from Callum Douglas. "Please do not leave on my account!" He turned from the landing. "I have some business that will keep me a while in the storage shed here. So it is *I,* you see, who must take my leave!" Another exaggerated bow to me and he disappeared inside the shed.

A sigh from Mr. Takarangi. Was it of relief—and if so, why? What was it between those two?

"Perhaps, Miss Newcombe, you will allow me to escort you back to town?" A slight hesitation. "I know you are pressed for time, but perhaps on your way, you might stop briefly and meet Mere—my wife. We are in Wanganui for a few days . . . I should like you two to meet."

"I should love that. Thank you!"

We walked companionably back along the river bank, Malvina and Reginald running on before us.

A wise glance down at me. "Those two—you have won their trust. They are fond of you . . . you have been good for them."

"You think so?"

A warm smile. "I know so. They loved Miss Inglewood, too, you know, but they still did not feel *safe.* When they came with her to the Mission, they would cling always about her skirts and send their secret looks one to the other, and that one," he nodded toward a laughing Reginald running ahead with his sister, "he would act his part, no matter what! They loved her, but they knew she could not protect them!"

"Mr. Takarangi . . ." I hardly knew where to begin and then pounced on the most surprising of his revelations. "You know about Reginald?"

"Of course. One has only to watch him in his secret moments when he thinks his behavior is unobserved — what intelligence springs then to those blank eyes!"

I took a deep breath. "You have not told anyone?"

A shake of the head. "No. There has been no one to tell. I observed this at the Mission, you understand, on the few times they visited. I have not as yet met Mr. Raven, though I hope to do so, shortly."

"Mr. Takarangi, why do *you* think the children are so afraid? And from what, or whom should they be protected?"

A silence followed by a sigh. "I wish I could tell you, but I cannot. My conclusions are based merely on what little I have observed, and of course on hearsay." A humorous glance. "We Maoris gossip quite as much as you pakeha — and there are several of my people at Ravensfall!"

"And Miss Inglewood?" I asked hesitantly, very much aware of the impropriety of talking about my employer's business with a stranger.

An understanding look from the deep brown eyes and a kindly hand patted my arm. "Ask what you will, Miss Newcombe, our conversation will go no further, I assure you. And you need, I believe, a disinterested person to whom you may speak in confidence. Now, about Miss Inglewood . . ." The broad brow wrinkled in thought. "A kindly soul . . . as I said, the children loved her . . . but there was something odd — that is to say, something out of place about . . . about . . . her demeanour . . . and then her clothes!" A brusque laugh.

191

"I know little about women's clothes, but as Mere said, Miss Inglewood's gowns, despite their dark colors and evident simplicity, always looked expensive . . ."

We stopped walking for a moment and looked at each other in silence. Somewhere above, a gull shrieked and the children's laughter floated back to us on the breeze.

"So, you think . . . ?"

He wiped a hand across his brow. "Who knows what to think! Except that the poor woman is dead. She was a good person, you know, whatever her motivation for being at Ravensfall. She meant well, I'm sure of that. But she did not have your strength . . . and then, perhaps, she loved too well one she should not!"

"Henare!"

A slight start, then a loving look. "My wife, Miss Newcombe. I told her where I should be and she has come along to meet me."

Toward us, walked a tall woman, younger—as far as I could see—than Mr. Takarangi by about ten years.

"Henare!"

A smile. "My name in Maori, Miss Newcombe— Henry." He turned toward his wife. "Mere, this is Miss Newcombe who has come to take Miss Inglewood's place at Ravensfall. I believe I told you about her?"

I was given a friendly smile. "I have heard all about you from my cousin, Ngaire!" Her voice was deep, a rich contralto.

Mr. Takarangi laughed his deep laugh. "You see—I

4 FREE BOOKS

TO GET YOUR 4 FREE BOOKS WORTH $18.00 — MAIL IN THE FREE BOOK CERTIFICATE T O D A Y

Fill in the Free Book Certificate below, and we'll send your FREE BOOKS to you as soon as we receive it.

If the certificate is missing below, write to: Zebra Home Subscription Service, Inc., P.O. Box 5214, 120 Brighton Road, Clifton, New Jersey 07015-5214.

FREE BOOK CERTIFICATE

4 FREE BOOKS

ZEBRA HOME SUBSCRIPTION SERVICE, INC.

YES! Please start my subscription to Zebra Historical Romances and send me my first 4 books absolutely FREE. I understand that each month I may preview four new Zebra Historical Romances free for 10 days. If I'm not satisfied with them, I may return the four books within 10 days and owe nothing. Otherwise, I will pay the low preferred subscriber's price of just $3.75 each; a total of $15.00, *a savings off the publisher's price of $3.00.* I may return any shipment and I may cancel this subscription at any time. There is no obligation to buy any shipment and there are no shipping, handling or other hidden charges. Regardless of what I decide, the four free books are mine to keep.

NAME

ADDRESS _____ APT

CITY _____ STATE ___ ZIP

(   )
TELEPHONE

SIGNATURE _____ (if under 18, parent or guardian must sign)

Terms, offer and prices subject to change without notice. Subscription subject to acceptance by Zebra Books. Zebra Books reserves the right to reject any order or cancel any subscription.

GET
FOUR
FREE
BOOKS
(AN $18.00 VALUE)

told you! There's nothing much that goes on at Ravensfall that we don't hear about!"

Mere Takarangi smiled again. She was an impressive young woman, hawk-nosed and slender featured, distinguished rather than pretty. Though she was darker complected than her husband, through the bronze sheen of her high cheekbones glowed a ruddiness of good health.

She was also, as I saw at once from the disposition of her draperies, in an "interesting condition." I turned my eyes politely away only to be awarded a deep musical laugh. "Due any time, now, Miss Newcombe. That is why we came down to Wanganui—I wanted to be with my mother."

She was as forthright as her husband. I smiled at the delightful lack of hypocrisy.

"I was telling Miss Newcombe about Miss Inglewood," Henare Takarangi explained to his wife.

Mere's brown eyes were serious suddenly, her face still. "Poor Miss Inglewood. Ngaire said she would wander round Ravensfall like a lost soul, but what she was in search of, we could never guess . . . and toward the end, you know, she became so pale and nervous and jumped, so Ngaire said, at the slightest sound."

"She was afraid of something?"

"We think so . . . but of course she never confided in us. But at the time of the flood, on the evening when she was drowned, Ngaire said she went running out of the house like a wild thing."

"Was she crying . . . did she say anything?"

Mere was silent for a moment, biting her lip, as if not quite sure what to say. We had almost reached

Moutoa Gardens and in the distance we could hear the rattle of traffic over the Town Bridge.

"Yes, she did say something," Mere admitted finally. "But no one would believe Ngaire when she said what it was. They said that in light of what happened afterward that she must have misinterpreted what she thought she heard . . ."

"But what was it? What did Ngaire hear?"

A rumble of a laugh from Mr. Takarangi and I was aware that he was watching my face intently. Despite the laugh, his eyes were serious.

Mere looked ruefully at her husband. "Ngaire heard—thought she heard—something about Malvina . . ."

"Malvina?"

"Yes. Malvina . . . and the *taniwha*."

"*Taniwha!*" I could scarce believe what I was hearing. Unwillingly, I thought of Ishbel's sketchbook and the picture it contained of that mythical creature, half dragon and half snake, about its ghastly business.

"Miss Newcombe, you are unwell!"

I came to myself with a start. We had stopped walking and the Takarangis were peering at me anxiously.

I gathered my thoughts. "No, not at all . . . it's just. But what happened next? I mean, what happened after Miss Inglewood ran out of the house?"

Mere Takarangi continued with her tale. "Ngaire thought that something must have happened to Malvina, but before she could decide what to do, Malvina herself came down the stairs. So Ngaire ran out after Miss Inglewood to tell her that Malvina was all right. But . . ."

"But?"

"Miss Inglewood was already rounding the corner of the house, and before Ngaire could catch up she had run past the library and study windows and was on her way down to the River Walk . . ."

Mere paused a moment, perhaps like myself conjuring up the scene in her mind's eye — the beating rain, the gurgle of a river in flood, and a distraught woman disappearing down the River Walk into a shadowy tunnel of trees.

"And that was the last Ngaire saw of her?"

"Yes . . . but . . . there's more. You see, as Miss Inglewood reached the River Walk, Ngaire thought she saw someone else among the trees. It was too dark to see who it was, but it had to be someone from the house, of course, so Ngaire thought that Miss Inglewood would be taken care of. But, just to make sure, when she returned to the house, she tried to find Mr. Raven. He wasn't in his study so she checked the cloakroom and as his Burberry was missing, she thought that he was the one she had seen — and that naturally he would deal with Miss Inglewood. But . . ."

"But?"

"Well, you see, at dinner time when Miss Inglewood could not be found, Mr. Raven said he had not seen her, that he had not in fact, been out of the house."

"Perhaps Ngaire was mistaken about the Burberry."

"Oh, no, Miss Newcombe. You see, she checked again in the cloakroom and the coat was back on the hook that Mr. Raven always uses — and it was soaking wet!"

We looked at each other in silence.

A cough from Mr. Takarangi. "Perhaps, someone else had . . ."

His wife interrupted him. "Oh, no. Everyone was accounted for at the inquest — even Mr. Raven."

I looked at her in surprise. "Mr. Raven was accounted for?"

"Yes — by Mrs. DuPrès. She said that he had been with her in the drawing room all afternoon."

"Mere," Mr. Takarangi's tone was mildly reproving. "You never told me about all this!"

Mrs. Takarangi smiled sweetly. "Henare, you don't like gossip."

Three o'clock on a busy Friday afternoon. Dodging carts, horses, stray dogs, I shepherded the children across the dusty ruts and potholes of Victoria Avenue. My conversation with the Takarangis had made us late and I still had an errand to perform for Ishbel — I had promised to bring her back some rosewater from Kitchen's chemist shop.

"Oh, look, Miss Newcombe! Perhaps, we shan't be late after all; there's our gig parked right outside the chemist's!"

Malvina was right. Before us loomed a bored Hargreaves holding the head of the sprightly chestnut that had brought myself and Callum Douglas to the townhouse — had it been only a fortnight ago? It seemed scarcely credible!

"Good afternoon, Hargreaves!"

"Argh!"

"We're late. Do you think you could take us all back

196

with you?"

"Argh."

Cunningly, I tried a question that required more than a yes or no answer. I glanced toward the chemist's shop, an elegant red brick building with stone facing. "Who is within?"

A look of pure dislike suddenly dissolved into one of triumph. Silently, Hargreaves jerked his thumb toward the shop door.

"Oh there you are, my dear Miss Newcombe and Reginald and Malvina, also! How fortunate. Perhaps I can take you up and save you the walk back to Wicksteed Street?" Mrs. Mannering descended the steps in the midst of her usual babble.

I cut in quickly while I had the opportunity. "Thank you, that's very kind. Would you mind waiting while I make a small purchase for Ishbel?"

I started forward without waiting for an answer, only to be stopped by an apron-clad assistant appearing in the doorway. "Mrs. Mannering—you forgot the drops!" He started down the steps, holding a neatly wrapped package.

Mrs. Mannering had already descended the steps and to save trouble I reached out a hand, thinking to pass the parcel to her. Mrs. Mannering, however, turned quickly and snatched so suddenly at the package, it nearly dropped in the street.

"My drops, to be sure! I swear that if my head were loose!" A bland pale-blue stare through the pebble glasses. "For my eyes, you know—so very weak!"

There was a slight cough from the assistant where he still stood on the steps. The expression on his face could only be described as bewildered. Then, raising his hands — as if in despair — he returned to the shop.

When I entered, he was already engaged with another customer and I was attended to by someone else.

Excitement for me back in Wicksteed Street; my trunk had arrived at last!

I could hardly wait to open it. And yet once faced with it on my bedroom floor, I felt rather like Pandora and the box — and wondered what memories I would let loose once my trunk was opened; for I had not seen it since I had had it shipped from Liverpool.

"Miss Newcombe?"

Jenny's voice sounded through my half-open door.

"Come in, Jenny. You're just in time! As you can see, my trunk has arrived . . ."

"Oh, I know that, Miss! I was here when they brought it!"

She came in, bearing on her arm the material we had chosen the day before for my ball dress; rose-pink watered taffeta which we intended to trim with silver lace. I looked at it, still aghast at my extravagance.

Jenny giggled at the expression on my face. "It's too late, now!"

"Oh, Jenny, how could I?" I gulped. "It's not even suitable for . . . for the position I hold!"

She drew herself up. "This is a new country and you can do whatever *you* want to do. If Mrs. Mannering or Mr. Raven don't like your dress you can tell them to go to . . . you know where!"

"Jenny!"

"In the meantime, stand still! I need to see how the

material folds. I want to see it next to your skin."

I stood still. "But, Jenny—"

"But, nothing!" She knelt before me, twisting the folds of the taffeta this way and that, and now looked up at me, her mouth full of pins.

"I can't . . ." I looked at the gleaming rose-pink folds, "I really can't! I don't know what got into me!"

The blue eyes looking up at me crinkled. "The Devil?"

I caught my breath, remembering the Reverend Mr. Pugh wagging a stern finger before me, "My dear Harriet, the Devil temps us each and everyone; and in your case, you must be particularly careful! Your mother, you know, wore bright colors entirely unbefitting to her station and for the sole purpose, I believe, for catching the attention of men . . . 'Ah Vanity, Vanity, thy Name is Woman!' "

I looked at Jenny, "I'll wear it," I announced.

Her blue eyes smiled and, through the pins she mumbled, "Of course you will!"

She took the pins from her mouth and standing up, looked me over critically. "There now, I knew it! With a twist here and a pouf there . . ."

"Jenny, I thought we had already agreed on the pattern!"

Her eyes twinkled. "So we have—just one or two 'improvisations' you might say! Now then, that's all right and tight." With one swoop, she gathered up the taffeta in a warm glowing bundle and, depositing it on my bed, turned to me. "So let's have a look in that trunk!"

"Jenny!"

"Come on, now—so many straps on this thing—

199

how do you get it undone?"

Together, we undid the straps.

"And now the key!" Jenny looked at me sternly. I produced the key and unlocked the trunk.

Books, of course, and layers of newspaper and camphor balls swaddling those clothes and items that my Aunt Alice had determined I should take with me to those wild unattainable lands, the colonies. ("Three of everything, Harriet," she had intoned. "However, considering where you are *insisting* on spending the rest of your life, I rather think that you should take more!")

Jenny grinned at the highly practical — and ugly — drawers, chemises, and petticoats and shook her head over my plain sensible dresses.

"Well, we'll have to see what we can do! This mulberry cashmere might pass if it had some fresh trimming and we could make some pretty, lacy blouses to go with that heliotrope skirt . . . but what's this?" Her exploring fingers had found a flat square package stowed in the middle of a particularly ugly grey woolen jacket. She looked at my face. "Oh, sorry, I didn't mean to pry!"

"That's all right!" I took the package from her and unwrapped it. "My parents . . ."

Jenny looked down on the daguerrotype made shortly after my birth; my father and mother (holding a clearly reluctant me) staring solemnly straight ahead.

"But how like your mother, you are! The same high cheekbones, the same straight short nose, the same hair!" She glanced at my riotous mane. "So that's where you get it from!"

I could see that she wanted to ask more questions and I steeled myself. Instead, she smiled sweetly and handed me the picture. "I expect you'll want to find a place for this. Now, let's see, what have we here?" She plunged her hands back into the trunk and dragged out an especially hideous pair of rubber galoshes.

I looked about, deciding where to put the portrait—an emotional moment, because in the rectory I had always to keep it hidden. ("Mr. Pugh," Aunt Alice had warned, her face turned away, "would not wish to see your mother's likeness on display—even in your chamber . . .")

Perhaps the mantelpiece, I wondered, or the top shelf of the bookcase? I decided on the bookcase and as I was putting the picture down on the top shelf, I automatically registered the titles of the books below—*The Scarlet Letter, Jane Eyre, Vanity Fair, The Three Musketeers, A Tale of Two Cities*—a well read copy, as I could tell by the number of papers sticking out to mark the favorite places of the person who had been reading it.

I looked toward a still busily delving Jenny. "This room was Miss Inglewood's?"

Jenny looked up from her rummaging, her face apologetic. "I'm afraid so. You don't seem able to escape from her, do you? Her room at Ravensfall, her room here : . ."

"That's all right. I'm beginning to feel that Miss Inglewood and I are old friends." (Like a little mouse, I thought, slipping from room to room—and now, from house to house—what did she want of me?)

On an impulse, I turned to Jenny. "In fact, I was talking about her just this afternoon with Mrs. Takarangi, Ngaire's cousin. She told me that Miss Inglewood had said something about a taniwha when she rushed out of the house on the night she was drowned."

Jenny shook her head. "Oh, that Ngaire! She's so superstitious—I swear she believes in the old stories! It's her grandmother—she's always filling her head with nonsense!"

"Her grandmother?"

"Old Moana."

"I should have guessed! So, that's why Moana is always around at Ravensfall."

"Well, actually, now I come to think of it . . ." Jenny paused thoughtfully, "Moana is Ngaire's great-grandmother—Hemi, Moana's son, is Ngaire's grand-father."

"What happened to Ngaire's parents?"

"Her mother died of typhoid when Ngaire was just a baby and her father was killed in the Maori Wars— that's why Moana hates us pakeha so much. She keeps saying that one day we'll all be swept into the sea."

I remembered Mr. Takarangi talking of the Battle of Moutoa Island when we had first met. "You mean Ngaire's father was a . . ." I paused, trying to remember the name Mr. Takarangi had given the dissenting Maoris.

"Hauhau."

"That's right . . . I remember now, Mr. Takarangi said they were called that because of their battle cry." I shivered.

Jenny grinned at the expression on my face. "Oh don't worry, it's been over for years—at least twenty. You can sleep safe at night!"

"But what was it all about? Mr. Takarangi said it was to do with some quarrel over land."

Jenny started to put my unpacked undergarments away into the drawers of a walnut tallboy and I moved over to help her. "Yes, the wars were over the land . . . I don't rightly understand all the 'ins and outs,' but there was some treaty or other made with the Maoris when the first settlers arrived—something to do with the Maoris recognizing the old Queen and agreeing to sell some of their land for a fair price in return for protection. Something like that—and the Wanganui Maoris felt they were cheated."

She patted my chemises into a tidy pile and grinned suddenly, looking down at her bethrothal ring. "I mean to say, Miss, as Thomas—my young man—said, red nightcaps, jews'-harps and umbrellas are not exactly fair exchange for good farming country!"

I had a sudden riotous picture in my mind's eye of a group of Maoris all wearing red nightcaps, playing jews'-harps, and carrying umbrellas. "Yes, I see what you mean!" In an effort to quell my mirth, (for her Thomas was right; in my opinion, it had not been a fair exchange) I looked out my window at the sunlit back lawn and the tall hedge that disguised the alley beyond. "How tranquil everything seems now . . ."

"Now, yes. But in the old days, there was a real scare on. Thomas's family had a farm up-river and he remembers being carried in the middle of the night through a passage his dad had made under the house to a secret cellar."

"My goodness, were they attacked?"

"Their house was ransacked but they stayed hidden in the cellar. Shortly afterwards they went back to

Wanganui. The town was never attacked, of course, but Thomas says there was always the thought that they could be. And there were all sorts of stories — awful, awful stories — about what was going on in the outlying districts . . ."

I stared at Jenny and then at the quiet scene out the window. "It all seems so unbelievable . . . but I'm beginning to understand from what you tell me as to why Moana acts the way she does. Poor, old woman before the . . . pakeha . . . came, she must have had a quite different life and perhaps she didn't want to change . . . and then with her grandson . . ."

There was silence for a moment, then Jenny smiled at me. "You know, you are a truly understanding person. You really care about people and have sympathy for them."

"Oh, I hardly think . . ."

Ignoring me, Jenny rushed on. "Miss Inglewood, now, she was completely different. She was nice enough in her way — a proper lady, always 'please' and 'thank you' — but to her, Ngaire and I were just maids, there to serve her. And as for old Moana . . ."

"Yes?"

The blue eyes were thoughtful. "Miss Inglewood did not approve of Moana — and in a way, you can hardly blame her! That smelly old pipe Moana always carries and the way the slips in and out, so's you hardly know she's there — she sometimes gives *me* the creeps! Still, there's ways of dealing with people, isn't there?"

"What was Miss Inglewood's way?"

Jenny finished placing my underwear in the drawers and began to help me shake out my dresses before hanging them in the walnut wardrobe. "Miss

Inglewood's way," she said at last, "was to look down her nose at Moana and not speak to her — and she'd complain about her to Mrs. Douglas or Mrs. Mannering in Moana's hearing. I remember once . . ."

She paused to make a face at what Aunt Alice had described as my best gown: a lively dun-colored affair with black ruching. "Really, Miss, I don't know how you could even *think* of wearing . . . but, as I was saying, about Moana. I remember once, serving them all afternoon tea on the lawn — I remember particularly because the master was there, instead of in his study as usual and he was talking to Miss Inglewood — very affable, he was. You know, if you go by that portrait in the dining room, Miss Inglewood was very like the late Mrs. Raven, and we were all hoping, for the sake of the children, that, that . . . *you know* . . . and she wasn't exactly averse to him either!"

I suddenly remembered my afternoon walk by the river and the Reverend Mr. Takarangi's words about Miss Inglewood, "Perhaps, she loved too well, one she should not . . ."

"But, as I was saying . . ." Jenny's voice interrupted my thoughts, "there they were on the lawn, Mrs. Mannering and Mrs. Douglas, their heads nodding together and the children playing croquet with Miss Ishbel sketching away as usual, when Miss Inglewood suddenly looks over the lawn to those huge tree ferns and says in that — if you'll excuse me, Miss — that snotty upper-class accent of hers, 'There's that dirty old woman again, I just do not know how you can tolerate her!' And there was Moana standing among the ferns . . ."

"And Moana heard her?"

Jenny put the last of my dresses into the wardrobe before replying. It was almost as if she were reluctant to tell me what happened next. "Yes," she admitted at last.

"So, what happened, Jenny?" I could hardly curb my impatience.

A deep sigh. "Well, Moana—you know how bent over, she is? Somehow, she straightened up and stared at Miss Inglewood . . . oh, Miss Newcombe, if I believed in witchcraft, I'd swear. . . ."

"You mean, she looked spiteful, malicious?"

"No, nothing like that—it's hard to explain. She just stood there as still as a statue, with her face like carved granite and her eyes immovable as stones . . . and when she looked toward Miss Inglewood, it was as if she was not looking *at* her, so much as *through* her, as if, somehow, Miss Inglewood was transparent . . ."

"Did she say anything?"

Jenny shuddered. "Yes. And in light of what happened after, it makes you wonder, it really does!"

"What did she say?"

Jenny shut the wardrobe door decisively and looked toward my still half-full trunk. "We'd better tackle the rest tomorrow!"

"Jenny! What did Moana say?"

"Oh, this sounds so unbelievable, but she looked toward Miss Inglewood and she said quite calmly and clearly, 'Soon, it will be your turn and you will be gone.'"

I let out a long breath. "And what did Miss Inglewood say?"

"Nothing. She sat there, very still, with her teacup halfway to her lips. It was funny, really—as if she

206

were frozen!"

"And the others?"

"Ishbel laughed, you know, the way she does, and Moana looked at her, but before she could speak, Mr. Raven stood up . . ."

"And?"

"He didn't say anything, just looked at Moana until she slipped away into the bush—almost, as if they had some sort of secret signal—and then he said the oddest thing to Miss Inglewood."

"Yes?"

Jenny wrinkled her brow in thought. "He said, 'After all, she was here first!' "

"He meant Moana?"

"I suppose so. But what did he mean?"

I thought of the Master of Ravensfall and the last time I had seen him in the dead of night, slipping down the River Walk. I remembered his face, pale in the moonlight, looking up at my window, and shivered. There was something going on, something sinister, I was sure of it.

I shook my head as I helped Jenny move my trunk out of the way into a corner of the room. "The more I hear about Mr. Raven, the more I don't know what to think. What happened after that? I mean between Miss Inglewood and Moana?"

Jenny gathered up the taffeta from my bed and stood a moment at the door. "Miss Inglewood went on the same way as before—I mean, looking down her nose at Moana and refusing to speak to her; but we could all see that she was frightened of her. And then one night, we heard her screaming at the door of her room—Miss Inglewood, I mean—and when we rushed to see what was the matter . . ."

Jenny paused a moment, her hand on the door-knob.

"What had happened?"

"Someone had let loose a fantail in her room. Poor little creature; it was fluttering against the window pane — so someone must have put it in the room — because, you see, the window was closed. And of course, we all thought Moana had done it."

"But a fantail in the house means . . ." I could hardly bring myself to say the word.

From the open doorway, Jenny looked back, her blue eyes serious. "It means death."

Twenty

I miss the long English twilights. In New Zealand it is no sooner dusk, it seems to me, than it is dark. I had intended to work on my long-neglected novel, but after Jenny's revelations, Sir Percival's problems seemed remote and uninteresting, and as for the Lady Ariadne, she had become no more than what Aunt Alice would have described as a "mere simpering chit!" Perhaps, I thought humorously, I should simply take all the characters at Ravensfall and put them into a novel!

Looking out my window at the fading sunlight, I decided on impulse to go for a walk before it grew dark. Perhaps, I might have time to walk down Guyton Street to Victoria Avenue and back. If I hurried, I might even have time to visit Willis' Bookstore, though that was somewhat further down. I slipped on my ulster, for the late afternoon air was sharp, and pinning on my hat, I grabbed my gloves — and not wanting to be detained by any of the household seeking to ply me with errands — sneaked quietly down the backstairs.

I thought I had escaped safely when I heard voices on the driveway at the side of the house. However, they belonged to Jenny and a short wiry young man with a straggling ginger moustache; she introduced him . . . as Thomas McGregor, her intended.

Jenny giggled. "You won't give us away, will you, Miss? Mrs. Hargreaves doesn't allow followers!"

"You tell Mrs. Hargreaves what you want, Miss! My Jenny doesn't have to worry. These New Chums think they can rule the roost and as far as I'm concerned—"

"Get along with you, Thomas! Mrs. Hargreaves isn't a Pommey," Jenny looked fondly at the freckled face almost at eye level with her own. "She was born in Wellington when it was still called Port Nicholson, she told me so herself!"

The thin face was still flushed. "Well, I'm still not taking any nonsense from her." Under the sandy brows, the piercing bright blue eyes softened suddenly. "Me and my quick temper! I'm sorry, love!" Then, turning to me. "I'm sorry, Miss Newcombe, it's just that this is a new country and we don't have all that class nonsense that goes on in the old country and as I keep telling Jenny, she doesn't have—"

"I keep telling you," Jenny interrupted, "that I'm under obligation!"

"Oh, I know, I know—they paid your fare and your wages are good but . . ."

"When are you getting married?" I intercepted to prevent another argument.

"October," Jenny announced.

"September," growled Thomas.

They looked at each other and then at me and laughed. "That's one of the things we have to get sorted out tonight," Jenny explained. "Mrs. Hargreaves says that seeing that Thomas is in town, I can have the evening off after dinner. We're going over to his parents and later we're going to the skating rink."

"Skating rink?"

They laughed again at my astonishment. "What's the matter?" Thomas asked with pretended belligerence. "You think we're at the back of beyond? Of course Wanganui has a skating rink."

"Perhaps, I can take the children there while we're here. That would be a pleasant outing for them! Do you go there often, Mr. McGregor?"

"Only when I'm in town. I usually live up-river, not far from you, Miss Newcombe." He smiled at my surprise. "I am employed by Mr. DuPrès at his vineyard—learning the business, you might say—but not for long, love," he added, turning to Jenny.

Jenny sighed. "Poor old man. He's worse, is he?"

I looked at them, puzzled.

"Sorry, Miss Newcombe," Jenny apologized. "We should have explained. Mr. Joseph DuPrès has the property next to Ravensfall." She gave me what I can only describe as a "naughty look." "Mrs. Hélène DuPrès, his wife, stays at Ravensfall when her husband is away on business."

"Oh! Yes. Yes, of course. I remember now, Mrs. DuPrès saying something about a vineyard. But Mr. DuPrès isn't well?"

" 'Fraid so. Nobody talks about it, but he has consumption. He seemed to be getting better for a while, but lately . . ." Thomas McGregor shook his head, "You know how it is with consumption."

I did indeed. I still remembered my poor father with his cheeks flushed, not from health but from fever and his pitiable coughing.

"He shouldn't have gone off on that long trip," Jenny remarked indignantly. "Her High and Mightiness should have stopped him! Oh, sorry, Miss."

"That's all right, Jenny. But I must hurry if I am to have my walk and to get back before dark."

"Her High and Mightiness," I thought with an inward chuckle as I sped off down the street—what a glorious description of Hélène DuPrès! I wondered what her husband was like—"poor old man" Jenny had said—so evidently he was considerably older than Mrs. DuPrès who was no older than . . . I decided to be generous . . . about thirty or so.

I turned the corner into Guyton Street, and as I walked briskly down the hill, I began to play around in my mind with my earlier idea of putting all the people I had met recently into a novel. But who would be the heroine, who the hero, I wondered? And who would be the villain? After a little thought, I decided that Miss Inglewood was the obvious heroine. After all it seemed to be around her that most of the main action revolved and—I thought of one of my favorite novels, *Jane Eyre*—a governess would make a good chief character.

On the other hand, Jane Eyre, after her many trials and tribulations, had finally found happiness, but poor Mary Inglewood had not. However, Jane Eyre had been such an uncomplicated character with few secrets of her own whereas my Mary . . .

"Watch out, Miss!"

I found myself standing at the busy intersection of Guyton Street and Victoria Avenue, about to be run over by a huge grey carthorse pulling a dray.

My arm was clutched by a dashing young man wearing a bowler hat and brown tweed caped overcoat.

Disengaging myself gently, I peered up from under my wide-brimmed hat, one of Aunt Alice's more daring creations of dark grey velour swathed with jet braid and topped by nodding light-grey plumes. "Thank you, sir."

The brown eyes above widened and, to my astonishment, a monocle was inserted into one of them. "A young lady from 'home,' I do believe!" The voice was pleasant, a mellow tenor with a slight colonial accent.

"Yes, I have recently arrived from England. Thank you again, I must be on my way."

"I believe I am going in your direction. Allow me to escort you across the street."

"Thank you but from the way you are standing, with one foot still on the road, I have the distinct impression that you intended to proceed up, rather than down the avenue. Good day, Sir!"

The brown eyes gleamed and a kid-gloved finger and thumb twitched delicately at a silky fair moustache. "Allow me to introduce myself. My name is Alfred Smythe, Miss—?"

"Thank you, Mr. Smythe. Good day!"

I was almost across the road, when my elbow was clasped yet again. I whirled round, furiously angry. 'Unhand me at once or I shall call a constable!"

A hearty Scottish laugh followed by a well-known Scottish brogue. "My God, Harriet, you'll never get yourself a husband. Don't you know that young ladies are supposed to be demure, yielding, and placid? You could at the very least swoon into my manly arms!"

"Callum Douglas! I might have known!"

Another laugh as I was guided swiftly round a trap and an ancient cart to the wooden building on the corner that Reginald had informed me was the common school.

"Now, then!" The lean figure loomed over me. "What are you about raising your hackles at the best 'catch' in Wanganui?"

"What?"

"Alfred Smythe."

"I don't understand."

A patient sigh followed by a grin of pure mischief. "No, I don't suppose you do — or if you did, could care less!"

"I wish you would explain yourself!" I tried desperately to straighten my hat, which in my chaotic progress across the street had become somewhat dislodged.

"Harriet, will you keep still a moment. Those swaying feathers make me feel quite seasick!"

"I said to explain, not to insult!"

A contrite smile. "Sorry! To explain: Alfred Smythe is the lucrative answer to every mother's prayer for an unmarried daughter. You're supposed to be *nice* to him!"

"I may be unmarried, but I'm not in desperate need, as yet."

The blue-green eyes crinkled in laughter. "I give up! But never let it be said that I did not try to do my best for you. Come, now, I'm on my way to the post office. Would you like to go with me — and I'll walk with you back to Wicksteed Street."

We were about to turn the corner, when the school-house door was flung open and a small energetic figure clattered down the steps.

"Bonjour, Mademoiselle!"

The French accent was atrocious but I recognized at once the friendly freckled face of Reginald's *real* New Zealander friend, Jim Parker.

"Bonjour, Monsieur!" I responded automatically, while wondering how to continue with our game without giving away Reginald's secret to Callum Douglas.

I need not have worried. Under the mop of bright blond hair, the blue eyes smiled guilelessly past me. "G'day, Mr. Douglas!"

Callum Douglas smiled back. "Hello, Jim!"

"But what are you doing here?" I asked, feeling foolish. "I thought you lived at Ravensfall."

"Well, I do, Miss, and I don't. My mum, Miss, she died when I was 'so high.'" A hand was raised part way from the ground "and my dad hasn't been right since. So I live with my dad's married sister and her family and when I get too much for her to cope with . . ." he gave an exaggerated sigh, then winked. "She sends me up-river on a weekend. Specially now, with the *Waiwere* sailing so regular — to bother my dad, instead of her!"

I wanted to run my hand through the bright blond mop, to slip an arm about those proud shoulders, but of course could not. Instead, I looked at the school behind us. "Don't tell me you have just got out of school, Jim. Isn't it rather late?"

"Kept in!" He announced proudly.

"Kept in? Oh, you mean you had detention. But what did you do?"

He twinkled up at me. "Pea-shooter, Miss. At Eliza Harding!"

I nodded in understanding. "You shot peas at Eliza Harding—but why?" I cast about in my mind. "Is she a tell-tale?"

"Eliza, a tell-tale! Nah . . ." He thought for a moment, then blushed. "She said bad things about my dad," he admitted at last. "She said he's an . . . athee . . . something—you know, someone who doesn't believe in God."

"Atheist?"

"That's right." He grinned suddenly. "Well, of course, it's true, but she doesn't have to say so, does she."

I looked at him in awe. "You're quite right! However . . ."

"Yes, I know, I shouldn't shoot peas at a girl!" A shy smile. "Can I come and visit you, while you're here?"

"Of course! I hope you do!"

"Good-oh! That's all set, then. G'day, Miss! G'day, Mr. Douglas!" Waving cheerfully, he set off across the street, weaving his way expertly through the busy traffic.

"An interesting young man!" I remarked to Callum, as we continued on our way down the Avenue.

"Indeed!" He looked down at me thoughtfully. "How did you become so well acquainted with him?" He gave me an amused glance. "For him to address you in French!"

"If you call that French!" I paused a moment, wondering what to say. Though, I was feeling more and more the need to confide in someone, I felt I could not betray my promise to Reginald. "I met him on Sunday. He was visiting Reginald, who was sick in bed. I had quite a conversation with him: he informed me in no uncertain terms, that he was a *real* New Zealander!"

Callum laughed with me but he gave me a quizzical look and I wondered if he had noted my hesitation and wondered at the reason for it.

"Reginald?" Another quizzical look. "Sometimes, I wonder if that young man is as backward as he seems!"

I tried to keep my face expressionless. "What makes you think so?"

"Something that Mary Inglewood said."

Deliberately casual, I stopped walking to observe a display of cabbages outside a greengrocer's shop.

"Really?" I asked, keeping my tone of voice carefully level.

"Really!"

I stared fascinated at a decorative heap of oddly shaped root vegetables. "Those are not potatoes, are they?"

An impatient sigh. "No. Kumeras — a type of sweet potato."

"How interesting! One sees something new every day, does one not?"

"Yes, one does!"

Politely, I raised my hand to restrain a yawn. "You were saying about Miss Inglewood?"

An answering yawn, followed by a sarcastic grin.

"Yes, a notion of hers that seemed odd at the time . . . but, no doubt you are not in the least interested!"

I dragged my eyes away from a stack of celery. "I'm sorry, I had not intended to be rude. By all means, tell me about Miss Inglewood . . . and her ideas."

The mobile mouth crooked in another grin and the blue-green eyes gleamed with amusement. "About Reginald?"

I drew away from the shop and began to walk again down the Avenue. "Certainly," I replied, still keeping my voice level, "tell me of Miss Inglewood's notion about Reginald."

His tone was teasing. "You are *sure* you want to know?"

I managed an innocent smile. "Only if you want to tell me!"

"Harriet, if this were not a public place, I would quite cheerfully strangle you!" He fell into step beside me. "All right, about Reginald—you have noticed nothing strange about him? That is, with you, he has not shown signs of having a mind that is more astute than it at first appears?"

"I have only been here a week, you know," I temporized, very much aware of the watchful gaze above me, "though it seems much longer! And as yet, all I have done really is to try to find out where the children are with their lessons." I sighed and shook my head. "Reginald is very withdrawn," I added for good measure.

"I see . . . then, you haven't noticed anything, yet."

I gave myself a mental pat on the back for my cleverness. "Why, what did Miss Inglewood say about Reginald?"

"There were things that he said or did . . . that seemed out of place, considering his apparent lack of intelligence." A pause, as we worked our way around a group of shoppers intent on gossiping, then the wary gaze was upon me yet again. "Mary — Miss Inglewood — felt that Reginald lives in a state of fear and that is why he acts the way he does — as she put it — he hides behind a facade."

"But why should the poor child be so frightened?"

Callum hesitated and looked down at me, his eyes for once without their usual mocking light. "Mary believed he knows something vital about his late mother's murder; something that was not revealed at Mr. Raven's trial . . ."

We had reached the corner of Ridgeway Street where the post office was situated and now stood still a moment, gazing at each other. It was a busy street, but I was only vaguely aware of the passing traffic and the pedestrians scurrying by. "You mean," I asked tentatively, hardly believing what I was suggesting, "that Reginald could . . . could incriminate his father?"

Callum nodded. "So Mary believed."

"And . . . and his father knows this!"

"Yes."

I took a deep breath. "And so, Mr. Raven is . . ." I could not bring myself to say it.

The face above me was grim. "So, Mr. Raven, my dear Harriet, is in effect keeping his son at ransom and the price of his freedom is silence!"

In the middle of the intersection stood a large stone public drinking fountain, and I remember my eyes clinging to it as a kind of anchor as the four intersecting streets seemed to whirl around it like a fiery Catherine wheel.

"Harriet! You are all right?"

"Yes, It's just—I was thinking, that so much of what I have observed seems to fit in with . . ."

I found myself guided firmly across the road to the post office on the other side.

I was deposited neatly at the post office steps. "What have you observed?"

"Oh, nothing really. Just a host of little things that I am sure would not be considered important by a court of law."

A lean brown finger and thumb tilted my chin. "What little things?"

"Oh, I don't know—nothing I can discuss at the moment—I have to think . . ."

A brusque laugh. "That's my Harriet!"

"Callum Douglas, I am not your Harriet. I am no one's Harriet, except my own!"

The blue-green eyes smiled down into mine. "That's what I like about you, Harriet: your independence, your stubbornness. But . . . these are also the qualities most likely to bring you harm."

He looked down at me, his face serious, his eyes full of warning. "Harriet . . . I believe strongly that Mary Inglewood's death was not accidental. I believe she discovered what Reginald knows and that she was foolish enough to reveal her knowledge."

The sun had completely disappeared and I shivered in the cold wind that had sprung up. I looked up at the pale serious face gazing down at me earnestly. "You are telling me that Mary Inglewood was murdered and that Mr. Raven . . ." I could not bring myself to say the words.

Callum nodded. "Yes . . . at least, I strongly suspect it."

"Then why not go to the police?"

A bitter laugh. "On what evidence? What did you just say about a host of little details that would not stand up in a court of law?"

"But . . ."

He took me gently by the shoulders. "But one day I shall have enough evidence . . . and that will be the day . . ." He did not finish the sentence; there was no need—the cold blaze of his green-blue eyes was enough to make me shudder.

"Harriet!" His voice was urgent, the Scottish burr even more pronounced. "Please leave Ravensfall. Please—for your own safety."

"I am in no danger!"

"Harriet, that sharp mind of yours has already observed a 'host of little things.' How long do you think you can conceal what you know from *him?* The man is very cunning, you know."

"I know, but I can't leave Reginald. Surely he more than myself is in danger!"

"No, the child is sufficiently cowed by fear; and in any case, I don't think even Mr. Raven would actually harm his own son. But you are the one likely to be in danger. Don't worry, I shall take care of Reginald."

I thought of Ravensfall and its dark hallways and lonely rooms and I thought of Malvina, Reginald, and Ishbel isolated there in the power of a murderer. "I cannot leave, Callum. The children need me."

He sighed. "I knew that would be your decision— but I did my best!" He shook me gently. "At least

221

promise me one thing!"

"What is it?"

"That if you hear anything, see anything . . . at all
. . . *strange,* that you will come to me. And otherwise
keep the information to yourself!"

I thought of my promise to Reginald and the
awkwardness this had brought about. I shook my
head. "I don't like to make promises. However, I shall
more than likely come to you!"

An exasperated smile and another gentle shake.
"Take care, Harriet. Take great care!" Callum
Douglas said.

Twenty-one

"Good morning, my dear! I do hope you slept well!"

A white befrilled cabbage festooned with pink ribbons nodded at me around my partially opened door. It proved to be a night-capped Mrs. Mannering. Her pale blue eyes beamed at me through her thick spectacles.

What, I wondered with grim humor, would she say if I told her that I had spent the night tossing on my pillows, wondering how best to bring her murderous cousin, Marcus Raven, to justice.

Instead, I replied with a decorous greeting and opened my door further.

Giggling girlishly, she extended a plump hand from the voluminous folds of a fuzzy white shawl. "I am Cupid!"

"Excuse me?"

The plump hand opened to reveal a small envelope. "I have brought a *billet doux* for you, my *dear* Miss

223

Newcombe!"

"I . . . I see . . . a letter. For *me*, you say?"

The shawl was hugged closely round the plump shoulders and the blue eyes looked at me guilelessly. "So chilly here in the hall!"

"Please come in and . . . er . . . sit down!"

"Oh, I am so pleased you asked! I have to tell you all about . . ." A girlish simper. "The *author* of your letter, and, of course, the circumstances that brought it about. And naturally, I want to hear *all* about your meeting!"

I looked at her, dazed. "My meeting?"

A light tap on my arm. "You naughty girl, to try to keep it from us! Although, of course, you had no choice, as we were out when you returned and of course, when *we* returned, you had retired. Which, now I think of it, is why I am delivering this missive *now* instead of . . ."

"Pray, sit down!" I broke into the torrent before I was drowned in words. "I'm sorry, my fire has not yet been attended to; but here is an extra shawl and I believe, if I open my curtains and let in the sunlight . . . Oh!"

Outside, the sky was a bright clear blue and over the lawn and hedge shimmered a sparkling heavy frost. "This really is the most surprising place, Mrs. Mannering. One never knows what to expect next!"

"Quite, my dear! However, your letter!"

She was about, I could see, to explode with curiosity. I took pity on her. Opening the envelope, I removed a single sheet of thick, creamy paper. The letter was short, the writing heavily sloping, all flying dots and slashes.

"My Dear Young Lady,

How can I apologize enough for my persistence, this afternoon! I assure you, I meant no disrespect! I know that I should not have attempted to draw you into conversation, but once having gazed into your beauteous eyes, I found it impossible to depart! Please forgive me — and allow me to have the pleasure of meeting with you again!"

The signature — dashing, like the writer himself — was "Alfred Spencer Smythe."

"My dear, I am all agog!"

I was to be allowed no privacy, it seemed! I gave up and handed Mrs. Mannering the letter.

"Oh, my dear Miss Newcombe. How *utterly* charming . . . and such a delightful young man! He was my partner, you see, at whist — his dear mother held a card party last night to which we were all invited; cousin Marcus and Mr. Tavish having arrived in time from their trip to Wellington — and, now let me see, where was I?"

I resisted an impulse to scream. "You were telling me of your conversation with Mr. Smythe."

"To be sure! He inquired about the children, of course — always so polite, as he is! — so naturally, I mentioned you and one thing led to another and he asked for your description because, so he told me, he had seen a young lady walking off down the Avenue with Callum Douglas — and we thought it might be you!"

She paused at last and gave me a brilliant smile. "So I suggested to him that he write to you — and so

225

he did! Now, tell me, what did you think of him?"

I tried to be tactful. "I think he is very han—"

"Handsome! Precisely! And confidentially," she leaned forward, rubbing her hands together, "Quite the best 'catch' in Wanganui! There, now!" Sitting back, she regarded me with a self-satisfied beam.

I tried to think of something to say, but nothing I thought of seemed adequate.

Mrs. Mannering had more than enough words for both of us.

"Now, regarding your clothes, my dear, I have had a talk with Jenny, who as you know is an excellent seamstress, and she has agreed to alter a mulberry cashmere of yours for tomorrow . . ."

"Tomorrow?" I asked, faintly.

"To be sure. Church, you know—Mr. Smythe is bound to be there! Now, as I was saying, Jenny has agreed to alter the mulberry and I believe I have some silver buttons and ribbons that will suffice. And of course, you may wear my grey fur tippet. Now, as for your hat . . ."

She paused at last, but I was too dumbfounded to take advantage of the opportunity.

"You will excuse me, I hope, but . . ." she looked at me unhappily, "Jenny tells me that she saw you last night wearing a hat that was . . . er . . . quite remarkable! Feathers, of course, are in fashion. However, for one of your short stature, perhaps not quite so many. And a hat with a smaller brim?"

Gathering her shawl about her, she heaved herself up from the chair. "Well now, I'm glad that's settled?"

"Settled?" I choked out. "What is settled?"

"My dear Miss Newcombe, you have something

caught in your throat?" A helpful thump on my back.
"Settled, you ask? Oh, how my mind jumps about! I
meant only, that you and Jenny will visit Miss Clark's
establishment this morning. She is newly opened up,
you know, and has a splendid assortment of millinery.
I know this is short notice, but I am sure you will find
something. My friends all *rave* about her! She advertises
in *The Yeoman,* you know!"

"Indeed!" I tried to look suitably impressed, "But—"

"A toque!"

"What?"

"Your hat, my dear! Something smaller and close-
fitting, with perhaps *one* feather curling up from the
crown. I shall tell Jenny!"

She looked back at me from the door, her round
face crumpled up in a tentative smile. "You cannot
imagine how pleasant this is for me. Such fun! Akin
to organizing a campaign! I never had a daughter,
you see—my poor little Georgie, was of course, a
boy—and, naturally, Malvina is too young . . . and
poor Ishbel . . ."

The fuzzy shawl disappeared around the door at
last. My head in a whirl—as if *I* had done all the
talking! I sank down on the nearest chair. What had
happened to Mrs. Mannering's 'poor little Georgie,' I
wondered, with an inner giggle—had she talked him
to death? For shame, I reproved myself sternly for
making a jest about such a thing! Mrs. Mannering
only meant to be kind, I decided, and I should not
make fun of her. I could understand her need to have
a daughter—and after all, Malvina *was* too young
and . . .

I sat bolt upright. Ishbel, I thought! Why had Mrs.

Mannering referred to her as "poor Ishbel?"

" 'Where are you going to, my pretty maid?' "

At the bottom of the stairs stood Gideon Tavish in a brown vicuna suit complete with fawn waistcoat and a natty buttonhole of what to my astonishment, appeared to be a dandelion encircled by daisies.

I gritted my teeth. I was not in the mood for his attentions. I made myself be pleasant — it was not his fault, poor man, that my day had started off with Mrs. Mannering! " 'I'm going a-walking, Sir,' she said!' " I misquoted.

I was rewarded with a broad smile. "Perhaps, I could accompany you?"

"Well, actually, Jenny is going with me. I need a new hat and Mrs. Mannering seems to think that I should have a second opinion!"

Another smile through the beard and a warm look from the brown eyes. "I should be delighted to provide a third! There is nothing I enjoy more than advising ladies when they have momentous decisions to make! By the way, how charming you look today, if I may say so. That shade of blue is particularly becoming!"

I looked down at my old blue serge shirtwaist that I had rescued from my trunk and pressed the night before. "Thank you," I responded doubtfully. I had become so used to Jenny's derogatory remarks about my clothes, that I no longer felt confident.

"And that boater is just the kind of hat to complete your ensemble!"

Across the hall to the right, a door opened to reveal Marcus Raven, dressed for riding; much as I had seen him a week before, in tweed jacket, corduroy breeches, and highly polished boots. I had not seen him since the preceding Sunday night, when I had observed his progress down the River Walk. The next morning both he and Mr. Tavish had left, so we were told, on a trip to Wellington. I looked at him, now, remembering Callum's warning, "Take care — take great care!"

"Good morning," he announced to Mr. Tavish, then raising his eyes, he saw me descending the stairs. "Good morning, Miss Newcombe! I was just coming to find you before I rode out. I wonder if . . ." He stopped and gazed appreciatively at Mr. Tavish's buttonhole. "Malvina?" he suggested.

Gideon Tavish nodded benignly. "Malvina!" he agreed. "Dear child!" He coughed. "However, my dear Raven, I was just telling Miss Newcombe how delightful she looks today."

To my surprise, the sombre features softened suddenly and broke into a smile. "Indeed, yes — that boater is particularly becoming!" Then, while I looked at him in amazement, he added, quite without his usual brusqueness, "I see you are going out; unless your errand is urgent, I wonder if I might take a few minutes of your time?"

"Of course," I responded, somewhat in a daze at his continued amiability. "I am going with Jenny to buy a new hat. However our expedition can easily be delayed."

"Please allow me to be of assistance, my dear Miss Harriet!" Gideon Tavish's deep voice boomed through the hall. "I shall be waiting for you in the drawing room. I should be glad to ring for Jenny and explain the delay." He turned to Mr. Raven, "I have offered to accompany Miss Harriet to help her decide on her purchase!"

My employer's lips twitched. "I am sure that *Miss Harriet* is duly appreciative!"

Mr. Tavish disappeared into the drawing room across the hall, while Mr. Raven stood waiting for me to descend the remaining stairs.

I did so slowly, playing for time. I had known, of course, that I should have to continue to meet with Marcus Raven, and often alone. No doubt he would continue the charade of caring about his children, and Callum and I had decided that it would be best for me to continue as I had always done — but taking great care not to reveal what I knew about Reginald. However, now the moment had come, I felt a distinct lack of confidence.

"I only wanted to talk with you about my children's progress," he explained, as he ushered me into what appeared to be a small parlor comfortably furnished with bright chintz covered arm chairs and small oak tables, on one of which reposed a bowler hat, riding whip, and gloves. An oak whatnot stood in one corner holding a collection of sea-shell-covered ornaments and the most enormous aspidistra I had ever seen.

"Mrs. Hargreaves' pride and joy!" Mr. Raven remarked, noting my awe with some amusement. "Mrs. Douglas swears that she must feed it olive oil! I believe it won first prize in a local plant show."

"Are you not afraid that it will one day take over this room, and eventually the house?" I asked, as I settled into the chair he indicated by the fire.

A bark of laughter as he sat down in a chair

opposite mine and stretched out his long legs toward the grate. "I should not be surprised!"

What lay behind that apparently relaxed demeanor, I wondered. Why was he being so friendly? I remembered Jenny's account of Miss Inglewood's meeting with Moana—"very affable" Jenny had described Mr. Raven's manner toward Miss Inglewood—"and she was not averse to him!" And what was it Mr. Takarangi had said, that Miss Inglewood had "loved too well, one she should not?" Had Marcus Raven deliberately won Miss Inglewood's confidence and then . . .

"Miss Newcombe, you are shivering! Come closer to the fire. And I swear, you have not heard a word I have said!"

I was going to have to be careful, very careful! "I am sorry, Mr. Raven, I'm afraid my mind was elsewhere!"

He gave me an indulgent smile (definitely not his usual style). "I expect you are thinking about your new hat! Don't worry, I shall not keep you long!"

Could he really be such a monster, I wondered, and then remembered poor Reginald's pale little face and what Callum had told me.

"I was wondering if you needed new textbooks? If so, I have an account at Willis's that you may take advantage of while you are here in Wanganui."

"Thank you, the textbooks are more than adequate. Miss Inglewood," I added, watching his face closely, "was very thorough."

Was it my imagination, or did a muscle twitch in that saturnine face at my mention of Miss Inglewood's name?

His tone of voice when he replied was smooth, suave even. "Miss Inglewood was indeed an excellent teacher; although, at times, I felt that her approach was too serious. The children did not laugh and play with her, the way I understand they do with you. However, she did have some interesting ideas — about Reginald for example . . ."

The topaz eyes looked at me closely. Here it comes, I thought.

"Miss Inglewood intimated to me that Reginald may not be as backward as we had supposed!"

So that was it, I thought grimly, he was trying to catch me off guard! Let him try!

I sat back, apparently at my ease and kept my voice carefully casual. "So far, I have really only had time to find out where the children are in their studies."

A small frown wrinkled my employer's brow. "And Reginald?"

I gave him a bland smile. "He is, of course, a delightful child, but as for his intellectual qualities, it is rather too soon to tell!"

The face before me regarded me thoughtfully, the lean hawklike features restored to their more usual sombre lines. "I see."

There was a short silence during which I kept my face expressionless.

"And Ishbel?"

"Ishbel!"

"Yes. Ishbel McCleod. You are, I take it, acquainted with my stepdaughter, Miss Newcombe?"

I was furious to feel myself blushing. And I was convinced, from the twitch of my employer's lips, that he was enjoying my discomfiture — odious man! "I'm

232

sorry, I'm afraid my mind was on Reginald."

The pale eyes gleamed with what I can only describe as a mocking light. "Was it indeed?"

I attempted to recover my dignity. "You wish to know how I feel about Ishbel?"

A patient sigh, "I believe that was what I had intimated! You were, after all, in such a state of concern regarding her, that you felt obliged to visit my study in the middle of the night!"

I shrivelled at the memory and hastily gathered my thoughts together. "Yes, of course! We have been here—what is it, two days!—but Ishbel seems to be settling in very well. In fact, I believe she may have found a beau!"

"Indeed!" The Master of Ravensfall bent forward suddenly and his tone of voice was sharp. "And who is this young man?"

"No one you would disapprove of, sir! In fact, it is the gentleman who visited us last Sunday—Mr. Jonathan Turner. I believe he is quite taken with Ishbel!"

"Is he indeed!" The eyes watching me were not so much disapproving, as bleak.

At that moment, there was a knock at the door and in came the object of our discussion.

A glowing smile. "Good morning, Step-Papa! Oh . . . I did not see you sitting there, Miss Newcombe!" The glow diminished. "I'm sorry!"

I rose to go. "I expect you have something to talk about to Mr. Raven in private."

The glow returned and I was given a pretty smile. "Well, yes, if you don't mind!"

"Not at all. If that is all, Mr. Raven, perhaps, I could go?"

"Step-Papa . . ." Ishbel began to say as I reached the door.

"I do wish," I heard Marcus Raven reply, "that you would address me as Papa!"

"But you are not my Papa," Ishbel answered, her voice light and sweet. "My Papa is dead."

Twenty-two

"My dear Miss Newcombe, dearest Alfred has told me all about you!"

A lace-edged cologne-scented handkerchief was wafted before my nose and I gazed up in awe past a sternly whale-boned magenta bosom to a puce face crowned by nodding jet-black plumes.

"How do you do, Mrs. Smythe!" I managed at last.

Mrs. Mannering, glued to my side like a barnacle ever since we had left the precincts of the church behind us, beamed at me her satisfaction.

"You are, of course, of the Devonshire New-combes!" Mrs Smythe's stentorian voice announced, at last.

"Well, actually . . ."

Mrs. Mannering patted my arm. "No, dearest Euphemia, I believe I told you. Miss Newcombe is of the Lancashire Newcombes."

"Really? I don't think . . ."

Mrs. Mannering smiled blandly. "And how is Sir Albert? I do hope he is better!"

235

"Thank you, Papa is greatly improved. Doctor Earle says that it is a question of—"

"I'm so pleased! And here is your son! How well he is looking!"

Alfred Smythe, splended in dark maroon superfine, raised his grey silk top hat. "Miss Newcombe! Please say you have forgiven me!"

"Yes. Of course." Under Mrs. Mannering's pale, blue gaze, what else could I say.

"And may I say, how enchanting you look!" His gaze took in my mulberry cashmere, Mrs. Mannering's grey fur tippet, her pearl ear bobs ("I insist, my dear!") and the grey velvet toque that Jenny and Gideon Tavish had persuaded me to buy.

"I understand," he continued, drawing me to one side, while his mother and Mrs. Mannering discussed the hats and bonnets of various acquaintances, "that you are attending the Glenby's on Saturday. I hope that you will save at least three dances for me!"

"Mr. Smythe, you know that isn't proper!"

He sighed. "A waltz, then! Do say you . . ."

I nodded absently. Mr. Raven had emerged from the church porch and now stood frowning towards a group of young people by the gate opening onto Victoria Avenue. I wondered what had brought about his disapproval, then saw that the star attraction of the group was Ishbel. Dressed in blue velvet with a matching broad-brimmed hat, she looked particularly becoming. While she chatted merrily with two or three young men, Jonathan Turner stood to one side, obviously jealous.

". . . Into the countryside." Alfred Smythe's tenor penetrated my consciousness.

"Excuse me?"

"I was asking, if this afternoon, you would care to—"

"I'm sorry, I am engaged!"

"Perhaps, during the week?"

I smiled politely. "I have my duties to attend to."

Mrs. Mannering was of a sudden back at my side. "Dear Miss Newcombe. So conscientious as you are! I am sure that some arrangement can be made—is that not so, Cousin Marcus?" she appealed to Mr. Raven, who had just come up.

He frowned down at her. "Arrangement for what?"

"Why, for Miss Newcombe to be sure! To take a short trip into the countryside with a group of Mr. Smythe's friends."

"I can't possibly neglect—" I began.

"By all means—you must do whatever you feel fit, Cousin Lydia!" The words were polite enough, but the tone was absent. He was looking again toward Ishbel, who was laughing gayly. "I believe it is time we went home," he added somewhat abruptly. "I promised to talk with Callum Douglas before lunch and the Prebyterian church being so much closer, he should be back by now." He turned to me, "Please find Malvina and Reginald and I shall get Ishbel."

Sunday afternoon and a spruced-up Jim Parker to take tea with Reginald and Malvina Raven.

He ran a finger around the inside of his stiff white Eton collar. "Aunty Em made me wear it!" he explained disgustedly to Reginald. "And this too!" he continued, indicating a large floppy bow-tie in navy blue crêpe. "I feel a right sissy!"

Malvina and Reginald laughed—a sound that was becoming more frequent and that I loved to hear.

"Do you think, Miss Newcombe . . ." Malvina began hesitantly. She paused while she carefully handed Jim his cup and saucer—under my aegis, she was being "Mother" and taking care of the teapot.

"Yes, dear?"

"Well . . . I know that gentlemen are supposed always to be correctly dressed in front of ladies. But do you think that perhaps, this once, Jim might be allowed to . . ." she looked at me, greatly daring, "remove his collar!" she finished in a rush.

I was delighted; my Malvina was showing signs of independence. (I could almost hear Aunt Alice tut-tutting in the background!)

I pretended to give the matter great thought. "I suppose, this once!"

"Oh, Miss, may I really?" The face fell. "Nah! I can't!"

"Why not?" I asked, intrigued.

"It's my Aunty Em. When I go home, she'll ask questions you wouldn't believe, about what I said and what I done—did. And she's bound to ask if I wore my collar, like she told me to—because I created a fuss when she made me put it on. I can't lie to her, see, or I would. But she has this way of looking at you . . ."

I nodded understandingly. "I see. Your aunt sounds very strict. I'm glad she let you come!"

"Oh, she says you're a . . . a . . ." He twisted his face in thought, "civilising influence?"

I collapsed in a gale of laughter. "*Me!* Me, a civilising influence?" I took a sip of tea, still trying not

238

to laugh. "My aunt would certainly not agree with your aunt about that! However, do have a piece of this cake. Mrs. Hargreaves made it specially for our tea party!"

Inevitably, it was Dundee cake—which, I knew I would forever associate with Miss Inglewood. How I wished I could ask the children about her and about what was frightening them, but—I thought of Malvina's tense little face when I had tried to pry the secret out of her—I knew I could not. Not knowing the secret, according to Malvina, somehow protected me. "We told Miss Inglewood," she had said, "and she is dead."

I sat back listening to the children's idle chatter. How was it, I wondered, that only Reginald and Malvina knew? It was obvious from her evident affection for her "Step-Papa" that Ishbel did not—and I supposed, being so much older and only their half-sister, after all, the children were not so likely to confide in her. Perhaps they wished to protect her, too! And then there was Mr. Raven's attitude toward Ishbel: if she had an affection for him, he certainly did not entertain one for her? But there was something else, something I could not quite put my finger on.

With an effort, I brought myself back to the party in progress.

"And after tea," I asked. "What would you like to do? Play 'Blind Man's Bluff,' 'Hide and Seek' or perhaps you'd like to 'dress up' and pretend you're French aristocrats again!" A sudden thought struck me. "By the way, how do you know so much about French history?"

It was Reginald who answered; a bright normal Reginald I longed to hug, but of course could not — at least not in front of Jim Parker!

"Oh, that was Miss Inglewood. She said if we were to study the language, we should know all about the people, didn't she, Mally?"

Malvina nodded. "She used to read to us all the time; *The Three Musketeers, A Tale Of Two Cities . . .*"

"*The Man In the Iron Mask* and *The Count Of Monte Cristo!*" added Reginald with relish.

"And she used to tell us about her French grandmother who escaped from Nantes during the revolution," Malvina continued.

"Her grandmother was an aristocrat?" I asked, curious.

"Yes — and so was Miss Inglewood!"

"Is that what she said?"

Malvina giggled. "Of course not! But she kept telling us stories of when she was a little girl and how her family would travel between their estate in England and the one they had in France. And then she'd teach us French phrases for how to go through customs and deal with servants — things like that!"

"I see! Well, if you have all finished, perhaps we could stack the tea things ready for Martha and then you can all decide what to do."

In the end, because the sun was still shining, they decided to play "Grandmother's Footsteps" on the back lawn.

Though the drawing room had some well-stocked bookshelves, there was no library as such in the town house. I could have gone to the drawing room, of course, but did not wish to do so. I did not want to be detained by Mrs. Mannering and her inevitable chatter—the more especially as I had pleaded a headache when refusing to join her there to discuss her "campaign." Perhaps, what followed was a punishment for my "white lie"!

Instead, I went to the bookshelf in my room and ran my fingers over the obviously—from the look of their covers—oft-read tomes. I pulled them out, one after the other, all the books that Reginald and Malvina had quoted that afternoon, feeling somewhat strange, wondering if Miss Inglewood had been the last person to handle them. It was almost, I felt, that there was a link or a mode of communication—call it what you will—between Miss Inglewood and myself. A link that, whether I wished it or not, was becoming steadily more tangible.

I shivered and turned up the lamp. "Behave yourself, Harriet!" I told myself aloud, "You are a great deal too fanciful!"

I picked up *A Tale Of Two Cities* and several papers—apparently used as bookmarkers—fell out and lay beneath me on the rich Turkey carpeting. Most of them appeared to be torn strips of old writing or accounting exercises—Malvina's or Reginald's, presumably—but one was not and it lay on the carpet; pink, folded, and inviting.

I found myself scarcely breathing, as I bent from my chair to pick it up. Slowly, I unfolded it and looked at the writing: basically small and concise but the loops and dashes growing larger and bolder as the letter progressed.

Dearest Fan:

We are in Wanganui again, as you can see, and I have just picked up your letter from the post office—under my pseudonym, of course. How dearest Grandmère would be pleased to see the spirit exhibited by the granddaughter she had least hope for! But enough of that!

As for your first concern: yes, indeed, my likeness to poor Minna has been commented on—there is even a portrait of her in the dining room at Ravensfall! However, as I stressed before I left, there are any number of small-boned, fair women in this world. Who would guess that a poor governess (as I must appear) and a great heiress should be cousins. The more especially, as I was in India with poor dear Edward all those years and did not even attend Minna's wedding to James McCleod (unfortunate wretch!). Who is there left to recognize me? And now, my dearest friend, I hope you have your vinaigrette by you—for what we suspected about Minna's murder (and it was murder) is true! Oh, the horror, the tragedy of it—especially the tragedy, for Minna must have realized, when she married against all the advice of her friends, the risk . . . oh, what will happen to those poor children—and more especially, Ishbel! Dear Fan—you must put your mind to rest about me! I assure you, I have been very circumspect. I have been very careful and no one knows who I am or what I am here for . . .

Here the letter with a small splodge of ink ended. I sat looking at the blot. Mary Inglewood—or whatever her real name was—had been interrupted. She had taken the letter she had been writing and quickly folded it and hidden it in what she had at

242

hand, which happened to be *A Tale Of Two Cities* — which, of course, accounted for the blot. But, why had she not rescued the letter later, finished it and sent it off?

Something must have happened, I thought — but what?

There were footsteps outside my door and then a knock.

Quickly, I re-folded the paper and slipped it among some of the pages of the novel I was supposed to be writing. "Come!" I called.

To my relief, Ishbel entered.

An apologetic smile and a smothered yawn. "Excuse me for interrupting you, Miss Newcombe!" Her aqua glance took in the scattered papers on my table. "My goodness, are those lesson plans or letters you are writing?"

"Both," I answered with an easy smile. "Please sit down, Ishbel." I rose and moving over to the fireplace, stoked the embers.

"How cold it is in here!" She yawned again and shrugged more closely round her shoulders the blue and cream Paisley shawl she was wearing over her blue wool dressing gown.

She looked sleepy, I thought, and her eyes lacked their usual brilliance. "I'm sorry, I'm afraid I was concentrating so much on . . . my letters, that I let the fire die down." I put another log on the fire and some lumps of coal from the coal scuttle. "There now, that should do it!" I turned toward Ishbel inquiringly. "Was there something you wished to talk to me about?"

To my surprise, she was nodding in her chair.

"Ishbel?"

She came to herself with a start. "I'm sorry. These past few nights, it seems that once I'm ready for bed, I can hardly keep my eyes open! Now, let me see, what did I . . . oh!" Another yawn. "Cousin Lydia told me that you would be wearing pink and silver for the ball and she wondered if I would lend you my silver and seed pearl necklet and earrings . . . well, of course I would . . . but I forgot all about it till now."

"How very kind of you, Ishbel!"

"Not at all. Why don't you come to my room and look at them. I nearly brought them with me, but I decided you might like to look in my jewel box and see if, perhaps, you would prefer something else."

"Perhaps, I should look tomorrow — you are so very tired. I swear that at any moment you will be sleep-walking!"

Ishbell rose to her feet with an effort. "No, I'm all right!" She smiled at me drowsily. "It would be better if you had a chance to see them tonight. Tomorrow the dressmaker is coming early to fit my ballgown and then I'm supposed to be riding out with Jonathan — that is," she blushed. "Mr. Turner."

"Indeed! That young man has taken a great fancy to you, I believe! In that case, let us go to your room, by all means!"

I followed her down the hall, touched by her friendly offer. Though she was always agreeable to me and ready to make conversation, there was a withdrawn quality about Ishbel — it was almost as if she were continually on the watch. I remembered Miss Inglewood's reference to her in the letter I had found and wondered why she had seemed to be more worried about Ishbel than Malvina or Reginald — because, as Callum Douglas had told me, it was Reginald (and of course Malvina, but I had not revealed that to him) who knew the secret.

"Please come in!" Ishbel opened the door and ushered me in.

She had never invited me into her room before — either in the townhouse or at Ravensfall — and I looked about with interest, while she crossed to an oak dresser by the window and rummaged in a drawer.

Just like Malvina's and Reginald's rooms, this one was tastefully, even luxuriously furnished. A deep-piled blue and gold Turkey carpet on the floor and blue and gold hangings at the window and around the canopied four-poster bed. But, whereas Malvina had her dolls apparently participating in a tea party in one corner of her room and Reginald had his toy soldiers in battle formation all along the top of his dresser, apart from the toiletries usual for a young girl, Ishbel had nothing personal on display. The room, I thought, did not reveal Ishbel's tastes at all, could in fact, have belonged to anyone. The toiletries were, however, arranged with precision and there were no clothes or the usual odds and ends left on any of the chairs or tables. Perhaps, Ishbel was just an extremely tidy, careful person!

"Here we are!" From the drawer, she drew out an ornate teak box and set it down on a mahogany occasional table. "Do sit down, Miss Newcombe and take your time." She threw open the lid to reveal all shapes and sizes of boxes. "These are the necklet and earrings, I told you about. But as I said, you are entirely welcome to look through my other jewels."

"But these are lovely!" I exclaimed, looking down at the delicately wrought silver earrings and the chain twined about with seed pearls. "And Mrs. Mannering was right, they are just the thing!"

"Yes, they are pretty. They belonged to my mother and are among the few jewels I have from her. I receive the rest on my twenty-first birthday, along with my fortune." She yawned again. "But wouldn't you like to see what else I have . . . There might be something else you would prefer . . ."

She could hardly keep her eyes open, I noticed, and was already politely trying to restrain another yawn.

"Oh, no thank you, Ishbel—these are perfect! Now get into bed and I shall tuck you in!"

I escorted her across the room. Her bed was already turned down and the pillow dented. She must have been in bed, I thought, when she had remembered about her mission to me. I helped her up onto the high feather mattress and tucked the sheets and blankets about her. She snuggled down, her unnightcapped auburn hair spreading about the pillow and glinting gold in the soft glow from the lamp. What must it be like, I wondered, to be so beautiful and to know one would inherit jewels and a great fortune on one's twenty-first birthday?

"Good night, Miss Newcombe!"

"Good night, my dear—and thank you!"

She murmured something unintelligible as she drifted at once into a heavy sleep.

I turned to her bedside table to put out her lamp. It was then that I noticed the laquered tray holding a small plate with the crumbs from some shortbread and a porcelain mug that had evidently held hot milk.

I looked at the sleeping Ishbel — an Ishbel who surely had been unusually drowsy — and I thought of the words of Gideon Tavish last Sunday about the drops . . . about disguising them in milk, and I remembered Mrs. Mannering on the steps of the chemist's snatching the package so quickly from my hands and explaining quite unnecessarily that the drops were for her eyes. And I thought of the way the attendant had reacted to her explanation.

I could hardly believe that my earlier conclusions were apparently right, that there was indeed something sinister taking place.

Poor Ishbel, I thought, poor child!

I felt a great coldness.

Twenty-three

"Callum! Callum Douglas!"

I knocked on his window pane and peered at him through a chink in the curtains. His room, at the back of the house, could only be reached through the kitchen and I had to go around by the outside.

Wretched man, why did he not respond? I could see him clearly, seated at a table, dealing apparently with estate matters; for he had a large inkwell before him and was making notations into a large ledger.

"Callum!" Taking up a large stone, I pounded sharply on the window.

Thank goodness, he had heard me! He turned toward the window, and then to my surprise, in one fluid movement blotted and closed the ledger and turned out his lamp.

"Callum," I hissed as best I could through the window. "It is only I, Harriet!" What is the matt—?"

My words were stifled by a large hand over my mouth as my wrists were twisted behind me.

"My God—Harriet!"

The long face, made pale by the moonlight, gazed down at me ruefully. I was set summarily on my feet.

"Who did you think it was?" I asked angrily, "The Czar's least favorite anarchist?"

A loud guffaw.

"Callum Douglas, will you please be quiet!"

"Dearest Harriet, why on earth should I be quiet?"

I resisted an impulse to kick him on the shin. "My reputation, sir, if nothing else!"

"Your reputation!" He lowered his voice dramatically. "Of course, never let it be said that it was compromised!" A long lean finger touched me lightly on the cheek. "Is that why you chose my window instead of the door?"

"Your door leads from the kitchen—if any of the servants had still been up . . ."

The beginnings of another guffaw, quickly—aided by my urgent pummelling—brought under control. "What about the other door?"

"Other door?"

A heaving of the shoulders, quickly restrained. "Certainly—the one leading onto the lawn at the back."

"You mean there is another door?"

"Miss Newcombe, you are to be congratulated for your quick thinking! I do, indeed, have a back door. And if you had been present on the back lawn this afternoon to supervise your little charges, you would have seen it!"

"Little charges? Oh, you mean 'Grandmother's Footsteps'!"

He grinned and shrugged his shoulders helplessly. "Grandmother's Footsteps—is that what you call it? As

I recall, *Master* Reginald Raven suddenly flew at Master James Parker, and Miss Malvina Raven was obliged to separate them with a handy croquet mallet."

I laughed. "Oh, good!"

"Good?"

I looked up at the outraged face and laughed. "Yes!" I thought for a moment, then explained. "They are acting like true children at last!"

I looked up at him, standing straight and tall in the moonlight. "Oh, Callum, there is something I have to tell you. But it sounds so ridiculous; I can hardly believe it!"

Somewhere close, a dog howled in sympathy and a small creature scuttled across the grass into the hedge behind us.

He rested his hands lightly on my shoulders. "You're shaking! What is it?"

"It's about Ishbel."

The moon passed behind a cloud and in the darkness I could not see his face; but I could feel him stiffen and for a brief moment, his strong fingers dug into my shoulders. "We had better go inside."

He led me around the house to a door set in the side opposite the hedge.

I looked around as he turned up the lamp. The room was small but comfortably furnished with a brown and gold carpet, a single bed with a brown coverlet and gold and orange eiderdown, a washstand of course with a matching dresser, a wardrobe, table, and two chairs. On the table, which evidently served as a desk, was an assortment of papers and a pile of ledgers. A small clock by the ledgers showed the time to be half past ten.

"Sit down, Harriet. Take the armchair!"

I sank down with relief. He was right, I found with surprise, I have been shaking with the tension. "I nearly waited till tomorrow," I explained, "but then I remembered about her early morning cup of hot chocolate and I thought —"

Callum sat on the straight-back chair and rested his elbow on the table. "Cup of hot chocolate?" he asked, puzzled. "What do you mean?"

"Oh, Callum. I think they are drugging her but I can't imagine why. As I said, it all sounds so ridiculous!"

In the lamp's glow, the blue-green eyes blazed. "Drugged? Ishbel?"

I told him, step by step, what I had observed, ending with a description of Ishbel's drowsiness that night and the mug by her bedside that had contained hot milk. "Apparently," I finished telling him, "according to Ishbel, she has been feeling drowsy for days!"

The chair clattered against the table as Callum lurched to his feet, his face coldly furious. "The . . ." (he said a word, I cannot mention here). "I might have known he would think up something of the kind. Laudanum! It's what he did to Minna."

I rose hurriedly. "You mean that Ishbel —"

"Sit down, Harriet. We have to think! It's all right, Ishbel is in no immediate danger! I dare say that what he intends to do —" He broke off suddenly and began to pace slowly up and down. "Of course, that is why he gave in and let her come to Wanganui! And why he is giving her the laudanum now. Ishbel is to present a 'drowsy' face to the world and soon it will be put about that 'delicate' Ishbel McCleod is ill . . . has perhaps — just like her mother — come down with consumption. And then, after our return to Ravensfall, no one will be surprised to hear of her death!"

I looked at him in horror. "You mean that Mr. Raven . . . ?"

"Of course!"

"But, why?"

"Oh, Harriet! Think! Why do you suppose he murdered Minna?"

"For her money?"

"For what remained of it! He had already spent the greater part of her personal fortune paying off his brother's debts and restoring the Yorkshire Ravensfall . . . and now, of course, he needs more money. He has two estates to run, you know, and like his brother — as you can tell by the furnishings of his houses — he has very expensive tastes. Our Marcus Raven likes to live in luxury!"

I dislodged several pins, as abstractedly I ran my fingers through my hair. "But, I don't understand about Minna! If he had full control of her money, why should he — "

"Kill her?" He spat out the words brutally and stopped his pacing for a moment. "Because she had served his purpose. And because another fortune lay close to his hand — one that with Minna out of the way — he could control freely!"

"You mean?" I could hardly bring myself to say it. "That he hopes to . . . to . . . somehow control *Ishbel's* fortune?"

He sat down again, sighing heavily. "What else!"

"But, I don't understand."

252

"About Ishbel's fortune?"

"Yes . . . I mean, if Minna's fortune is already spent—"

The long lips parted in a mocking smile. "I told you to think, Harriet!"

I ran my hands through my hair again. "Callum Douglas, say what you have to say—you are driving me crazy!"

A short laugh. "Before Minna married Marcus Raven, her solicitors drew up a marriage contract making sure that a large portion of Minna's assets would be held in trust for Ishbel—particularly those assets that had come from Minna's late husband and Ishbel's father, James McCleod."

I understood at last. "Oh, so that's where Ishbel got her fortune from! But, Marcus Raven can't control it, can he? I mean, he is only her stepfather. And I've just remembered, Ishbel said something to me tonight about her not inheriting her mother's jewels and her fortune until she was twenty-one."

Callum Douglas gave me a pitying smile. "Yes, indeed, if she lives that long. Unless she marries of course. Which, with the way she is guarded, is highly unlikely!"

"I can't believe it!"

The face watching me was stern and cold like the face of a stone effigy of a knight long dead. "Why not? We know he has killed at least twice already. Why not Ishbel? She is not his daughter, after all. In fact, as you have no doubt observed, he is not even fond of her."

I thought of my beautiful delicate Ishbel and shuddered. "But surely, if Ishbel should . . ." I could hardly bring myself to say the word, "die . . . Mr. Raven would *still* not have control of her money?"

"No?" An eyebrow was raised ironically. "According to the Trust, if Ishbel should die before she becomes twenty-one, her fortune will go to Malvina and Reginald—and Marcus Raven will have full control!"

I shook my head. "And the irony of all of this is the fondness Ishbel has for her stepfather—almost like a schoolgirl crush."

A mocking twist of the mobile mouth. "The Master of Ravensfall has a certain attraction for the 'fair sex,' I believe! As I said, Harriet, think! Whose husband is dying and who do you think would like to be mistress of Ravensfall?"

"Hélène DuPrès!" I remembered the last time I had seen her in that diaphanous wrapper. "You mean that she is also . . ."

He shook his head. "I don't know. But it gives us one more reason as to why our respected employer should dispose of Ishbel just now. The vineyard that our Hélène will inherit is not doing very well and Hélène also has expensive tastes!"

"But what about Mrs. Mannering and Mr. Tavish? I can hardly believe—"

"Harriet, grow up! You have heard them; you have seen them. You have remarked upon their subterfuge! Mrs. Mannering is a childless widow in straitened circumstances! As for Gideon Tavish . . ." he hesitated. "I don't know, but I have always felt that he is not what he seems."

I remembered my walk with Mr. Tavish in the garden at Ravensfall and my own mixed feelings about him. I nodded my agreement. "Yes, I have always felt that way. Oh, Callum, what are we going to do?"

"First, we must make sure she does not take the drops!"

"We had better warn her!"

"No, I'll take care of it, somehow. I don't want Ishbel put into a state of terror." The blue-green gaze was suddenly intense with emotion. "I shall watch out for her and protect her as I have always done. I've known her since she was a baby, you see, and she looks upon me as an elder brother. I would do anything in the world for her . . ."

Twenty-four

"Sheep!"

Mrs. Smythe's mannish voice boomed through her drawing room with all the delicacy of a blasting cannon. "Sheep!" she exclaimed again, "can't stand the creatures — too stupid! However, one must agree they have their uses!"

It was Tuesday evening; she stood in front of the huge marble fireplace of the mausoleum that was her drawing room, laying down the law to Jonathan Turner.

I restrained a giggle. Apart from her puce-colored face, she was not, I thought, unlike a sheep herself that evening! I looked with awe at her grey hair arranged in astonishing puffs and fluffs and whirls under a much be-laced white silk cap with nodding mauve bows of taffeta ribbon, and at her dinner gown of grey quilted velvet trimmed with innumerable ruffles of grey fur.

"Mother is in fine form, tonight, is she not?"

The gentlemen had just rejoined the ladies and

Alfred Smythe oozed a distinct aroma of brandy and cigars—especially brandy. Nodding my agreement that Mrs. Smythe was indeed in fine form, I moved away a little. He followed.

A slight hiccup. "Did I tell you, Miss Newcombe, how delightful you look tonight?"

"Yes."

"That . . . blouse," he announced indistinctly, gazing at the *café au lait* satin and lace blouse Jenny had made to go with my heliotrope skirt, "is par . . . partic . . . par-tic-u-lar-ly fetching!" he finished at last in triumph.

I restrained a temptation to applaud and moved away again. He followed.

"Of course," Mrs. Smythe declaimed from across the room, "my husband visits our various properties frequently, but I rarely accompany him . . . roads are dreadful, and when one is there . . . nothing to look at, just sheep . . ."

"So pleased you could come tonight," Alfred Symthe breathed heavily. "Sorry we could not ride out into the country, but these southerlies sometimes last for days."

As if in agreement, the drawing room door which he had left open banged shut in the draft and the heavy gold plush portières swayed in the brisk breeze seeping in through the French doors behind.

To my relief, two maids appeared with coffee trays.

"Perhaps, Mr. Smythe, as coffee is about to be served, we should sit down. Those chairs over there look inviting."

As he led the way, I slipped off in the other direction and hid behind a potted palm.

Secure in my refuge, I could watch the proceedings

without interruption.

I was reminded of my first night at Ravensfall and the welcome I had been given in the drawing room. What a lot had happened since then — and in just over a week's time! Sometimes, I felt that I was caught up in a raging torrent that was carrying me swiftly and inevitably toward a terrible doom . . . almost, as if, somewhere out there, lurked my own personal taniwha.

I pulled my scattered wits together, telling myself not to be so fanciful, that I needed to be on guard for Ishbel's sake. I looked about the room, seeking her out.

She had rescued Jonathan Turner from Mrs. Smythe and now they both sat, sipping their coffee, on a plum-colored damask love seat, sufficiently far away from the others to be private.

Dressed in the lavender and white striped gown I had first seen her in, she looked particularly charming. Even from such a distance, I could observe the glow of her wild-rose complexion and the clear gleam of her extraordinary eyes. No drowsiness, there, thank God!

Before he had left to return to Ravensfall on Monday, Callum Douglas had sought me out to tell me he had solved the laudanum problem. He had slipped into Mrs. Mannering's room and exchanged the laudanum bottle he had found on her dresser, with a similar bottle he had purchased at the chemists. "No laudanum in *that* bottle, though, Harriet," he had remarked with a wicked grin. "But be careful; this is only a temporary measure — they're going to wonder why the stuff's not working — but perhaps, by that time, we shall have enough evidence to go to the police! Be careful, Harriet. For yourself as well as Ishbel!" He kissed me quickly on the cheek with a light laugh, and then was gone.

Ishbel's bell-like laugh chimed through the room. How good it was to see her enjoying herself in the company of a pleasant and suitable young man! I looked over to where Marcus Raven, resplendent in his usual dark but perfectly cut dinner suit, sat chatting idly with Mrs. Smythe's widowed sister. As Ishbel laughed, he looked in her direction and frowned. Jonathan Turner was at that moment whispering something in her ear and their heads were close together.

I remembered what Callum had said about Ishbel receiving her fortune if she married before she attained the age of twenty-one. So that was why Mr. Raven discouraged suitable young men! I determined to do my best to help Jonathan Turner. Perhaps, I thought, later in the week, I could arrange a joint outing! I shuddered, when I realized that in order to do so, I should also have to invite Alfred Smythe, as he was the only suitable young unattached man I knew!

Mr. Tavish, who unfortunately for him was caught in the crossfire between Euphemia Smythe and Mrs. Mannering, was also looking toward Ishbel and Mr. Turner—though, in his case, his facial expression was blandly benign as usual. Who was this man, I asked myself yet again. I was *certain* he was not what he seemed. I had a sudden and daring thought. Perhaps, when he was out of the house and I could be reasonably sure of not being caught by the maids, I could search his room!

I stifled a horrified laugh! What had come over me in the bare ten days I had been in New Zealand? What had happened to the demure (well, almost!) Harriet, trying so hard under Aunt Alice's guidance to become a conventional young lady? Aunt Alice was right, I should never have left England!

Isbel's laugh rang out again, joined this time by the counterpoint of Jonathan Turner's melodious tenor. I looked toward them, at their glowing faces — Mr. Turner gazing with obvious adoration at Ishbel. Nonsense, I told myself, Aunt Alice was wrong! If I had not come, I would not have been able to help Ishbel . . . perhaps, my coming would save her from a dreadful fate!

Quarter to five on a Wednesday evening, a freezing southerly gale battering the house, sporadic bursts of rain beating at the windows — and Harriet Sherlock Holmes Newcombe creeping down the hall to the room of Mr. Tavish.

You must be mad, I told myself, absolutely insane! I debated whether or not to go back. I went on.

It was, of course, the wrong time of day to "examine" a gentleman's chamber in his absence — much too dark and about to grow more so. But I had no choice. I had kept an eye out as best I could, while carrying out my duties, on the comings and goings of Gideon Tavish; but wretched man, he had kept about the house all day. It had been a chance remark that I had overheard from Jenny and Martha, about Mr. Raven and Mr. Tavish being out for the evening with friends and leaving early, that had alerted me. I knew that I had better seize the opportunity when it was presented.

I had put on an extra petticoat against the cold, plus a blue woollen spencer, and a pair of fingerless crocheted mittens. In one pocket of my black bombasine skirt I carried a candle stub and a box of Lucifers. I was well prepared!

Gideon Tavish's bedchamber was situated next to Ishbel's at the front of the house. I stood for several moments in the freezing hall trying to find enough courage to enter. Finally, I made myself open the door and, after looking nervously over my shoulder, stepped inside. I was careful to leave the door open an inch or two to let me hear anyone coming along the hall — although I realized the howling winds outside would probably disguise any sound inside the house. I knew I would have to work fast *and* be very careful.

The room was much like Ishbel's; the same dark panelled walls, rich blue and gold Turkey carpeting, and heavy highly polished mahogany furniture. I looked about nervously, wondering where to start first. At the bedside table, in the drawers of the huge chest, in the pockets of the clothes hanging in the wardrobe? Not for the first time, I felt a sense of distaste for what I was going to do and had to take myself seriously to task; telling myself, yet again, that my efforts were all for Ishbel's sake.

In the end, seeing some books and papers on the bedside table, I decided to start my search there first. As I made my way across the room, a sudden squall of rain beat against the window and outside the sky darkened under the massive rushing clouds. Hurriedly, I lit my candle and stuck it in the candlestick on the table.

In the meagre light cast by the flickering candle flame, the papers proved almost impossible to read. They seemed to be notes of some kind, written in a small, crabbed handwriting that was almost illegible. There did, however, seem to be some phrases in what looked like Latin; I wondered if the writer was using a type of code. I would take the papers over to the window after I had examined the books, I thought, and see if in the little light remaining, I could decipher at least a few sentences.

Putting the papers back down on the table, I took up the books. There were four of them: De Quincey's *The Confessions of An English Opium Eater*, Flaubert's *Madame Bovary* (printed in French), a book with a title I could not understand because of the German gothic lettering, but the author—if I had deciphered the name correctly—seemed to be a Sigmund Freud; and—of all books—*A Tale of Two Cities!*

I held the last book in my hands and felt my heart beat faster. Was there to be *no* escape from Miss Inglewood? Slowly, I replaced the books exactly as I had found them and bent to pick up the papers, turning as I did to the door to check the hall. To my consternation, through the gap I had left, shone the wavering glow of a lamp, as someone turned from the stair landing further down the hall.

It was too late for me to escape—I did the only thing possible to prevent my discovery. Hurriedly replacing the papers, I blew out the candle and holding the smoking stub in my hand, dived under the bed.

I was only just in time. From under the edge of the bed valance, I saw the glow from the lamp lighting up the room as two pairs of masculine galoshes entered. Because of the pounding rain and the whistle of the wind outside, I could not hear the words but I recognized the deep tones of Gideon Tavish as he crossed to the fireplace. Someone, who I guessed to be Marcus Raven, replied; one pair of galoshes then approached the bed.

I lay rigid, scarcely daring to breathe.

"My Dear Raven . . . yes . . . warm up soon . . ."

The bed sagged as Gideon Tavish sat on it and began to remove his galoshes. The wind still howled but the rain pounded less.

"Excuse me? James McCleod?"

An answering voice.

"Oh, yes, definitely."

The wind died down for a moment.

Marcus Raven's baritone. "I don't believe she is taking the drops . . . We shall have to think of something else."

"I agree with you, my dear fellow. By the way, it's the oddest thing, but can you smell candle smoke?"

A short silence as Marcus Raven's galoshes approached the bed.

"Have your papers been disturbed?"

A riffling sound. "It's hard to tell—but they're all here and in the right order."

Another silence.

Marcus Raven spoke again. "I believe, my dear Tavish, that you would be wise to keep them locked up—and also that box of drugs, you have!"

"My box? Do not distress yourself. *That*, I always

263

keep locked! However, it had not occurred to me to do the same with the papers; but you are quite right. I shall do so immediately!"

"In that case, if you will excuse me, I have an errand. I am sorry about our trip!"

"My dear fellow, I understand perfectly! In this weather, it would be most unwise. Perhaps we can meet in the small parlor in a few minutes to continue our discussion?"

There was silence as Gideon Tavish moved about the room. At long last the door opened and shut and he was gone. I made myself stay still for at least five minutes before I dared scramble out from under the bed. Brushing down my rumpled skirts and pushing back my tousled hair, I crept to the door and opened it. All clear! I slipped out onto the landing and started to sidle down the hall. A door opened behind me.

It was the door to Ishbel's room and in the opening stood Marcus Raven.

"Ah, Miss Newcombe. A moment, please!" He turned to the room behind him. "Now, remember what I said, Ishbel!"

A voice sounded from within the room.

"Yes. Very well, Cousin Lydia . . . yes . . . I quite agree! Yes, Cousin Lydia. I shall see you later!"

He closed the door firmly and turned to me. "I was just—" His eyes widened as he observed my disarranged hair and rumpled skirts and held up the lamp he was holding, the better to observe. "No doubt you have been playing 'Hide and Seek,' Miss Newcombe?"

"I . . . I . . . have . . . been 'turning out' my room." I managed at last, trying to keep my voice from shaking.

Marcus Raven regarded me expressionlessly, then with what seemed a deliberate slowness, looked first at the door to Mr. Tavish's room, then to where I had been walking in the hall when he had seen me.

I thought desperately, then came up with a brilliant explanation.

"I wanted to see Ishbel but when I arrived at her door, I heard voices. I decided not to interrupt!"

He looked down at me gravely. "No doubt you did not wish to be seen in your present state!"

"Just so, sir!"

Reaching behind him, he opened the door. "In that case . . . I assure you there is only Mrs. Mannering with Ishbel."

"But . . ."

A sarcastic smile.

Holding my head high, I entered the room.

Mrs. Mannering and Ishbel looked at me in astonishment but before Mrs. Mannering could make one of her interminable speeches, Marcus Raven had one last riposte. "Have you ever thought of writing a novel, Miss Newcombe?" he asked pleasantly.

Somehow I thought of something to explain my presence to Ishbel, and then, making my excuses, returned still shaking to my room.

As I moved about changing my clothes and tidying my hair, I thought about the conversation I had overheard between Gideon Tavish and Mr. Raven. Perhaps, I thought, it might be a good idea to write down what I remembered.

Taking a notebook, I sat down by my fire. The box

of drugs, of course: I wondered briefly, if that had been the box I had seen Mr. Tavish bringing from Mrs. Douglas's room on my first morning at Ravensfall. Hadn't she said something about "a nostrum"? And then of course they talked about "the papers" but not in any way to elucidate for me what they were about. But there was something else . . . something I noted at the time but was in too terrified a state to pay attention to it. Something odd. Of course! In my excitement I bit the end of my pencil. "James McCleod" one of them had said—and surely James McCleod had been Ishbel's father?

I thought of Miss Inglewood's letter that I had carefully stowed away among my papers. If I remembered correctly, she had referred to James McCleod as a "poor wretch"—but at that moment, I had not really paid attention to the phrase. In fact, I really had not had the time, as directly afterward I had found out about the danger Ishbel was in . . . and then, of course, I had gone to Callum.

I rose and went to the table to fetch my novel. I remembered that I had hidden the letter among its pages.

The pages of my novel were disarranged.

The letter was gone.

I remembered Mr. Raven's sarcastic question. "Have you ever thought of writing a novel?"

Twenty-five

Outside the storm still raged, and I shivered as I paced up and down my chamber.

What was I going to do?

It was almost midnight but though I had carefully locked my door, I was too over-wrought to prepare for bed. I looked at the door. Somewhere in the darkness on the other side lurked the man I was convinced was a murderer.

Pull yourself together, Harriet, I told myself, succumbing to a fit of the vapours will certainly not help either you, the children, or Ishbel. The best thing, I decided sternly, was to think things through logically. What, after all, had the letter revealed? Nothing really, except that in Miss Inglewood's *opinion* there had been a murder. In other words, the letter had revealed nothing that could incriminate Marcus Raven — had not, in fact, even referred to him by name! Therefore, there was no reason why I should be a threat to him. And, I thought with a shiver remembering those cold light eyes, if he had considered me a threat, he would never have made a sarcastic reference to my novel. He would simply have bided his time and then . . . I shuddered.

In fact, the more I thought about it, the less I could imagine the Master of Ravensfall—villain though he undoubtedly was—stooping to search among a lady's papers. Of course, Mr. Tavish or Mrs. Mannering could have done so. After all, I had not looked at my novel since Sunday night when Ishbel had interrupted me. Anyone could have entered my room since then when I was about my duties, but somehow, I could not . . .

Perhaps, I thought, Mr. Raven's remark was really what it seemed, with no undercurrent of threat. What was it, he had said? "Have you ever thought of writing a novel?" A comment made after my creative answers to his insinuations; after he had observed my disorderly appearance and had looked meaningfully toward Mr. Tavish's room. Thank God, I thought, that like myself, he had no real proof!

No, I could not imagine Marcus Raven or either of his minions—and yet, my papers *had* been disarranged and the letter *was* missing—so what was I to think?

On the other hand, I thought suddenly, perhaps my papers had been examined and he had asked his question about my novel simply to gauge my reaction. To find out what—if anything—I knew!

I did not know what to think.

I looked toward my bed, at the plumped feather pillows and bright patchwork quilt turned invitingly back and told myself that I ought to start undressing—but never had I felt less like sleep. Outside the wind roared and there was a light splatter of rain against the window pane. I wished I had the courage to make my way down through the darkness of the house to the storm-tossed garden. A short walk through the battling elements would have cleared some of the cobwebs from my mind, I thought, and a brief struggle against the freezing, gale-force winds might have relieved some of my nervous tension. I looked regretfully toward the door and knew that I would never have the courage to unlock it.

Instead, I wandered over to the window and slipped behind the swaying curtains. Outside, in the uncertain light from a cloud-tossed moon, the garden was a well of shifting shadows: the dense blackness of the wind-ruffled hedge at the back, the lighter darkness of the swaying elm tree in the corner, and a moving pattern of muted light and shadow across the lawn as the moon sailed in and out among the clouds. As I watched, one of the shadows took substance and, emerging into a sudden pool of light, slipped past below my window in the direction of Callum Douglas's room at the back of the house.

Callum Douglas, I thought, thank God! Someone, at last, I could confide in!

I found myself rushing to my wardrobe and pulling out my ulster and galoshes. It was not until I was winding a long mauve woollen muffler about my head and neck, and facing again my locked door, that I had second thoughts. Callum, I remembered, had told me that he was going to be at Ravensfall until after the ball. What, I wondered had brought him back? And more to the point, how in this gale had he managed to canoe down the river?

What if it were not Callum Douglas?

Who else could it be? Surely not Mr. Raven or anyone within the house. If Mr. Raven or Mr. Tavish had been out, they would naturally have returned through the front door.

Perhaps Callum had returned from Ravensfall before the worst of the storm. Or he may have traveled down on the *Waiwere* and spent the intervening time elsewhere, before coming back to the town house.

I looked at the locked door. Did I have the courage to open it? I thought of a pair of blue-green eyes and how their mocking light could soften to tenderness. I thought of a lean brown finger gently touching my cheek.

I unlocked the door.

Beyond the light pouring out from my room, the hall was deep in shadow. Regretfully, I closed the door behind me and found myself in utter blackness. I had decided against taking lamp or candle. I was afraid that a light might attract attention and in any case the route I was going to take—the back stairs (close to my room) and the passage past the kitchen to the side door—was well known to me.

The air was dankly chill and I drew my coat closely around me. The house creaked in the wind, but I could hear no other sound. "Courage, Harriet!" I murmured to myself. I reached out a hand and began to feel my way along the panelled wall to the backstairs.

Once down the stairs and in the passage, I debated briefly whether or not I should approach Callum's door through the kitchen. I decided against it. Although it was unlikely, one of the servants *might* suddenly decide to fulfill a need for a cup of tea. More importantly—horrible thought—supposing I knocked on Callum's door and someone else should open it!

I decided to keep to my original plan and slip out through the side door. If there were a light at Callum's window, I would try as I had done before, to peer through the curtains. If the curtains were firmly closed, then I should have to determine what further action—if any—to take!

The chains and bolts on the back door were hard to undo and when I had finally managed to turn the reluctant key and stiff knob, the opening door nearly pushed me off my feet as the force of the wind pushed it inwards.

Strange to say, it seemed warmer outside—perhaps because the rushing wind stirred up the air, preventing the build-up of that dank, icy chill that seeped throughout the house. Somehow I managed to pull the door shut and then stood briefly at the top of the steps and peered down the side of the house.

A soft glow shone through the curtains in Callum's window. I heaved a sigh of relief and, struggling against the wind, I made my way down the path and, climbing onto the cut-off tree trunk I had used before, peered inside. The curtains had been pulled close but they swayed in the stiff breeze filtering through the window frame, intermittently fluttering apart and allowing me glimpses of the interior. In this manner, I was allowed a glance, first of the orange and gold eiderdown on the bed, then of the ledgers on the lamplit table, and then of the person seated beside the ledgers.

271

It was Hargreaves.

Hargreaves! I could hardly believe my eyes! As the curtains fluttered to and fro in the breeze, I could see that he was seated at an open ledger and making notations as he referred, every so often, to a tattered slip of paper.

He was wearing a brown tweed jacket and collarless shirt, I noted—hardly appropriate clothes for the storm outside. The door opening into the kitchen, I observed as I leaned hard against the glass and peered round a suddenly deflated curtain, was partly open. Therefore Hargreaves had entered Callum's room from inside the house. His had not been the shadowy figure I had seen beneath my window.

I decided to return to my room; but before I could do so, Hargreaves stretched, yawned, and folding the slip of paper, placed it in an inner pocket. He then leaned forward and turned off the lamp.

Left in complete darkness, I clung to the window sill a moment as to a life raft and then, hit by a sudden drenching shower of rain, I dropped to the mud below. Somehow or other, keeping one hand against the side of the house and the various plants and trees in between, I managed to squelch my way back to the side door.

Try as I might, the stubborn knob would not budge.

From out of the now driving rain, a well-known baritone. "May I be of assistance, Miss Newcombe?"

A strong arm seized me about the waist, the door was opened and I was propelled along the dark passage to an even darker kitchen.

"For God's sake, woman, don't scream!" The savage

272

voice hissed into my ear. "I am not about to murder you—at least, not yet! I'm just looking for—" My wrist was seized in an iron grip and I was dragged abruptly forward. Some muffled scrapes and thuds, then a lamp shed a welcome light over Mrs. Hargreaves's orderly kitchen.

"Sit down!"

I was thrust into a chair by the stove. A white-faced Marcus Raven towered above me. "What are you about, Miss Newcombe?"

"What?"

"I said . . ." the words came slowly, as if ground out through a particularly difficult mill, "what are you about?"

"Well . . ."

"Take that off!"

"What?"

"That . . . that what-ever-it-is around your neck and head!"

"My muffler!"

"Precisely!"

"But—!"

"And your coat!"

"My ulster?"

"If that's what you call it! Good God, woman, it's ringing wet! I know those things are supposed to be waterproof but *not* in a storm such as this! Now are you going to take it off or am I going to take it off for you?"

I took it off—and the muffler also. He was right; both were "wringing wet." I was glad to get both off— but not, of course, glad to admit it!

I stood before him in my galoshes and my simple—

and somewhat damp—blue serge. "And, now, sir, your Burberry!"

"My Burberry?" He paused in his ministrations to the stove.

"If that's what you call it! Good God, sir, it's wringing wet!"

He grinned suddenly and his lean features relaxed. He looked, I thought, exactly like Reginald when he had been caught out in a prank. He dragged off his dripping coat and hung it on a row of hooks by the kitchen door.

Over his white dinner shirt, from which he had removed the cravat, he wore, of all things, a deep violet velvet smoking jacket, decorated with silver braid.

"Please excuse my lack of formality," he apologised, "I was smoking in the small parlor, when I decided to . . . to go out . . . In any event, I hardly expected at such a time of night to meet a lady!" Dexterously, he settled a tea kettle on the now glowing stove.

I watched as he moved about the kitchen, finding teapot, cups, and saucers. Could this man, I wondered yet again, really be such a villain? I remembered Callum's warning, I thought again of the remarks I had overheard and—glancing toward the hook with the dripping coat—I remembered Ngaire's tale of a terrified Miss Inglewood rushing down to the flooded river . . . rushing down to her death. I shuddered. Had poor Miss Inglewood also doubted his evil? Again, I remembered Mr. Takarangi's remark that "she had loved one she should not." Had it been Mr. Raven she had loved? I thought again of my favorite novel, *Jane Eyre*. Had Miss Inglewood thought

274

of Mr. Raven as a kind of Mr. Rochester, gloomy because of his wife's fate. Except Mr. Rochester's wife had been mad, while Mr. Raven's wife had been murdered!

I watched my employer now, as he carefully rinsed the teapot with hot water from the nearby boiling kettle and wondered if he had done likewise for Miss Inglewood. Had she been won over by that easy charm that on occasion he seemed able to produce? It was almost, I thought idly, watching him emptying the pot and measuring the tea leaves, as if he were two people. Was there not a form of madness, I thought suddenly, where the one afflicted would assume another personality?

Was it a deep-seated madness, rather than greed, that had caused Marcus Raven to kill twice and perhaps to contemplate a third murder? If so, had the taint passed to his children — poor Malvina and poor Reginald, so much like his father! Oh, poor little creatures! Which was worse, to know one's father was a murderer or a madman? At least, Ishbel was not affected, I thought thankfully, her father having been James McCleod. The mysterious James McCleod that, for some reason, Mr. Tavish and Mr. Raven had discussed that evening, and that Miss Inglewood had described in her letter as an "unfortunate wretch."

Of course! That was it! I sat up straight, scarcely able to restrain my excitement. During our walk through the garden at Ravensfall, Mr. Tavish had admitted knowing Minna McCleod while her first husband was still alive. James McCleod had died and Mr. Raven had married his rich widow. Had there been yet another murder? Is that why Miss Inglewood had referred to James McCleod as an "unfortunate wretch"? Were Mr. Tavish and Marcus Raven long-time conspirators?

". . . harboring, Miss Newcombe?"

I came to myself, to find my employer regarding me quizzically.

"Excuse me?"

A slight smile. "You have been sitting there silent, for at least five minutes. I asked you what deep thoughts you were harboring!"

If only you knew, I thought! "Oh, nothing of any importance," I replied aloud. I watched as he poured the now boiling water into the teapot. "You certainly make a good cup of tea, Mr. Raven," I added, attempting with light smalltalk to disguise my nervousness and to lead the conversation away from myself. "I understand," I added for good measure, "that in America it is almost impossible to find a properly brewed pot of tea!"

"Really!"

"Yes!" I warmed to my subject. "Apparently, the Americans do not understand about the importance of boiling water nor the necessity of allowing the tea to brew after it is made!"

"How very well-informed you are, Miss Newcombe." His tone was serious, but I could have sworn his shoulders heaved as he turned to pour the tea into the cups.

I was annoyed. I could see nothing amusing in my dissertation, which after all was true!

"As I recall, you like just a little milk?"

"Thank you. Apparently," I returned tenaciously to my topic. "This ignorance has something to do with

276

the Boston Tea Party—"

I broke off as a plate bearing a large slice of rich chocolate cake was presented. I suddenly found that I was exceedingly hungry and unable to resist taking a large bite before continuing with my subject. "Since then, most Americans have drunk only coffee!" I concluded at last, dusting the crumbs from my lips.

"How fascinating," exclaimed my companion, in a suitably serious tone. "And now that we have exhausted the topic of American tea-drinking habits, what shall we discuss next? Perhaps," he continued with a politeness that was almost deadly, "we could discuss your tendency to take midnight walks—and this one in particular, that led you out in the middle of a southerly gale to Mr. Douglas's room?"

I swallowed a piece of chocolate cake a little too quickly and coughed. Hurriedly, I sipped some tea, all the time aware of my interrogator sitting opposite, one eyebrow raised ironically.

"I assure you, sir," I uttered with great dignity, "that I had no nefarious purpose in mind when I left the house!"

"No, I am sure, not. I cannot imagine *you* being . . . er . . . *nefarious*, Miss Newcombe! No doubt, you had a perfectly good and, naturally, totally *innocent* reason for your expedition, that I am sure you will reveal in your own good time! Please continue. I am 'all ears'!" Sitting back in his chair, he folded his arms and waited expressionlessly.

I suddenly had a Brilliant Notion.

I hid my excitement by taking a sip of tea. With deliberate casualness, I replaced my cup in its saucer and sat back. "It concerns the novel, you know, that I am writing!"

I watched my employer's face carefully for some sign of guilt at the mention of my novel. To my disappointment, his face did not change expression. That is to say, his mouth trembled just a little — but no doubt, this was on account of a sudden cough he restrained politely behind one hand.

"I believe, Miss Newcombe," he continued at last, "that I *suggested* you write a novel. I did not know at the time that you were actually writing one . . . but how pleased I am that you have found such a use for that undoubtedly original mind of yours! What kind of novel are you writing? An adventure story? A romance — a children's story, perhaps?"

If he had looked through my papers, he would undoubtedly know that I was writing a romance. I watched his face carefully as I made my reply. "I am writing a mystery story."

"A mystery story! Of course! A wonderful outlet for one of your considerable talent!" His eyes did not flicker with disbelief and his face betrayed no expression other than the surprise that might have been expected on hearing that an employee of his was a secret writer of mysteries. "And so," he continued, "you were writing your story, when you suddenly had an urgent need to consult with Mr. Douglas about some point or other. No doubt your story takes place on a country estate and you wanted to make sure that your facts were correct about a point of management?"

"Oh, no! Nothing like that!"

"No? Miss Newcombe, you *do* surprise me!"

I sipped my tea and regarded him sternly over the

rim of my cup. I remembered his remark in his study at Ravensfall, about attack being the best form of defense. "Mr. Raven, you may laugh, but writing is a serious business—and not easy!"

A contrite face. "Pray forgive me. I do not mean to mock! But do go on. I assure you, I am completely fascinated!"

I looked at him narrowly, but could not discern any signs of amusement. Mollified, I continued with—I blush to admit it now—my series of well-constructed lies. "I was attempting," I explained, "to write, but I suffered an impasse!"

"An impasse!"

I looked at him suspiciously but could see no hint of a smile. "Yes, sometimes writers run out of ideas . . . or more precisely, not exactly run out of ideas—but for a time be unable to develop them . . ."

"Now, you really *do* surprise me! But, pray continue!"

I frowned at him, but his face was perfectly serious.

I continued. "I was at that point tonight. It is very frustrating to be in such a case, you understand!"

He nodded in reply.

"And sometimes a short walk in the open air will suffice to clear away the cobwebs in one's brain . . ."

"Ah. *Now,* we come to it!"

I tried to look suitably downcast. "I know it was foolish of me, at such a late hour and in such weather, to venture out but . . ." I hesitated apologetically.

"Please continue—I am completely fascinated!"

"Well, the backstairs being so much nearer my chamber, I decided to go down that way and then, of course, along the kitchen passage and out the side door . . ."

He leaned forward in his chair. "And then?"

"The wind was too strong. I realized it as soon as I had managed to open the door, and I planned to go back inside the house. It was then that I glanced down the side of the house and saw the light in Call—Mr. Douglas' room and wondered . . ."

I blushed, but though his eyes narrowed momentarily, Marcus Raven made no reference to my near-use of Callum Douglas' first name.

"And you wondered?" he prompted me politely.

"I knew, of course, that Mr. Douglas was supposed to be at Ravensfall and was not supposed to return until after the ball on Saturday. So therefore, I wondered . . . naturally . . . if there were a burglar in his room!"

"Naturally!" The Master of Ravensfall gave me a look of what I could only describe as admiration. "Thank you, Miss Newcombe for your very . . . er . . . *comprehensive* explanation! How I should like to read your novel!"

"Yes. I should of course, be glad to show it to you, but unfortunately, I have mislaid it somewhere . . ."

"Mislaid it?"

"That was why it was so frustrating tonight," I explained mendaciously. "I wanted to look back at a certain chapter but when I went to fetch my novel, I could not find it anywhere. I last saw it, I believe, on Sunday evening. With preparing for the ball and going out to dinner last night, I have not had the time, you understand, to write." I took a deep breath and then added daringly, "And what is particularly frustrating, is that Miss Inglewood's letter is with my

280

papers!"

The silence was so complete, I could hear the kitchen clock tick—could hear, in fact, the beating of my heart.

Marcus Raven stared at me with a look, I could almost swear, of complete amazement.

"You mean," he asked at last, "that you knew Miss Inglewood and that she wrote to you before she . . ."

"Oh, no! Nothing like that," I hastened to assure him. 'It is simply that I was looking through some old books in my room and came upon an old letter that I assumed was Miss Inglewood's—I know her writing, you see, from exercises she corrected for the children."

He leaned forward. "And this letter? You apparently consider it to be of some importance."

I gave him an innocent look. "That's just it, you see! I don't know whether it was or not because before I had time to read it, I was interrupted. Ishbel came to my room to invite me to look at some jewelry that she thought, dear girl, I could wear at the ball. So I re-folded the letter—it was written on pink paper as I recall—and placed it among my papers and, as I explained, with everything that has been going on, I completely forgot about it till this evening!"

Marcus Raven studied me silently, a slight frown between his dark brows.

Was his amazement genuine, I wondered? Or did he know about the letter? Perhaps he had it at that moment in his possession. And if he did have the letter, did he believe my story that I had not read it?

Twenty-six

Thursday morning and a pale blue sky awash with
scudding clouds. The storm had abated leaving behind only an icy gust or two, a ghostly reminder of its
former freezing presence.

I peered out my window, then looked at the clock
on my mantel shelf. A quarter past seven . . . perhaps
another half hour? I returned to bed.

"Miss Newcombe!"

I struggled to raise a heavy eyelid and half exposed
what I was sure a very bleary eye.

"Miss Newcombe!"

"Um . . ."

"Miss Newcombe. Are you sick?"

The voice was tremulous; the voice in fact was
almost hysterical. The voice belonged to a nearly
frantic Malvina.

Malvina!

With great resolution, I managed to heave myself
from my pillows. "What is it, sweetheart?"

An audible sigh of relief. She stood by my bed in

her blue merino dress, a tangerine velvet Alice band about her fair curls and a wavering cup and saucer clutched precariously in her small hands. "Martha said to give you this!"

It was a cup of tea. "Thank you, dear!" I took a sip, it was tepid. "Lovely!" I forced myself to take another sip and smiled my appreciation.

A movement in the doorway and an anxious Reginald peered in.

"You are sure you are quite well?" Malvina asked again.

"Of course! What makes you think that I am not?" For the first time, I looked at the clock; it lacked a quarter to nine. "Oh, my goodness, I had no idea it was so late!"

"You see," Malvina explained, "when you did not come to breakfast, we began to worry because you are *always* on time. And then, when you did not come at all, we peeked around your door and you were . . . were not . . . *moving* . . . just like . . . just like . . ."

Hurriedly, I put my cup and saucer on my bedside table and reaching out, took Malvina in my arms. "Oh sweetheart, I just over-slept, that's all!"

"That's what Martha said." Reginald had crept into the room and now stood close by my bed. I reached out a hand and took one of his.

"She said you were 'sleeping it off,' " he continued.

"She said *what?*"

"Sleeping it off—because of your novel, you know. She said you had probably been up all night writing!"

"My novel! How do *you* know about my novel?"

"Reggie!" Malvina, her tears forgotten, turned angrily to her brother. "You know we were not supposed to say. We promised!"

"*You* did — I did *not!*" Reginald gave an unrepentant grin.

Malvina took a look at my flabbergasted face. "You see, Miss Newcombe, it was an accident — really, it was! Wasn't it, Reggie!"

Reginald nodded.

"Just how did this *accident* happen?" I tried to look stern.

"It was just before we left Ravensfall. You had left the folder with your papers in it on the schoolroom table, by a pile of our books and papers . . . and Martha came in to help us pack and tidy up . . .'

I nodded, beginning to understand. "Go on!"

"Well, somehow, your folder fell on the floor and all the papers were scattered about. Well, of course, we would never have dreamed of reading them!"

I gave her a hug. "Of course not!"

"And neither would Martha, would she Reggie? Except that, as she picked the papers up, she happened to notice that one of them was headed up with a chapter and a number so she 'knew it was not a private letter or a diary . . . and then, we all worried that perhaps, we'd got all your papers out of order; so we set to work to sort them out . . . and I am afraid that we just could not help reading . . . Oh, Miss Newcombe, is the Lady Ariadne really going to elope with Sir Percival?"

"And what about Sir Percival's duel with Lord Dunsany?" asked an anxious Reginald.

Malvina blushed. "We know we shouldn't have —

but we asked Martha to take another peek when she was dusting in your room. And she said she tried, but it did not look as if you had written much more. And that anyway, she did not have time to read as she could hear someone coming down the hall.

"We're sorry, Miss Newcombe, we really are. It was just that we were so interested . . . and we were scared to tell you, because we thought you might be offended!"

"My dear, you have just said the magic word. All writers like to know that their work is interesting. And of course, I understand how all of this came about. However, it was wrong of you to ask Martha to look again and wrong of her to do so. But I am glad you had the courage to tell me all about it. I am sure you are not likely to do such a thing again. Now off you go, both of you! I must get dressed!"

When, I asked myself as the children left the room, had Martha last "taken another peek" at my papers — and had she noticed a folded pink letter among them?

A busy morning followed by a busier afternoon. Four o'clock at last and some time for me to be by myself. Oh, the luxury of it — to be able to sit and think undisturbed in my own room! Even with all the turmoil, I thought, the doubts, the fear, I would still far rather be "my own woman" in Wanganui, New Zealand, than be in that awful rectory in Manchester, at the beck and call of my Aunt Alice and (I shuddered) the Reverend Mr. Pugh!

A knock at my door.

I could scarcely restrain a laugh—so much for solitude!

The knock was so soft and hesitant, I decided that it must be Malvina. It turned out to be Martha, her whey face tinged with pink along the high cheekbones.

I had often read the phrase that someone was "wringing his—or her—hands" but had never actually seen this action. Martha was wringing her hands, in her apron.

"Oh, Miss . . ."

"Now, now, Martha, I know what you must have come about! And do stop that, you are going to ruin your apron!"

"Oh, Miss Newcombe, I didn't think. I mean, I never . . . and when the children told me you knew . . ."

"It really doesn't matter, Martha. I can quite see how it all came about."

"Well, yes, it *were* an accident, see! But I should never have let them make me look again . . . and among your private papers . . . though I didn't think of that at the time. And to be honest, Miss, they really didn't *make* me do it. I just wanted to find out whether . . ." an embarrassed look and a rare shy smile.

"Yes?"

"I know it's silly, but I just had to find out whether or not Lady Ariadne was . . ."

"Going to elope with Sir Percival?"

Her face lit up expectantly. "Yes!"

"Oh, I *hope* not! Sir Percival is such a nincompoop!"

286

Total outrage. "How can you say such a thing, Miss! Sir Percival is . . ." She hesitated and gave me a doubtful look. "What do you mean, 'you hope not'? Don't you know? I mean you're the one who's making up the story!"

"Well, yes, but . . ." I gave up trying to explain. "But, in any event, I cannot go on with it at the moment, I seem to have mislaid my folder. Are you sure you put it back on the shelf?"

"Oh, yes, Miss! I was just going through your papers, trying to find what you had written last and I heard someone in the hall, so I put the folder back right away."

"And this was . . ."

"On Monday morning, Miss, when I was dusting your room."

I took pity on the anxious face. "Oh, that accounts for it, then, for I did not miss my folder till afterward."

Utter relief on the pale face. "Oh, I'm glad! That is, I'm sorry you've mislaid your papers, but . . ."

"I understand! Perhaps, you might ask the others if they have seen it? I am sure it will turn up somewhere."

I waited as she turned to go. "Just one more thing, Martha—I am becoming so absentminded—but do you recall seeing a *pink* paper in the folder. I seem to have lost that, also!"

She stood a moment in thought. "No, I'm pretty sure I didn't—and I would have noticed it, wouldn't I—a pink paper in amongst the white ones?"

My folder, I thought, would have to be hidden!

"O what a tangled web we weave,
When first we practice to deceive."

One of Aunt Alice's favorite quotations — usually directed toward myself, when she had found some forbidden book concealed in my room! I had to admit grudgingly that in this case, she — or rather Sir Walter Scott — was right.

I hated the stories, or rather, *lies* (at least be honest to yourself, Harriet, I told myself!) I found myself telling. But at that time, I could not see what else to do! My folder, for instance, had to be hidden to give credence to my story. What if the person who had taken the letter decided to search my room to check what I had said? For that reason, I should have to hide my papers in some room other than my own — in some place where they could easily be "found."

I thought for a moment. Not in the school room, as obviously if I had really mislaid my novel, that would have been the first place for me to check. The drawing room? A possibility — I had spent a little time there by myself on Monday morning, looking through the bookcases. However . . . of course, I thought suddenly, the sunporch!

I should have thought of it before, I chided myself. It was a long narrow room on the first floor that stretched almost the entire length of the back of the house. With large windows designed to catch the winter sun, it was strictly informal and furnished

288

mainly with bamboo couches and wicker chairs. It was used by the family mainly in the mornings after breakfast.

At such a late hour—I glanced at my clock, half past four—it was almost bound to be empty.

No sooner thought than done! I swathed myself in my black crocheted shawl and concealed beneath it my papers—and as an afterthought, some corrected exercises of the children's. I would take the back stairs, I decided. Feeling slightly foolish, I quietly opened my door.

"Ah, there you are, my dear Miss Newcombe!"

I found myself under the full scrutiny of Mrs. Mannering's pebble glasses.

"You naughty girl, where have you been hiding yourself! We have to meet—*I insist*—for our 'campaign,' you know! Dear Euphemia, Mrs. Smythe, is quite taken with you, *I am convinced!* In fact, when I met her quite by chance at the Emporium just this afternoon, she told me, indeed *insisted* that I bring you along to her 'at home' tomorrow afternoon! There now!"

She paused at last and peered past me into my room.

I gave up. "Perhaps, you would like to . . . ?"

"I should love to—however," she indicated Ishbel's open door at the other end of the hall, "Ishbel and the dressmaker are waiting for me. Great decisions have to be made, you know!"

I sighed with relief.

"However, perhaps later . . ."

"I am afraid that I . . ."

"But now I come to think of it, I am engaged. Cousin Marcus wishes to meet with me in the parlor to discuss the ball and poor dear . . ." She clasped a hand to her mouth. "Goodness gracious, how I do run on! However, what I meant to say first . . . but then, my mind went quite astray . . . was that Alfred Smythe is, I am *sure,* quite *smitten* and that if you . . . well, of course, I must admit that he has a *slight* problem . . . but I am sure that the *right* young woman would bring him about. Which is why dear Euphemia . . . but I really must go."

With a bustle of her black skirts, she sped up the hall. At Ishbel's door she turned, and I was aware of her watching me as I made my way to the back stairs.

To my relief—and surprise, for that matter, considering how my afternoon had passed—the sunporch was quite empty. Quickly, I stowed my novel on the under-shelf of an occasional table situated by a bamboo chaise lounge in the far corner, and for good measure arranged the children's corrected exercises on the table top.

I was turning to go when I heard footsteps. I hurried to the door. Emerging from the well of the first-floor landing, was Gideon Tavish. I had not seen him, or rather his galoshes, since the day before and considering what I now knew about him, I had no desire to see him. Luckily, my black shawl merged with the shadows in the dark hall and he did not discern my presence. Thankfully, I slipped off down the backstairs.

As I was so near the kitchen, I decided to visit Mrs. Hargreaves to arrange some cooking lessons for Malvina. As I walked along the passage, I thought briefly about Hargreaves and his role in my adventure of the night before. On reflection I decided that he probably helped Callum with the accounts of the town house. After all, he had been making notations in the ledger and there had been nothing stealthy about his actions. It was the role of the Master of Ravenswood that intrigued me. What had he been doing at that time of night out in the storm?

"Drown them!"

I came to myself with a start. So immersed had I been with my thoughts, that I had not realized that I was almost at the open kitchen door.

"Drown them, I say! There's nothing else for it!" The voice belonged to Mrs. Hargreaves and Hargreaves made his usual expressive reply.

"And *you* will do it . . . you hear me!"

"Argh!"

I could not believe what I was hearing. I approached the door softly and peered round.

"I certainly don't have the heart for it. Poor innocent little things!"

Mrs. Hargreaves was standing at a marble-topped table, apparently making pastry. Hargreaves was seated to one side, immersed in the pages of *The Yeoman*. On the floor near his feet was a basket containing a large tabby cat and a squirming heap of kittens.

"Excuse me!"

Mrs. Hargreaves turned her sour face toward me.

"I had wanted to arrange for those cooking lessons we talked about earlier, Mrs. Hargreaves, but I could not help overhearing your conversation."

A loud sniff from Mrs. Hargreaves. Hargreaves ignored me.

I tried again. "I suppose you are referring to those kittens. What a shame . . . can't you give them away?"

Another sniff as she gave her pastry a thump and turned it over. "You think I *want* to drown them! I've given away as many as I can. They're not easy to get rid of, kittens!"

She seized her rolling pin and whacked the pastry. Hargreaves looked at me contemptuously over the top of his newspaper.

"How many do you have left?"

Another thud as the pastry was turned again. "Two."

"Well, that's wonderful! Why don't I take them for Malvina and Reginald?"

The pastry was again attacked by the rolling pin. I tried to keep a pleasant smile on my face.

At last her slit of a mouth opened to reply. "That's as maybe!"

"Excuse me?"

"That's as maybe! You'll have to ask Mrs. Douglas!"

"Well, it's not worth sending all the way to Ravensfall to ask about two kittens! I am sure Mrs. Douglas will not object. Ravensfall, I am quite sure, is large enough to accommodate a herd of elephants, never mind two kittens!"

The pastry was given a final thump and then

wrapped in cheese cloth. The sour face turned toward me. "I'm telling you, Mrs. Douglas won't have them — kittens nor puppies neither."

"But, why not?"

A long silence as the pastry was transported to the pantry.

She returned at last, wiping her hands on her apron, while I tried to keep my temper.

"Malvina had a kitten once. It was found hanging . . . by its tail. It was dead."

Hargreaves lowered his paper and smiled.

Thursday evening at last. But now that I was seated alone by my fire, I kept seeing in my mind's eye the poor little hanging kitten, described by Mrs. Hargreaves. I was relieved when there was a knock at my door and a smiling Jenny entered, my pink watered taffeta draped over one arm.

"You're going to look lovely, Miss! I just want you to try it on one more time before Saturday . . . just to make sure!" My blue serge was whipped over my head and replaced by the ball gown.

Jenny stood back, eyeing me critically. "It fits perfect . . . absolutely perfect!"

"It's beautiful, Jenny! I wish I were as clever as you with my fingers. But don't you think it's a little low?" I looked dubiously in the glass at my neckline.

She shook her head and smiled. "Not on your life! Low necklines are all the rage for evening wear. Besides, you're not so much showing as hinting!"

"Jenny!"

"Well, you've got a good figure! No sense hiding it, is there? That dusky shade of pink really compliments your complexion," she added, twitching the puff sleeves and straightening the bodice. "Miss Ishbel has a cheval glass in her room. Let's go along there right now so you can see how pretty you look!"

"Perhaps, if she is in her room . . ."

"Oh, she is . . . with Mrs. Mannering. They're looking over her jewelry for the ball."

Ishbel and Mrs. Mannering were seated by an occasional table examining the contents of Ishbel's jewelry box.

"Tah-rah!" exclaimed Jenny from the doorway to announce my grand entrance.

"My dear! How charming . . ." Mrs. Mannering rushed into her usual spate of words, while Ishbel, her eyes widening for a moment, remained silent. Of course, as I told myself, with Mrs. Mannering present, she really did not have much choice!

Mrs. Mannering at last relapsed into a semi-silence made up of little sighs and appreciative murmurs at Jenny's handiwork. I studied myself in the glass and glanced over my shoulder at Ishbel. She was looking at me frowningly.

"You don't like my gown, Ishbel?"

The pretty lips pouted into a smile. "Of course, dear Miss Newcombe. That color is very becoming!" She turned to Jenny. "How clever you are! But don't you think that neckline is a little low?"

Jenny pinched my arm to keep me quiet. "Not at all, Miss . . . not for evening!" She turned me round, adjusting the silver lace of one of the frills. "But what's all this about you being a writer, Miss?"

If Jenny had wanted to change the subject and take attention away from my neckline, she succeeded.

Exclamations from Mrs. Mannering. A thoughtful look from Ishbel. "So that's why I always see you writing! My dear Miss Newcombe, how exciting!"

"You naughty girl—not to have told us, before!" Mrs. Mannering gushed. "Just think how dearest Euphemia will be impressed. And just what are you writing?"

"A book," I answered, while I could get a word in. Was it my imagination, were the pale blue eyes behind the glasses suddenly watchful? I wondered whether or not Marcus Raven had told her already about my papers and if she were testing me. For good measure, I added, "Unfortunately, I have mislaid my folder with my papers in it, sometime on Monday, I think! And it's the oddest thing . . . I would have told you before . . . but with mislaying my papers, I had quite forgot!"

Deliberately, I turned back to the glass, pretending to adjust my neckline. That Mrs. Mannering had managed to remain silent so long, was in itself, interesting!

"Forgot what?" asked Ishbel, interested.

"As I said, it's the oddest thing . . . but as I was going through the books in my room, looking for something to read," I stopped to adjust my hair, while looking at Mrs. Mannering's face reflected in the glass. "I came across an old letter that I believed must have belonged to Miss Inglewood!"

"Miss Inglewood?" Was Mrs. Mannering's start of

surprise real or pretended? Her tone of voice was certainly rather dramatic, I thought. Unfortunately, she turned her head slightly and her spectacles reflecting the glow from the lamp disguised the expression in her eyes. Did she know I was watching her reaction through the glass?

In contrast Ishbel, though obviously interested, was more restrained. "What did the letter say?" she asked.

I turned back to her. "That's what's frustrating! You see, I did not have the time to read it. There was a knock on my door and I put it with my papers, intending to read it later." I paused and smiled. "In fact, you, my dear Ishbel, were the culprit! Or rather, Mrs. Mannering!"

"Me, the culprit!" There was a distinct quaver in Mrs. Mannering's voice. She leaned forward in her chair.

I smiled sweetly. "Yes, of course, because you were the kind friend who suggested to Ishbel that she lend me her necklet and earrings! And I was so excited about her generous offer that I forgot all about the letter!"

Twenty-seven

Never had I seen Ishbel look more exquisite! She stood gracefully in front of her cheval glass while Jenny and Martha checked her over carefully.

"You look lovely, Miss!" Martha sighed admiringly, her plain little face lacking any sign of envy for the splendor of her employer's beautiful stepdaughter. "You were right to choose the lilac sarsenet, it compliments your hair. And that white tulle overdress makes it all filmylike. You look," she continued hesitantly, "like a fairy that's just stepped out of the mist!"

A muffled snort from Jenny. She stood back and observed Ishbel critically from head to foot. "Aye," she said, reverting to her native Lancashire dialect, "Ye'll do!" She adjusted a rosette of dark lilac-colored ribbons on Ishbel's left shoulder and pulled forward a lock of her shining, auburn hair.

"The amethyst and pearl earrings, Jenny?" Mrs. Mannering asked anxiously.

"Yes. And the bracelet." Jenny surveyed Ishbel judiciously. "But not the choker—a single strand of pearls only!"

A sigh from Mrs. Mannering. "You are right, of course!"

The single strand was duly secured about Ishbel's long slender neck.

Jenny turned her eyes toward Mrs. Mannering. "Now, you, Madam!"

"Me!"

"Yes. Too much jet!"

"Too much?"

"Entirely too much!" Jenny signalled Martha. "Miss Ishbel's evening cloak!"

The cloak was produced — black velvet lined with swansdown — and Ishbel was duly enshrouded.

Jenny nodded her head toward the door. "Martha, give Miss Ishbel her chatelaine and make sure it contains a vial of rosewater and a fresh handkerchief. Then take her down to the drawing room to wait for Mr. Raven." She looked at Ishbel, "and you, Miss, make sure you sit still while you're waiting — I don't want those skirts crushed!"

Martha gave Ishbel her chatelaine and both she and Ishbel left.

Jenny studied Mrs. Mannering again. "Yes, too much jet. And that cap will have to go!"

"But it's my *best* cap, Jenny, that I bought in London."

Mrs. Mannering was no match for Jenny. She was seated at her dressing table and de-capped within seconds.

"Now, Miss Newcombe, seeing as Martha is downstairs, would you mind helping me, please?"

I wondered with a private grin, what would have

happened if I had declined. "Of course, Jenny!"

"Thank you. In that drawer over there you'll find a cap of Brussels lace. If you wouldn't mind looking for it, I'll go about removing some of this jet!"

"But it's my best Whitby jet, Jenny!"

"I know, Madam," Jenny whipped off two of the many necklaces dangling from Mrs. Mannering's plump neck. "There now, that's better!" Taking up a long-tailed comb, she began to fluff up Mrs. Mannering's soft white curls.

"Thank you, Miss!" She took the simple cap of fine Brussels lace that I handed to her and, arranging its thin black satin streamers into a bow, set it on top of Mrs. Mannering's head.

A gratified Mrs. Mannering peered at herself in the glass and nodded. "You were quite right, Jenny! The other cap was too . . . too . . ."

"Fussy, Madam. Also, the lace of this cap compliments the lace about your collar."

She turned to me. "Now, Miss, if you would please hand me that black cashmere shawl, I believe Mrs. Mannering will be ready to join Miss Ishbel in the drawing room. And then I shall have time to attend to *your* hair!"

In no time, Mrs. Mannering was enveloped in the shawl and bundled through the door.

"Jenny, how do you manage it!"

An innocent grin. "Manage what?"

"You know perfectly well what I am talking about! Manage to get them all to do what you want without any fuss. And most of all, manage to keep that woman from talking!"

"Oh! There's nothing to it. It's . . . it's like being a

299

dog managing a flock of sheep. You ignore all the baaing and nip at their heels till they do what you want! Now, sit down, do . . . or I won't be able to get your hair done in time!"

Quickly my hair was brushed back and up, and then arranged into a fall of soft ringlets that were allowed to cascade from the top of my head down to my pink taffeta shoulders. A silver ribbon was threaded through my topknot and Ishbel's silver and seed pearl earrings and necklace were put in place.

"Jenny, you have wrought another miracle! And Ishbel's jewelry just gives that extra finishing touch. How kind it was of her to lend it to me!"

A sniff.

Startled, I looked at the face behind me in the glass. "Why, Jenny, what is it?"

"That one, *kind?* Never!"

"But she did lend me . . ."

"It was Mrs. Mannering who told her to make the offer." She grinned wickedly. "After I put the idea in her head!"

"Jenny! So I have *you* to thank! But I don't understand why you should feel that way about Ishbel. She is always perfectly obliging."

Another sniff. She was beginning to sound like Mrs. Hargreaves. "Always obliging, yes—when it suits her! But not *kind.* When Miss Ishbel does anything, it's always for her own ends."

"How can you say such a thing?"

"Think, Miss! Does she ever go out of her way to do anything for anyone? Think of Malvina and Reginald—poor little soul—and their loving ways. Now *those* two are loving and kind . . . always pleasant and

300

helpful and *warm*." She paused a moment to smooth a last ringlet and arrange kiss curls in front of each ear. "I grant you she's always laughing . . . but it's my belief it's just for effect."

"What do you mean?"

"Look at her eyes, the next time she laughs . . . and you'll see that they're watching you."

The Glenby's house was situated at the top of a long sloping lawn on upper Victoria Avenue. It was large and rambling, not unlike a smaller Ravensfall without the cupola. The "ballroom" which turned out to be three interconnecting rooms with folding doors in between, overlooked the back lawn which, in its turn, sloped down into what in the lamplit darkness appeared to be a small wood.

"Orchard, my dear Miss Newcombe!"

The voice belonged to the son of the house, an amiable fair-haired young man with watery blue eyes. He was examining my dance program, while we stood by French windows that opened onto a terrace and an urn-bedecked balustrade, its stone steps connecting the house and lawn.

"There are so many of us, that Father tries to provide for all our needs in any way he can!"

"So many?"

"I have nine sisters!"

"I see!"

He grinned at me impishly. "Have you read *Pride and Prejudice?*"

. "Certainly!"

"So, now, you see the reason for this ball!"

"You mean?" I could barely restrain a laugh, "that your parents are hoping that your sisters will all meet suitable young men and therefore . . ."

Another grin. "Be married off! Believe me, this is a carefully orchestrated campaign! Of course, only four of my sisters are 'out.' Three are at school and two are still in the nursery . . . so, it could be worse. But, oh dear—here's Mother on the warpath! Perhaps I could have this polka?" He quickly scribbled his name in my program.

"Jeremy!"

A small, brown-haired birdlike woman approached us. "Jeremy . . . oh, excuse me, Miss . . . er . . ." Her bright brown eyes examined my ensemble. Was she worried about any possible competition I might provide for her daughters, I wondered, restraining a smile.

"Miss Newcombe, Mother!"

The brow cleared. "Of course, how stupid of me! You are Miss McCleod's companion, are you not?" She looked consideringly at her son. Her thoughts were almost palpable—eligible son, unmarried heiress! "I trust that Miss McCleod . . ."

The weak blue eyes directed a humorous glance at me. "Miss McCleod, I assure you, Mother, is well taken care of!"

We all directed our gaze toward a laughing Ishbel fending off a covey of young men, all intent on engaging her attentions.

The belle of the ball, I thought fondly. How glad I was that Marcus Raven, whatever his true intent, had allowed her to "try her wings."

"And you have . . . ?"

"Engaged Miss McCleod for a schottische, Mother."

Mrs. Glenby sighed—thankfully, it seemed to me. "Good . . . good." Then remembering her duties as a hostess, she turned to me.

"A polka, Mother!" Jeremy Glenby answered, without waiting for the question.

A bright smile, followed by a look of steel. "Good! Now, however, you must attend to your sisters. Annabelle still has three dances unbespoke and poor Dora . . ."

"I shall take care of it, Mother. Trust me!"

Doubtfully, Mrs. Glenby watched her son depart. "Such a good boy," she murmured, "it's just . . ." She glanced at me and pulled herself together with an obvious effort. I was, after all, companion to the heiress! "Jeremy is so responsible," she chirped. "Always so caring for his sisters! However, enough of my family . . ." She looked about the room. "I wonder if you have met—"

"Dearest Miss Newcombe. Mrs. Glenby, my apologies for my interruption!"

Before us, stood the "best catch in Wanganui."

I stifled a groan and forced a smile.

In the background, the small orchestra—five serious young men armed with a piano and various stringed instruments—had started up the first strains of a quadrille.

A white-gloved hand was raised to the fair moustaches—now carefully waxed. "My dance, I believe!"

I gave in gracefully.

I did not know any of the three other couples making up our "set." However, in the set adjoining, I noted Marcus Raven leading out a glowing Ishbel.

At a pause in the music, Ishbel's laugh rang out and I looked over at her as she gazed up at her stepfather. How could Jenny have made such a judgment, I wondered, about Ishbel's eyes? As they looked up at Mr. Raven, they shone as if they were on fire.

A fifteen minute interval had been allowed to enable the orchestra to take a well-deserved refreshment break. I withdrew quietly from the chattering group of young people I had become a part of and made my way over to an alcove beside some French windows. Jenny would be pleased when she saw my program, I thought. It was completely full! I had never danced so much in my life. I needed a few minutes to "catch up" with myself.

It was not to be! No sooner was I safely in my alcove, then I found myself being approached by a hesitant Jeremy Glenby.

"I say, Miss Newcombe, you seem a capital sort of a person — someone a fellow can trust!"

Restraining a smile, I looked up at the earnest blue eyes. "What can I do for you?"

He had the grace to flush. "Don't quite know how to put it! But the fact is . . . I am in love!"

"My goodness, but we have only just met — how *very* flattering!"

The flush deepened. "That is to say —" He gulped. "What *can* I say —"

I took pity on him. "I was just teasing you! You don't need to say anything!" I followed his glance toward a certain sprightly young lady who appeared to be studying with enormous interest a nearby display of spring flowers.

"Phoebe Jones . . . Isn't she pretty?"

I looked at the dark curls and saucy tilted nose and had to agree that she was. "Indeed, yes! And your mother does not approve?"

"No. Phoebe has to work for her living, you see. She's an assistant in Miss Clark's millinery establishment. Mother feels that I can do—But how did *you* know about Mother?"

"I have a sixth sense! And that, of course, is why Ishbel was invited to the ball. Another part of your mother's 'campaign'?"

A gloomy look. "I expect so. Of course, Miss McCleod is as beautiful . . . as . . . as a goddess! But I had met Phoebe already—got to know her quite well, in fact, despite Mother—and I feel so very comfortable with her!"

"Mr. Glenby, you do not need to apologize! I understand perfectly! I am, as it happens, the object of a concerted 'campaign' myself!"

The blue eyes twinkled and peered short-sightedly past me to where Alfred Smythe, a wine glass in his hand, had been detained by Mrs. Mannering.

It was my turn to be surprised. "How did you know?"

Another mischievous grin. "Absolutely nothing escapes Mother—and Wanganui is a small place, you know! However . . ." He looked at me inquiringly, his glance flickering between me and Alfred Smythe. "You mean you are averse to . . ."

"Quite definitely averse!"

"But that's capital!"

"Excuse me?"

He bit his lip apologetically. "It's Mother again, you see!"

Light dawned and I could not restrain a laugh. "Oh, you mean, she would like . . ."

He laughed, then gave me a rueful look. "You are quite right! Mother was hoping to . . . er . . . *obtain* Mr. Smythe for Eloise!"

"Poor Eloise!" I exclaimed before I could help myself. "Oh, please excuse me." I blushed in my turn. "But—" I paused delicately, not quite sure what to say.

"Please, Miss Newcombe. There is no need for embarrassment! Mother is quite aware of Mr. Smythe's—weakness. But she is determined that the . . . er . . ."

"Right young woman will bring him about? But what does Eloise think?"

"Eloise? Oh, spare no pity for Eloise; she's an idiot! She and Alfred Smythe should deal very well together! However . . ."

"However, you wished a favor from me, I believe? Could it have to do with that polka we are engaged for? Do you know, Mr. Glenby, that I have danced so much this evening that I feel quite exhausted. Do you think that we could sit this one out—perhaps," I glanced at the open French doors behind me, "we could chat a moment or so outside. It has become quite warm in here, I do declare!"

Jeremy Glenby laughed ruefully, then gave me an admiring look. "How splendid you are! You see Phoebe and I have danced twice together and . . ." He looked ruefully at the chaperones on the daïs at one end of the room, "Our dancing again would be remarked! However, we did not wish to leave you

306

partnerless and a friend of mine—"

I laughed up at him. "No, please! I meant it, when I said I was exhausted! Why don't you introduce me to Miss Jones and for the benefit of the chaperones, we will, all three of us, go out onto the terrace together. But please be quick!" I nodded toward Alfred Smythe, who having escaped from Mrs. Mannering, was headed determinedly my way.

We were outside in a thrice, and leaving the grateful lovebirds together, I discreetly re-entered the room by another set of French windows.

The interval was over and the orchestra was busily tuning up for the polka. Alfred Smythe, I noted with relief, was partnered with a brown-haired girl, who, from her likeness to Mrs. Glenby, I took to be one of the four marriageable daughters. I wondered with a giggle, if she was the idiotic Eloise!

I looked around for the Ravensfall party. I soon distinguished Mr. Raven's tall sombre figure bent over Mrs. Mannering's chair at the side of the room. Ishbel, however, was nowhere to be seen. She was probably in the ladies' cloakroom, I thought. Perhaps, like myself, she was in need of a rest! As far as I had observed, (for of course, I had been somewhat occupied with my own activities!) Ishbel had not only had a partner for every dance, but in between times had always been surrounded by admiring young men. In other words, she had enjoyed tremendous success and I was very pleased for her!

Across the hall from the ballroom, in a room set aside for cards, were tables providing light refreshments to sustain the guests until supper was served. I decided to relieve my thirst with a glass of lemonade.

Like the ballroom, the cardroom was decorated with bowls of early spring flowers and temporary arches entwined with ivy and other trailing, green plants brought in from the outside.

Some of the arches had been arranged to form little booths that gave a sort of semi-privacy to those who wished to disport themselves at the encircled tables.

Piling a plate with some small ham and egg savories, a deviled egg, and a slice of rich dark fruitcake, I daringly had the attending maid pour me a glass of claret cup, instead of the lemonade I had originally intended to ask for. Why should I not indulge myself for once, I thought, as I gazed about the room looking for a quiet place where I could sit comfortably and eat undisturbed.

I finally decided on an empty booth, not too far from the refreshment table. With a sigh of relief, I deposited my plate and glass on the card table inside the booth and sank down on a chair at the back. I had not realized how tired my feet were! I raised my glass to my lips.

"So you're the filly!"

"Excuse me?"

"Alfred's intended!"

I choked as I sipped my wine. "What?"

Before me stood perhaps the oldest person I have ever encountered; an ancient gentleman with silver slicked-back hair, twirled (I swear!) silver mustachios and amidst the wrinkles, extraordinarily shrewd, bright blue eyes twinkled.

"Alfred's intended," reaffirmed this vision.

I put down my glass. "If sir, you are referring to Mr. Alfred Smythe, I do not believe that he has as yet asked for my hand in marriage!"

A bark of a laugh. "Hoity-toity!" The voice was gravelly with age, but appreciative. "Euphemia was right — got a spark to you!"

"What!"

"Euphemia. My daughter, y' know! Alfred's mother!"

"Of course! You must be Sir Albert Spencer . . ."

"Alfred's grandfather! Quick thinker, ain't you!" He winked at me. "Mind if I sit down?" He lifted his coat tails expertly and sat before I could answer, on the chair next to me. He observed my heaped plate. "Like a gel with a good appetite — healthy! Yes, Euphemia was right. She usually is. Good gel, Euphemia! I said he should try for the heiress and she said she lacks bottom . . . too highly strung y'know. She'd blow away in a breath of wind. Now, *you*, you've got good lines . . ."

I decided to interrupt this extraordinary monologue before it got completely out of hand.

"Sir Albert, I believe you are under a misapprehension! I am *not* going to marry your grandson!"

"Eh? What's that? Why not? He's rich, ain't he?"

"That has nothing to do with it!"

A shrewd look from the bright old eyes. "I know what worries you — but the right gel will . . ."

"Bring him about." I finished. "No thank you. Find another 'gel.' How about —" I thought frantically, "Miss Eloise Glenby?"

"She's an idiot! Wouldn't do, you know, with Alfred an idiot as well. Think of the children!"

I thought and shuddered. An inspiration came to me. "Miss Dora Glenby?"

He looked at me admiringly. "Ye've a good head on you! I'll say that! Ye're right, of course—*she'd* make him walk the straight and narrow—but he'd do better with you! What about it, eh?"

I sighed. "Sir Albert, I will *not* marry your grandson!"

"But, why not?"

I gave up. "I do not like him!" I took a sip of claret to fortify myself.

"Good God, m'dear, neither do I, but what's that to the purpose!"

He edged closer and before I was aware of what he was about, laid one hand on my shoulder, and the other on my knee. "Now, look'ee here, m'dear . . ."

"Miss Newcombe!"

Towering over us was Marcus Raven. His pale eyes, icy with disapproval, noted first my wine glass and then Sir Albert's intimacy.

I shrivelled; then, with an effort, rallied. Putting down my glass and edging away from my companion, I gazed coolly up at my employer. "Mr. Raven, I should like to introduce Sir Albert Spencer. Sir Albert, this is Mr. Marcus Raven, my employer!" I turned what I hoped was a limpid look up at Mr. Raven. "Sir Albert was just . . . er . . . talking to me about his grandson!"

I could have sworn that the stern lips above me almost relaxed into a smile. But I must have imagined it, for the baritone when next it issued, was deadly cold. "Sir Albert. How do you do?" The sombre glance was next turned on me. "Miss Newcombe, I wonder if you could spare a few moments?"

Sir Albert, who had been watching this exchange with lively interest gave another bark of laughter, and as I was trying to rise, dug me suddenly in the ribs, almost causing me to lose my balance. "So that's the way of it, is it?"

It is of course, entirely improper for a lady to lose her temper, the more especially in public — but I Had Had Enough! "I would thank you, Sir," I hissed at Sir Albert, "to keep your hands to yourself!" With as much dignity as I could muster, I struggled around the table. "And you, Sir," I glared up at the Master of Ravensfall, "will please escort me from this room!"

An arm was presented. "That had been my intention, Miss Newcombe!" I looked up at him suspiciously, but could discern no sign of amusement.

Another bark of laughter. "Got the bit between her teeth, has she? You'll have to keep *her* on a tight rein, my boy!"

"I shall not, Miss Newcombe, ask you how it was that, completely unchaperoned, you were drinking wine in the company of an elderly rake. I am quite sure, that given the opportunity, you would provide me with an answer both marvelously detailed and ingenious in its logic!"

Out in the hall, Marcus Raven glared down at me; his eyes pale ice. "I have only two questions to ask, Miss Newcombe," he continued with terrifying polite-ness, "both pertaining to certain instructions that I gave you recently. The first question is, 'Where is Ishbel?' and the second is, 'Why are you not with

311

her?' "

"Ishbel!" I had completely forgotten about her—but of course, could hardly admit as much. "I . . . er . . . believe she is in the ladies' cloakroom."

"You *believe?* You mean you don't *know!* Miss Newcombe, you do recall the terms of your employment! You do understand the primary reason you are here tonight?"

The baritone was cutting and I hung my head, blinking back the tears. He was, of course, quite right. Whatever his reasons—whether sinister or not—for keeping such a close watch on Ishbel, I had been employed as her chaperone and had neglected my duties!

An impatient sigh and a firm finger was inserted under my chin. My face was raised and dabbed at expertly by a fine cambrick handerkerchief. "Do you think, Miss Newcombe, you could possible enter the ladies' room and see if perhaps Ishbel is there?"

Ishbel was not there.

In the ballroom the polka had concluded and the musicians were relaxing a moment before starting up for the next dance. Ishbel was nowhere to be seen—and neither, I suddenly realized, was Jonathan Turner. Biting my lip, I looked up at Mr. Raven. To my surprise, the expression on his face was not so much angry as anxious.

He looked toward the French windows. "I believe we should try the terrace." Taking my hand, he led me quickly through the chatting groups across the dance floor.

The terrace glowed in the uncertain light of the string of Chinese lanterns. My lovebirds, I noted fleetingly, were still in one dark corner, their heads too close together for propriety. From the other corner, Ishbel's laugh rang out.

A non-committal grunt from Mr. Raven. He started forward. So did I. As my hand was still firmly held, I had no choice.

"And, so you see, that is the reason why he wears his belt! Look up there—at those three bright stars ... Oh, Mr. Raven and ... er ... Miss Newcombe! I'm afraid, I did not hear your approach!" Jonathan Turner's tenor spoke out apologetically.

"Dearest Step-Papa! Mr. Turner was telling me all about the constellations of the stars and of Orion, in particular!" Ishbel's voice, musical as always, pleaded.

"How interesting!" Marcus Raven's voice was non-committal. "However, I do believe the next dance is about to begin!"

"I'm sorry, Mr. Raven!" Jonathan Turner was quick to apologize. "I had not realized that we had been out here so long! Time spent in Miss Ishbel's company always passes so quickly." Taking Ishbel's arm, he guided her toward the French window.

Ishbel turned back a moment, the light from the ballroom playing about her red-gold hair and sifting through the delicate tulle of her overdress. "Don't forget, Step-Papa," she pleaded prettily looking from Mr. Raven to me and then back to him again, "that you are to dance the Lancers with me!"

Marcus Raven abruptly released my hand that he was still holding and when he spoke, his voice was expressionless. "I have not forgotten!"

In the ballroom, the violins struck up a waltz and Ishbel with one last look at her stepfather, turned at last, and drifted inside.

"Come, Miss Newcombe, no doubt you have a partner waiting!"

Why was it, I wondered, that his mood seemed to change so swiftly? I remembered his almost tender gesture of only a few minutes before when he had dabbed at my tears; and I could still feel the grip of his hand upon mine; and now — as I had experienced in the kitchen at Ravensfall — a complete turn-about from a friendliness that was almost approachable to a stony complete withdrawal. Was it guilt, I asked myself, over his treatment of his stepdaughter? Were these mood changes further evidence of his sinister intentions?

We stood a moment at the French windows, watching the dancers, a laughing Ishbel among them, whirl by. She was partnered by a handsome young man, who was obviously not averse to her charms. A disconsolate Jonathan Turner stood alone nearby.

"Come now, Miss Newcombe," Marcus Raven's baritone broke into my thoughts. "Who is your partner for this dance? I'm quite sure," he added, with the glimmer of a smile, "that you *have* a partner. Except for the polka, I believe you have . . ."

At this moment, a disgruntled Jeremy Glenby with a flushed Phoebe Jones were ushered from the terrace by an irate chaperone. On seeing me, Jeremy's face lightened. "Thank you for being such a good sport," he murmured, grinning. Phoebe looked back at the terrace and giggled.

"Miss Newcombe, what have you been about!" Mr. Raven's voice was shocked, but there was an amused gleam in his topaz eyes. "As I was saying, I believe you have been partnered for . . ." he looked back at the terrace, "*every* dance; so there must be an anxious gentleman somewhere, wondering where you are. Come, my dear lackwit, is it not time that you looked at your program?"

I looked at my program. "You are quite right Mr. Raven, I do have a partner for this waltz and the gentleman concerned is close by!" In response to his raised brows, I added. "It is you, sir!"

"I . . . see." He stood a moment looking at the dancers.

"If you would rather sit this dance out, sir?"

"Not at all, Miss Newcombe. However, it is a trifle warm in here. Do you have any objections to dancing on the terrace?"

Without waiting for an answer, he seized me by the waist and waltzed me through the French windows.

Aunt Alice had never allowed me to waltz and now I understood why. "The close proximity of the sexes and the intimacy of a gentleman's hand about a lady's waist is apt to lead to Certain Feelings, my dear Harriet, which oftentimes result in behavior which is Most Improper!"

I hated to do so, but I was obliged to admit that Aunt Alice was right! I had danced all evening with good-looking—even handsome and charming gentlemen—but had never experienced this . . . warmth . . . this sudden tremulousness about my heart . . . a tremulousness that seemed to extend down my arms to the points of my fingertips as they nestled either in Marcus Raven's hand or against his shoulder. I was acutely conscious of the warmth of his white-gloved hand resting against my back . . .

I dared to look up and was lost. The lights of the colored lanterns, the stars above and the topaz eyes of my partner seemed to merge into one vast whirling kaleidoscope.

"Miss Newcombe, you are unwell?"

The music had stopped and I found myself resting my head against a strong chest. "Oh, please excuse me!" I forced myself to raise my head from the chest, only to find myself supported by two strong arms.

"You are dizzy from the constant whirl of the dance, I expect!" The baritone lacked its usual ironic tone, was indeed, to my surprise, almost tender. "How beautifully you dance . . . as light as . . . as gossamer . . ."

There was a cough from the direction of the French doors. We found ourselves under the sour gaze of one of the chaperones. Nearby, an amused Jonathan Turner watched us thoughtfully.

"As light as gossamer" . . . the words kept recurring again and again in my head as I danced—with somewhat more decorum—throughout the rest of the evening. Why, I asked myself, should I feel so ridiculously happy at a compliment—and probably not an unusual compliment for a polite gentleman to pay to a lady—from my employer; a man who, I reminded myself sternly, was dangerous and not to be trusted!

I watched him now, as he led Ishbel through the last "figure" of the promised Lancers; sombre again, the other Marcus Raven, as I had come to think. Which was the true one, I wondered? Perhaps, they both were—like a kind of Doctor Jekyl and Mr. Hyde.

Even in the culminating "grand chain" when the distraught chaperones had to exert all their authority to maintain proper decorum, my employer managed to look as cheerful as the chief mourner at a funeral!

The dance was over at last, a ten minute interval was called. I noticed with amusement that Mr. Raven withdrew from the chatting throng to stand a silent, disapproving Jove against one wall.

"Dear . . . indeed . . ." A hiccup. ". . . Perhaps, I might even say . . . my *darling* Miss Newcombe!"

I groaned inwardly. A slightly swaying Alfred Smythe was standing before me, to claim his second dance of the evening.

"No, you may not!"

"What?"

"You may not," I answered, enunciating every word slowly and clearly, "call me darling — especially, *your* darling!"

"Oh, would that I might . . . dearest Miss New . . . no, away with all thish . . . for . . . form . . . for-mal-i-ty!" He glanced down at me, roguishly daring; white-gloved finger and thumb fingering his waxed mustache. "Dearest Miss *Harriet*, I wish you would . . ." he swayed toward me, "let me call you darling, esh . . . espec-i-a-ll-y *my* darling!"

One poke of my finger in his chest, I thought longingly and he would fall over backwards. With difficulty, I restrained myself.

"Perhaps," he continued, "you would care to take a walk on the terresh . . . ter-race? I have Something Speshel, I par-tic-u-lar-ly wish to say to you!"

"No."

"Oh, please, *darling* Miss Harriet, say that you

317

will!"

"No."

A sigh and a cunning look. "Grandfather approves of you, you know. And So Does Mother!"

"I am flattered."

"Grandfather shays . . . *says* that you are a girl of shpir . . . spirit and that you will bring me about!"

"I have no intentions of bringing you about," I was beginning, when the music started. My hands were seized and I found myself dancing the wildest polka of my life.

"Let me go!" I hissed, as, with a close shave we missed two other couples and danced straight into a wall.

"Only . . . only, my *darling* Harriet, if you will allow me to take you onto the terresh!"

I bowed to the inevitable. Perhaps, I thought, I would have more control over him outside. "Very well, if you would care to sit . . ."

My hands were grabbed again before I could finish the sentence.

"Darling, *darling* Harriet, let ush dance our way to happinesh!"

We rocketed right through the French doors and across the terrace. I saw the balustrade approaching. I saw the steps. I managed to pull my hands away at last, but unable to stop the momentum of our insane jig, I lost my balance, and catching my heel in a crack, toppled straight down the steps, cracking my head sharply at the bottom.

I lay in a state of semi-consciousness, vaguely aware of the throbbing pain in my head and of a rush of feet down the steps.

"Harriet!" a vaguely familiar baritone interrupted the pain, "you little demon! What scape have you got yourself into now? Harriet?"

A pause as my head was examined by skillful fingers. I was lifted gently and allowed the luxury of resting against a strong chest. "Oh, Harriet, what *are* you about?" The voice was soft, caressing even, and to my groggy astonishment, I felt what could have been a kiss on the top of my head.

I dragged my eyes open. I was, of course, in the arms of Marcus Raven. At the top of the steps, gazing down at us with a mixture of shocked horror and amusement were the other revellers, foremost among whom were Ishbel and Jonathan Turner.

Twenty-eight

A young man wobbled past on bicycle, as I hurried down Victoria Avenue trying to reach the post office before it closed.

"G'day, Miss Newcombe!"

The bicycle rocked precariously, as a bowler hat was raised and a hand waved at the same time.

"Mr. Glenby! Good afternoon!"

To my relief, he scrambled down from his bicycle and wheeling it along the pavement, fell into step beside me. "Mother says she met Mrs. Mannering at church yesterday and that the word was that you had quite recovered from your fall. Must say you're looking well!"

"Thank you!" I smiled up into the earnest face. The blue eyes were framed, I noticed, by round moon wire-rimmed glasses.

He noticed my glance and adjusted the spectacles self-consciously. "Mother won't let me wear these. Says they hide . . ." he grinned, "my best feature! But a fellow's got to see, you know!"

I studied him for a moment. "I'm afraid I do not agree with Mrs. Glenby! Your spectacles actually bring attention to your eyes—like picture frames, you know—and, if anything, give you an air of distinction!"

He chuckled, highly delighted. "That's what Fanny says! Says I'll impress my clients!"

"Fanny?"

"My favorite sister—my twin, actually—the only one of all my sisters who doesn't look like Mother; bunch of sparrows! You can't imagine what it's like at home sometimes!"

He put on a gloomy look and looked so comical, I burst out laughing. "Truly, Miss Newcombe. The place is like a bird house, twitter, twitter all day long! Except for Fanny." He sighed. "Poor girl is in love!"

"Poor girl? You mean, like her twin, her attentions are engaged by someone your mother considers unsuitable?"

"Oh, no. Nothing like that! In fact, Mother had high hopes—until he met the heiress!" He flushed. "I beg your pardon, Miss McCleod, I should say!"

"You mean that Fanny is in love with . . ."

He nodded gloomily. "Yes. Jonathan Turner!"

"Oh, poor Fanny! I am afraid that young man is completely infatuated with Ishbel!"

"Yes. It's Ishbel this and Ishbel that until a fellow's nearly driven out of his head!"

I laughed. "You know Mr. Turner well, then?"

"Yes. We went to Collegiate together—that's the boys' school up the Avenue—and now that I'm studying for the bar, Jon's father has taken me on." He

321

peered down at me through his spectacles. "There's not much hope for Fanny, is there?"

"Not at the moment, I'm afraid! Mr. Turner does seem to be a very serious young man."

He grinned. "Oh, he is! Once he has his mind set on something, there is no stopping him. In fact, he enjoys the challenge!"

I looked up at him, amused. "Does he consider Ishbel a challenge!"

"Not precisely . . . rather, her stepfather!"

I thought of Marcus Raven's lack of encouragement and was obliged to nod my head.

There was silence for a moment, as my companion looked down at me, quite obviously wondering whether or not to tell me something.

"What is it, Mr. Glenby?"

He swallowed. "Fact is, shouldn't be mentioning this. But, Miss McCleod told Jon you would all be returning to Ravensfall soon and so I thought . . . well . . . that if there really is some sort of danger, then you ought to know about it!" He took a deep breath and flushed.

I looked up at him, startled. "Danger?"

He nodded. "Dare say it will sound far-fetched, but when Mr. Raven's background is considered . . . you *do* know about the late Mrs. Raven and Mr. Raven's trial?"

"Yes."

A sigh of relief. "Good! That's what worried me you see—revealing a client's private affairs—but if you know about it, already! Jon's father handles Mr. Raven's New Zealand affairs, you see. And Jon being interested in Miss McCleod . . ."

"I understand. Please go on!"

Another deep breath. "Were you also aware that Miss McCleod's fortune, if she should die unmarried, would be inherited by her half-brother and half-sister—*and* that Mr. Raven would be in full control?"

"Yes, I knew that!" In answer to his inquiring look. "Mr. Douglas told me . . . Ishbel's cousin."

"Mr. Douglas . . . of course, Mr. Raven's manager. And Miss McCleod's cousin, you say—and surely, with her best interests at heart?"

I thought of the cold fury of those blue-green eyes. "She looks upon me as an elder brother," Callum Douglas had said, when I told him of my suspicions. "I would do anything in the world for her!"

I looked up at Jeremy Glenby. "Oh, yes. In a way, Callum and Ishbel are like brother and sister!"

He sighed with relief. "Then there is someone at Ravensfall you could go to if . . . ?"

"If what?"

He hesitated again. "This sounds so preposterous . . . but Jon believes that Mr. Raven means to get his hands on Ishbel's fortune. And you know, there is only one way he can do that!"

I thought of that way and shuddered.

We had reached Ridgway Street and now stood for a moment looking at the big white drinking fountain on the intersection. Had it really only been a week, I asked myself unbelievably, since Callum had made his revelations to me at almost the same spot?

"Why should Mr. Turner think such a thing?"

An embarrassed glance. "A lot of little things, really

323

. . . As I said, it all sounds so preposterous! And frankly, knowing Jon as I do and his bull-headedness when it comes to him obtaining what he wants, I wondered at first, if it were not all just wishful thinking on his part!"

I tried to maintain my patience. "What little things?"

He reached up a hand and adjusted his spectacles, then looked down at me, his blue eyes serious. "First of all, there has been a great deal of talk as to why Ishbel — such a beautiful young girl — should be kept so isolated at Ravensfall. And it was noted that when the family did come to Wanganui, that Mr. Raven or Mrs. Mannering was always present at any social function to which Ishbel was invited." He grinned suddenly. "Good heavens, Miss Newcombe, my mother is strict enough in such matters with my sisters, but she certainly allows them to attend alone any function that she knows is suitably chaperoned!"

I decided to play "Devil's Advocate." "Perhaps they are wary of fortune hunters?"

"Then why do they not make sure that she is introduced to suitable young men? Why keep her so *isolated?* And then there is the matter of Miss Inglewood!"

He looked thoughtfully down at my startled face. "Those suspicions are not all new to you, are they?"

"I have to admit, that I have wondered . . . But pray continue. What about Miss Inglewood?"

"At the Inquest her death was found to be accidental, but there were a number of stories at the time. One of the maids at Ravensfall put it about how terrified Miss Inglewood was . . . and of course," he stopped and grinned, "she also mentioned something about a *taniwha!*" Laughing, he shrugged his shoulders. "As for that . . .! However, the point is, that Miss Inglewood was afraid and that she was evidently running from something!"

"Why do you think she was afraid?"

He shook his head. "Who knows? Jon thinks she may have discovered some sinister plan or other to do with Miss McCleod and had foolishly allowed her suspicions to become known." He scratched his head and again adjusted his spectacles. "And then there's Miss McCleod herself and some of the remarks she has made to Jon."

"*Ishbel* suspects something?"

"Not precisely . . . that is, she has never said and of course, Jon could hardly . . ."

"What has Ishbel said?"

"For one thing, when Jon was sounding out her feelings toward him, she made the strangest remark . . . that she felt that Mr. Raven did not intend for her to marry . . . and then, at other times, she has hinted at . . ." He paused flushed. "This next is hardly suitable for your ears, Miss Newcombe!"

I answered with some asperity. "Then you should have thought of that before you started this conversation! Pray go on, do you want me to die of curiosity?"

He smiled apologetically. "I'm sorry! It's just that, Ishbel has hinted that Mr. Raven is apt to be . . . let us say . . . *overly fond* . . . of unsuitable ladies?"

"So?"

Another embarrassed look. "Such ladies, Miss

Newcombe, are usually expensive to maintain and if Mr. Raven had control over Miss McCleod's fortune . . . In the newspaper accounts, that Jon managed to obtain, money was the suggested motive for Mrs. Raven's murder." He looked at me anxiously. "As I said, it all sounds so preposterous. I do hope that I have not offended you . . ."

"Not at all. I know you mean well and as a matter of fact, I have been extremely worried because you see—"

"My dear Miss Harriet!" A familiar booming voice with its faint Scottish burr.

I had been about to tell Jeremy Glenby about the drops and my own worries about Ishbel. Now, looking up at Gideon Tavish's bearded smile, I could have screamed with frustration.

"But excuse me, I believe I am interrupting a conversation?" Mr. Tavish raised his hat and waited expectantly.

I gave in. "Mr. Jeremy Glenby, Mr. Gideon Tavish."

I looked warningly at Jeremy Glenby. "Mr. Tavish is a guest of Mr. Raven's. He has just come from Scotland."

"How do you do, sir! But what a pity you missed our ball! I am sure that if Mother had known you were a guest of Mr. Raven's she would have sent you an invitation. We are always eager to hear first hand news of 'home.' "

"Thank you. Mr. Raven did offer to procure me an invitation, but, having a great many personal papers to attend to—I am here to write a book about New Zealand birds, and have sadly neglected my duties—I

326

was obliged to decline! But dear Miss Harriet, I see you have a letter in your hand and I believe . . ." he looked at the clock in the post office tower, "that the post office is about to close! Do let me escort you across the road and afterwards I should be honored to walk with you back to Wicksteed Street!"

A shriek as Malvina, followed by Reginald, followed by a stick-waving Jim Parker fled through the hall past my room.

"Children, children!"

Jim Parker slid to a stop and grinned up at me. "Sorry Miss Newcombe. We're playing at pirates. And I'm Bully Hayes!"

"Bully Hayes?" the name seemed familiar to me. Where had I heard it before?

"Yes, Miss. My dad told me about him, he had a cousin sailed with him to Fiji. He used to ship guns to the Hauhaus—you know, during the Maori Wars."

"Your father's cousin used to ship guns!"

"No, Miss, Bully Hayes. And then when he left, he'd take the whisky."

"Whisky?"

"That my dad's cousin made—out in the bush." He studied my face a moment. "Look, Miss, I ain't funning. It's true! The tunnel's still there."

"Tunnel?"

"That led to the whisky still, Miss!"

"I see. Silly of me to ask!"

He looked at me suspiciously, before, with a blood-curdling yell, he took off down the backstairs.

I looked at my clock as I entered my room—twenty minutes past five—a half hour at least to myself, to think things over. Jeremy Glenby's warning had thoroughly disturbed me. What was I going to do?

As I settled down by my fire I glanced, not for the first time during the past few days, toward my parents' likeness on the bookcase. My father's face, straggly-moustached and delicately-boned stared back at me, the serious, compassionate eyes about to twinkle into one of those smiles that even after all those years, I still—with a tug at my heart—remembered.

"Be true to yourself, Etta," he would have said. "If you are true to yourself, then all else follows! And remember," he would add, after it had become obvious that his life was about to come to a close, "and rememeber, above all else, that I love you and if God wills it, I shall always be with you in spirit . . . you will never be alone, my darling child . . . You have brought such joy to me," he breathed at the last.

"Be true to yourself!" I thought of all the lies I had told during the past few days and gulped. But what would have happened, I asked myself—especially in light of what Jeremy Glenby had imparted—if I had told Marcus Raven the truth—that I had gone out into the storm because I thought that Callum Douglas had returned and that I wished to discuss with him the possibilities of our employer's villainy toward his stepdaughter?

I looked closely at the picture again, at the likeness of my mother. "And Mother?" I had asked my father. He had smiled at me. "She came into my life when I needed a ray of sunshine," he had replied, ruffling my curls, "and she gave me you. And at this moment, God is looking down on her, as He does on all of us, and, I am sure, giving her His blessing! Always think well of your mother, Etta, and pray for her — she is an *honest* soul, my Millicent!"

Honest, I thought irritably. Always honest. And I certainly had been less than honest! But what else could I do? I thought of Malvina and Reginald and of poor dear Ishbel. Though I had been strictly brought up to believe otherwise, surely in this case, the end justified the means! My conversation with Jeremy Glenby certainly seemed to confirm this. And for that reason, it was a great relief to know that someone other than myself and Callum had realized that something was wrong, and that the conclusions we had drawn were not just based on disordered thinking on our part!

And yet?

There *was* a fault in our reasoning. I was sure of it! There was something I had missed but try as I might, I could not think what it might be.

"Be true to yourself!" I seemed to hear my father's voice. Be honest, Harriet, I told myself. Could it be simply that you do not *want* to believe that the Master of Ravensfall could be responsible for such dastardly conduct?

I thought again of his strong arms and that tingling tremulousness that had seemed to surge throughout my limbs when he had lifted me after my fall and held me close to his chest. These, I was sure, were those Certain Feelings that Aunt Alice had warned me led to Improper Behavior . . . and that all *ladies* should strive to avoid! I looked guiltily at the picture of my mother. Mr. Pugh had insisted she was a woman of low virtue. Had I, as he had implied, inherited her weakness?

What was I going to do?

You are wanted in the small parlor, Miss!" A giggling Martha peered around my door.

I groaned inwardly. Mr. Raven was probably the last person on earth I wanted to see at that moment . . . especially alone!

I tidied my hair and turned toward the door.

Another giggle.

"What is so amusing, Martha? Do I have a smudge on my nose?"

She made an effort to be serious. "Oh, no, Miss. In fact you look very nice." She looked at the new blouse Jenny had made me, of lavender silk sprigged with small daisies and trimmed with white lace, and for some reason giggled again. "Sorry . . . it . . . it's just—"

There were shrieks out in the hall.

"Oh, those children. I'd better quieten them down!" With a look, it seemed to me, of relief, she disappeared through the door.

Gloomily, I made my way downstairs to the small parlor. I should just have to talk to the man, the way I had always done, I decided—and above all, guard against my Weakness! I knocked sharply on the door and turned the knob.

"Oh, dear Miss Harriet! Please, please say you have

330

forgiven me!"

The odious Alfred! And on his knees!

I was so relieved, I could have laughed. Instead, I arranged my features in a cross look. "For goodness sake, get up! What do you mean by coming here? I told you quite distinctly that I never wanted to see you again!"

A bunch of daffodils was thrust into my face as my unwelcome suitor staggered to his feet.

"My little love! You were quite right to say what you did!"

"I am not—thank God—your little love! Now, please leave!"

"But, dearest Miss Harriet, I have something to tell you!"

"Nothing you have to tell me, could possibly interest me!" I started for the door, but the wretched man having seen my intentions, stepped in front of me, completely blocking my way.

"Remove yourself, sir, and allow me to leave!"

An earnest look, while the fair moustache was fingered nervously.

"*Please* hear what I have come to say!"

"Oh, very well. Get it over with!"

"My *dearest* Miss Harriet, Mother says that you were quite right to speak to me as you did and that you are a young lady not only of great delicacy but also considerable strength of character and that I should be grateful for what you have done for me!"

"Done for you?"

Under the moustache, the mouth assumed a resolute line. "I am no longer the man I was. Because of your . . . your . . . *angelic* intervention, I have reformed!"

I was stunned.

A soft knock. The door opened to reveal Mrs. Mannering.

"My dearest girl, I see that Mr. Smythe has given you his news! Is it not romantic to think that *you* are the one who has inspired him to . . . And not only that, but . . . however, we must not keep Mrs. Smythe waiting . . ."

"Mrs. Smythe?"

"Yes, of course, and Sir Albert, also. In the drawing room, you know, with Cousin Marcus and dear sweet Ishbel. When Alfred announced his good news, nothing would do, but they should all come right away to assure you that what he says is true and not only that," the pebble glasses glared sternly up at Alfred, "but that he will hold by his decision!"

After such a speech, it was almost a relief to reach the drawing room at last!

An arm was flung about my shoulders. "All is forgiven!" Alfred Smythe announced.

I removed myself from the arm to cope with booming congratulations from Mrs. Smythe, a bark of laughter from Sir Albert, and what could only be described as an amused stare from Marcus Raven.

"Do sit down, Miss Newcombe," my employer invited, "Ishbel has just rung for some tea."

"Did dearest Alfred tell you," inquired his mother, her puce face even darker than ever, "that he has signed the Pledge!"

A bark of laughter from Sir Albert.

"Be quiet, Father! As you know, my dear Miss Harriet — if so, I may now address you — the Pledge of the Temperance Society is for life!"

Another snort of laughter from Sir Albert.

"Be silent, Father. So we know," she turned a forbidding glare toward her son, "that from now on, dearest Alfred will live a life of rectitude and decorum!"

She opened her mouth to say more, but luckily there was a knock at the door.

A shy Malvina entered clutching two kittens — and my folder!

"I'm sorry Papa. I did not know you had visitors!" She turned to go.

"What is it, child?" For once, Mr. Raven's voice was gentle.

"I thought I should give this to Miss Newcombe right away, as I know she is worried about it . . . and anyway . . ." A mischievous look at me. "I want to know what happens next!"

"My goodness," gushed Mrs. Mannering. "Is that Miss Newcombe's novel? Did I tell you, dear Euphemia, that we have a writer in our midst? You would not believe how clever —"

"Thank you, Malvina," I cut in quickly to prevent an endless babble. "Where did you find it?"

"We were playing with the kittens in the sunporch. Martha said we had to quiet down! And two of them escaped and that's when we found your papers on an occasional table, with some of our exercises. I dare say you were correcting them and you were called away and afterwards, you forgot."

"Yes, I dare say, it could have happened that way," I

333

agreed, blushing at my prevarication. To hide my embarrassment, I opened the folder and riffled through the papers. Halfway through, I glimpsed something pink.

"Miss Newcombe, whatever is the matter?" Marcus Raven's baritone was concerned.

"Miss Newcombe, you have gone quite pale," Ishbel chimed, "Is your head bothering you again?"

Mrs. Mannering coughed and I looked up to find her pebble glasses turned full force on me. "My dear girl, did I see a pink paper there? Is that Miss Inglewood's letter you were telling us about? Do read it. I am all agog!"

In the circumstances, what could I do? I found the paper and unfolded it. It was Miss Inglewood's hand-writing, I recognized it at once—but it was *not* the same letter. It appeared to be the answer to an invitation—obviously it had never been sent—to someone in Wanganui.

Fortunately at that moment the kittens caused a diversion, enabling me to some extent to disguise my bewilderment.

I joined with Malvina in the chase: one little grey monster, evidently considering Alfred Smythe to be a tree, had climbed up his trouser leg; the other, grey and white, not so courageous, had sought refuge under Sir Albert's chair.

"Kitty! Kitty!" this gentleman cooed in a surpris-ingly soft voice. "Ouch!" Unwisely, he had inserted a hand under his chair.

I laughed. "Malvina, you had better rescue him, he knows you best!" I looked toward an amused Marcus

Raven, who with Ishbel was watching our maneuvers from the sidelines. "I was just telling Mrs. Hargreaves, that we could do with some kittens at Ravensfall for Malvina and Reginald—"

I was interrupted by a gasp from Malvina. "Oh, no, Miss Newcombe!" On her face was a look of pure terror. She made an attempt to recover herself. Looking toward her father, she added. "In any event, these are bespoken by Mr. McGregor, Jenny's young man—his parents are going to look after them until he and Jenny are married." She paused a moment and then continued. "I expect that Mr. McGregor will take them tonight. "Yes, tonight!" She spoke slowly and with resolution, as if she wished to assure someone present that the kittens would indeed be removed.

Marcus Raven sighed and looked toward Mrs. Mannering while Ishbel drifted back to her chair by the fire.

Malvina and the kittens departed, the tea tray arrived, and conversation was resumed.

I only half listened, so much did I have to think about. In fact, so disturbed was I by all that had happened, my head was aching again.

"Miss Newcombe?"

I was being addressed by Marcus Raven. "I asked, if you were quite well, Miss Newcombe?"

"I am sorry . . . I really am quite well; it's just that my silly head is aching again!"

"I thought so! Then it is just as well that Mrs. Mannering and I have decided that you and the children should have a short holiday."

"Holiday?"

"Yes, I have a small cottage in Castlecliff, at the beach. I should like you and the children to spend a few days there . . . the sea air will do you good!"

"But what about Ishbel?" Without thinking, I spoke more urgently than was wise.

A long considering look. "You do not need to concern yourself about Ishbel, Miss Newcombe."

Was there a veiled warning in those chilling tones?

His face completely lacking expression, Marcus Raven added, "Ishbel will return with us to Ravensfall on Wednesday. She will be well taken care of, I assure you!"

Twenty-nine

A tinkle and a series of thuds.

I dragged myself out of a deep sleep. Another thud. I pulled aside the covers and staggered over to the window.

Outside, a bright moonlit night — and, on the back lawn, looking up at me, a pale face with a pair of blazing, blue-green eyes.

Callum Douglas.

Thank God!

I struggled with the window and finally raised the sash. A blast of cold air and a hiss from Callum.

"Harriet! Come down and let me in. The side door!"

Haste and secrecy, it would seem! I stepped into my slippers and pulling on Aunt Alice's brown woollen dressing gown, I left my chamber and felt my way down the back stairs.

He was already waiting at the door, his long lean body outlined against the moonlight. "Thank you, Harriet! Leave the door open till I get a lamp lit."

I stood at the open side door, until a glow of light from the kitchen informed me that he had found a lamp.

"Brrr, there is going to be a frost in the morning!"

I looked at the clock, three-thirty. "It *is* morning!"

He grinned at me, his devilish grin, the light from the lamp setting his red-gold hair on fire. "I am sorry, but I had word . . . that is . . ." He hesitated a moment, while he picked up the lamp. "That is, I have to see Mr. Raven later today, and as it's a clear bright night, I decided to come down early. I have a number of errands to perform on my own account . . . so thank you, Harriet. I am afraid the outside door to my room was stuck. I would not have disturbed you, otherwise. Would you like me to light you up the stairs?"

"Callum! I need to talk to you about Ishbel!"

"Ishbel?" His face tightened at the urgency in my voice. "You had better come in here." As he spoke, he turned to the door leading to his room, off the kitchen, and fished a key out of his pocket. "I always keep my room locked when I am away," he explained to my puzzled face. "I do not want the maids interfering with my papers."

"But surely, Hargreaves . . ." I began, as the door was unlocked.

"Hargreaves? The tone was abrupt and the face turned toward me was tense. "What do you know of Hargreaves?"

"Nothing. It's just that he was in your room the other night — Wednesday, I think it was, the night of the gale."

338

As I spoke, the door swung open. Apart from some tarpaulin-covered boxes in one corner, the room appeared much the same as when I had seen it before. I noticed, however, that the outside door was firmly barred on the inside. Before I could remark on this, Callum, with a muffled curse, stepped back sharply and closed the door.

"What am I thinking of, Harriet! Inviting you alone to my room, at such an hour!"

I felt myself blushing. He was, of course, quite right. I had become so free in my behavior lately, I chided myself, that I had not given a thought to my sitting, clad only in night attire, alone with a gentleman in his bedchamber!

"Come," a light pat on my shoulder. "Sit down and I shall set this stove to rights and soon have a fire burning. "Now, what was this you were telling me about Hargreaves?"

"Hargreaves? Oh, yes, Hargreaves. Nothing, really. "Only, I saw him in your room, through the window, you know, and he seemed to be entering something in one of your ledgers." I looked up at him, troubled. "I had thought, perhaps, that it must be some detail about the management of Mr. Raven's town house . . . But you said something about keeping your room locked . . ."

The beginnings of a laugh, quickly muted as a blue-green glance was cast toward the ajar kitchen door behind us. "No mystery! You are, of course, quite right, Harriet. One of Hargreave's functions is indeed to keep me informed of the financial details of Mr. Raven's town house, so naturally he had a key to

339

my room." He raked the embers in the stove and added kindling. "But, why were you observing him through my window and in the midst of a gale, I think you said?"

"Oh, as for that! I dare say, it sounds very silly now; but I thought I saw you crossing the lawn and I so desperately needed to talk to you, I came downstairs only to find it was Hargreaves in your room and not you, as I had expected!"

The kindling caught and warmth issued from the stove. Callum turned toward me inquiringly. "So it was Hargreaves you saw on the lawn?"

"No . . . Mr. Raven!"

Callum added coals to the stove and then turned to me. "I believe, Harriet," he said, his Scottish burr rolling the r's in my name, "that you had better give me a detailed account of what has been going on!"

He sat quietly, his eyes intent on my face, as I told him everything that had happened since he had been away at Ravensfall. When I finished, he sat back with a sigh.

"I'm sorry about the letter, Harriet. Really sorry!"

"You mean, that it was stolen?"

His eyes serious, he shook his head. "No, that you found it in the first place!"

I looked at him in bewilderment. "But surely it confirms what we had suspected?"

"Precisely! And the person who took the letter from you, now realizes that *you* know more than is good for you!"

"But, the second letter—surely that was put there because whoever it was—Mr. Raven, I suppose—

thought I had not read the first one."

"Oh, Harriet, be serious! Considering the circumstances, do you think it likely that Marcus Raven really would believe that you had not read that letter?" He gave a sarcastic laugh. "I certainly would not! No, the other letter was put among your papers for two reasons. One, as you carefully told everyone that you had not read the first letter, you can hardly go about saying that this one is different. And two, it is probably meant as a warning—to let you know that you are being watched. I dare say he is trying to frighten you into leaving."

Despite the heat from the now glowing stove, I suddenly felt quite cold.

"Dear little Harriet!" Callum bent forward and took my hands in his. "Please take heed! You did not believe me before, when I warned you. But you *know* now: there is danger at Ravensfall, not just for Ishbel but for you as well. Ishbel, I can take care of. I always have and I always shall. But your safety, I cannot guarantee!"

He looked down at me, in his eyes a deep sadness.

"Harriet, I want you to go upstairs, right now, and write a letter of resignation. Leave while you are still in Wanganui. Do not go back to Ravensfall on Wednesday!"

To say that I was not tempted to do as he asked, would not be true! I thought of the dark passages of Ravensfall, its isolation in the bush, and the river in which Miss Inglewood had drowned. And then I thought of Malvina and Reginald and straightened my shoulders resolutely.

"I cannot do as you ask, Callum. I just cannot bring myself to leave the children! However, I shall not be returning to Ravensfall on Wednesday. Mr. Raven told me that I am to stay with Malvina and Reginald for a few days in Castlecliff. Who knows what will have happened in that time? After all, we are no longer alone in our belief that something is wrong! Perhaps, with someone else to help, you will find enough evidence to go to the police!"

I then told him about the suspicions of Jonathan Turner.

"Do you think I could take off my hat?" a sailor-suited Malvina asked hesitantly.

I smiled down at her. "Yes. And so shall I!"

Aunt Alice, I thought, laughing to myself, would have a fit! "A true lady, Harriet, *always* wears a hat; the more especially at the seaside—quite apart from the sake of propriety, one must always guard one's complexion."

I took a deep breath of the salty, sun-drenched air. Callum Douglas had been right, the day had started with a frost, but it had melted early and now down at the beach at Castlecliff the sun beat down from a deep blue sky. Shimmering blue-green sea as far as the eye could see, edged a coast that swept in a huge curve from a hazy horizon in the south, where a faint blur indicated the South Island, all the way to a snow-capped mountain peak far away to the north.

"Mount Egmont," Malvina explained.

"Moana calls him Taranaki," Reginald added.

342

I laughed. "Him?"

"Oh, yes—he is one of the mountain gods," Reginald explained. "Moana told us that long ago he lived with the other gods—they're all volcanos, really—in the middle of the island."

"You mean, he *moved?*"

Reginald nodded. "Yes. You see, he fell in love with another mountain's wife—who, of course was a mountain, also."

"Of course! Then what happened?"

"The other mountain fought Taranaki and Taranaki lost!"

"So, Taranaki ran off," Malvina continued, "and as he ran, he left a deep trench in the earth which the other mountain filled with water—and that is how the Wangauni River was born." She bent to pick up an oddly-shaped piece of driftwood, carefully dusting off the sand.

"I don't think I'll ever get used to the idea of black sand!" I exclaimed as I watched her, "although, it's not precisely black. In fact, sometimes in the sunlight, it sparkles like silver!"

A group of barefooted children—accompanied by a large, brown, shaggy dog—ran laughing down to the sea.

"You know, it is so warm, I believe you might remove your boots and stockings!"

Reginald grinned and Malvina looked at me in awe. "You mean, go barefoot, Miss Newcombe!"

"Why not! If you go into the sand dunes, you may take off your things in private. And then, if the water is not too cold, you may paddle!" I fished two hairpins

343

out of my hair and twisted them together. "Here, I believe this will serve as a passable hook to get your boot buttons undone!"

I watched enviously as the children emerged from the sand hills and ran barefooted to the water's edge.

A daring idea entered my head. Well, why not, I asked myself? In the privacy of the sand dunes, I struggled with my boot buttons, slipped off my stockings, and hitching up the skirts of my old blue serge, I ran happily out onto the beach and down to the sea, where I joined the children splashing in the tide.

The shaggy dog soon joined in with our romping and through him, Malvina and Reginald made friends with the other children, "real" New Zealanders, I observed by their speech, a Maori brother and sister and a pakeha assortment of two boys and three girls. One of the children had a ball and before long, using a piece of driftwood as a bat, a game of rounders was organized and naturally I joined one of the teams to make the numbers even. Unfortunately, the dog—Stinky by name—decided to accompany me, when, after hitting the ball into the sand hills, I ran madly from base to base in order to make a full "run." Just as I slid into the sand at the last base, Stinky, overcome with joy at my well-earned success, cannoned into me and sent me flying head over heels into a pair of grey tweed trousers.

Above the trousers, a grey and navy checkered Norfolk jacket.

Above the jacket, a bowler hat.

Beneath the hat, the saturnine features of the Master of Ravensfall.

"You have very pretty toes, Miss Newcombe," this presence uttered.

A strong hand helped me to my feet and I stood before my employer, very much aware of my bare lower limbs, my tumbled hair, and the fact that the first three buttons of my bodice had come undone.

Gather your wits, Harriet, I told myself in my mind, you have every right to play with the children on the beach if you so want. And if you become somewhat dishevelled in the process, that is to be expected. Now raise your head, you are not a small child after all, and look this undoubted villain in the eye!

The undoubted villain looked down at me gravely.

"Good afternoon, Mr. Raven!" I greeted him with dignity.

He raised his hat. "Good afternoon, Miss Newcombe!"

"As you can see, sir, the children and I were engaged in a game of rounders. Unfortunately, Stinky," I indicated that engaging scoundrel, now busily sniffing Mr. Raven's highly polished shoes, "became somewhat excited and caused me to fall."

"So I saw."

"Rounders, sir, is a highly educational game, besides exercising the body, it also encourages coordination between hand and eye."

"Indeed!"

"In fact, I understand that in America, they have a variant of this game that they have named baseball. I am told," I continued, warming to my subject, "that the game is taken very seriously, the players wear special uniforms and great sums of money are placed as bets . . ."

I stopped. My employer, who having turned aside, had taken out a large white handkerchief and appeared to be restraining a cough. "How very knowledgeable you are concerning the habits of the Americans, Miss Newcombe! However, I wonder if we could step aside for a moment, I am here for a particular purpose." He eyed the staring circle of children and glanced down at Stinky who was now investigating his ankle, "Perhaps . . . Stinky? . . . could serve as your substitute?"

We walked up the beach to a sand dune.

To my surprise, Mr. Raven removed his jacket and laid it down on the sand. "If you have no objections to my taking off my jacket, I believe we would be more comfortable if we were sitting down!"

We sat down on the spread-out jacket.

"What a glorious day and so warm. Most unusual in the middle of winter! I feel positively over-dressed!" He eyed his shoes dubiously. "I wonder, Miss Newcombe, if you would mind my removing my shoes? I very much doubt that the sand and salt are good for the leather! And perhaps, before the air chills again, I could join my children at the water's edge . . ."

Before I could answer, he slipped off his shoes. His socks followed suit. He then turned up the edges of his trousers.

"Now that we are comfortable, if somewhat unconventional, let me come to the reason for my visit. A

346

certain gentleman of your acquaintance wishes to pay you his addresses and he has asked for my help in this matter. My dear Miss Newcombe, you look distinctly cross! I realize, of course, that I am only your employer, but you are a long way from your family, and I do feel a certain responsibility!"

"If, sir, you are referring to Alfred Smythe, I wish to have nothing to do with him! And so you may tell him!"

An amused glance. "At least let me present his case! He assures me that he abominates his former . . . er . . . weakness and is now a totally reformed character and that with your help, he is sure that so he will remain! Not only that, but his family background is impeccable. He is, his mother tells me, related to the Somerset Smythes and the Norfolk Spencers!"

"How truly marvelous!"

"I am glad you are impressed. In addition, he is an only son and will inherit several properties. In fact, Mrs. Mannering—who sent me down here, post haste, when she heard of the matter—tells me that he is the . . . er . . ."

"Greatest catch in Wanganui?"

"Precisely!"

"Mr. Raven," I began, attempting with dignity to rise to my feet, "please tell Mr. Smythe—" Unfortunately, I caught my feet in my skirts and fell into my employer's lap.

Directly above me, Marcus Raven's face, his topaz eyes sparkling in the sun and about his head, an aureole of light. I felt his arms about me and experienced immediately that wild tremulousness I had sensed before, this time accompanied by a delightful giddiness.

With an effort, I dragged myself away, and sat still for a moment, very much aware of Marcus Raven's physical proximity.

"I take it that you wish to refuse Mr. Smythe's offer?" The words were ordinary enough but the baritone, to my suddenly sensitive ears, lacked its usual steadiness. "Come then. Now I have done my duty!" He scrambled to his feet and held out a helping hand to me.

His hand was strong and at his touch, a great warmth swept throughout my limbs. I knew then that I was lost. This man might be a murderer, might be the most despicable villain in the world, but . . .

"Miss Newcombe? Papa?"

Before us stood Malvina. "Could Reggie and I go out with Philip and Betsy?" She indicated two of the children she had been playing with. "They say they are going home for afternoon tea and that their mother would not mind if we went with them."

I pulled myself together with an effort. "Yes, of course, providing that their mother *really* does not mind. If she does, you must come home at once!"

I turned to Marcus Raven and tried to keep my voice steady. "Perhaps, sir, you would like a cup of tea?"

He took out his watch and flicked open the lid. "I should like that very much, Miss Newcombe. I believe I just have time. I am returning to town on the four-thirty-five train." His voice was steady and completely without expression. "In any event, I should be glad to have the chance to tidy myself!" He looked ruefully down at his sandy feet and trousers. "I believe I shall leave off my shoes until we reach the cottage, the idea of traveling with sand-filled socks does not appeal to me!"

Mr. Raven's weatherboard cottage — what most New Zealanders, I found, called a "batch" — stood on a small street just across the sand dunes. It was small, only having two bedrooms, a living room, and a kitchen.

"Please forgive the disorder!" I apologized as we entered, barefooted, into the small but cheerful living room, "The children were having a pillow fight and one of the pillows burst!" I indicated a trail of feathers that led from the black and red living room carpet through the open door of Reginald's bedchamber to the bed with its disarranged patchwork quilt and wild tangle of pillows. "I really should have made them tidy up before we went out, but it is such a beautiful sunny day and I did not want them to miss any of it!"

"No need to apologize! Perhaps, I could leave my things in Reginald's room?"

"Yes, of course, and then after you have had your cup of tea, I shall bring you some hot water for you to bathe your feet."

I watched him as he hung his jacket on one of the knobs of Reginald's brass bedstand and placed his shoes neatly on the hooked rug beneath.

How stilted our conversation sounded, I thought; it

was as if we were in a play and making up the dialogue as we went along. A polite and completely artificial dialogue that was designed to keep our true thoughts from surging into the open.

I glanced at the clock. My goodness, almost four o'clock, I had better be quick. Hurriedly, I set my hat on a convenient glass dome containing a stuffed partridge and dropped my shoes and stockings on a chair by the door.

In the kitchen, after putting the kettle on the stove to boil, I quickly buttered some scones and heaped them generously with blackberry jam.

"Malvina's specialty," I explained to Marcus Raven as he watched me from the doorway. "Mrs. Hargreaves taught her how to make them. She is really becoming quite a good little cook. I nodded toward a steak and kidney stew simmering gently on the stove. "She prepared the stew with hardly any directions from me."

"But why are you doing the cooking? Where is Mrs. Jenkins?"

"She has a sick grandchild to look after and I told her not to worry about us. I am very good at fending for myself!"

"So I have noticed." Reaching out, he selected a scone.

"Watch out, they are a little crumbly," I was beginning, when the inevitable happened. The scone broke in two and a trail of blackberry oozed down his cravat and shirt.

"Oh, dear! I am sorry!" I seized a damp cloth. "Let me have your cravat and here is a bowl of hot water.

Why don't you go into Reggie's room where there is a mirror and tidy up your shirt. Luckily most of the jam seems to be on your cravat . . ."

"Oh, Harriet Newcombe, what am I to do with you?" As he spoke, he took the bowl and I felt his fingers tremble as they touched mine. He stood a moment, looking down at me, his eyes questioning. Suddenly, as if he had found an answer, he turned abruptly and left the room.

Could this be the cravat of a murderer, I asked myself, as I sponged away the blackberry stain. I thought again of Marcus Raven's tenderness on the night of the ball and his gentle raillery when we were alone together. I just could not believe that the man could be vicious—unless, as I had fancied before, Marcus Raven was mad and had two personalities, the evil one of which, he kept concealed! I thought suddenly of Mr. Pugh. "Beware the devil, Harriet, he comes in many guises . . . and you are particularly susceptible, my dear!"

Harriet Newcombe, I informed myself sternly, you must be more circumspect! What do you think you are about . . . you know perfectly well that the sensations you are experiencing are Highly Improper and not to be countenanced! Firmly, I took up the cravat and marched out of the kitchen.

Marcus Raven, his damp shirt open about his lean brown throat, came out of the bedroom to meet me. I held out his cravat, but instead of taking it, he rested his hands on my shoulders and drew me to him. For a moment, I was in another world. I could *hear* the clock ticking on the mantelpiece; I could *hear* children

351

playing somewhere near our open door and the sounds of approaching footsteps along the street outside . . . but all I was *aware* of was Marcus Raven's beating heart.

"Harriet! There is something I must tell you . . . it concerns Ishbel." He tipped my face up and gazed down at me, his eyes heavy with guilt. "Oh, Harriet, her mother would never forgive me but—"

A cough from the door. A scandalized Jonathan Turner looked about the room, noting first our compromising position and disheveled appearance, then my shoes and stockings on the chair and finally, the bedroom behind, with Mr. Raven's shoes beside a wildly disarranged bed.

My employer gripped me closely. "Good afternoon Jonathan!" You must be the first to congratulate us. Miss Newcombe has just agreed to become my wife!" My arm was firmly pinched. "Have you not, my love?"

"Sir . . . I don't believe—"

"Of course, my dear. I entirely agree!" He turned to Jonathan Turner. "For the time being, we have decided to keep our engagement a secret. Miss Newcombe feels that the children need a little more time to become used to her."

To say that Jonathan Turner was surprised would be an understatement. His voice, when he spoke, was stunned. "My felicitations, Miss Newcombe. Sir—"

Mr. Raven smiled pleasantly. "I am afraid you have caught us at a somewhat informal moment. We have just returned from the beach as you can see!"

Jonathan Turner looked dubiously at our bare feet.

"And the children, bless their hearts, have not as yet tidied up after their pillow fight!"

"Just so, sir." Mr. Turner politely turned his eyes away from the bedroom behind us. He coughed and, with apparent relief, changed the subject. "I am here at the direction of my father. You were not at home when I called earlier this morning, but Mrs. Hargreaves told me you would be in Castlecliff later today. As in any event, I had to inspect some properties down here, my father suggested that perhaps we could travel back together and I could explain things before you came to our chambers. There are some papers for you to sign."

"I see, thank you!"

Marcus Raven turned to me. "My love, if you would bring me that warm water, you spoke of. I believe I am obliged to return with Mr. Turner." He paused a moment and then added with a wicked smile, "We shall continue our plans when you and the children return to Ravensfall!"

Thirty

Ravensfall again. Four o'clock on a chill, grey Friday afternoon. Apart from an occasional spatter of rain, the trip up-river had been uneventful, but now I walked about the breeze-blown garden in a state of high nervous tension. What was I going to say to Marcus Raven?

The question had been plaguing me ever since he had announced our "engagement" to Jonathan Turner. That the engagement was merely a ruse on Mr. Raven's part in an attempt to restore my reputation, I was, of course, aware. But I could not forget the look in his eyes as he had held me in his arms . . . I could not forget that wicked smile.

Shame on you, Harriet, I kept telling myself in no uncertain terms. Think of what you have observed, and of what Callum Douglas has told you, and remember the conclusions drawn by Jonathan Turner. Marcus Raven has quite possibly murdered at least twice and is apparently considering doing so yet again!

I could not believe it.

Think of Miss Inglewood, I told myself. What had Mr. Takarangi said? That she had loved one she should not? Miss Inglewood had loved and she was dead!

Clutching my ulster against the cold, I rounded the side of the house and began to pace down the lawn past the library.

And what about his revelation concerning Ishbel, I questioned for the hundredth time? Had not his eyes been full of guilt. What had he been about to tell me, I asked myself again. And even more intriguing, why had he decided to tell *me?* Being aware of my suspicions, had he been going to tell me some made-up story to allay them? Or . . . a dreadful thought occurred to me, had he been feigning his emotions toward me? Was he trying to make me his accomplice? I thought with a sickening feeling of Hélène DuPrès.

"Harriet!"

Marcus Raven appeared at the side door.

"Harriet," He strode toward me and before I knew what he was about, took me in his arms. "I saw you pass the library window," he murmured into my hair, "and I could not resist . . . oh, my dear, forgive me if I act coldly toward you in public, but soon this will be all over . . . I must explain—"

Suddenly, he stiffened and moved away from me. I followed the direction of his eyes toward the huge old tree with the unpronounceable name that Mr. Tavish had called the New Zealand Christmas tree. There in the half-light, almost a part of the grey gnarled trunk, was Moana. Slowly, she looked from one to the other of us and then bared her teeth in a soundless cackle.

"Mr. Raven!"

Ngaire came to the door. "Mr. Raven, Mr. Takarangi is here to see you. He says it is urgent!"

I followed Marcus Raven into the house. At the door, I turned back. Moana still stood there watching.

"Good afternoon, Miss Newcombe!" Mr. Takarangi's pleasant deep voice interrupted my thoughts.

I pulled myself together. "Good afternoon! I wonder, Mr. Takarangi, if I might see you after you have spoken with Mr. Raven? I have something for your new baby. I understand, it is a little boy?"

His broad features lit up with pleasure. "Thank you, Miss Newcombe! Yes, a splendid son. We have named him Wiremu." He smiled at me and added, "Maori for William."

The two men entered the study.

"We have found the cave," I heard Mr. Takarangi say as the door was closing. "It is in the bush above the landing . . ."

As I made my way to my room, I thought about what I had overheard. What cave, I wondered, and why was Mr. Takarangi so urgent about it?

I gathered up my present—a baby's small jacket I had crocheted in soft white wool—and making my way down again, arrived back at the study, just as the door was opening.

"In that case, we shall have to act quickly . . ." Marcus Raven was beginning. He saw me and stopped. "Ah, Miss Newcombe, you have your gift, I see."

I gave the little coat to Mr. Takarangi and all three of us moved to the side door.

"*Tena koe!*" Mr. Takarangi greeted Moana, who having left the tree, was approaching us over the lawn.

A musical laugh rang out from the direction of the River Walk. Moana, instead of returning the greeting, spat out a word I did not understand and gliding over the grass, disappeared into the bush.

Beside me Mr. Takarangi stiffened, then shrugging his shoulders laughed a little.

On the path leading from the River Walk, Ishbel appeared, accompanied by Jonathan Turner.

I looked at Mr. Takarangi. "What was that all about?"

"A word, I'm afraid your pakeha tongue will never get around, Miss Newcombe, *patupaiarehe!*"

I laughed. "I'm afraid, you are right! But what does it mean?"

He bit his lip thoughtfully before replying. "Moana is very old, you know, and still remembers the ancient ways . . ."

"Yes?"

"The word closest in translation is 'fairy'; but it does not refer to those small winged creatures in your *pakeha* picture books, but rather to a race of innately evil creatures who have magic powers. They are said to live in the misty highlands . . ." He looked at the approaching Ishbel and hesitated. "I am afraid that these creatures, who look just like humans, are said to have light skins and red hair!" He turned to Marcus

Raven and shrugged apologetically.

"Think nothing of it, my dear fellow! It is understandable that Moana should think the way she does . . . life has not been easy for her. I really do not blame her for not liking us very much!"

"Malvina," I said hesitantly to Mr. Takarangi, "says Moana believes that all of us pakeha will one day be swept into the sea!"

"An old Hauhau belief, Miss Newcombe. And not one to which I subscribe!" Mr. Takarangi smiled down at me. "It is true that this land has been taken over by a people of a different race, but if it had not been the British, it would have been the French or some other nation. That is the history of the world, is it not—one people constantly taking over the territory of another. Think of your own nation! You British are the result of a constant mingling—the Celts, the Saxons, the Norse, the Normans. You may still squabble among yourselves, but you are—largely—one nation."

"Do you think, then, that this will happen in New Zealand? That the races will mingle?"

He nodded. "Eventually, yes . . ."

"But don't you think it a pity for all the Maori traditions to disappear?"

A deep rich laugh. "I said a mingling not a taking over! Don't worry, Miss Newcombe, the best—and, I'm afraid, human nature being what it is!—probably some of the worst features of both races will be preserved!" He nodded affably to the approaching Ishbel and turned to Mr. Raven. "I must be going, Mere will be wondering where I am. As for that matter, we spoke of . . . I think that possibly, late tomorrow afternoon?"

Thanking me again, he left.

I waved to Mr. Takarangi and turned to find that Jonathan Turner and Ishbel had reached the door. Jonathan, a small frown between his brows, looked thoughtfully at myself and Mr. Raven. Placing an arm about Ishbel's shoulders, as if she needed protection, he drew her away from us through the door. Ishbel looked back at me over her shoulder and, her beautiful eyes completely expressionless, gave me a brilliant smile.

At Mrs. Mannering's insistance, I joined the family in the drawing room that night for coffee after dinner.

"I know you have your novel to write, dear girl, but all work and no play . . . and, in any event, dearest Euphemia wants me to speak to you. She has not given up hope, you know, and neither has dearest Alfred, who, as I must tell you, my dearest girl, has become a most Reformed Character and goes about performing Good Works . . ."

Was it possible that I had been in New Zealand scarcely four weeks! I looked about the drawing room; at the pink and mauve carpet, the plum-colored chairs, and remembered how on my first evening, this room in the blaze of light from the chandeliers and wall sconces, had seemed such a vivid and astonishing contrast compared with the dark wet bush outside.

I had felt, I remembered, like Prince Florimund, struggling through a dark forest to find an enchanted world within. A somewhat bedraggled Prince Florimund, I thought with amusement. What was it Ishbel had said afterward, that I had looked like a bird blown out of its nest in a storm? I looked down at my mulberry cashmere with its trimming of silver ribbons and thought that not only had I found an enchanted world but I had also become a part of it!

However, enchanted worlds, I reminded myself, were worlds of darkness as well as light and inhabited by elfin folk adept at spinning webs of shimmering magic that cunningly concealed the deceit within.

I came out of my revery to find Jenny offering me a cup of coffee.

I looked over the rim of my cup at the Master of Ravensfall, standing as usual in front of the fireplace. Which was he, I wondered, thinking of my fantasy, one of the creatures who spun the web or one who was caught in it?

Beside me, Mrs. Mannering, busily knitting what appeared to be a grey muffler of extraordinary length, was engaged in one of her interminable conversations with Gideon Tavish and Mrs. Douglas.

Mr. Tavish, politely nodding his head in between restrained yawns, was watching the children seated on the floor near by. As on my first evening, they were quietly playing "Cat's Cradle." Definitely creatures caught in the web, I thought with a shiver. Poor little things!

Mrs. Douglas, like Gideon Tavish, nodded her head politely, even occasionally managing to get in a word or two, but her eyes were directed across the room where her son and Ishbel were engaged in quiet conversation.

How alike those two were, I thought again. It seemed scarcely possible that they could only be cousins and such distant ones . . . Which remote ancestor did they both take after, I wondered?

Ishbel's laugh rang out. She was dressed in mauve silk and, as usual, with her auburn curls glinting in the soft light, her beauty glowed. Though she talked amicably enough with Callum, her eyes kept glancing toward her stepfather. Poor Jonathan Turner, I thought! He had no chance of engaging Ishbel's affections while she still harbored her schoolgirl crush for Marcus Raven.

At least Jonathan—bull-headed Jonathan, as Jeremy Glenby had called him—had Ishbel's interests at heart and would prove a good protector. No doubt that was why he was visiting his brother this weekend. He had traveled up on the *Waiwere* as I had done, but when I approached him he had avoided me and of course, having Malvina and Reginald with me, I had not been able to pursue him. Embarrassed, I remembered the situation in which he had discovered Mr. Raven and myself and the distrust he had displayed to me afterward. Surely, I thought with sudden horror, he could not regard *me* as part of the plot against Ishbel!

No doubt, I thought with relief, Callum would soon put him right! Before I had left for Castlecliff, Callum has assured me that he would seek out Jonathan Turner and ask him to join forces.

Callum smiled at me from across the room. Thank God he was there! I would have to speak with him privately somehow, and the sooner the better. He had an office in the house, I knew; but it might be better to see him in his private quarters—a small cottage over by the stables, next to Jim Parker's dad.

I also needed to speak with Mrs. Douglas, I thought. Sipping at my coffee, I wondered how much she knew or if indeed she suspected anything at all. Callum had said that for her own protection, he had told her nothing. "Look at what happened to Miss Inglewood, Harriet," he had replied when I suggested we talk to his mother. "And look at the danger, you—with your constant interference—have got yourself into!" He had looked at me thoughtfully and then had added, "In any event, now that the laudanum has been abandoned, Ishbel is safe enough in the house. I dare say they will try to arrange an 'accident' in the bush somewhere. And of course, either Jonathan or myself will be on the alert for that!"

Now, thinking over his warning, my hands shook so much, I was obliged to put down my cup and saucer. Callum was right, of course, but surely, if I questioned Mrs. Douglas discreetly without her being aware of my purpose? For instance, she of all people could probably provide information about Ishbel's father and give us some idea as to why Gideon Tavish had mentioned his name. Was there yet another fortune involved, I wondered?

My hands trembled again as I attempted to pick up my coffee cup.

"You are feeling chilly, Miss Newcombe?" Marcus Raven was looking at me, his hawk features sombre.

What had he said, out there on the side lawn before Maona had interrupted us . . . about treating me

362

coldly in public? What game was he playing? What devilish plot was this man hatching? All of a sudden, all my doubts returned in full strength. Was he the one spinning the web with myself caught in its deceitful magical threads?

My cup clattered, as I put it down again. "I am a little chilly," I admitted, "I believe it is the dampness in the air . . . it's raining quite hard, now, I can hear it, even in here."

Mrs. Mannering paused from her knitting and was silent for once, her head cocked, listening. "I believe you are right, my dear. I do hope we do not have a flood. When we do, we are quite isolated, you know, as the river becomes too difficult to handle!"

"That is because of the taniwha," Ishbel observed. "They like whirlpools and floods, you know, Miss Newcombe!" She laughed suddenly, a tense laugh that chimed like tiny brittle bells. "And that is when they are at their most dangerous."

"I believe," Marcus Raven interrupted, "that taniwhas are not necessarily evil. That, in fact, they often act as guardians and attack only when the mana of the river is threatened."

"In any event, my dear Miss Ishbel," Gideon Tavish remarked soothingly in his deep Scottish voice, "they do not really exist, do they?" He laughed comfortably and then added, "Have you ever *seen* a taniwha?"

"I asked Moana that, once," Malvina's soft voice suddenly surprised us all. "And she asked me . . ." Malvina hesitated, her thin face pale with fear, "she asked me, if I had ever *seen* the wind!"

At this auspicious moment, the door opened to

admit Jenny carrying a silver tray bearing an envelope.

"Bad news, I'm afraid, sir," she warned Mr. Raven as she presented the tray. "Mr. DuPrès has been taken bad. Mrs. DuPrès fears he is dying!"

Marcus Raven opened the envelope and read the note inside. "I am afraid that is so!" He looked toward Mrs. Mannering. "She asks for the comfort of . . . our . . . presence."

"Oh my dear Marcus, of course!" We shall leave immediately!"

"If you'll excuse me, Madam," Jenny spoke up, "but it's raining something dreadful now . . . a real deluge . . . and the poor lad who brought the note is wet through. He rode down the bush track," she added, "because the river was too dangerous. I told him he'll have to wait till morning to take back the answer. It's so dark out there now, you can't see your hand before your face!"

"In that case," Mr. Raven agreed, "we shall have to ride over first thing in the morning. Cousin Lydia, myself, Mrs. Douglas, and of course, Ishbel . . ." He paused a moment and exchanged a long look with Gideon Tavish. "What about you, my dear Tavish?"

"I should be glad to offer my support!"

"Good, that's settled then! Miss Newcombe, you will remain here with the children. The journey would be too difficult for them, and in any event, you are not well acquainted with Mrs. DuPrès!"

At last the evening had come to a close, but before

I could catch him, Callum had slipped off into the night.

I *had* to see him . . . I was so worried about Ishbel. I kept remembering how Marcus Raven had looked at Mr. Tavish before asking if he wished to accompany them to the DuPrès property. Were they planning, as Callum had feared, an "accident" for Ishbel in the bush? It would be easy enough in such awful weather! All they had to do was to separate her from the rest of the party and then, on some steep muddy slope in the middle of a tangled growth of trees and undergrowth . . .

I shuddered and pulled myself together with difficulty. Callum would have thought of all that, I assured myself. But I had to see him, just to settle my mind!

Upstairs in my chamber, I changed into a blouse and one of my black bombasine skirts that I hitched up at the waist in an effort to avoid the mud. I twisted a black scarf about my head and after slipping on my ulster, I made my way to the cloakroom downstairs. My galoshes were there and also some hurricane lamps kept there against an emergency.

Once outside the door, I stood still a moment, guarding the light from the lamp. I really had no fear of being seen. It was hardly likely that anyone else at that time of night would venture out in the pounding rain.

Thank goodness for the lamp, I thought. Without it the darkness would have been impenetrable and I should never have been able to find my way to the stables, situated behind a screen of bush off to one side of the house. Taking a deep breath for courage, I made myself set off into the night.

To my surprise, the door to Callum's cottage was open, the light streaming out into the night. As I approached, I saw Callum, rising from a ledger-piled table. He was dressed for the outside in a thick coat and with his slouch hat pulled down over his eyes. He picked up a hurricane lamp and stood for a moment glancing about the room, which besides the table and chair contained a number of shelves bearing books and various oddments. As I reached the steps leading up to his door, he moved suddenly over to one of the shelves and setting down the lamp picked up a couple of earthenware bottles which he then placed in a tarpaulin-covered box off to one side in a corner.

"Callum!"

He whirled to the door, his blue-green eyes blazing. "What are you doing here?"

"I . . . I'm sorry, if I startled you! It's just that Ishbel—"

"Ishbel?" His face tensed. "What about Ishbel?"

"I am worried about her journey tomorrow!"

His face relaxed. "Oh, as for that . . . I have it well in hand . . . In fact, that is why, as you can see, I am going out again tonight. I am going to send word to Jonathan Turner to meet with me tomorrow and we will . . . er . . . trail them in the bush!"

"But how will you send word? You cannot cross the river on such a night!"

He stood for a moment, looking at me silently. "Oh, Harriet, no wonder Marcus Raven finds you such a menace. Your mind is far too sharp. I have

366

arranged to send signals with my lantern of course! Now, I shall escort you back to the house. You have been standing in the rain long enough!" He came out onto the steps and closed the door. "By the way, how long have you been standing there?" he asked casually, as he took my arm, "you look quite drenched through!"

The next morning the rain had eased a little, but a filmy mist, rising from the river, enshrouded the house and garden.

As I descended the stairs into the hall, Callum Douglas came through the green baize door and I was reminded of our first meeting at Ravensfall when Malvina had introduced him as her cousin. Now, as then, the white light streamed through the stained-glass windows, illuminating St. George and the dragon-besieged maiden.

Callum stepped round the stairs and stood waiting for me—fittingly, I thought—in front of the St. George window. A true St. George, I thought, about to rescue Ishbel from . . . from what? Don't tell me, Harriet Newcombe, I chided myself, that you have doubts, even now! I reached the foot of the stairs and the newel post where the great carved raven was pinning down its prey.

They had gone into battle, Ishbel had told me about her stepfather's ancestors, with their raven banners flying; and I remembered Marcus Raven telling me with evident enjoyment of his Uncle Josiah and his association with Bully Hayes and then, with a start, I thought of his wolfish grin as he had warned me that night in the kitchen only two weeks before, that despite his . . . how had he described it? Civilized veneer? That a pirate still lurked beneath!

My doubts vanished.

Callum stepped forward and looking about to make sure we were alone, spoke softly. "All is in hand, Harriet. Don't worry!"

"But how will they travel through this mist?"

"The track leads up over a hill; the mist will be lighter there, and in any event, it will ease later. Harriet . . ." His voice was urgent and his eyes anxious as he looked down at me. "Take great care! I am just as worried about you, as I am about Ishbel. You see too much, my dear, and you draw too many conclusions . . . I have a feeling . . ."

"Yes?"

He hesitated. "You see, you will be left all alone. I have a feeling that Raven will slip back and seek you out and. . ."

I gulped. "But he will think you are here!"

He shook his head. "That's just it, my dear! He has given me directions to go to the Turner property to make arrangements about some sheep we are buying. So you see, he will think that I am out of the way!"

He paused and laid his hands lightly on my shoulders. "Listen carefully, Harriet! If you should see Raven, go immediately to Hemi and tell him to take you at once to Wanganui. When I cross the river, I shall send Hemi back with the canoe and he will leave it tethered by the landing!"

Footsteps sounded in the hall leading from the

study.

Callum Douglas stepped back. "Take care, Harriet! Take great care!"

An anxious morning followed by a fearful afternoon! To the surprise of Reginald and Malvina, I had kept them all day in the drawing room, knowing that from there I could see the driveway that led to the edge of the bush, where the track started. If Marcus Raven turned back, I reasoned, there was no other way on horseback that he could approach the house unseen.

At four o'clock, I sent the children upstairs with strict instructions to stay in the schoolroom. I then paced up and down in front of the drawing room window, before deciding to do what I should have done after Callum's warning.

I decided to confide in Jenny.

I had not done so before, strictly because the whole idea of Marcus Raven coming back to Ravensfall solely to murder the teacher of his children would to her ears—without the benefit of what I had seen and heard, and without Callum's warning—have sounded utterly fantastic.

Apart from Mrs. Rawlins and a sleepy Hemi dosing in a chair by the fire, there was no one in the kitchen. As there was barely anyone in the house, Mrs. Rawlins told me apologetically, she had given the servants leave for the rest of the day. Ngaire had taken Martha to visit her cousin Mere and Jenny's young man had come to take her across the river.

Dispirited, I returned to the drawing room.

In the end, it was Ishbel who came, just as the afternoon light was waning; a distraught and disheveled Ishbel seated on a tired, mud-spattered horse.

As I watched, instead of taking the path to the stables, she rode her horse around the side of the house, evidently on the way to the kitchen.

I hurried into the hall and through the green baize doors. As I entered the kitchen passage, Ishbel emerged at the other end.

"Miss Newcombe, thank God, I've found you! Look, there isn't time to explain, but I cannot believe that Step-Papa . . . I just cannot . . ." Weeping, she cast herself against me and I took her in my arms, feeling cold suddenly and utterly bereft.

"You mean . . ." I could not bring myself to say it.

She looked at me through her tears. "Yes. He . . . he tried . . . but Callum came upon us and he had brought his gun, you see, so he shot . . . at . . . at Step-Papa . . ."

"He . . . killed him?"

"No . . . he missed . . . and Step-Papa ran off into the bush. Callum was going to run after him, but his horse slipped in the mud, and Callum fell and broke his leg. Oh, Miss Newcombe, I am so afraid! Not only for myself but for Callum! I didn't want to leave him, but he said the best thing I could do was to go to Wanganui. He has left the canoe by the landing and I was to tell Hemi . . ."

I sighed with relief. "So that is why you rode around to the kitchen?"

"Yes, Hemi is on his way now, down to the river. Oh, dear Miss Newcombe, Callum told me that you

370

know all about . . . about . . ."

"Yes, I'm afraid so, my dear . . . But come, we must not waste time. I expect that Callum is worried that Mr. Raven will make his way back to Ravensfall before help arrives."

Clutching each other's hands, we rushed back through the hall, pausing only long enough for me to grab an ancient coat from the cloakroom.

"We'll go out the side door," I panted, as I pulled Ishbel down the passage, "and then down the lawn to the River Walk."

"Miss Newcombe!" a frantic voice called to me, as we emerged from the house and began our mad rush down the lawn. "Miss Newcombe!"

I stopped and looked back. From the third-floor landing window, leaned an hysterical Malvina. "Miss Newcombe, don't go—"

Her next words were lost as Ishbel pulled at my hand and hissed urgently. "Quick . . . pay no attention to Malvina . . . She'll be all right. She's Step-Papa's favorite, after all!"

"But Ishbel—"

"Miss Newcombe, he might be here at any moment. We must go!"

We started to run. As we reached the River Walk, I saw movement further down. Thank God, I thought, Hemi must be there waiting for us! I looked back over my shoulder. Malvina was still at the window screaming. To my astonished ears, the word she was crying out with such terror, was *taniwha!*

"Ishbel," I began, as she dragged me after her. She looked back at me critically, then pulling at my hand, she led me off the path into a tangle of bushes and tree ferns near the cliff edge. "You need to rest a moment to get your breath . . . but we had better hide here off the path, in case he comes and sees us!"

"Ishbel, Malvina screamed something about the taniwha!"

"Yes. Well, she would, wouldn't she! She's thinking about Miss Inglewood, you see. I suppose, she thinks I am going to send you after her."

"After her?"

"Yes. To the taniwha." Ishbel spoke softly, as if to a small and rather stupid child. Her words were all the more dreadful because she spoke completely without expression.

Too late, I realized that she had positioned herself between me and the path. Behind me, only a few feet away, was a long drop to the swiftly flowing river.

"You mean," I began, trying to edge past her, "that *you* . . . er . . . sent Miss Inglewood to the . . .?"

"The taniwha. Yes." She stepped in front of me.

If only she were not so tall, I thought frantically. I decided to try to play for time by humoring her. "But why, Ishbel?"

"She got Malvina and Reginald to tell her about Mama," she explained reasonably, "that I gave Mama the overdose of laudanum, you know."

"Why did you do that, Ishbel?" I tried again to sidestep around her.

For the first time, her face showed expression. When she spoke her words were full of hate. "She had my Papa—my true Papa—put in a bad place! So it was her fault that he died. And then almost as soon as

372

he was dead, she got Marcus Raven to marry her . . . and she did not deserve him!"

Hoping that her sudden display of emotion had distracted her, I started to edge past her, a little at a time. "You cannot marry Mr. Raven, you know, Ishbel. The laws of our church forbid the marriage of a stepfather with a stepdaughter."

She moved suddenly, stepping in front of me again. "If I cannot have him, then no one else will!"

I stood still for a moment, pretending to be defeated. "Was Miss Inglewood in love with Mr. Raven? Is that another reason why you killed her?"

She laughed her tinkling bell-like laugh. "Oh, Miss Inglewood was not in love with Step-Papa—although, I did wonder about him, because of her likeness to Mama, you know—no, my dear Miss Newcombe, Miss Inglewood was in love with my brother!"

She laughed again and stepped back a little, evidently in order to enjoy the expression on my face.

"Your brother?"

"Yes. Callum Douglas! Miss Inglewood told him what she had discovered, you see. And naturally, Callum warned me. He always tells me everything, you know!"

I looked at her completely stunned. "Callum Douglas is your brother?"

"Half-brother, really. Honestly, Miss Newcombe, you prod and pry and you think you know everything, but you don't, do you! You come to all the wrong conclusions. Callum and I often laugh about it. You're really not very bright, are you?"

She paused a moment, looking down at me consideringly. "But now, you have got to go. You have been chasing after my Step-Papa. You have even, so Jonathan Turner tells me, snared him into an engagement!"

I suddenly thought of a hawk-featured face and a pair of topaz eyes. "Attack is the best form of defense," he had said.

I was going to have to act fast. I eyed Ishbel, so much taller than myself—however, she was wearing a heavy full-skirted riding habit, the hems, for modesty's sake, in case they blew up in a wind, weighted with lead—whereas under the coat I had borrowed, I was wearing my rather skimpy old blue serge. Act quickly, Harriet, I told myself.

Before Ishbel knew what I was about, I slipped off the ancient coat and threw it up at her face. I had hoped to cover her head, but unfortunately did not quite manage to do so. However, while her attention was distracted, I threw myself forward and grabbed her firmly around the knees.

We fell to the ground in a desperate struggle. I had hoped once Ishbel was down, that I would be able to get up quickly and make my escape, but she was too quick for me and grabbed at me before I could rise. She was impeded by her heavy skirts but her arms were strong and so we rolled over and over as each of us tried to gain the advantage.

As we struggled I was vaguely aware of shouts from across the river and of pounding feet flying down the River Walk, but so desperate for my life was I, that I continued to struggle. Finally, near the edge of the cliff, I managed to free one arm and reaching up, I grabbed her by the nose. She let go of me abruptly and I rolled away only to realize in horror that my sudden action had sent Ishbel rolling in the opposite direction over the edge of the cliff.

Somehow, she managed to hang onto the edge with her hands. Desperately, I struggled to my knees and crawled toward her. I grabbed her hands but she was too heavy for me. The footsteps I had heard, finally reached the place where we were, but as the bushes separated, Ishbel's hands parted from mine and weighted down by her heavy skirts, she dropped into the swirling waters below.

Callum Douglas rushed past the bushes, dragging off his jacket. His blue-green eyes blazed at me. "If you have killed her," he snarled, as he approached the cliff edge, "I shall come for you!" He dived off the cliff and I leaned forward to see him drop into the river.

He was too late. There was no sign of Ishbel.

More footsteps. Another frantic parting of the bushes.

"Harriet!" a well-known baritone exclaimed.

I found myself fainting into the arms of the Master of Ravensfall.

I recovered consciousness to find myself lying on a sofa in the study, an anxious Marcus Raven hovering in the background, while Gideon Tavish sat beside me, feeling the pulse in my wrist. As I opened my eyes, he gave a sigh of satisfaction.

"Ishbel?" I asked.

His voice was gentle. "I am afraid my dear

that . . ." He did not need to finish the sentence, his sad brown eyes told the story.

There was an abrupt movement from Marcus Raven.

"My dear Raven, it is better that Miss Harriet be told the truth and at once, rather than to be left in a state of anxiety or to suffer a setback later on, when she discovers what really happened. I assure you that this method has brought about the best results in the recovery of other patients of mine."

He leaned forward and patted my hand. "I am a doctor, my dear, called in by Mr. Raven because of his anxiety over his stepdaughter."

"But, why . . .?"

"Why did I act . . . *incognito,* as it were?" He smiled down at me. "Because of the nature of Miss Ishbel's malady. Her father, you see—James McCleod—died in an asylum for the insane. Mr. Raven did not, of course, *at first,* suspect Miss Ishbel of being responsible for her mother's death. However, her morbid tendencies and her growing possessiveness toward himself made him wonder if perhaps she had inherited her father's illness."

Pausing a moment, Gideon Tavish patted my hand again. "But then," he continued, "with the death of Miss Inglewood in such peculiar circumstances, coupled with Miss Ishbel's preoccupation with morbid subjects such as the taniwha, as illustrated by her sketches, he wondered if perhaps . . . and so he called me in. I attended her late father, you see."

I shuddered as I thought of Ishbel's sketchbook with its picture of the taniwha.

Marcus Raven spoke to me for the first time. "That is why, Harriet, I was careful when Ishbel was present, always to treat you with extreme formality. Doctor Tavish thought that Ishbel's possessiveness toward myself may have been a cause leading to Miss Inglewood's death . . . but unfortunately, Harriet, you were too much for me! As far as you were concerned, I could not restrain myself!"

His face suddenly relaxed into a smile and I thought again, how much he resembled his son. How could I ever had doubted him, I wondered?

I had a sudden mental picture of a pair of blue-green eyes. "Callum. Is he . . ."

"Dead?" asked Marcus Raven harshly. "Not he! When he could not find Ishbel, he swam off downriver and is now lurking somewhere in the bush."

Gideon Tavish smiled down at my puzzled face. "Mr. Raven suspected that Douglas was illegally distilling whisky in an old cave used for that purpose by the late Josiah Raven."

I had a sudden memory of tarpaulin-covered crates both at the town house in Wanganui and in Callum's cottage at Ravensfall. "Of course! I exclaimed and then added. "And Hargreaves was helping him. That's why you were looking through Callum's window that night!"

My employer nodded. "Yes. It was Greg Parker—the father of your friend Jim—who alerted me. He was the one who told Callum that he suspected that Josiah—just like Parker's cousin—had smuggled whisky to Bully Hayes. Parker, of course, did not know where the old still was and neither did I . . . my

377

uncle was a reformed character when I stayed with him . . . But apparently Callum discovered where it was. Parker saw him with some bottles one night and he thought that Callum may have been using some youths from the mission to help him load and transport the whisky down the river to our storage shed. Hargreaves was then responsible for getting the whisky shipped to Wellington for distribution!"

I groaned. "Oh, what a fool I have been. So that was why you wandered about so much at night?"

"Yes. I was checking on Callum. I tried to follow him to find where the cave was, but he was too clever for me. So I was obliged . . . considering that mission youths were involved . . . to call in the services of Mr. Takarangi. And that is why we were up in the bush just now instead of the DuPrès vinyard. We had hoped to catch Callum Douglas off guard. Thank God, we looked down and saw you with Ishbel!"

Ishbel had been right, I thought. I had prodded and pried, but I was not bright enough to come to the right conclusions! I remembered another piece of information that Ishbel had stunned me with; something else that should have been clear to me.

"Callum!" I asked. "Ishbel told me that he was her brother!"

Marcus Raven nodded. "Her half-brother."

"Then Mrs. Douglas . . .?"

"Mrs. Douglas is not Callum's mother. You see, shortly after Minna—my late wife—married James McCleod, she saw a small boy . . . an exact replica of James . . . living in deplorable circumstances in a run-down cottage on the highland estate. She made inquiries and found out that James had . . . that is, the boy was James' son . . . but not . . . er . . . legitimate!"

I hid a smile at his sudden delicacy of expression. "I see . . . but Mrs. Douglas?"

"She is indeed Minna's cousin. She was a widow in straitened circumstances and as Minna—who had a soft heart—wished to help both the boy and her cousin, she had them both brought to the estate. Mrs. Douglas was to act as nurse to Ishbel and then later to Malvina and Reginald. And a polite fiction was invented that Callum was her son!"

"I understand . . . at last!"

Gideon Tavish handed me a small glass containing some liquid.

"What's this?"

"Just a little something to make you sleepy!"

I looked at him suspiciously. "Is this what you gave Ishbel."

He laughed delightedly. "How did you know? I wanted to give her the drops to see if they would help calm her especially during the night and later when I discovered that she did indeed have her father's malady, I thought that until we could have her admitted to a home in Wellington, they might possibly keep her out of mischief . . . but she was too cunning for us and stopped taking them!"

Thirty-one

Soon it will be dawn. My last candle flutters in the candlestick and in the restless shadows forever shifting about the walls, I seem to see again the faces of those I have loved best at Ravensfall: Malvina and Reginald—and Marcus Raven, the man whom I have promised to marry.

I hear that baritone again:

"I must go back to Scotland, Harriet, now that there is new evidence to clear my name. Will you wait for me? Will you look after Ravensfall while I am gone? And when I return, we shall be married."

He gathered me in his arms and tilted my chin. I studied again his hawk-featured face with the topaz eyes I loved—and that wicked pirate's smile. And I felt again all the familiar tingling tremulousness as I nestled against his chest.

I did not want him to leave me; but I knew that if he did not take this chance to prove his innocence and regain his honor, that he would regret it all his life. So, I did not tell him of Callum's threat or that

Callum—now a fugitive from the law—had been seen prowling in the bush near by.

With one last kiss, the Master of Ravensfall had left for Scotland, taking his household—and Doctor Tavish—with him. Even the children, now free from Ishbel's terrible threats, were ready to give evidence freely.

Oh, Ishbel! My beautiful, glowing Ishbel, with her terrible malady. What would have happened, I wonder now, if in the beginning, I had expressed my fears to Marcus Raven and had answered him truthfully? How could I ever have told myself that in this case that "the means justified the end"? If I had not told a series of lies, I ask myself now, would Marcus Raven have been warned in time? Would Ishbel's life have been saved?

"To what purpose?" I can hear Gideon Tavish's deep, Scottish voice in my mind. "The poor child was quite mad, you know!" Does such a state justify her death? Am I absolved from guilt?

Jonathan Turner, Bull-headed Jon, would not have agreed! "Harriet Newcombe is a murderess," he told the police. "I was on the river bank opposite, when I saw Harriet throw herself at Miss McCleod and she was the one who caused Miss McCleod to fall off the cliff! Harriet Newcombe," he had insisted, "after agreeing to marry Marcus Raven, conspired with him to murder Ishbel McCleod in order to gain control of Miss McCleod's fortune!"

Of course, with the evidence given by Mr. Tavish and Mrs. Douglas, the case against me was dismissed. But Jonathan had done his work well; there are still some who call me murderess.

And now, as I write here in my chamber at Ravens-fall, I wait for that other who loved Ishbel and who now hates me. If I look down from my window now, will I see him? Will I see a pale moonlit face gazing up at me from the River Walk?

Post Script

New Year's Eve and a fine summer's night. I sit here at my chamber window for the last time as Harriet Newcombe.

Soon, Jenny—dear Jenny, now Mrs. McGregor—will come to help me dress.

"Well, of course, I had to come," she had exclaimed, when I greeted her at the landing. "Thomas would have come, too, if he could. But he can't leave our vineyard." She paused a moment, watching the *Waiwere* sailing around the bluff; then taking my arm, as we ascended the River Walk, she had added, "Oh, to think of all that has happened . . . but, still, that's all in the past, isn't it? And now that Mr. Raven is free of his troubles . . . oh, I am so glad for you both! Of course, I always had a feeling . . ."

I look now at the satin folds of my wedding dress laid across my bed and at the veil—a cobweb of

Brussels lace. And I think of the Master of Ravensfall, waiting for me in the drawing room, the Reverend Mr. Takarangi nearby, ready to officiate and Mere, his wife, at the piano.

I remember Marcus returning from Scotland and feel again that familiar giddiness as he had taken me in his arms. "Let us start a new life," he had murmured into my hair, "in a new year . . ."

My dear love, I think now, how could I ever have doubted him?

Outside, the ruru calls and I look out into the night, thinking of a pale face with a blaze of blue-green eyes. Somewhere out there in the moonlit bush, danger still lurks—but here at Ravensfall, with Marcus Raven to protect me, I shall be safe.